FREE TO BE

A Novel

Gracie L. Chandler

Published by *Life Everlasting Press*
Jacksonville, Florida

Cover by Marion Designs
Cover Art: *The Goddess of Hope & Mercy,* by James Denmark, Oil and Collage
Hurricane Katrina Artist Relief Initiative

www.gracielchandler.com
ISBN 10: 099618080X
ISBN 13: 9780996180801
Library of Congress Control Number: 2015907352
Life Everlasting Press, Jacksonville, FL

Dedicated to

Tommy J. Chandler, the calmest, most confident man I know. Your show of faith enriches my Belief. Thank you.

AUTHOR'S NOTE

When I told an acquaintance—a resident of Beaufort, South Carolina—that I was writing a novel about the freed people of St. Helena, she immediately sent an item she knew I'd need, a book entitled *Gullah Fuh Oonuh (Gullah For You)*, by Virginia Mixon Geraty, (© 1997). It became one of my primary go-to-resources.

Prior to the results of a twenty-year study done by African American linguist Dr. Lorenzo Dow Turner, Gullah speech was deemed substandard English. Because of Dr. Turner's work, Gullah speech is now classified as a true language—Gullah Creole—subjected to the rules and nuances of all languages. It is for this reason I've tempered the dialogue of the freed people's characterizations. *Ef me ain done dis, oonuh hab haa'd time fuh know wuh me say.* Translation: If I hadn't, you would have struggled to understand what I'd written.

Since language is a huge part of culture, I've included elements of Gullah Creole in the book. The verbs *go, going,* and *gone* have been replaced with the Gullah Geechee verb, *gwine. Been* and *be* are used instead of the verbs *are, is, was,* and *were.* Pronouns *he, she, I, me, we, us,* and *our,* are often written in reverse syntax.

In 2013, The Ritz Theatre and Museum in Jacksonville, Florida, presented "Word, Shout, Song: Lorenzo Dow Turner Connecting Communities through Language". The exhibit, on loan from the

Smithsonian Institution's Anacostia Community Museum, traces the cultural links between the Gullah Geechee communities in the Southeastern US coastal states and the West African countries from which the enslaved people were transported.

The following books provide authentic insight into the Gullah Geechee culture of the Sea Islands:
Bailey, Cornelia Walker. *God, Dr. Buzzard, and the Bolito Man*, Doubleday Publishers, (2000).
Campbell, Emory S. *Gullah Cultural Legacies*, 3rd ed., Gullah Heritage Consulting Service, (2008).
Johnson, Michele Nicole. *Sapelo Island's Hog Hammock*, Images of America Series, Arcadia Publishing, (2009).

For more information, visit the Gullah Geechee Cultural Heritage Corridor, U.S. National Park Service website, http://www.nps.gov/guge/

CHAPTER 1

CRECIE

The boys darted between the rows, their wooly little heads barely visible above the waist-high bolls. "The Big House!" they yelled, "Miz Alina say ya'll must come now!" As their high-pitched voices faded in the distance, the yard bell's incessant clanging began, summoning the workers from the fields.

Crecie, bending over the Sea Island cotton, stood tall, puzzled by the breach in rigid plantation routine. A glance at the sun revealed it wasn't time for the short morning break, yet the other workers were already rushing along the rows, leaving the field. Her impulse to join them passed quickly; it was against her nature to leave work undone. Not because of the overseer's whip—a rarity for any slave on Ivy Oaks Plantation—but because she despised slackness. Hard work, the pride the master took in her labor, was all she knew. She kept picking, listening as the hands' animated voices drifted her way.

"I wonder why Miz Alina send fo' we."

"How I know? Since the war start, ain't no telling."

"Yeah, with them Yankee ships blockading everything coming and going...."

"A change coming; I can feel it in my bones!"

1

The change had begun in April, when the South Carolina militia routed federal Ft. Sumter. President Lincoln had labeled the attack a rebellion, calling on volunteers to quell it. But after eight more states joined the seven that had already seceded, and a Baltimore secessionist mob stoned Union troops, killing four, Lincoln retaliated by blockading all Southern ports. The simmering skirmishes between North and South exploded into all-out civil war.

The sight of Union gunboats anchored off-shore had encouraged the slaves' hope for freedom. It was all they'd talked about for seven months and Crecie was sick of hearing it. To her, the concept of living without boundaries simply didn't exist. But her shelves of fruit preserves did. She couldn't see freedom, but she could see her yard garden and jars of healing herbs. The bit of money the master allowed her to keep when he hired her out was real, too. Besides, where would she go? St. Helena Island was her home, where she was born, and when the time came, where she'd die.

She continued along the billowy row, her rhythmic touch firm but delicate; as delicate as the fine linens and lace the cotton was destined to become. Reaching the end of row, she emptied the sack into the receiving basket and started for the Big House. The others were long gone.

She'd just entered the manor road when her mate, Isham, reined Rex into the fork. A battered straw hat shielded his olive-toned face and he sat tall in the saddle. In spite of Isham's tattered clothes, his regal bearing gave the sturdy Marsh Tacky a certain grace. As the plantation's slave driver, Isham monitored the workers, assigning their daily tasks. He'd never abused his authority, but he wasn't shy about using it either. Many a slacker, slow on completing a task, had felt the tip of his whip. A few had even spent a night or two in the slave jail.

He dismounted and Crecie ran to him. "Isham!" she said, grabbing his muscular arm. "Why Miz Alina send fo' we?"

"Why you take so long, Crecie? Everybody else—."

"Tell me, Isham! What be happening?"

"Word come from Beaufort. A hundred Yankee gunboats heading straight to Ft. Walker, fixing to attack."

"Attack Ft. Walker? Why, that be right on the sound, at Bay Point!"

"That's why the white folks getting off St. Helena. They leaving Beaufort, too; and Edisto, Hilton Head—all the islands—even Sapelo down in Georgia."

"B-but they gwine go, just like that?"

"White folks running scared, Crecie. They know them rebel soldiers can't stave off all them Yankee ships."

Scared? I ain't never see one scared buckra, let alone hundreds o' 'em. "What about the missus—she going?" Crecie was certain the black-haired Alina Boson feared no one. But she also recalled the packing had begun at the Big House the same day the blockading ships moved closer into Port Royal Sound.

"Oh, she leaving alright," said Isham. "Done already rent a place up 'round Spartanburg, gwine run us inland to work it, same as the other planters gwine do. I guess they figure to come back when Johnny Reb win the war—*if* they win it."

"Spartanburg!" Her mind went straight to family. Her grandmother, Bentoo, was still spry, but too frail for such a long trek. Sham, their oldest, was big for his thirteen years and strong as an ox. He could go the distance, but Mistress Alina might not want him along. Seven year-old Leona might be able to keep up, but the baby, four-year-old Willie, was too young. "And what about the cotton?" she asked. "There still be plenty to pi—."

"She ain't taking everybody, just the full-hands—like we."

"But Isham, that mean us got to leave our chillun and Bentoo. And the food we lay-by for winter—how us gwine tote all o' that?"

Isham, hoping to change the subject, fumbled with a cedar box lashed to the saddle. "Everybody at the Big House been busy all morning; they ought to be through loading up by now."

But she would not be deterred. "What about our rooster and biddies?"

Isham ignored the question. "Miz Alina come looking for you the minute she got word about the gunboats."

Crecie was trained by her grandmother and both women had healing skills that even amazed the medical community. When Mistress Alina suffered one of her moody spells, she'd summon Crecie or Bentoo before sending for the doctor.

"Who—what she say? What she want?" Not knowing what frame of mind the mistress would be in, she felt her anxiety rise.

"I don't know—just say fo' you to come. With all the rushing and packing, I figure she must need a potion or something."

The young woman turned on her heels, toward Oak Avenue and the Big House. But before she could take a step, Isham grabbed her wrist. Shocked, she struggled against his hold. "What be the matter with you? The missus sent for me!"

He held tight. "We ain't going, Crecie. We ain't leaving Ivy Oaks."

CHAPTER 2
THE DECISION

Crecie stared at Isham, shocked by his words. "You must be crazy—us *got* to do what Miz Alina say."

"Listen to me. I know Massa Lincoln say they fighting to save the Union, not to free our black a—."

"And that be the truth, too. Ain't no white folks gwine take side with we."

"No, Crecie, you wrong. Let Massa Lincoln call it what he want, but I *know* this war be about we. Freedom coming, and us gwine get some land, too; you'll see."

Crecie had known Isham almost as long as she'd known herself, but never had she heard the word *freedom* escape his lips. Never had he mentioned owning land or spoken with such fervor. She exhaled noisily and added him to all the other changes she'd been forced to accept.

He released her and she glared at him, massaging her sore wrist. Although she was reluctant to test the lure of freedom, she knew that having land was the only way they would survive if it *did* happen.

"We already twixt a rock and a hard place," he said. "Johnny Reb on one side, Yanks on the other. I gwine take a chance with the Yank."

"But the chillun? Where—."

"Don't worry, they fine; Miz Alina taking a lot o' mamas to Spartanburg, so she leaving *all* the lil' ones with Bentoo."

Isham rearranged the wooden box to make room for Crecie. "We ain't the only ones staying put; plenty folks done already take to the woods." He mounted Rex and reached to give her a hand up. "C'mon. Us gwine hide with the others 'til the missus leave the island."

She ignored the gesture and looked toward Oak Avenue, a flowery, tree-lined road leading to the Big House.

"C'mon, let's go," he insisted.

Crecie remained stock-still. She'd never, in all her twenty-eight years, had to decide anything of worth; even Isham had been chosen for her. How could she follow his half-cocked dream of freedom? To follow him, a slave, meant denying generations of beliefs that reached far deeper than chains and shackles. The seeds of indoctrination had borne fruit—fruit that declared the master's way better, his water sweeter, and his fire hotter. As far as Crecie was concerned, freedom wasn't worth a dead gnat if the master hadn't declared it to be.

Isham sighed and withdrew his hand. "I can't rightly explain it, Crecie, but I feel bad for you." His voice was tremulous, but he kept it in check. "You...you just try to do so much, and you end up fitting nowhere. One part of you sidling up to Massa and them, trying to please however you can; and the other part, bracing against what you *truly* be—a slave, just like the rest o' we."

Crecie knew he was right because she'd prayed for the war to end, bringing back the sameness of her days. But just like the avenue's fading oleanders, hope for the war's swift end grew fainter day by day. She felt Isham's eyes hard upon her.

"I ain't gwine go with the missus, Crecie. You do what yo' mind tell you, but I ain't leaving this island." He jangled the reins. "Giddy-up, Rex."

She felt bewildered. Watching the horse amble towards the forest's secret spaces, she waited until Isham disappeared then turned to face Oak Avenue. The landing was five miles to the west, beyond the Big House. If she cut through the trees, maybe she could catch up with Miz Alina.

She entered the woods, ducking thick vines and low-hanging limbs. But the brambles still reached out, scratching her, ripping her already tattered dress. Made of osnaberg cotton—commonly known as nigger cloth—the dress had been coarse and sturdy when Master Boson doled out the material six months ago. As she trudged toward the landing, memories of that day filled her mind.

It was a few weeks after the rebels had commandeered Ft. Sumter, a balmy May day. In spite of the Union's embargo, the plantation was doggedly festive, replete with red and blue streamers. After the cloth had been distributed, a band played patriotic music and Malcolm Boson, scion of Ivy Oaks Plantation, appeared on the Big House's bunting-draped balcony. The gray tailor-made uniform gave stature to his stocky frame and his jacket's brass buttons glinted in the noonday sun. He gave a signal and the music ceased. Two hundred or so slaves stood shoulder-to-shoulder in the piazza, their solemn faces trained upward toward Boson and his wife, Alina.

He began his farewell speech by deriding the Union. "I'm going into battle, to fight for you and our way of life. Don't listen to those damn Yankees; they're horned devils who will sell all ya'll—young and old—send you to Cuba. Your new masters will work you from dawn to dusk—in gangs, not half-day tasks like you do now. And the sun will be fiery hot all year long. That's where you'll be for the rest of your born days, chopping sugar cane in the burning sun." He railed for more than an hour, ending the tirade by admonishing the Negroes to remain faithful. "Many of your people were among the first Africans brought to St. Helena; this is your home, too. You must continue to take care of Ivy Oaks just as you've always done."

He motioned for his wife to stand beside him. Alina McIntosh Boson, a coal miner's daughter from the hills of North Georgia, smiled down at the upturned faces. Crecie, one of the few who knew the smile came from her head, not her heart, refused to look up.

"Miss Alina is now your mistress *and* master," said Boson. "She will continue to take care of you just as I have—just as generations of Bosons have always done. Do as she tells you, and above all, continue as if I were still here."

Unlike the master of Ivy Oaks, the mistress had no generational ties with the people, but she *could* manage a plantation and they knew it. Stepping forward, she drawled sweetly, "I have only this to say: Ivy Oaks will persevere; this little war will be over so soon, the master'll be back home in time for supper."

The Negroes offered a lack-luster cheer and the band struck up a lively tune. Boson climbed on his horse and galloped off, leaving behind a steely-eyed wife and slaves listlessly waving miniature Confederate flags.

Lost in thought, Crecie pressed on until a thick, low-hanging vine blocked her path, returning her to the present. She yanked it. Her sleeve immediately ripped loose so she snatched it completely off. "Ain't nothing but a rag now, no how; been wearing it for seven mont's."

Finally, she reached the bluff, seeing boats and skiffs—piled high with crates and luggage—sailing in the distance. The last lumbering barge was floating away from the bank. Poultry, pigs, cows, and goats, teetered among the cargo as slaves shouted above the cacophony, frantically steering the animals from the craft's low edge. Crecie watched the pathetic flotilla disappear around the river bend.

A choice, as usual, had been made for her. Still, she agonized over things of which she had no control—the war, the Yankees, Johnny Rebs—and where was Isham? A blue fly landed on her exposed arm and she brushed it aside, worried about clothes for the winter. Yet, as she headed for Slave Row and her grandmother's cabin, she found comfort in one thing: with or without a master and a mistress, Ivy Oaks was still home, and for now that was all that mattered.

CHAPTER 3

BENTOO

Malcolm Boson's ancestors had left nothing to chance, platting the slave communities for optimal efficiency. The housekeepers lived close to the main house and the washerwomen near the cisterns; husbandry workers dwelled quite a distance away, among the smells and squeals of slaughterhouses and hog sties. Isham and Crecie dwelled in Midway—home to the carpenters, shoemakers, and other tradesmen. The slave hospital was also located there.

Bentoo's cabin, the nursery, was in the settlement known as Slave Row. The nursery's proximity to the fields saved time when mothers came to breast-feed their babies. Located in the outlying areas, it was home to the plantation's largest work force—the field hands. A long row of two-room cabins fronted each other to form a narrow dirt road. Sizable yard gardens, measuring a fourth of an acre, flourished behind the cabins, supplementing the slaves' meager rations. Beyond the yard gardens on one side of the road, lay a meadow, surrounded by dense woods. Across the road, behind those cabins and yard gardens, vast fields stretched for miles, farther than the eye could see. Cotton barns, granaries, and tool sheds dotted the landscape, defining the nature of the crops grown there.

Crecie hurried along the unusually quiet street. The cabins were deserted; their rickety doors and shutters swung wide open. Tools usually stowed in the sheds were strewn about, abandoned. A fishing pole, propped beside a long-handled hoe, defined the slaves' self-time from that demanded by the master. Crecie assumed the inhabitants were hiding in the woods or had been forced to go upland. Wherever they were didn't concern her. She just wanted to gather up her children and go home to Midway, as far away from the forts as possible. Since Missus Alina was leaving all the little ones with Bentoo, she felt it would be wrong to saddle her grandmother with her own three children as well.

She eyed the scattered rubble as she walked along, silently denouncing broken tools, pilfered lumber, and bits of casting nets. Though she didn't approve, she knew why the clutter existed; for people who had nothing, everything had potential, and the slaves were ingenious in making-do.

Crecie cut through one of the front yards and, skirting the black laundry pot straddling a mound of cold ashes, approached Bentoo's cabin. An array of dried plants hung from its narrow eaves; other plants grew in pots bunched close against the cabin's whitewashed tabby walls. She took quick inventory of the medicinal herbs and decided she already had plenty of lavender, deer tongue, and life-everlasting. The aroma of Hoppin' John, a one-pot mixture of black-eyed peas and rice, wafted out into the yard. When it was available, a piece of streak-o-lean was added as seasoning; but meat, purchased from western states, was in short supply since the war began.

She opened the door and Bentoo rushed to shush her, indicating a baby and four toddlers asleep on moss-stuffed pallets.

"With all this commotion going on, I give 'em celery tea with a bit of honey," said Bentoo. "Calm 'em right down, too."

11

Leona and Willie ran to Crecie, nuzzling against her flimsy skirt. She gave them a quick hug and they hurried back to their shell game in the corner.

"You got your hands full here," said Crecie glancing at the sleeping children. "I gwine take Sham and them back to Midway."

"No, leave Sham; he sleeping sound now. He been agitated all morning so I give him some tea, too. But I got a couple other lil' scoundrels you can take." She nodded toward two wide-eyed toddlers, then slowly shook her head. "They belong to Hester and Maggie...po' lil' things. Seem like they know their mamas gwine be gone for a long spell."

"I can take 'em with me; that be two you ain't got to see about."

"Thank ya. I 'preciate that," she said, easing into the rocker chair. The enormous castoff from the Big House dwarfed her petite body. "Sit," she said, indicating one of four high-back, slatted chairs, also castoffs.

Crecie looked askance and remained standing. "Ain't you hear what be going on? The Yankees fixing to shoot at them two forts on the bluff."

"'Course I hear—can't you see all these young-uns Miz Alina done put on me?"

Crecie sighed and sat down. "Well, all I got *is* a minute. I got to get home with these chillun."

"Why ain't Isham come for 'em?"

Crecie carefully considered her reply. Bentoo's feelings toward Isham ran hot and cold. She hadn't even attended their jump-the-broom ceremony nine years ago, even though Mistress Alina had allowed the quasi-wedding to take place at the gazebo. But then Bentoo ran hot and cold with everybody. Sometimey. That's what the slaves called people like that: sometimes nice, sometimes nasty. Crecie decided to ignore Bentoo's question and changed the subject.

"Is it true, this war gwine free we?" she asked.

The old lady took some rabbit tobacco from a pouch and tamped her hand-carved pipe. Her movements were slow, and Crecie wondered if she, too, was avoiding an answer.

"It depend," said Bentoo finally.

"On what?"

Bentoo leaned into the hearth and took a light from the embers. The fire cast a glow over her smooth, honey-brown face and she appeared younger than her sixty-six years.

"It depend on who win what they fighting fo'."

"And what that be?"

"Well, Massa and them say the United States ain't they country no mo'; done set up they *own* country with they own president—Jeff Davis. And that be what they fighting fo'. Now, if *they* win, fo' sho' they gwine be taking us with 'em." Bentoo paused and gestured around the cabin. "And this'll be we lot 'til the day us die."

Crecie stared into the fire, listening.

"Now the North say *they* fighting to keep the Union and everything else the same way it always been; that mean we still gwine be slaves. So, even if the North *do* win...." She gestured around the cabin again, nodded, then puffed her pipe. The tobacco flared red and died to smoky gray. "But however it be, I see a better chance at getting free if the South get whopped. We *know* where we stand with them; wind might blow a little calmer from the North."

"Ever since they start fighting, ain't nothing been the same," said Crecie. "You never know what gwine be from one day to the next."

"Yeah, you right about that," said Bentoo. She continued to puff as she rocked, her short legs barely touching the solid dirt floor. Master Boson had offered to lay in wooden planks and she'd conceded for the adjoining nursery. But the floor on her side of the two-room cabin remained the old-timey African way, hard-packed dirt, smooth as wood. A comfortable silence fell over the room and one of the wide-awake toddlers, Ossie, wandered over to Crecie.

He rested his head in her lap and she caressed his back. Staring into the fire, its glow warming her face, she recalled her own childhood winters by the double-sided fireplace, playing with the little corncob dolls Bentoo had made for her. She was just five when her grandmother let her help tend the babies. Even at that young age Crecie had instinctively known how to hold the little ones, speaking nonsense words to soothe away their fussiness. Out of all her early jobs, she liked the nursery best.

"You got time for me to feed Willie and Leona?" asked Bentoo. "I already give the other chillun their gruel."

Crecie's stomach reminded her she'd worked through the breakfast break and she was tempted. "That pot smell good," she said standing, "but, no, I got to go. I'll fix something when I get home." She stooped and lifted Ossie, then Louise, placing one on each hip. "C'mon Leona, Willie; we got to get on home to Midway."

CHAPTER 4

THE BIG GUN SHOOT

Crecie ushered the hungry brood inside. Glancing around the cabin, she was satisfied with the proof of her hard work. Fruit preserves and jars of vegetables—part of the family's winter store—occupied most of the space. A stack of neatly folded quilts shared a shelf with belts and wallets made of rattlesnake leather. Her ever-plentiful jars of herbs and remedies rested on one of the room's two tables.

She had just lit the hearth, preparing to cook rice and okra, when the house shook. The children screamed and ran to her. The Union attack had begun.

Crecie hastily created a shaky little fortress, slamming the rough-hewn table and rickety chairs to the floor. Crouching behind the crude barrier, she drew everyone near and they pressed in even closer. Leona and Willie, just children themselves, each held a toddler. The next thunderous blast exploded, and the two-year-olds screamed again. But this time Leona and Willie, eyes wide and questioning, were too terrified to make a sound. Even if they had, their shouts could not be heard above the booming missiles. The battle was miles away, too far to reach the cabin, but its petrifying bedlam convinced Crecie that the entire island and everything on it was being destroyed.

Rivulets of sweat, brought on mostly by fear, coursed along her body; her long straight hair, damp and unbraided, lay plastered on her shoulders and down her back. She tried to pray, but her mind couldn't focus. So she fought the panic by mumbling curses at the Feds and rebels, wishing to hell she'd left with Miz Alina. Or with Isham—at least they would've died together. Her arms ached from cradling the children, but she couldn't let go lest she lose the strength that togetherness brought. They sat motionless and Crecie was certain that each new blast would bring sudden death. What good was freedom to dead people?

The ships' powerful guns fired on Fort Beauregard at Bay Point, rotated on the sound's smooth waters, then turned to bombard Fort Walker on Hilton Head. The fleet sailed to and fro in perfect formation while Federal soldiers watched the spectacle from troop ships anchored just outside the sandbar. The one-sided skirmish started mid-morning and could have ended sooner if the Confederates, though outnumbered and low on ammunition, had not continued fighting. Finally, four hours into the battle, they sent up the white flag of surrender. The rebels' last defenses against the Union blockade crumbled. Federal forces now controlled the entire South Atlantic coast, occupying the islands from North Carolina to Florida. Except for a few Unionists and diehard Southern civilians who'd refused to leave, the majority of the Sea Islands' inhabitants consisted of ten thousand abandoned slaves. Neither the fleeing plantation owners nor their bonds people realized that November 7, 1861 marked the beginning of the end of their way of life.

Finally the barrage was over. Crecie tried to stand, but her cramped arms and legs resisted. Willie continued to cling, and she nudged him aside. Fighting the needle-sharp pain in her limbs, she hobbled to the splintery shutter. Even though Midway was shrouded in ashy, acrid smoke, she could see that the buildings—cabins, shoe shop, carpenters' sheds, tanning yard, slave hospital—were still standing. The vibrations from the big guns had displaced some of Crecie's many herbs and potted medicines, but the pecan and pear trees were untouched. A crow, perched high in a pine, signaled an all clear and immediately the other birds, including the chickens, took up the cry. Indian summer gnats and whining mosquitoes emerged from their hiding places and whizzed through the shutters and door.

Crecie massaged her throbbing head, trying to knead away the pain and confusion. Was Bentoo safe? And Isham. Where was he? In the woods, at the Big House? She wrapped her arms about her slender waist; physically holding herself together, she struggled to control her unsettling thoughts. *They dead—everybody dead!* Her body rocked side-to-side, but the movement brought little comfort. A pat on her back, light and timid, broke the rhythmic spell.

"Ma," Leona whispered.

Crecie's inner turmoil had manifested as shrill shrieks. She looked down; four tear-streaked faces brought her back to reality, reminding her of priorities. "It gwine be alright," she assured the children and went to rekindle the fire. Measuring the rice, she mentally noted how much remained; everything had to last through the coming winter. Then she hung the pot on a hook in the fireplace. That simple act, the smallest of routines, brought a sense of peace.

Just as the rice began to boil, a shadow fell across the door and Isham stepped inside. He looked as if he'd been hurled into a briar patch. Bits of leaves and cock-a-burrs clung to his kinky, rust-red hair; his freckled skin was smudged with dirt.

Leona and Willie ran to him, hugging his legs so tightly he almost lost his balance. Even the two little cousins, Ossie and Louise, held on fast.

"Papa! Papa!" Leona exclaimed. "It been thundering but it wasn't no lightning."

"And no rain, neither," piped Willie.

Crecie joined the fray and ran her hands over his chest, reassuring herself he was all in one piece. "Where you been? You alright?" she asked.

He drew her close. "You still here," he said, "you ain't leave with Miz Alina and them." He sounded relieved, happy even, and Crecie, comforted by his presence, didn't bother to explain she'd missed the boat.

She removed the cock-a-burrs from his hair and wiped at the dirty smudges. "I been too scared fo' you. Where you go hide?"

Isham frowned and unwound the children from his legs. "Leona, ya'll go to the other room."

"What be wrong?" cried Crecie, alarmed. "Bentoo? Sham? They dead—I know they dead!"

"No, no; everybody alright—far as I know." He paused and drew Crecie to him. "I...I had to go to the cemetery."

The word cemetery hung in the air and Crecie stepped away, instinctively wiping her hands, ridding them of some unseen, supernatural contamination.

"That's where I been when the Big Gun Shoot start." Isham was one of the few islanders, black or white, who gave short shrift to St. Helena's reputed ghosts. But Crecie *had* encountered them, had witnessed their wandering presence.

"Wh...why you had to go *there*, Isham?" Her knees buckled and she eased into a chair, nervously clasping and unclasping her hands. "Why you had to go stir up them haints?"

"'Cause ain't no darkies—buckras either—gwine be poking around the graveyard. That the safest place to be anyway—dead folks ain't got no knives and guns."

"They don't need none; they got other power."

"Aww, Crecie, that foolishness just in yo' mind," said Isham.

She knew differently, but kept quiet. Even as a child, she had heard the disembodied voices, seen the fleetingly real apparitions. As an adult, healing the sick, she had witnessed miraculous cures and eerie transformations. Crecie *knew* the spirit world existed, was as real as the one she lived in.

"Ma," said a small voice. Neither Isham nor Crecie noticed Leona had quietly returned to the room, the others lined up behind her like little ducklings. "They say they hungry."

Well, the living still got to eat. She turned to Isham. "You hungry, too? I ain't cook nothing…it been too much going on. I been scared to death, all that shooting."

"Me, too. I thought that noise was gwine wake the dead!"

His little joke brought a slight smile to her lips.

"Yeah, I could eat a lil' something," he said, glad to see she'd brightened a bit. "But I got to go to the Big House first, make sho everything alright up there. Then I gwine ride over to Slave Row; get the word out fo' everybody to meet up in the morning, see where we headed, what we gwine do now."

Can't tell what the next day gwine bring no more, she thought.

They walked out to the yard and the children followed, pleading to ride Rex.

"I'll let ya'll ride *one* time, and then I got to go," said Isham.

He placed each child firmly on Rex's broad back. Crecie watched as he guided the horse around the area's well-trotted path. But she felt something was different, out of kilter. Suddenly it came to her—riding Rex was a Sunday treat, their only day off.

But today was Thursday, a day for picking cotton, mixing potions, or washing clothes, with the children running about underfoot, supposedly helping. Isham would still be inspecting the day's tasks, not riding the children around the yard. She turned and hurried into the cabin. *Ain't nothing the same no mo'—nothing!*

CHAPTER 5
NOW WHERE WE STAND?

I t was early the next morning and Crecie reached the edge of
the crowd just as Isham stepped onto the cotton barn's loading
platform. He held up his hands and the nervous whispers of field
hands, tradesmen, and other workers quieted down. Isham's voice
was reassuring, a perfect match for his easygoing nature.

"I know the Big Gun Shoot on yesterday be the first thing on
everybody mind," he said. "It be on my mind, too. I ain't seen no
army folks, so we need to plan we next step, keep Ivy Oaks running
like we always do."

An approved murmur came from the crowd. As the slave driver, Isham had been third in command, after Boson and the white
overseer. But overseers had short tenure and the people, especially
the field hands, knew that Isham was the real reason for the plantation's success. He was fair in his assignments, giving each hand a
task he or she was able to perform. In the evening he checked their
work—planting, weeding, harvesting, whatever the assignment for
the season—making sure the jobs had been done to standards. He
was a leader whose decisions made the difference between a well-
run plantation and a poor one. This year's cotton crop had been
especially bountiful.

"I know Miz Alina ain't give out the winter cloth or nothing befo' she run away. But don't ya'll be fearful o' that, us'll make do," he said. "I know some of you scared, wondering what gwine happen now that Massa *and* the Missus gone. But ya'll know that ain't nothing new. They leave every summer anyway, head off to Beaufort or the pine lands. Us look out for self then, us look out fo' self now."

Fo' true, thought Crecie. No white person dared remain on the islands during the dreaded malaria season. In May, at the first sign of hot weather, all the planters fled what they called the malaise, leaving the islands totally in the slaves' control. Ivy Oaks—self-governed by blacks—became Isham's domain. In addition to overseeing the livestock, the food crops, and the moneymaking cotton crop, Isham also supervised the other areas of plantation work and nothing was overlooked. The corn stalks were stripped for fodder, public roads filled with dirt, repairs made on the manor house, and slave cabins whitewashed and spotlessly cleaned. A sense of pride and ownership prevailed throughout the plantation, especially in the slave settlements. On their return in late September, the Bosons would find their property in perfect condition, better than they'd left it. Yes, Isham *had* proven he could run the plantation without white oversight.

"...and then they come back," continued Isham, "and it be time to harvest the cotton, it be time for Massa to take in all the money, too. But if it don't be fo' we, won't be no money." He gestured toward the cotton field. "You see that out yonder—that be white gold—worth more money than I can think of, and us done it! The biggest crop we ever growed, and even if Massa and Missus ain't here, that cotton can't go to waste, us done work too hard. *Somebody* got to sell it and it might as well be we!"

Crecie shifted nervously. She was certain of Isham's ability when following Master Boson's well-ordered plans, but now he stood alone, seemingly with a plan of his own. Could he carry on without a white person's say-so? Would the people follow his lead?

"Ya'll know Massa gone to war and many of the hands gone to the other side with Miz Alina. No telling *when* they coming back. That cotton can't wait 'til they do; us got to finish getting that harvest in and *everybody* got to pitch in."

As slave driver, Isham had walked a thin line between a demanding master and reluctant slaves, but the people knew his true loyalties were with them. Now it was his turn to discover theirs. Could he handle the job, keep Ivy Oaks going? Crecie wanted to believe in him, but what about the others, what did they think?

The people stood silent, seemingly unwilling to even pick up a croaker sack without white directive. Indeed, after Master Boson went to war, if Isham hadn't had the mistress's backing, many chores and tasks would have been left undone.

Amos, one of the carpenters broke the silence. "Listen, Isham, I ain't trying to talk fo' nobody except me, but I never picked too much cotton when Massa was here, and I fo' sho ain't picking none now he gone!"

A general hum of agreement came from the crowd. Dahlia, Amos' mate, went to the stand. "I want to have my say," she said, stepping on the platform. "I been working cotton *and* rice ever since I been knee-high to a duck; start out by carrying water and food to the fields—bucket so big, had to half *drag* 'em. When I turned twelve, Massa, he say to me, 'Dahlia, you big enough now to be a half-hand, take on a fourth acre task.' Well, I couldn't do it, I just cry and cry. My ma, she didn't want me to get the whip, so she double up, did her work and mine 'til I could do a quarter task by myself. I been work full task since I was 15 years old—setting out plants, weeding, picking that cotton. All my life, it been cotton, cotton, cotton! And I sick o' it!" She turned and gestured toward Slave Row. "Now, if me and mine can just lay claim to ten, twelve acres—plus that yard garden back of my cabin—that gwine take care my family and that be fine with me. I don't bear no account to this white man plantation!"

The crowd began to grumble and the dissension grew louder as some workers proclaimed loyalty to self, and others to the land. Crecie's mind struggled between both sides of the argument, and as usual straddled an emotional fence.

"All ya'll hush!" Bentoo's raspy voice rose through the commotion and she reached a hand out to Amos. "Help me up here, boy!" she demanded.

The young man half lifted her onto the platform. Her hooded eyes stared directly at him. "You new at Ivy Oaks, so I excuse you. But you, gal!" She leveled a knobby finger at her great niece, Dahlia. "You my sister grandchild; your roots go too deep for that foolish talk."

Dahlia looked away, but Amos spoke up.

"No, Aunt Bennie," he said. "I ain't new here; I been brought to this island twenty or so years ago."

"What I say? You *new* blood. What be twenty years against a hundred or mo'? My pappy and his pappy be slaves here; grandpa come straight from Africa—Guinea. The slave catchers bring him to the slave auction in Charles Town." She turned and faced the crowd. "When the first old man Boson buy him, bring him to the island, no Ivy Oaks been here—just woods, all jumble up with briars, full o' snakes; 'gators been soaking in the creeks. And my grandpa and them, they the one who clear the brambles and the swamps, turn all this into rich land. They be slaves, true, ain't had *no* power against the white man, but they had strength o' mind and if it don't be for them, this plantation ain't gwine stand here today."

"Tell the truth, Aunt Bennie!" exclaimed a female voice.

"Who then bear account to this land?" continued Bentoo. "The one who say so on paper or the one who blood mark the ground? The one who sip tea in the shade or the one whose sweat water the fields? My grandpa, *your* great-grandpa—all o' them who come ahead o' we—this place be to *their* making. If we leave this land fallow, then they labor be in vain and they toil be fo' naught!" She started towards the edge of the platform then paused, pointing at Dahlia again. "I tell you this one last thing—I ain't work this land all my life to die for naught; not if I got a thing or two to say about it!" The people applauded as Amos helped her down.

"Bentoo right," said Isham. "Us labor done paid for this land a thousand times over. The time come now for the land to pay we."

Ever fearful of Isham going beyond his bounds, Crecie watched anxiously as he scooped up a handful of soil; then he raised his fist and slowly released it.

"Look at this! This our life—right here in this dirt! Massa gone, but the land ain't. It left up to we now, to work on we own and take care o' self."

A man's gruff voice vowed, "I with you and the land, Isham!" Others joined in; encouraging shouts ringed the field.

Crecie stood quietly, shamed by her doubts. Isham had stepped forward, laying claim to *all* their labor. He'd dared to own it, pushing the rest of them to do the same. And why shouldn't they benefit? Truly the need was there. For the first time in her life, she recognized what her husband *could* achieve if given the chance, saw why he craved the internal release that freedom offered. She started to go to him, to try to put her feelings into words, but the thunder of galloping horses stopped her. Everyone watched the dust cloud approach.

CHAPTER 6

THE ARMY LANDS

The soldiers pulled up close. Their uniforms were blue and Crecie wondered how their small caps covered their horns. The one up front wore a suit with many shiny buttons, so she figured he was the leader. His deep-set eyes gazed calmly upon the crowd as the other riders gawked, openly staring. Their straight-line lips snarled in contempt, making her feel ill at ease. Yet she could not help but stare back. The men's ash-gray skin looked like a flounder's underbelly, lacking the reddish tan of the whites to whom she was accustomed. One of them reached to remove his cap, and Crecie held her breath; when he wiped his smooth, hornless brow, she exhaled in relief. The rider with the buttons spoke.

"I'm General Thomas West Sherman," he said, addressing no one in particular. "All of the Sea Islands, from Hilton Head to Edisto are now under the jurisdiction and protection of the United States Government. The government, under the Confiscation Act, has classified you as contraband of war." His words were rote, but his voice held a warm, slightly hoarse quality.

Amos raised his hand. "Beg pardon, suh, but what kind o' act you say—confisband?"

"No, no, the *Confiscation Act.* It's a law that says—." Looking out at the sea of blank faces, the general paused and started over. "Have you heard of the Fugitive Slave Law?" he asked Amos.

"Yes, suh. That mean master can lay claim to his slave even if he *do* make it up North to freedom; law say he can bring him back South."

"That be if he can *find* him," someone in the crowd yelled.

"That's right," said Sherman. "But the Confiscation Law changes that. The law says that if the United States Government captures the rebels' land, then his weapons, livestock, tools, even you, his slaves—anything that will help those traitors win the war—the government has the right to use it, too. It's called contraband, and all of that is under the government's control."

Isham had made his way from the platform and now stood beside the general's horse.

"So if the gov'ment control we, us still be slaves then?" he asked.

"Who are you?" asked General Sherman.

"My name Isham, suh. I be the driver here."

"Ah, the Unionist at Pender Plantation told me about you. It was because of you Ivy Oaks didn't suffer as much damage as some of the other plantations. Good job, Isham."

"Thank ya, suh."

"Well, to answer your question, you are no longer slaves." A general murmur rippled through the crowd. "Slavery is illegal in the United States, and these islands are now a part of the US, *not* the Confederacy."

"We be free then," said Isham.

General Sherman paused and he seemed taken aback by the statement. He dismounted and stood tall, but Isham was still half a foot taller.

"Well, no, you're not *exactly* free," said General Sherman. "My orders are to reassure the planters that the army will not interfere with social customs or the way the civilians carry out their business."

"But you say you own—er, *control* everything here," said Isham. "All the plantations, the fields, the livesto—."

"Yes, everything!" said General Sherman.

"And what about we? If us ain't slaves and us ain't free, where we stand?" he asked.

The hands fidgeted, mumbling Isham's concern.

"You are no longer your *master's* slaves, but as contraband the government needs your labor to help us win the war," said General Sherman.

"But this war ain't about we, though," said Amos. "The way I hear tell, it be to save the Union."

"But the war *could* lead to your freedom," said the general. "That is if President Lincoln chooses to sign the emancipation law."

"E, e-man *what*, suh?" asked Isham.

"Emancipation; that law will make you free—as free as I am!"

Crecie gasped and eyed the general suspiciously, wondering why he'd lied, saying blacks could be free like whites? To her, his words were mere foolishness.

"So," Isham continued, "if Massa Lincoln don't sign no paper to free we, an' Massa don't own we, what gwine become o' we. Us ain't got no land, ain't got nothing—not clothes even."

"I'm sure the government will make some provisions for your welfare. Right now our main concern is to hire workers to get that cotton baled and shipped up north."

"But what about us who don't work cotton? I be a carpenter, what I gwine do?" said Amos.

"Oh, I can assure you there'll be plenty of work!" Sherman replied. "Yesterday the United States Army transported over 13,000 troops and 1,500 horses to Hilton Head. In the coming months over 50,000 men will be on these islands. An army supply base and hospital will soon be built on Hilton Head. I'm sure you will find a way to make a living."

The general turned and mounted his horse.

"My orders are to secure the islands and take stock of the properties, which, of course, includes you," he said. "My report will go to Washington. All I know is that you are now the responsibility of the United States Government, under the army's control and protection."

He reined his horse and looked down at Isham. "Once things are settled, the government will place Northern white men to properly manage these abandoned plantations. Until then, I expect you to carry on, keep Ivy Oaks operating. Well, if there are no more questions, we're moving on, there're many more farms to inspect." They galloped away like they'd arrived—in a cloud of dust.

Crecie watched Isham's once hopeful face become reticent and she knew he was struggling to safeguard his thoughts and feelings. She went to him, but he brushed her aside and walked away. She listened as the newly labeled "contrabands" pondered their ever-changing lives. Their doubts and frustrations echoed her own. But through it all, she held on to one strong thought: without the people the land was worthless, and without the land, the people would also perish. No matter what, she decided—the land, the people, the government—they all needed each other to survive.

CHAPTER 7
GOVERNMENT COTTON COLLECTION

The hoarfrost crunched under the soles of Crecie's paper-thin shoes. She drew the flimsy layers of tattered garments close, but the rags offered little protection against the early December chill. Shifting her weight from one foot to the other, she waited as Isham assigned the workers' tasks. Watching the ragged mix of mainland runaways milling about, she realized that even in her deprived state, she was better off than they were.

The runaways had begun trickling onto the Sea Islands in April, immediately after the navy's blockade created a shortage of goods. Then four months later, with the passage of the Confiscation Act, they became more emboldened, risking life and limb in search of food and clothing. Although the Sea Island slaves hadn't exactly welcomed their mainland counter-parts, they'd done their best by them; sharing their meager food and hiding the runaways from their own overseers and masters. That had been the situation until November and the Big-gun Shoot. The smoke from the cannons had barely settled before the slave grapevine falsely spread the word that freedom, shelter, and rations could be had for those who made it to the Sea Islands. Using the Union ships to buffer their escape, hundreds of naked, emaciated runaways arrived daily, overwhelming the military. General Sherman immediately hired those able to work and appealed to the government and Northern sympathizers for food, medicine and clothing. Then he placed former slave drivers such as Isham in charge of the plantations, relying heavily on their expertise.

Crecie eyed the crowd, studying the gaunt newcomers. Most were in no condition to work, a few so sick they'd be dead before noon. She wasn't even sure how long *she* would last. She struggled to maintain her orderly work patterns but with so many changes, she did chores haphazardly, if at all. She longed for the days when her labor was clearly defined and she was certain where she would be and when she would be there. She wanted the return of orderly routines and the customs—Christmas mornings when they'd all put on their Sunday best and gather outside the Big House, shouting "Christmas gift!" And Massa and the Missus would come out and give presents to everybody—whisky for the men, scarves for the women, candy for the children. She wanted to be among her own Ivy Oaks people—no matter how reticent they were—not compelled to work with half-starved strangers. Most of all, she wanted the respect due her as a medicine woman and status as the driver's wife. And though she would not admit it to anyone, she wanted the security of her value as a slave, the knowledge that she was worth something, not some name she could hardly say—*contraband.*

Lost in her musings, she was startled to hear Isham say "Morning suh." She looked up to see her husband, General Sherman, and a strange white man standing nearly three feet away. Intrigued, she sat on the damp ground and pretended to fiddle with her croaker sack.

General Sherman said "This is Lieutenant Colonel William Reynolds, Isham. The Treasury Department has placed him in charge of collecting all the Sea Island cotton; he'll give your orders from now on."

Crecie watched Isham's confident air collapse and his face morph into a mask of slack-jawed acquiescence.

"Yes suh," he said, doffing his weather-beaten hat.

Reynolds ignored the gesture and pointed to the fields. "Why is so much cotton still unpicked? The workload has to increase or the government is going to lose money."

"Uh, excuse me, suh," said Isham, "but we be short-handed since Johnny Reb take some o' the hands to work fo' them in the war; and then Miz Alina take some o' them upland. Lot o' these people come from the Main, half-starve and sick. Even some o' the Ivy Oaks workers falling by the wayside."

General Sherman turned to Colonel Reynolds. "Isham's right. What's worse, hundreds more arrive daily."

"Well, something will have to be done; send them back or something. I don't see how we can win this war and take care of negs, too," said Colonel Reynolds.

The general frowned. "I agree, but if we *don't* take care of them, who is going to pick that cotton—you? Anyway, they're not your concern. Secretary Chase has chosen the perfect man to oversee the contrabands' needs."

Crecie's ears perked up and she saw Isham, hearing that bit of news, grip his hat.

"Oh, really. Who?" Reynolds' surly tone contradicted the question's simplicity.

"Didn't Chase tell you? He's hired another agent to look after the contrabands, someone who will guide them, prepare them for freedom. God knows these ignorant brutes need all the help they can get."

"From what I've seen of them so far, there's a definite need alright. But tell me, who *is* this guiding light Chase has appointed?"

"His name is Pierce, Edward Pierce. I heard he's an abolitionist, like Chase. Anyway, he has connections in the private sector; religious affiliations, too, I believe."

"So then he really *is* a guardian angel," Reynolds sardonically replied.

"Angel or no angel, someone has got to get these Negroes fit to work or the government stands to lose millions. The cotton will rot—."

"The cotton *will* be collected," Reynolds interrupted.

"Rot on the bush," concluded the general. "If these people aren't working, they'll be on the dole, dependent on the United States government." The general turned to Isham. "What kind of timetable are we looking at for the next crop?"

"Well, suh, soon as most of the cotton's been picked, the men can start getting the ground ready for the new crop while the women and chillun do the ginning and packing."

"What do you mean, 'getting the ground ready'?" asked General Sherman.

"That mean the fields got to be fertilized with salt marsh grass; if the land lay fallow past the middle of Feb'rary, it ain't gwine be much of a crop."

"I see," said the general.

"Plenty strong hands be needed to tote that marsh grass to the fields," said Isham, "spread it all over. If the land ain't got that rich mud, you won't see a yield like out yonder." He pointed to the fields.

"That's quite a production; hopefully that's all," said the general.

"Oh no, suh. Then the soil got to rest; just sit there and soak up that muck for about a mont' or so. Then sometime in late March—April at the least—the women and chillun can start laying in the seed."

The general turned to Reynolds. "So you see, Colonel, it is vitally important the Negroes are well enough to work. You and Pierce will have to work closely together; make certain—for the sake of the treasury—there's a crop next year."

"You can be assured, sir, the project will be successful."

The two men walked away and Isham came over to Crecie. "You hear what they say?"

"Yeah," she replied, scrambling to her feet. "It be something different every day."

"Ain't nothing change, though; us still ain't got no say about nothing."

And never will, thought Crecie, trudging after him.

CHAPTER 8

ISHAM TAKES A STEP

Crecie was dressed, about to wake up the children when Isham unexpectedly entered the cabin. "Why you still here?" she asked. "I figure you to be in the field by now."

Isham didn't answer until he'd poured a cup of hot, brewed peanut coffee and sat down. "I ain't going," he said, taking a sip of the rich, brown concoction.

Crecie's mind raced, watching him silently taking another sip. She tried to read his face. *What done happen now? Maybe the rations ain't enough...or the wages.* "Isham, I know three weeks gone by, and we ain't get no pay yet, but Colonel Reynolds say—."

Isham slammed the tin cup down, sloshing the liquid over the rough table. "Reynolds! Don't say a damn thing to me about that buckra. He done put that crazy colonel to be next in charge under him."

Crecie grabbed a rag and dabbed at the spilled coffee.

"Who? Nobles? The one the general hired befo' Reynolds come here?"

"Yeah, he the one; he done brought in his friends and put 'em over we, send *we* to the fields, picking."

"Where they come from, up north…?" She hung the rag on a nail and stood beside the mantle.

"They dumb as a doorknob, don't know a damn thing about cotton—not a damn thing! Then Nobles got the nerve to change our work from task labor to gang lab—."

"Gang labor! Working from sunrise to can't see no mo'?"

"I ain't doing it, Crecie. Gen'ral Hunter say us almost free, and to go back—working in gangs—that's *worse* than befo'."

Crecie sat down, facing him. "Well, free or slave you still gwine have to work. If you ain't working for the gov'ment, who you gwine work for—the army?"

Isham leaned in, his voice barely above a whisper. "I got a plan, Crecie."

The words by-passed her ears and went straight to her heart. It skipped a beat, then thumped a double beat. *A plan! Oh, Lordy, no! He ain't got no business with a plan.* She waited for him to go on, knowing instinctively that whatever he was thinking didn't include white folks. It was a terrifying thought.

"You know that land out near Possum Point? Muddy Creek run along the north end."

She meekly nodded.

"Well, us can hire two or three of them runaways to help we get that land ready for spring planting."

Us *can hire?* "But ain't that Massa land? What leeway you got to plant on it?"

"You see any massa around here?"

"But the Gen'ral…*he* be in charge o' everything now."

"He can be in charge all he want; land ain't worth spit if us don't work it."

"I know that, but Isham—."

"What he gwine do if us clear a few acres at Possum Point and plant on it—dig up the seeds?"

"But you got to pay them runaways if you call yourself gwine hire 'em to work fo' you."

"Oh that ain't no worry; I got some—." He stopped mid-sentence. "I'll find a way…maybe give 'em a share o' the crop."

"And what they gwine be eating in the meanwhile, while the crop growing in the ground?"

Isham walked over to the well-stocked shelves. "We got lots more food than this stored away—rice, potatoes, corn. We can share…ration it out." His voice took on a ragged edge. "Why you got to down everything I try to do, Crecie?"

"That ain't what I aiming fo', Isham, but that be a heavy burden on we, trying to take care o' other folk; us can barely take care o' self. And besides, you ain't give the new white man a chance, the one the gen'ral say coming to help we. Maybe he can—."

"Damn it, Crecie! *White man!* That's all you know!" He banged his fist against the shutter. It flung open and the morning chill rushed in.

Crecie had had enough, and she pushed away from the table, so vigorously the rickety chair fell backwards, clattering to the pine-wood floor. She stood nearly eye-to-eye with Isham and her voice came on strong. "You know, Isham, I sick and tired o'yo' mout', telling me *I* don't know if I be a slave or what; saying *I* try to act like Miz Alina and such. But now here *you* go, trying to be like Massa— gwine plant on *his* land, hire slaves to work for *you!* Them white folks might done fool *you* about being free, but I know my place, and 'til such time, I gwine stay in it!"

"What place, Crecie? Just 'cause Massa say you be a slave, you plan on staying one? Boson gone, you ain't got no massa no mo'!"

"It ain't just about him, and you know it! It be about *all* o' them. I don't care if they come from north or south—they still be white; and the white man gwine rule the darkie no matter what!"

"Ain't you been listening—Gen'ral Sherman say us free now, and 'til somebody tell me different, that's the only thing I'm going on."

"You a fool if you think they gwine let we—."

"*You* the fool, scared to even wipe yo' behind 'til they tell you to. No, Crecie, the time done come and I fixing to move on—something you ain't got sense enough to do."

"I got plenty sense; sense enough to know who still holding them damn reins, and it sho ain't yo' po' black ass!"

Isham glared at her, flexing his fist. Suddenly he picked up a potted lavender plant and smashed it against the cabin wall. "Damn you, Crecie! With you or without you, I gwine plant them acres!" He tramped out the door.

Soft whimpering came from the pallets shoved in the corner. Crecie rushed over and snatched the quilts off the cowering children. "Ya'll get up! I got to get to that cotton field befo' the sun rise!"

CHAPTER 9
JUST ABOUT WORKED OUT

Crecie glanced at the inky January sky, thankful for the waning moon. *Won't be no picking by moonlight tonight.* She left the sack of cotton at the weigh station then trudged through the dusky shadows, headed for Slave Row.

As she approached the nursery, she spotted Bentoo and her young charges in the sweet potato patch. Leona saw Crecie coming and glanced at her great-granny. Bentoo nodded, and the little girl raced toward her mother, yelling, "Here come Ma!"

Willie followed, with the toddlers, now secure in the family, close behind. Sham waved and shouted, "Hey, Crecie!"

"Hey, all ya'll," she hollered back, smiling. No matter how hard the days or moonlit nights, the children's greetings always lifted her spirits. Remembering when the bone-weary mothers trekked from the fields to get their children, it was reassuring that at least *some* things hadn't changed. Their offspring had run to them, too, and none but the most irritable woman would remain hard-faced, refusing a playful hug.

Leona reached her first, wrapping her thin arms around her mother's waist.

Crecie recalled her own nursery days and was filled with mixed emotions. There had never been anyone for her to run to, making her feel different from the others. At first she thought it was because of her skin—blacker than a crow's blue-black iridescence. Then she imagined her long hair was the reason; her braids reached down her back even when she was a little thing. Bentoo had entwined rags in the silky plaits to keep them from unraveling. The women in the quarters said Crecie had *Indian hair,* and rightfully so, since her mother, Polly, was half Seminole.

But over the years, she'd come to understand it wasn't about her skin or hair. It was Bentoo's exacting measures—a spotless cabin, junk-free yard, lush vegetable garden—that had set Crecie apart. After toiling all day, few families had enough energy left to match Bentoo's rigid standards. Meal times were particularly isolating, as Crecie ate honey cakes from a milk-glass bowl and the others slopped at the trough, mush oozing between their dirty fingers.

She became a loner early on, preferring the company of corn-cob dolls rather than real playmates.

Crecie reached the potato patch, the children dogging at her heels.

"Come on, chillun," Bentoo admonished, "ya'll ain't through digging up these taters."

She turned to her granddaughter. "Look here, Crecie; this basket o' taters be fo' you."

Sham, holding a huge, oddly-shaped potato, said, "This be fo' you." He extended the dirty tuber, his arm rigid.

Crecie chuckled and accepted it, drawing her firstborn close. "You gwine go to Midway tonight?" she asked, knowing full well the answer.

Sham squirmed. "No! I stay with Bentoo tonight!"

She smiled. Sham often stayed with Bentoo. She'd delivered him, helping Crecie through a difficult labor. The young mother knew her son was different the moment she laid eyes on him and along with Bentoo's help, immediately accepted the challenge—prodding, training, coaxing—whittling at his limitations. He'd balked at each new hurdle, struggling to conquer simple milestones. But the women persevered, and through their loving will, he learned how to walk and talk. Finally he was able to feed himself and, in due time, could dress himself, too.

Crecie released the boy and arched her body; an attempt to smooth her kinked, aching, muscles. "Oh, my back, my legs! I just hurt everywhere," she said, frowning. "I done work hard all my life, but Lord know, I ain't never been through nothing like this befo'." She walked over to the nearest stump and eased down. "This gang labor got to be the hardest work I ever done! And that Colonel Nobles—he a mean one alright, a down-right snake. Put me on the first gang, the hardest one...working from sun up to can't see no mo'. I too tired to even plant my winter crop and you *know* that ain't like me!"

Bentoo removed a small vial of flaxseed oil from her apron pocket and handed it to her.

Crecie gently rubbed the oil on her calf muscles. "*Mmm*....That already feel better." She stood and hefted the basket, balancing it on her head. "I 'preciate this; used the last o' the summer crop to make tater bread."

"Oh, you welcome," said Bentoo softly. The older woman had been unusually quiet, but now she began to talk. "Colonel Nobles come here and say all the nursemaids gwine have to go in the field, work on the second gang. If not, ya'll got to pay we to keep the chillun."

"Pay! Pay what?" Crecie set the basket back down. "He slow paying we wage, and when he do, done already take out for that watered-down molasses them vendors sell. Who gwine look after all these chillun?"

"That's what I ax him. He say he ain't got nothing to do with that; but *everybody* got to pick that cotton, even ol' Mose, and his knees so bad he can barely walk. Nobles say Sham got to pick, too, even though he can't study a string bean long enough to pop it."

All at once the anxiety that had begun last April caved in on Crecie. She sat on a stump and cradled her head. "It just be too much," she mumbled, "do this—no do that—I try and try, but don't know what tomorrow gwine bring."

The children had begun a game of ring-tag and their loud shrieks echoed through the dusk dark night, bouncing off Crecie's throbbing head.

Bentoo gently massaged her granddaughter's tensed neck. "You should o' quit when Nobles made them drivers go work in the fields; you should o' leave like Isham done."

The words struck a nerve. Crecie woke up guilt-riddled each morning, knowing Isham needed her help. "That ain't nothing fo' we to talk about," she said, standing abruptly.

Bentoo's hands fell away. "That be the trouble with you," she retorted, "don't ever want to talk truth!"

"What truth you talking about, Bentoo?" She stared down her grandmother. "I don't know what the truth be no mo'. The army saying us free, able to do anything us want. But then the gov'ment saying us ain't—got to work for *them.* Then the gov'ment say they gwine pay wages, but the truth be told, I ain't see no sign o' money." She folded her arms, bracing against the night air. "We would o' had winter clothes by now—and a warm blanket, too, if Massa Boson still be here."

"Be that as it may, Crecie, he ain't, and I be just as dumb-fumble as you since he gone. But I know one thing fo' sho: Isham ain't waiting for no massa to give *him* nothing. He moving on, staking a claim for things to come."

"How he know what be coming? He could be working that land for nothing!"

"Nothing? That all he *ever* worked it fo'."

"But Bentoo, how—."

"You ax me about truth, Crecie, and I'm telling you—your place be next to Isham.

That be yo' truth right now." She turned and headed for the cabin, calling the children. "Shaaam! Leooona! All ya'll! Get in here out this cold!"

The January darkness overtook Slave Row and Crecie shivered, watching candles being lit. One by one their splintery glow flickered through the cabins' shuttered openings. Bentoo's words echoed in her head… "Your truth be with Isham." But that was according to Bentoo. *What be my own truth?* she wondered. Hard work was the first thing that came to mind. *Sho as the sun rise and set, that be the only truth I know.*

Crecie was aware of work long before she was aware of self. At age three she's stood at Massa's dinner table, fanning flies. When she was five, Bentoo put her to work in the nursery. Then there was work in all-girl groups when she was eleven, learning how to grow cotton. Now a grown woman, her days began at dawn—planting, hoeing, harvesting. Then well past midnight, there was always the washing, sewing, canning. In between, she'd cook, clean, mix potions, tend the sick, and deliver babies. Work *was* her truth, her life's only constant.

But why? Why did she strive so hard, going even beyond a slave's infinite toil? Her mind wandered as she dared to seek her own truth: *What if…what if I had o' done all that fo' my own good, not fo' Massa good?* Her heart instantly triple-thumped and she leaped from the stump. The thought of possessing her own labor terrified her. Rejecting the foreign notion, she fled to the cabin. *Time fo' work be here befo' I know it.*

CHAPTER 10
TREASURY AGENT PIERCE

I t was two months after the Union invaded the Sea Islands and
Edward Pierce wasn't sure what to expect at Port Royal. He certainly didn't think he'd be jouncing around the islands in an ox-
drawn army wagon. His enthusiastic driver, Mose, also assigned by
the army, seemed to know everything and everybody. He turned to
Pierce as they approached Slave Row.

"Mind if we stop, suh?"

Pierce hesitated. Stopping was the last thing he wanted to do.
"What on earth for?"

"Well, the people know the gov'ment send somebody to help
'em, so they looking to see who it be."

Pierce felt as if he'd been taken to task. After all, he *had* been
sent to aid the people. "Well, all right," he curtly agreed, "but make
it brief, I have much work ahead."

Indeed there was a lot to do, and the first thing on his list was a
thorough inspection of the two hundred or more plantations scattered throughout the islands. He wanted his report to Treasury
Secretary Chase to be impeccable.

At the end of the tour, Pierce was glad he'd granted permission
to stop. His brief exchanges with the former slaves had given him

insight as to their needs—both physical and emotional. He also came to the conclusion they were the most reticent, self-effacing people he'd ever met; he knew immediately that Port Royal was the perfect place to carry out his social experiment. After all, if *these* people, so confined and ill-advised, could be taught to assimilate into the general populace, surely it would be easier to incorporate those from the mainland, slaves who had been less isolated. The project at Port Royal would serve as the model for emancipation, proving to skittish northern whites that the freeing of four million or so slaves was feasible. Pierce was certain that by allaying white fears, the northern citizenry would support the cause of abolition and hopefully shorten the war.

Mose interrupted his musing. "This here place called Midway, it gwine be we last stop." He pulled the reins, turning into a yard dotted with leafless trees; empty gourds swung lazily from their stick-like branches. The men alighted from the wagon and started toward a whitewashed tabby cabin. Bits of uneven oyster shell jutted from its rough surface. The construction was the same as the other two-room cabins, only a little larger, identifying it as the slave driver's dwelling. Unlike some of the other cabins, it was free of broken tools and yard debris. Potted plants and hibernating hydrangeas clustered against the limestone walls, patiently awaiting spring. Pierce had the feeling a sense of orderliness and pride lived here.

A statuesque woman stood at a rickety, waist-high table, tacking something to a board. She stopped when the men joined her and Pierce saw she was securing a snake skin.

"This here's Mr. Pierce; the gov'ment sent him to see about we," said Mose. "And this here's Crecie, Mr. Pierce."

Pierce stared, drawn into the abyss of Crecie's impenetrable blackness. Her skin's raven patina, the jet of her hair, even the pupils of her deep-set eyes, coalesced into one ebonized plane. Two high plum cheeks and a softly rounded chin accentuated her oval face.

Pierce found the presence of mind to tip his hat. "Hello, Crecie."

No man, black or white, had ever tipped a hat to her. "Afternoon, suh," she said, staring at the ground.

"You remember Isham?" asked Mose, "The one clearing the field—he be her man."

"Oh, yes." Pierce readily recalled the tall, well-spoken man, noting his leadership ability. He'd made a mental note to hire him when the plan was in place.

Mose turned to Crecie. "You fix my tonic yet? My knees been hurting powerful bad."

"It been ready since last week. Ya'll want to come in?"

They followed her inside. The room, approximately eighteen by eighteen feet, was lined with plants and shelves. Medicinal herbs—bottled, freshly picked, or in the process of being ground—covered one of two tables. Plants sat on the crude mantle piece and lay drying on the blackened hearth. Even the wooden floor was lined with sweet grass baskets, brimming with blackberry root and sassafras. The shelves held jars of food, quilts, and items made from snakeskin. The only clear table stood in the center of the room, reserved for eating and cooking.

"You have quite a bit here," said Pierce, surveying the room.

"Yessuh."

He picked up a strikingly beautiful snakeskin belt. "Did you make this?"

"Yessuh."

"She make a lot 'o things," said Mose. "This here wallet, and snake-fang earrings for the ladies; Massa and the Missus give 'em to they city friends in Beaufo—."

"How much do you want for this?" asked Pierce, holding up a snake leather belt.

She straightened an errant fold on one of the quilts.

"I ain't want nothing for it, suh. It be a gift to you."

Piece started to protest, but thought better of it.

"Well, Crecie, I do appreciate this fine gift. Thank you for your generosity."

She ducked her head, self-conscious. "You most welcome, suh."

"I've got to be going," he said, moving towards the door. "Mose, are you ready?

"Yessuh, boss; got my tonic right here."

"It be a strong batch," said Crecie, "so take it slow, real slow first time around."

"Sho will," said Mose. "I'll do just that."

CHAPTER 11
PIERCE MEETS REYNOLDS

When Edward Pierce learned his soon-to-be partner, United States Treasury Agent William Reynolds was a colonel, he had cause for concern. Rightfully so; Pierce's short stint as an army private had made him leery of martial authority. The military, arriving on the islands before any other group, had assumed proprietorship, controlling space and shaping policy to their own advantage. Reynolds had taken his assignment to a higher level, extending his cotton collection authority to confiscate houses and furniture. In his zeal to seize anything of value, Reynolds had even shipped Beaufort library's profuse collection north, incurring the wrath of army generals.

Pierce's distrust was further confirmed during the cursory visits he'd made upon arriving. He'd readily discovered a shortage of seed and farm implements—the very tools he needed to supply the contrabands. Conditions at his personal quarters, assigned by Reynolds, were not much better. Before Mose left, he'd told Pierce that the small house was fully furnished when the overseer lived in it, but now the bungalow contained little more than a bed, a chair, and a crudely constructed desk.

Pierce was standing at the desk when Colonel Reynolds and Colonel Nobles barged into the room.

Neither man offered to shake his hand.

"You must be Pierce," said Reynolds.

"Well, yes," he replied.

Nobles immediately lunged for him and Pierce veered into the desk, spilling the books to the floor.

"I told you that's who it was!" exclaimed Nobles. "Snooping around, asking questions!"

"Settle down, Nobles," said Reynolds, stepping between the two men. "Just go back to the house; I'll handle this."

Nobles glared at Pierce before stomping away. "You see to the darkies, *I'll* take care of the cotton."

"Who was *that?*" asked Pierce, brushing himself off.

"Colonel Nobles. He's second in command and in charge of Ivy Oaks—a responsibility he takes very seriously."

"Extremely so, I'd say!" He extended his hand. "I'm Edward L. Pierce, attorney-at-law and recently appointed United States Treasury Agent."

Their hands briefly touched.

"I've been expecting you. I'm Colonel William Reynolds, Treasury Agent in charge of the Division of Confiscated Cotton."

And everything else that isn't nailed down, so I've been told, thought Pierce.

Reynolds bent to retrieve one of the fallen books. "I apologize for Nobles; he's a bit possessive about his territory." He thumbed through a copy of *Uncle Tom's Cabin; Life Among the Lowly,* then plopped it on the desk.

"Abolitionist, are you?"

"I don't regard people as property," said Pierce.

"And I don't regard niggers as people." Reynolds glowered at Pierce.

The young lawyer defiantly stared back. He'd heard how Reynolds had substituted General Sherman's original arrangements with his own shifty measures—replacing the Negro plantation managers with inexperienced white agents. Pierce felt that the colonel's most despicable deed was the low wages promised—a dollar for every four hundred pounds of cotton picked, but had yet to pay. The promised wages barely equaled the scant food and clothes the master had provided; with no means of obtaining goods on their own and no masters to provide even basic necessities, the contrabands were at his mercy.

Pierce ended the staring impasse. "How's the cotton collection progressing?"

"I've done an excellent job. The cotton's over half collected and most of it's already baled. Half of the bales been shipped to the ginning mills up north."

Pierce couldn't mask his surprise. He'd planned to gin the cotton locally, providing work for the field hands. By sending the cotton north, he was certain Reynolds had cut a deal with northern textile owners.

"I don't see that as a wise move, Reynolds. Cotton has always been ginned on the plantations, then sent north. I feel the people should continue the work they're accustomed to performing."

"Oh, you do? Well, listen, Pierce, I'm in charge of cotton, and it's cotton that's being shipped north. By the way, exactly what *are* your duties, your orders from Chase?"

Pierce stalled as he aligned the books, stacking them in a neat pile. The orders in his coat pocket directed him to report to Reynolds, making the colonel his superior. "I'm not quite sure," he lied. "I'll be meeting with Secretary Chase two weeks from now; I'll know definitely when I return." He then dropped the ginning protest, changing the subject. "I noticed there's a shortage of seeds and tools."

Reynolds half-leaned against the desk, his arms folded. "I have the seeds and tools safely stored—I'll be needing them for my plan."

"*Your* plan? What plan is that?"

"I propose to lease the abandoned plantations to honorable white men. They'll plant cotton for exportation to England. That'll put money in the treasury immediately. And they'll farm sustenance crops, too—corn, potatoes, and the like."

"I see. How will the Negroes be involved?"

"They'll provide the labor, of course."

"Will they be compensated?" asked Pierce.

"Oh, maybe we'll give them a share of the food crop, or set up some sort of distribution system; it'll have to be worked out. I'm certain you can handle it."

Reynolds had already put a similar plan in place by supplying the contrabands with molasses and fatback, deducting the cost from their proposed wages. Pierce wasn't sure how the arrangement worked, but decided not to confront Reynolds, intent on addressing all the issues when he presented his own plan to Secretary Chase.

Reynolds stood up straight. "If there's anything you need...."

"I'll be most appreciative for free access to the plantations. The Secretary has requested a full report, including an inventory."

"Very well. I'll let the agents know to expect you. *Especially* Colonel Nobles," said Reynolds and his lips formed an effortless smirk. "Let me know when you receive your orders. Have a good day."

Pierce squinted through the grimy, curtain-less window, thoughtfully stroking his beard as Reynolds galloped away. The colonel's plan *was* more cost effective than his, but it amounted to little more than re-enslavement, giving no thought to the Negroes' current situation. On the other hand, the Port Royal project encompassed the entire abolitionist movement, serving as a model for the emancipation of thousands of slaves. Pierce frowned, and his dour, narrow face mirrored his inner turmoil. His plan *had* to succeed. But it was doomed if he lacked absolute authority to carry it out. Pierce knew his most pressing problem was time. If the seeds weren't planted by late March, early April, the plan would definitely fail for want of a crop. He consulted his calendar; he had barely two months to initiate the project and get the seeds in the ground.

He sat down and drafted a letter to his mentor and friend, The Hon. Salmon P. Chase, informing him of the difficulty he'd had with Reynolds. He told the Treasury Secretary he would soon be sending a plan for approval and asked that his orders be amended, making him the primary authority for the Negroes' care and moral support. He assured the Secretary that Port Royal was the perfect place to prove to the world that freed men, given the proper tools, guidance, and opportunity, would work independently, and were capable of taking care of themselves.

But the people, lacking food and clothing, were barely fit to work. He wrote another letter, appealing to his Boston contact, the Reverend Jacob Manning, for help. He also stressed the need for talented, enthusiastic people to work as teachers and plantation superintendents.

Satisfied he'd done all he could up to now, he prepared for a good night's sleep. An exhaustive two months stretched ahead.

CHAPTER 12

TITUS AND HAMP

I t was mid-January, time to start fertilizing the cotton fields. The seasons were beginning to overlap, but Reynolds, already short of workers and under pressure to finish last season's abundant crop, could not spare the stronger hands to do the laborious mud work. He'd already mustered everyone to pick, pack, and transport cotton—even the elderly.

Bentoo and Crecie worked side-by-side and much to Crecie's surprise, her grandmother held her own. Isham took the children to Possum Point with him each day, but Crecie worked with a worried mind. The long hours of gang labor, coupled with Nobles's nasty temper, kept her on the edge of an emotional breakdown. As the tension between her and Isham escalated, headaches and stomach cramps became a part of life. None of the herbs helped, and the pain grew more intense daily. Finally, when her stomach became knots of burning agony, she succumbed and stayed home from the fields.

The outhouse sat at the far edge of the clearing, and although Crecie had already visited it twice that day, she felt a third gut-wrenching attack coming on. She frantically fumbled with the ramshackle door and, plopping down on the splintery seat, barely made it in time. As wind whistled through the privy's disjointed walls, she tapped her cold feet and pulled her ragged cloth coat close. A gentle massage to her griping abdomen gave her a small measure of relief. Shaking her tingling feet awake, she hurriedly finished her business and spent the rest of the day in the wall-bed.

The worst of the pain had eased by the next day but she still sent the children with Isham. Lying in bed gave her chance to think about what she called Isham's foothold and how she'd been so set against it. But he and a few other squatters had persisted, helping each other clear the thickets they'd claimed. *I been wrong about all o' that, worrying about what buckra gwine say. But white man ain't say nothing—no soldiers, no gov'ment—nobody run 'em off.* She got out of bed, muttering as she searched for more rags to layer on. "I done make my mind up, can't let worry send me to my grave."

Crecie huddled against the wind as she trudged along the road. Unsure of what she would say when she got to Isham's field, she knew for certain she wasn't going back to work for Nobles. She passed the fork leading to the contraband camp and, deep in thought, was unaware of the two young men who'd entered the road behind her.

"Morning," they chorused.

She turned and faced them; one glance caused her to her stop suddenly. Neither wore a hat, and their thick hair lay matted in uneven clumps. Tattered remnants of shirts and pants served as clothing. The ragged layers barely covered their emaciated bodies, and Crecie clearly saw patches of skin and knobby bones peeking through. Threadbare pieces of rugs, tied with frayed twine, served as coats. They'd wrapped bits of burlap to their shoeless feet, and she'd never seen anyone, not even slaves, as wretched as these youths.

"Who you? What ya'll name?" she asked and resumed walking.

"My mama name me Titus," said one of them, his complexion nearly as dark as Crecie's. "But everybody call me Dusty because that what Massa Riley call me."

"H-h-Hamp," said the other young man, stuttering. "Buh-b-but my name b-be Hampton."

She addressed the first youth. "Well, what name *you* go by— Dusty or Titus?"

He didn't immediately answer. Then after taking a few long strides, he said softly, "Titus. Dusty be a slave name, and I ain't no slave no mo'...my name Titus."

"You got family, Titus, kin folks?" she asked.

The question opened an eager floodgate.

"Old Massa Riley sold my Pa long befo' the war, but my mama and brothers and sisters still on the plantation. It be seven o' us. I'm the oldest."

Crecie looked at him closely, figuring him to be eighteen, nineteen. "So how you come to be here?"

"Well, this day I been in the rice field, doing mud work, and then I see the Union boat patrolling the river, loaded with runaways. By the time ol' Massa see me, I been on the river bank. 'Come back!' he holler and then I hear him shoot the gun. I had to pick between him and the river—I pick the river."

"And h-h-he can't swim a l-lick," said Hamp.

"What?" said Crecie.

"Billy Yanks on the boat been yelling fo' me to keep coming, so I keep wading out; but the water got mo' deep, 'til my head start bobbing under."

"Huh-he just about d-d-drown," said Hamp.

"I would o' too, if you ain't jump off the boat and save me. I too thankful. Now I be a free man."

Crecie stopped in the middle of the road and stared at him. "You mean to tell me you can't swim, and you jump in the river just to get here? To St. Helena, so's you can say you be free?"

"Fo' sho; and gwine do it again, if need be."

"Muh-muh-me, t-t-too," said Hamp.

"From the looks of you, I don't know why," said Crecie. "Seeing as bad off you be, you should o' just stay on the mainland. Where you from, anyway?"

"Mulberry rice plantation. But times just as hard on the Main—."

"Muh-muh-maybe worser!" said Hamp.

"And I rather die starving *free*, than die starving *slave* any day!"

"Where ya'll headed fo'?" she asked.

"Nowhere, just trying to find work, food," said Titus.

They continued in silence and she mulled over the risks the youths had taken for freedom's sake. When they reached the field, Isham was on the far side, busting sod. The children sat astride Rex as Sham lead him around the field. Crecie waved and Isham started toward them.

"My man Isham need some help. Talk to him, see if he'll take you on."

"That be a kind offer…what your name be?" Titus asked.

"Crecie."

"Thank you kindly, Miz Crecie."

She glanced around nervously. It was the first time she'd ever heard a black woman referred to as Miss, and the forbidden words—*Miz Crecie*—hung in the air.

Then she relaxed, realizing that changing times had made the boy bold. A slight smile played on her lips. "You welcome, Titus, but just call me Crecie."

Isham reached the group. "What you doing here?" he asked his wife. "And who these men?"

She didn't waver. "I come to work, Isham; and here be two mo' to help. Things moving fast these days, and somehow or another, I got to catch up to 'em."

At first, Crecie feared Nobles's reprisal and worked with one eye looking over her shoulder. But when he didn't come for her, she fell into a comfortable work routine. By the end of January the first winter crop—cabbage and Irish potatoes—had been planted and everyone looked forward to the harvest in March.

Titus and Hamp received scant compensation, compared to the amount of work they did, but they were grateful. Isham had scrounged up enough tattered clothes to keep them from freezing and the meager rations he provided kept them alive, even adding a little meat to their bones. They looked on as Crecie carefully bundled their sparse weekly provisions.

"Take yo' time eating this," she admonished, bringing two jars of pears out of the shed. She gestured towards the half-filled sacks of rice, corn, and sweet potatoes before giving them their precious food bundles. "You know this lil' bit o' food got to last we."

"Y-yeah, us know," said Hamp. "You t-tell we the same thing every time."

She eyed him sharply and Titus hastened to speak up. "Oh, but it ain't no harm fo' you to keep on telling we, Crecie. Us so glad fo' what you and Isham do fo' we."

"Yeah, I muh-mighty 'blige to you," said Hamp.

"Me and Isham ain't do that much; would o' been a smaller crop if it don't be fo' ya'll. *I* be the thankful one!" She secured the shed's rusty lock as the young men headed for the contraband camp.

CHAPTER 13

ON TO WASHINGTON

Treasury Secretary Chase moved swiftly from behind the massive Federalist desk. "Welcome, Edward! Welcome," he said, beaming.

"Thank you, sir," said Pierce. "It's a pleasure to see you again."

Chase grasped his former secretary's elbow, steering him toward a pair of wing-back chairs. "Here, please sit."

Pierce settled into the chair and Chase sat in the one beside it. "Now, tell me, Edward, what is the news at Port Royal?"

"Ahh, where do I begin," replied Pierce. "The whole area is bustling; so much so Commodore Du Pont remarked that the islands are teeming with collectors—cotton, statistics, and religious—all with one aim in mind: abuse the generals!"

Chase chuckled. "I gather you've met the military aristocracy."

"Oh, yes. General Sherman made sure of that. He called a meeting with everyone, all the generals *and* their abusers. His instructions were clear: we're to find a solution for what *he* termed, the Negro problem. As far as I'm concerned the biggest problem is Colonel Reynolds, and he was the only one to offer a solution."

"Leasing land to cotton speculators, correct?"

"Yes, that's right, with the lessees being white men only; no thought of post-slavery support for the freedmen."

"That's what I surmised. I received your proposal last week. I'm pleased to see it provides training for them, guidance toward self-sufficiency."

"Thank you, sir. With tools, supervision, and education, my proposal would benefit everyone; but it requires time and money. That's why I sensed General Sherman favors Reynolds's solution; his plan would bring a quick profit, readily put money in the treasury."

Chase leaned back in his chair and crossed his long legs. "At this point you need not be too concerned about what Sherman favors."

Pierce arched his brow and leaned forward. "Oh? Why not? He commands the Department of the South, doesn't he?"

Chase nodded, but remained silent.

"He appears to be doing a good job," Pierce continued, "making public appeals to northern societies, seeking food and clothing for the Negroes. But I feel his efforts are for the sake of expediency, not heartfelt. I think he lacks fervor for the work at hand."

Chase uncrossed his legs and leaned in closer to Pierce. "Apparently you're not the only one who senses that. Military gossip has it that powerful abolitionists are pressuring the War Department to remove him from that post; they want someone whose views are more in keeping with their own. Besides, except for a few skirmishes now and then, there's little military engagement on the islands."

"Yes, I realize that; and based on what I've heard, Sherman craves action. Do you know if anyone's been appointed?"

"It's not official, but it's rumored the abolitionists favor David Hunter. He's a bit eccentric, but very much an anti-slavery advocate."

"Mmm, never heard of him."

"Right now he commands the Department of Kansas."

"Well, if he can handle Bleeding Kansas, he should be well-suited for Port Royal. Maybe he'll give the northern newspapers something positive to say about emancipation for a change," Pierce said.

"Well, I doubt he'll do anything to tarnish it." They lapsed into a comfortable silence, then Chase spoke. "Tell me, did you meet my friend the Reverend Mansfield French? He was in the islands the same time you were, doing some reconnaissance work for the American Missionary Association."

"Oh, I almost forgot; he asked me to give you his warmest regards. He and I were outnumbered by the army and at the complete mercy of your cotton agents. Consequently, we formed an alliance. He's going to appeal to the AMA in New York, get them involved in the Port Royal project—if it meets your approval, that is."

"Why, by all means you have my approval; but the final word comes from President Lincoln. I've already arranged an appointment for you; tomorrow, I believe. Speak with my secretary regarding the specifics."

"Thank you, sir."

The men rose and shook hands.

"You're very much welcome. I know you're going to do a fine job."

And it will have to be in a very short time, thought Pierce. "I appreciate your confidence in me, sir. It was a pleasure seeing you again."

Edward Pierce waited in the anteroom with the other fifty or so favor-seeking petitioners. They clustered in small groups, chatting or restlessly pacing the floor. A few loitered near the huge oaken door, wrangling with the doorkeepers for permission to enter.

An hour passed before the door, which led to a broad corridor, finally opened. The crowd gravitated towards it, grudgingly stepping aside for those who already had entry rights. Pierce clutched his official pass and pushed to the front of the throng. He presented Chase's note and walked through the door unquestioned.

The stairs at the end of the large hallway led to the President's working office. Pierce tapped on the slightly opened door and a weary voice responded, "Come in." He entered, and through the wide row of windows, saw soldiers milling around their encampments. The Washington Monument, initiated twenty-five years earlier and still two-thirds unfinished, loomed in the distance.

The President sat at the smaller of two desks, his head down. He seemed to be in deep concentration. Pierce, waiting to be acknowledged, surveyed the shabby, over-furnished office. Fire crackled in the marble fireplace and weak light emanated from the gas lamps. A large walnut table, piled with maps and volumes of military history, sat in the center of the room. Wooden wobbly-looking chairs, pushed neatly under the table, awaited Cabinet members. Two antique chairs flanked a tall pigeonholed mahogany desk; its numerous openings bulged with notes, letters. Pierce surmised they were from persistent constituents, maybe even those waiting in the anteroom.

The President looked up, his face solemn and forlorn. Pierce had read about the children. Other than war reports, the story headlined the news. Both of the President's sons, after drinking contaminated water, had contracted typhoid fever. While Tad, the younger boy, slowly continued to improve, Willie's condition had steadily worsened.

The President stood. He stared down at Pierce, not inviting him to sit. "Well?" Lincoln sounded ill-tempered and he pursed his lips shut.

Pierce's frustration rose. Treasury Secretary Chase was the sole Cabinet member showing concern for the Negroes' plight, recognizing the crucial role they played in the nation's economy. Congress, except for Senator Sumner's tireless anti-slavery appeals, had turned a blind eye on the issue of emancipation. When Pierce approached those statesmen he personally knew, they had listened politely, but didn't offer their support. In fact, they didn't seem concerned that much of the Northern economy depended on the mills receiving a steady supply of cotton. The President was Pierce's last hope for an ally. *I can't give up,* he thought. He began to speak of the Negroes' situation, stressing their desperate conditions and immediate needs.

"Hundreds of slaves escape to the islands daily; they come with nothing, just the clothes on their backs, rags really. Food is in short supply and sickness—."

"I don't think I need to be bothered with such details," Lincoln impatiently interrupted. "Why is there such a great itching to get the Negroes into our lives, behind Federal lines?"

Pierce bit his lip, reminding himself that he was standing before the President of the United States. He regained his composure then continued. "These people did not ask to be in our lives, sir; and no one invited us into theirs. Besides, the Negroes at Port Royal have always lived there, long before we occupied their domiciles."

Lincoln did not reply, but sat down, scribbling something on a card: "I shall be obliged if the Sec. of the Treasury will in his discretion give Mr. Pierce such instructions in regard to Port Royal contrabands as may seem judicious. A. LINCOLN. Feb.15, 1862." He silently extended the card.

So, surmised Pierce, *as history must write it, the President approached the great question of slavery slowly and reluctantly.*

As if he had heard Pierce's thoughts, Lincoln spoke. "Do what you feel is honorable, but I will not decide the Negro issue on public opinion alone."

"I'm very appreciative for the privilege to serve, sir, and I shall continue to pray for your sons' good health. Good day."

"I thank you for your prayers," he uttered. Then, bowing his head, returned to his private angst. Pierce gently closed the door.

⊶⊷

Congress's response to Pierce's proposal was apathetic at most, leaving him apprehensive and frustrated. The assembly had reluctantly approved the plans for the Port Royal Experiment, and had inadequately funded it. The only thing the cash-strapped government initially provided for was the superintendents' and teachers' transportation and housing. Benevolent societies and private donors would have to provide capital for seeds, equipment, and salaries until the current cotton crop was sold. Then there was the destitution—the Negroes' dire need for food and clothing. Pierce dreaded the trip to Boston, worried his appeal in their behalf would meet opposition there as well.

CHAPTER 14

AT THE END OF THE DAY

On an unusually temperate day in February, Crecie packed a lunch of hard-boiled eggs and crackling cornbread and took the children fishing. As she rowed out into the middle of the creek, she realized it had been months since she'd had the time or energy to do anything with her family. Ossie and Louise, lulled by the boat's gentle sway, quickly nodded off. But Leona and Willie sat quietly as Crecie dipped the line into the water; they watched wide-eyed each time she unhooked the flopping fish, throwing them into the bucket. After she'd caught enough for supper, she showed the children how to bait the hook and lower the line. A fish took Leona's bait right away.

"Ma!" she screamed. "I got one!" Her shrieks startled the sleeping toddlers, and they stood, rocking the boat.

"Sit! Sit!" yelled Crecie. "I can't swim, and this too much water to drink!"

"Ma! Ma! I see 'em!" squealed Willie. "He be a big one."

Crecie steadied the rocking skiff then helped Leona land the fish. It *was* a big one, a catfish, the biggest catch of the day. After all the excitement, Crecie decided it was time to return to the shore. It had been a good outing, a fun day.

They had almost reached the quarters at Midway when she heard Rex's heavy gait coming from behind. She turned, surprised that Isham had left the field so early. He'd kept the same daily routine as when he was the driver at Ivy Oaks, rising before dawn and working until dusk—even on a day like today—Saturday.

He dismounted and the children clamored around, all trying to tell him about the fish. Crecie got his attention first.

"Where you going this time of day?" she said.

Isham took the pail of fish from her and strapped it onto Rex.

"I got to thinking," he said, lifting Leona and sitting her on the horse's broad back. "Isham, you be a free man, now...."

"Almost free," said Crecie.

"Well, close enough," he said, placing Willie in front of Leona. "Anyway, I say to myself, 'Isham, you free now, done work hard; why not hang up yo' hat fo' the rest of the day, go see if any o' that crackling bread left." He placed the last two children on the horse.

"But Papa, you too late," said Leona, "we done ate it all up."

"Yep! Aaall gone," repeated Willie.

Ossie and Louise mumbled a gibberish agreement.

"What! No crackling bread left?" Isham playfully snarled. "Who ate all that crackling bread?" He tickled Leona, asking her, "Did *you* eat it?"

"Nooo," she squealed between giggles.

Then feigning a grimace, in turn, he crept up on each child. "Let me see..." he said, tickling each of them. The question stayed the same—"Who ate my crackling bread?"

The children waited in delicious anticipation, hoping against hope to be his next victim. Each choice brought another round of tickling, along with giggling denials.

"Me, me!" said Ossie, as both toddlers raised their arms to be tickled.

"Don't worry, Isham," said Crecie laughing. "I saved you some crackling bread; hid it real good, too."

The family entered the road leading to their cabin and was surprised to see a wagon in the yard. "That look like a army wagon," said Crecie. "I wonder why Mose here?"

Isham stopped and stared at the ground. Crecie followed his gaze, seeing boot prints in the dirt. The two quilts she'd hung on the line to dry were gone.

"Stay here," Isham said as he ventured toward the wide-open door.

Crecie ignored his orders and, leaving the children on Rex, followed closely. She became alarmed when she walked past the army wagon; it was loaded with the food from the shed, their winter store.

Isham stood in the doorway, having caught the Union soldiers red-handed. They'd stripped the shelves bare but continued to stuff the last of the preserves inside their duffel bags, unrepentant.

Isham spoke softly. "I thought ya'll come fo' help we, not teef we food and things."

The soldier closest to him responded. "Help *you?* A damn darkie? Hell, I'm just here for the thirteen dollars a month army pay."

Crecie warily watched him heft the bag to his shoulder. His hair was the whitest she had ever seen on so young a person. She studied his gaunt face and ill-fitting blue uniform, realizing that he and the other men were about as bony as the contraband refugees. He walked towards the door and Isham took another step into the room.

"No, Isham, no," Crecie whispered, grabbing his arm. "Let th—."

Isham jerked away, blocking the door.

"I don't want no trouble, suh—."

"Then step aside and you won't get none," said another soldier, standing near the fireplace. His thick, russet beard made him appear to be the older of the two.

"I ax ya'll kindly to please put we things down," persisted Isham.

A third soldier came out of the other room. "Who gonna make us, darkie?" His eyes—piercing blue slits—signaled the other two for backup; the three of them then stepped forward, surrounding Isham.

The bearded man spoke. "I'm telling ya for the last time, Sambo, get the hell outta the way!"

But Isham stood his ground. "Naw suh, I can't let—."

They gang-rushed him and Crecie screamed. "No! Stop!"

But the soldiers continued, pummeling Isham to the floor.

Frantic, she darted from one to the other, shrieking, "Stop! Please suh; take it, take what you want!"

Ignoring her, the white-haired man led off with a sharp kick to Isham's side. He groaned but managed to twist the soldier's foot and send him sprawling to the floor. Then Isham struggled up, half kneeling.

Red beard lifted his rifle. "No!" screamed Crecie, grabbing his arm.

"Get off me, you wench!" He boxed her; she careened into the wall, hearing the gun butt smash against Isham's temple. Blood oozed from the wound and he fell back, barely conscious. The men continued to kick. As their hobnail boots found their mark, sickening thuds echoed throughout the room.

Finally, breathing hard from their exertion, the soldiers stepped over Isham's motionless body, joking and laughing as they left.

She knelt beside her unconscious husband. "Isham, Isham," she pleaded, slapping him. When he didn't respond, she grabbed the water dipper and doused his face. He groaned and struggled to move.

"My head, my hea…." he murmured, then fell still again.

From some distant place Crecie heard screams, but didn't know if they came from her or the children trapped on the big horse.

Suddenly Amos and others crowded inside the cabin. The young carpenter knelt beside the unconscious man. "He just got the wind knocked out a little bit," he said, attempting to reassure Crecie. "He be alright d'reckly." But she knew, watching Isham's blood drip onto the floor, that his injuries amounted to more than shortness of breath.

Someone had taken the children off the horse, and they ran inside, crying and gently touching Isham. "Papa...wake up, Papa," Leona gently pleaded.

Crecie let them be. "Amos," she said, "please, *please* go fetch Bentoo."

CHAPTER 15
COMING FO' TO CARRY ME HOME

B entoo knelt beside the low wall-bed, gently probing Isham's swollen abdomen. She suspected he was bleeding inside, a bad sign. "They beat him terrible," she mumbled, shaking her head. Crecie knew as much, but had prayed that she was wrong.

"I told him, Bentoo...I told him to let them solders be, but he—."

"Hand me that candle," Bentoo ordered. Holding the light close, she raised Isham's eyelid, the one not swollen shut. His pupil contracted slightly. *Well, that's better than nothing*, she thought. Tentatively she touched the knot on the side of his face. "How fast this lump been swelling up?"

"Real fast. It be two times big now."

Bentoo dabbed at the head wound. "They split he skull open, too. I'll clean it while you put together a poultice. Hurry—I don't want infection to set in." But it wasn't infection that worried her.

Crecie rushed over to the medicine table. She was rummaging among the hodgepodge of plant elixirs and herb jars, when she touched a fluted milk-white bowl. "Oh, no!" she exclaimed, snatching her hand away. *The crackling bread—Isham crackling bread...what if—oh no! no!* She spun around, facing Bentoo.

"He gwine be alright ain't he, Bentoo," she pleaded. Her voice quivered. "Please say he—."

"Quit sniveling Crecie, and get that poultice together!"

Bentoo's firm rebuke kindled her resolve to be strong and she turned back to the table. Careful to avoid the fluted bowl, she located the elm bark, comfrey leaves, and other plant matter and heaped them into the mortar. Her hands trembled as she ground the herbs then slowly added warm water. She stirred the fine powder until its consistency was just right, then handed the mortar to her grandmother.

Bentoo placed a clean muslin cloth on the wound and began spreading the mixture on it. Isham's ragged breathing stopped. Crecie gasped and reached for him, but Bentoo waved her away. "Leave him be, the medicine getting through." The irregular rhythm started up again.

Bento placed her hand on Isham's stomach and prayed. "Oh, wise and all knowing God, in your mercy way, please bring healing to Isham. I got the faith, Lord, and I know you got the power. In the name of Jesus, I ax that yo' healing power enter he body. Amen."

Crecie sat stunned, trying to scrutinize her grandmother's unexpressive face. "I ain't never hear you pray befo'; never see you in no church neither, not even when the *black* preacher come to Slave Row."

Bentoo continued applying the paste. "I use to go to church all the time, befo' Massa bring yo' mama to the plantation."

"Polly? What she got to do with church? And you praying?"

"Polly show me what a true Christian be."

"Why you never tell me none of this befo'? And you ain't never say too much about Polly...or Randy either."

"You ain't ax."

"I axing now."

"Alright, then; make a pot o' ginger tea while I finish with Isham and I gwine tell you."

Crecie prepared the tea and the two sat at the table.

"Well, you see, Massa always bring the preachers fo' we, sometimes the white one, sometimes the black one. 'Course *he* always tell 'em what to preach, to tell we the yoke of iron be cast around the servant neck, and how the Bible say the white man born to rule the black man. Massa hard set against slave knowing how to read and write, because the Bible say the truth gwine free you, and Massa ain't want none of us reading about being free."

"No, he don't want that," Crecie agreed.

"Preacher always say us must work hard for Massa and our reward gwine be in heaven; but Jesus say the will of God be done on earth like in heaven."

"Uh-huh. Now what that mean?"

"Polly say God want us to have good things *now*, on earth, not wait 'til we die and go to heaven." Bentoo paused, slurping the hot tea. "*All* the massas get real mean, nasty when it come to reading and writing; slave that know how to read and write know as much as they do, won't be so set to obey they massa then, neither." Bentoo took another sip of tea.

"Polly tell you all that?" asked Crecie.

"Yeah, she tell me and yo' pa Randy a lot o' thing. Sometimes I wonder if that be why he run off, she make it sound so good. He been a riverboat pilot, travel all over. One day the steamboat come back, but he ain't on it. Don't know to this day what happen to him; whether he dead or what. But oh, how he love his self some Polly; and she love him back, too. Then Polly, she...she...die. You and the great grands," she paused glancing at the bed, "and Isham, all the close family I got now."

"Why Polly kill herself?"

The words hung in the air and the silence lengthened. Bentoo stared into the dying fire, then rose to feed it a piece of wood. She stoked the embers and the blaze was reflected in her glistening eyes.

"I'm sorry, Bentoo," said Crecie. "I didn't—I mean it been so long ago, I just thought...."

"That kind o' hurt just won't leave," said Bentoo, returning to the table. She poured another cup of tea, but this time she added moonshine to it.

"Want some?" She offered Crecie the cup.

She shook her head.

"I don't know fo' sho why she did that, Crecie. I just know she born into this world free, and when the slave catchers snatch her from the settlement, they take her life, too...."

Crecie sat quietly, thinking about how she'd been struggling with changes for the past ten months.

"Befo' she be a slave, she be buried in her grave," said Bentoo.

From freedom to slave or from slave to freedom—change be hard. Polly couldn't do it...not even for me.

"But I never mention that to you, the thing that happen to Polly. Who tell you about it?"

Now it was Crecie's turn to remain silent, and her mind went back to a sunny, fall day, when she was seven years old. "I'll take that 'shine now," she said, pushing her cup over to Bentoo. "You ain't the only one got secrets." She gulped the homemade brew and then began her tale.

Crecie was seven years old, chasing autumn leaves in the slaves' burial ground as Bentoo foraged in the woods nearby. Suddenly the child heard a strange voice call her name. She looked around but saw no one. Frightened, she started to run towards the woods, to Bentoo. But just ahead, under a magnolia tree, she saw what looked like a floating cloud. Curious, she slowed to a walk; the closer she got, the less fearful she became. She reached the tree and looked up. The cloud was a woman, dressed in white, dangling from the lowest tree limb. Her head, bent slightly forward, leaned to the side, and her eyes were closed as if asleep; but the noose had snapped her neck, forcing her tongue from the back of her throat. It hung long, protruding from a twisted mouth. Crecie blinked, and the fleeting vision vanished. That was the first of many times the mother who had abandoned her in life came to her in spirit. Crecie had not known what it all meant, so she'd kept the apparitions a secret and learned to live with them.

"Nobody tell me about it; I see her for myself," said Crecie. "See her hanging in the magnolia tree, and I just know it be Polly."

Suddenly a chill enveloped the room and a faint tapping sound, seven in quick succession, came from the direction of the bed. The women jumped. There was no earthly explanation for the sounds since Dahlia had taken the children to her cabin.

"You hear that?" whispered Bentoo.

Crecie scowled and nodded. "Bentoo, I be *forever* hearing something," she said, hurrying over to Isham's bed. His breathing had become more labored, and his lips trembled as he struggled to speak. She bent low, her ear close to his mouth. Bentoo hovered near, watching.

"Gr...gra...yard," he whispered.

"Graveyard?" said Crecie. "No, no, Isham, don't say that!"

He tried again to speak, but all she felt was a wispy, wordless puff against her ear.

Bentoo edged Crecie aside and, kneeling by the bed, once again held the candle close. This time Isham's pupil remained rigidly still. She felt for his pulse, but finding none, gently folded his arms across his chest.

"No," said Crecie, hastily unfolding Isham's arms. "Isham ain't...ain't—he just—oh no, Lord; don't let it be!"

CHAPTER 16
CRECIE'S GRIEF

"Wake up, Isham," Crecie demanded, patting his battered face.

Bentoo, preparing an elixer-filled potion, kept a keen eye on her granddaughter.

"Isham! Isham!" said Crecie, shaking the body. *"Wake up, I say!"*

Bentoo hurried over. Pulling her away, she placed the elixir-filled cup to Crecie's lips. "Here, drink this."

Crecie struggled against the older woman's grip. "No! I got to tend to Isham."

Bentoo held fast. "Drink it!"

"No!"

Bentoo tried a different approach. Speaking softly, she slightly loosened her hold. "Drink it, chile, then I free you."

Crecie gagged on the first sip. Bentoo had mixed the moonshine and herbs to its highest potency.

"Keep drinking," she coaxed, "take it all down."

The young woman frowned into the cup; then glancing over at Isham, gulped the rest down. It burned her throat and the bitter brew took effect immediately. She steadied herself against the table. "I got to...go...see about...." She slumped into a chair, fighting to keep her head up. But the potion, a calming balm, took control; she'd fallen into an impenetrable sleep within minutes.

It was late evening when the sound of muffled voices outside the window awoke her. Family and friends, ensconced on crude wooden benches, had come as soon as they'd finished work in the fields. They came to offer comfort, but also to wait and watch. Sitting helter-skelter around the yard, they eyed the body, alert for the slightest life-sign—a finger's tremor, the whisper of a groan, an eyelid's tiny tic. The people had a saying: "Every shut eye ain't sleep; every good-bye ain't gone." In reference to the dead, the old adage spoke legends, because now and then, when someone slipped into a death-like trance, it was possible to be buried alive. The wake would last three days, and until the burial, Isham would never be left alone.

Crecie made her way into the yard and staggered to the body. "Isham don't need no cooling board," she declared, "bring him inside!" She grappled with the corpse, causing the wooden boards to tilt. Dahlia and Lizbet, strong women with strong hands, rushed over and gently led her away.

"Come, Crecie," said Dahlia. "We gwine take care you while Bentoo see about things."

She didn't resist when they walked her back to the cabin. The women took a stance near the door and Crecie sat by the window, her hands folded in her lap.

"You feel like talking, Crecie?" Dahlia asked.

She shook her head—an emphatic "no"—and began to speak. "He ain't dead, you know." She focused out the window, on the body. "Just you wait—Isham gwine be talking, laughing—sitting around just like we—soon as…as…."

The two care-givers exchanged glances, but said nothing.

"Us should o' gone," Crecie muttered. "If us been with Miz Alina, Isham wouldn't be hurt now." She stood, eyeing the door.

Lizbet moved near, blocking the opening. "It ain't nothing you done, Crecie," she said. "Them demon soldiers be at fault; they the ones done that evil."

Soldiers! Oh, Lord, them soldiers! In a flash the grisly memory burst through her fogged brain, corralling her thoughts, and like yesterday's reality, she was powerless to stop it. Over and over it went—the resounding clack of hobnail boots as they dislodged teeth and cracked ribs; the nauseating thud when the boots assailed the liver and collapsed the lungs. Crecie covered her ears, desperately trying to drown out her own piercing shrieks of "Why, Isham! Why!"

Hearing Crecie's lamentations, the elders rushed in and embraced her in prayer; but the sickening images would not go away.

Suddenly, she spotted the jug, the elixir. She snatched it up and downed a mighty swig, drinking until the mind-numbing potion dulled her senses. As Lizbet helped her to the pallet, one lucid thought entered Crecie's mind: *Nobody, not even Isham, could o' live through what they done to him.*

It was the night of the funeral and Crecie had been drunk, or close to it, during the entire three-day wake. Sitting at the table—head slightly bowed, hands pressed against her throbbing forehead—she struggled to clear her mind. The neighboring women had cleaned everything, scrubbing the floor with lye soap. But a stubborn rust-brown stain remained. *Isham's blood—it be bull-headed, just like him... him should o' just let things be—let 'em take and go.* The sorrow rose within and she longed to forget, to drink into oblivion. She fought the urge and, folding her arms on the table, rested her aching head. *If I drink and if I don't—it ain't gwine change what happen.*

Bentoo, hovering near, placed a jar in front of her. "I made you some herb tea," she said.

Crecie gratefully downed the soothing drink.

"You feel better?" Bentoo asked, gently massaging her back.

"I...I be fine," she lied. "The chillun, how they been holding up to...everything?"

"They ain't been here too much, Dahlia been keeping 'em. 'Course, Ossie and Louise too young to understand. I told Leona and Willie their papa gone to Heaven."

Crecie furrowed her brow. "What they say?"

"Willie...po' little thing...want to know when he coming back...."

Me, too, Willie... me, too.

"But Sham," Bentoo said, "can never tell what he thinking, him so slow catching on to things."

"Leona? What she say?"

Bentoo sighed. "I think she the only one that truly know. It be hard on her."

Crecie didn't respond, just rubbed her forehead. The women sat quietly, each coping in her own way. After a while, Bentoo went to the window and looked out to the road.

"Folks been coming since first dusk."

"I know," said Crecie, although she'd been only dimly aware of their presence.

The mourners had come from plantations near and far. Some walked, some drove ox-carts, and some rowed from adjacent islands. After toiling all day, they came just as they were—ragged, hungry, weary—intent on paying their last respects. It was late night by the time they'd all assembled, bracing against the February cold. Everyone knew what had happened to Isham and wanted answers, but who would they ask? Before the Big Gun Shoot, the line separating friend and foe was clearly marked. True, the bondsmen had suffered at the master's cruel hand, but rarely to the point of death; why would a man destroy his own property? But now the army, untested and untried, was in control. The soldiers stole, raped, murdered; yet they were shielded by the same generals who'd promised to protect the people. The former slaves had many questions, but that had to wait. Now they had to see that Isham got a proper send-off, one according to custom.

"It look like they about ready to go," said Bentoo. "You got something shiny to mark the grave with, something him been fond o'?"

Crecie nodded and retrieved the milk-glass bowl from the medicine table. The crackling bread she'd hidden away was stuck inside, moldy. "This been Isham lil' crackling bread bowl—won't eat crackling out o' nothing else."

Bentoo picked up the stone pestle. "You got to break that bowl so he spirit stay in the graveyard." She slyly eyed Crecie. "But *you* see 'em anyhow, ain't it?"

Crecie shrugged, scraping the dried food out of the bowl. "Sometimes I do, sometimes I don't."

"Here, take this pestle," Bentoo insisted. "Nobody want him roam—."

Suddenly Sham burst into the room, yelling, "Come see! Come see!"

Crecie hurried to him. "What wrong with you, boy?"

"Outside—all them people!" His angst-filled body scurried around the room. "Isham shut up in that box and I fixing to get he out."

"Oh, no," exclaimed Bentoo, blocking the door.

The boy shoved her aside and bolted out into the yard.

"Come on, Bentoo," said Crecie. "We got to catch he fast."

"I coming," she said, grabbing an elixir.

Amos and Hamp joined the chase, cornering the boy. He fought mightily as the men held him, but the women gently coaxed, getting him to swallow the elixir. He calmed down and soon fell asleep. The men stretched him out in the wagon next to the coffin, and the people lined up for the processional.

CHAPTER 17
THE VALUE OF LABOR

Congress approved the Port Royal project, but only funded transportation and housing. Pierce felt apprehensive—uncertain about resources for salaries, tools, equipment, and provisions for the freedmen.

He returned to Boston on the verge of giving up but discovered he'd worried needlessly. Rev. Manning had printed his letter in the *Transcript,* appealing to the public for help. Boston—along with New York and Philadelphia—rallied to the call, collecting tons of food, clothing, and medicine. Several of Boston's most influential abolitionists formed a new organization—The New England Educational Commission for Freedmen—and its well-heeled members volunteered to underwrite the salaries and equipment until the current cotton crop was sold. Pierce was heartened by the progress, seeing the divergent abolitionist groups working for a common cause.

But one thing lessened his enthusiasm—the death of the President's twelve-year-old son, William Wallace Lincoln.

⊷⊶

Pierce was so focused on fertilizing and bed rebuilding—key steps in producing superb Sea Island cotton—he barely listened to the young interviewee's responses. *It's already the middle of February and the land has to rest for a month after it's fertilized. Time is fleeting,* he thought.

Then, as if mocking his misgivings, the cuckoo bird sprang from the wall clock, sounding five times. The last interview of the day had gone past schedule. Pierce frowned, trying to conceal his annoyance. But the job-seeker, a young woman, took the clue and quickly stood.

"Thank you for seeing me, Mr. Pierce. I do hope you will consider my application."

"Yes, of course, Miss Winsor; I will give it my utmost attention. Good day."

He scanned the applicant list and drew a line through her name, muttering, "Too young." Pierce viewed women as incompetent for the project and had initially excluded them; but the Education Commission and Rev. Mansfield French, representing the New York AMA, insisted they be included. Only two women had passed Pierce's meticulous scrutiny, and he'd mentally placed them under Rev. and Mrs. French's supervision.

He sat studying the new superintendents' roster—all staunch New Englanders who would transform the rustic South into industrialized townships. They were well-educated dedicated abolitionists, committed to their beliefs. The array of engineers, doctors, clerks and teachers included Samuel Phillips, a medical student and nephew of fiery abolitionist Wendell Phillips. Harvard divinity student William Channing Gannett, son of a high-ranking Unitarian minister, was also on the list. None of the twenty-five new hires possessed the barest of farming experience, but Pierce wasn't concerned about their lack of agricultural skills. Farming would be left up to the Negroes. He was confident his hand-picked recruits would transform the former slaves into reputable freedmen.

Edward Hooper, an abolitionist scion, entered the office. The young man had just earned his law degree and was among the first to volunteer for Port Royal. Pierce immediately assigned him as his personal aide.

"Wasn't she the last applicant?" asked Pierce looking up.

"Yes, but a Mr. Philbrick is here to see you."

Pierce scanned the list of applicants. "Philbrick...Philbrick," he uttered. "He's not here. That's strange—I *know* this name, but the application fails me."

"That's because I didn't apply." Edward Philbrick, short in stature, but impressive in appearance, had entered the room unannounced. His gaze was steady and Pierce matched it head-on.

"Have we met?" Pierce asked.

"No, not formally. But we do travel in the same circles. My father was Samuel Philbrick."

Aha! Philbrick—pioneer abolitionist, founding member, Massachusetts Antislavery Society....

"Yes, of course. Your father was a man of great presence. Please be seated, Mr. Philbrick." Pierce turned to the waiting Hooper, "Oh, that will be all, Edward."

Philbrick remained standing. "Mr. Pierce, I do apologize for this impromptu visit, but Governor Andrew assured me that once you heard me out, my rude manners would be forgiven."

Massachusetts Governor John Andrew—President of the Educational Commission? Of course you're forgiven!

"Oh, no, you're not intruding," Pierce said, pulling a chair forward. "Please, sit. How may I help you?"

Philbrick accepted the seat and used a white handkerchief to dab at his broad forehead. Pierce noticed he wore a gold wedding band.

"Thank you; it *has* been a rather busy day," said Philbrick. "Perhaps we can help each *other.*"

"Please, continue."

"As you are aware, many white Northerners zealously defend the institution of slavery..."

Pierce nodded, looking beyond Philbrick's thick, sandy beard, trying to guess his age. *Early to mid-thirties,* he surmised, *same as me.*

"...their greatest fear is emancipation: What will happen if four million slaves are unleashed, free to come North? Many feel that they will displace white workers, run amok and rape our women. And should the white man retaliate...."

"Oh, rest assured it will not come to that," said Pierce. "On the whole, these people show a willingness to please; they love the land and will never leave it. They consider the entire plantation their home."

Philbrick leveled his eyes on Pierce and leaned forward. "I beg to differ; there were stories in the *Transcript,* citing they'd rioted and destroyed their masters' abandoned property last November."

"Well, there *is* a slight truth to that," admitted Pierce. "A few *did* go into Beaufort and perform a bit of mischief; but most of the Negroes remained on the plantations, content to busting up cotton gins and farm equipment."

"But there were pictures of the damage in the newsp—."

"That was the soldiers' doings—*they* went on a rampage—willfully looting and destroying everything in sight. If General Sherman hadn't immediately stopped it, the whole town would've been decimated," Pierce said.

"Oh, I see," replied Philbrick, leaning back in the chair.

"It was all a proslavery ploy, designed to portray the Negro as violent savages, undeserving of emancipation. While our abolitionist voice is more powerful than it was thirty years ago, we must remain ever vigilant."

"Yes, we still encounter anti-abolitionist sentiment; however, when the time comes, the government can't just tell the Negroes, 'Go! You're free!'"

"I sincerely doubt that will be the course of action," Piece replied.

"I assume, since you're custodian of the Port Royal Negroes—a new master, so to speak—you know what that course will be."

"Oh, I'm far from being anyone's master. My obligation is only for four months, until the end of the planting season. Prior business commitments dictate my return to Boston. "

"But what about your plan? I heard you were conducting an experiment for emancipation."

"Yes, that's true; but when I leave in June everything will be firmly in place. Right now, my main concern is providing food, clothing, medicine for the freedmen. They're in no condition to work and we need their labor; a third of the nation's economy comes from cotton."

Philbrick nodded. "The *world's* economy even depends on the staple."

"After emancipation we'll need the freedmen to sustain that economy. Not under the lash, of course, but under a wage-based system—"free labor"—if you will. As free laborers, the blacks—whites, too, if they so desire—will have the right to their own labor; working freely of their own volition, for their own personal gain."

Philbrick excitedly bobbed his head. "That's my exact premise! Give men the right incentives and they'll work harder; the harder they work, the more productive they'll become. Greater production means greater profits. That's what I aim to prove—that free labor will produce more cotton—cheaper, too—than slave labor."

"The Port Royal experiment is certainly headed in that direction. We're hopeful it will be the model for free labor at the end of the war." Pierce opened a portfolio and removed several files. "This part of the plan covers *Operations*," he said. "Former black slave drivers will be hired as foremen, ensuring the work is carried out in a systematic fashion." He then explained plantation management, describing how white superintendents would oversee purchases, equipment, supplies. "These learned young men will lead the Negro into freedom."

Philbrick picked up a file labeled *Schools.* "I see you're providing teachers, schools, books for the children—good!"

"Adults, too, if they care to attend."

"How will they be housed?"

"The army is establishing contraband camps for the refugee workers. The native islanders will live in their cabins, rent free. All of them will receive rations and initially paid small wages. After they're accustomed to a free labor system, their wages will increase and they'll be on their own, no longer given anything."

"This fits perfectly with my theory," Philbrick said. "But success depends upon free laborers—be it black men or white."

"Well, poor white trash won't work cotton; they feel it's beneath them."

"So that leaves the Negroes." Philbrick dabbed at his brow. "I'm an engineer by profession, but a businessman by design. This country exports over 350 million dollars worth of cotton and cotton goods annually." He tucked the damp handkerchief into his coat pocket. "I've heard that the black man won't work without the whip—that he's indolent. If that's true, our economy will lose 350 million dollars yearly."

"Balderdash!" protested Pierce. "The Negro doesn't need the whip any more than you or I. Why, when I supervised contrabands in Virginia, at Fortress Monroe, they readily set to hard work—digging trenches, building breastwork—with only the promise of a soldier's rations…beans, rice, sugar, and the like."

"Well, then," said Philbrick, "if they exerted that much effort for rations, how much more will they work for merchandise, for all the things they were denied as slaves? Think about it, four million new wage earners entering the market place, clamoring for dishes, clothes, furniture —shoes that fit. Why, factories will have to run night and day just to keep up with the demand."

"Exactly! And in the final phase, after the Negroes prove their independence and self-sufficiency, they'll be given the opportunity to purchase land—using money from their wages."

"Your plan is well structured," Philbrick said.

"Thank you," replied Pierce. "The premise is to elevate the Negro—upgrade his thinking, his work ethics. When we're through, he'll be a model of New England rectitude."

"That should placate Northern whites," said Philbrick, "seeing the Negro as a rehabilitated, civilized member of society."

The time passed quickly as the young abolitionists delved into political economics and the merits of free labor versus slave labor. Both felt that slavery was immoral—not only because it violated innate human rights—but because it infringed on the laws of economics. Once the South accepted the ideology of the new labor system, the economy would be governed by the invisible hand of the free market, solving the Negro problem.

"I envision the freedmen content with the free labor system and their manufactured goods and luxuries," said Pierce.

"I'm confident your plan will succeed," said Philbrick, "so much so, I'm donating $900.00 to the project."

Pierce was taken aback. "Why, thank you for such a generous, gift; it will certainly help the cause."

"Also, I want to be a part of the experiment—as a volunteer of course."

"We're honored to have a man of your stature; we need more like you."

"And women? Are the islands safe for them? I plan to send for my wife once I'm settled in."

"The pickets appeared to be well-maintained when I visited," said Pierce, "but in times of war...."

"But since the army has a huge coal refueling operation on Hilton Head, I know the Educational Commis—."

"The Commission!" Pierce stood abruptly. "I'm addressing them tonight—at the governor's mansion."

"And I've stayed past my welcome." Philbrick extended his hand and Pierce shook it warmly.

"To the future," Pierce said.

"A productive fiscal future," Philbrick replied.

CHAPTER 18

SAYING GOOD-BYE

The processional stretched almost a quarter of a mile, as hundreds of people, standing two-abreast, waited silently behind the wagon. Crecie noticed that someone had placed blinders on Rex and his ears stood up, alert, like when Isham let the children ride him. The fun-filled memory sharpened her despair. She quickly shifted her view to Mose, sitting in the driver's seat; but just behind him lay the coffin. Right away her knees buckled and she yearned for strong drink. But Bentoo's firm hands held her upright, guiding her toward the processional. Crecie took her place directly in front of the procession; she was surprised by the comforting presence of the mourners standing behind her.

Mose snapped the reins. "Giddy-up!" The slow walk to the graveyard began. Every fifteenth person or so carried a pine-wood torch; furtive shadows danced in their eerie glow. The people sang as they tramped to the cemetery—"Swing low, sweet chariot; comin' for to carry me home…." When the song ended, someone started another. The singing continued until they reached a jungle of thick vines entangled in massive live-oaks. The area, a muddled maze of palmetto scrub and underbrush, hadn't been worth the master's time or money to make arable. But the people, as usual, made do, clearing space as needed to bury their dead.

Cattle wandered among the unfenced burial ground, grazing and expelling dung over the slaves' final resting places. Cedar trees marked many of the death mounds, with a variety of sea shells—sun-bleached ocean symbols—scattered on top. None of the graves had headstones, but stick-crosses, in various stages of decay, listed crookedly over a few of the mounds. The graves were marked with mirrors, glass, or shiny metal objects—things the deceased once held dear—in the belief their reflection would light the way to a new spiritual home. All the items had been deliberately broken, 'killed' in the belief that their 'dying' would prevent the departed from leaving the graveyard to dwell among the living.

The men removed the casket from the wagon, and Crecie checked on Sham. Assured he was sound asleep, she stared off into the dense, moss-draped forest, waiting for Mose to begin. Her hands sweated as she clutched the little bowl's fluted rim.

Mose got down from the wagon and stopped at the edge of the woods. "Ancestors of the spirit world, we humbly ax permission to enter this sacred ground." He waited a few seconds then proceeded into the vine-entangled overgrowth. The coffin-bearers fell in behind him, and Crecie, with downcast eyes, slowly followed. Once inside, the people jockeyed for position and Crecie stood as far away from the coffin as she could.

A grave, four feet deep, was already dug and a trestle table placed beside it. As was the custom, the dead had been uniformly buried east-west. The men positioned the coffin on the table, making certain Isham faced east, toward Africa. Mose stood next to the coffin and solemnly intoned the funeral song:

"Come quickly, we must work hard; the grave not finish yet; Isham heart not cool, not at peace. Come quickly, we must work hard; the grave not finish yet; let Isham heart be cool at once."

Amos carried a cedar tree to the head of the grave.

"Death come quick and cut down the trees," continued Mose. "Let death be satisfied; let death be satisfied at once."

Amos filled in the dirt around the tree, firmly anchoring it.

"Death come quick and cut down the trees; a voice speak from far away," said Mose.

Amos spoke, saying, "Let this tree be the sign of a living spirit, traveling to the other side. Death is not the end of life, the spirit live on."

Crecie kept her head bowed, but the grunt of heavy lifting and the sound of unrestrained weeping signaled Isham had been lowered into the ground.

Mose bent down, scooped up a handful of the excavated dirt, and invited the people to do the same. "Come...come show Isham one last kindness on this side of the Jordan." He threw the dirt upon the coffin and the others followed suit—singing and extolling Isham's virtues as they bid him good-bye.

No one noticed that Crecie had slipped farther away, standing beside a patch of thorny bushes. She listened as the people circled the grave, saying farewell. But she couldn't fathom what was in that coffin. It wasn't Isham—Isham could laugh and talk and love. But if he wasn't there, then where? Her mind answered: *He be gone; everything he be...just gone forever.* The finality of death lay heavy upon her, stripping her of all hope.

The sound of dirt hitting the casket told her the men were filling in the grave. She held tight to the white bowl and, clamping a hand over her mouth, struggled to repress her grief. But one person could no longer stifle her pent-up emotions, and Leona's anguish echoed through-out the cemetery.

"Papa! Papa!" she screamed, running toward the grave.

"Leona!" Crecie tossed the bowl aside and sprinted to her child. The men stopped shoveling and looked to Crecie questioningly. She nodded in reply. The men resumed their task, and

Crecie stared boldly upon the coffin. Holding Leona close, she shielded her from the gaping hole. The child's sorrow diminished the grave's importance. *That body down there, it don't mean nothing if it ain't got life. Life—that what make the body mean something.* Leona wept inconsolably, and Crecie cradled the girl's head to her breast. *And he still living through these chillun—he blood running warm in they veins.* Then, for the first time since the murder, Crecie cried. Not only to mourn Isham, but to celebrate her mother. *Polly take she own body from this earth, but not she life. That gwine go on forever—through me, through these chillun, and they chillun after that.*

Crecie watched the last shovelful fall, heard the spade's pat-a-pat, tamping the dirt into a high, smooth mound. She still grieved, but the determination to fulfill Isham's dream strengthened her. She spoke to the grave. "It gwine be alright, Isham; I promise you, us gwine finish what you start." Immediately a spiritual reconnect surged through her body, displacing the physical void she'd felt.

She turned away from the grave just as Sham, awake and disorientated, called her name. Lifting the still-distraught Leona, she carried her to the wagon, joining Bentoo who was trying to calm the disoriented Sham.

Mose hurriedly scattered sea shells over the mound, ending the ceremony. "The sea bring we," he proclaimed, "and the sea gwine take we back." He then led the procession out of the cemetery. The little milk-white bowl lay forgotten in the briar patch—unbroken and, according to ancient beliefs—alive.

CHAPTER 19

LET HIM ALONE

The assembly room at the governor's mansion was nearly filled by the time Pierce arrived. He looked for a seat, surprised to see such a diverse group of abolitionists in the audience. Some, like him, sought to end slavery via political-economic solutions. Others urged its demise by immediate emancipation. The back-to-Africa adherents advocated colonization. Now here they all sat, side-by-side symbols of doctrinal tolerance. The war and its promise of emancipation had indeed created strange bedfellows. Pierce found a seat just as Governor Andrew stepped to the lectern.

"Good evening, ladies and gentlemen, I'm John Andrew, president of The New England Educational Commission for Freedmen—welcome. This organization, created solely to prepare the Port Royal contrabands for freedom, has arranged a series of lectures for your discernment. Permit me to present our members." He gestured toward the dozen or so men seated behind him. None of them needed introduction, their abolitionist work was so eminent. William Lloyd Garrison, publisher of the *Liberator,* was especially renowned. The men stood as Andrew announced their names. "Special recognition is given to our valiant officers, men who have agreed to chart our group's course—Edward Everett

Hale, chairman; William Endicott, treasurer; Edward Atkinson, secretary; and yours truly, John Andrew, President."

Pierce joined in the polite applause. *A very influential group,* he thought; *especially Massachusetts governor Andrew.*

"Seated among you," continued Andrew, "is Mr. Edward Pierce, newly appointed Special Treasury Agent in charge of the contrabands at Port Royal. As a former army private at Fortress Monroe, Mr. Pierce supervised the Negro laborers, qualifying him for his new position. He is one of Massachusetts' native sons and an ardent worker for freedom's cause. I present to you Special Agent Pierce." Scattered applause rippled through the audience.

"Good evening, gentlemen," said Pierce gripping the podium. "This past November, Union forces captured the Sea Islands and Southern planters abandoned over two hundred plantations, leaving eight thousand slaves to fend for themselves. They were not given piece goods to make their one winter outfit; they now wear rags, what's left of the summer allotment.

"The planters used most of the land to grow cotton and imported ninety percent of their food, primarily from the Midwest. The Union blockade is fully operating, causing a scarcity of everything; food, clothes, tools—*everything.* Plantations on the mainland are managed primarily by wives and mothers who can barely feed themselves, let alone their slaves. Hundreds of half-starved Negroes escape from the mainland daily, seeking food and freedom on the Sea Islands. They wait near the shoreline, wading out when Union vessels approach. The waters are tricky and many drown. Those caught trying to escape are shot by civilian patrols, or even by their owners. But they still risk their lives. There are approximately ten thousand souls on the Sea Islands, and that number grows rapidly.

"These new arrivals are in much worse condition than the island inhabitants, who at least can remain in their own cabins. But the refugees have nothing. Sick and malnourished, they're unable to work. Their clothes are rag *remnants*, and many die from exposure soon after they reach the isla—."

Pierce paused as the rear double doors flew open. The standing, overflow crowd created a pathway and a tall, light-complexioned man entered the room. Straight away, whispers of excited recognition permeated the room. Governor Andrew motioned him forward and all heads followed the man's progress. The late arriver appeared slightly embarrassed as he addressed Pierce.

"I apologize, sir, for this unseemly interruption. Please continue."

Pierce nodded slightly. "Thank you, Mr. Douglass, but an apology is not necessary." He turned back to the audience. "Yes, as I was saying, the Union blockade went into full effect in November. Relief organizations such as the Education Commission are spearheading food and clothing donations. The government is providing tents for the refugees, and will soon establish permanent camps.

"My duty is to help the Negroes at Port Royal survive these extreme conditions and aid in their eventual transformation into freedom. The plan is to hire astute superintendents to guide the people, making certain they adhere to the proper amount of labor, cleanliness, sobriety, and better habits of life. We want to ensure they continue the labor to which they are accustomed, so a paternal discipline is in place for the time being, with the prospect of better things to come."

He looked out over the racially mixed audience. Each person seemed attentive, but gave no indication of his or her personal views.

"Teachers will be provided and schools established for the children. As the workers show themselves fitted for the privileges of citizenship, they will be dismissed from this system, free to work in any employment they choose, and encouraged to purchase land.

"You have been more than generous in your outpouring of goods and tools for this worthy undertaking. We will continue to rely on your giving nature, as the need is monumental. Thank you."

As he took his seat, the applause, though short, seemed genuine. Pierce was convinced the plan was in the Negroes' best interest.

John Andrew's introduction of Frederick Douglass was brief yet effusive, emphasizing the former slave's importance as a voice for his people. The renowned abolitionist strolled to the lectern, basking in the audience's warm reception. He raised his hands; the sound of his rich baritone glided over the audience.

"I came here tonight, as I often come to these affairs, not as a speaker but as a listener, knowing there is always so much wisdom to be gleaned in Boston. But some of my friends—" he turned to Governor Andrew and smiled, "even when they *know* there is a difference of opinion between me and the scheduled speakers, still call me out upon the platform." Then his deep, dark eyes fastened on Pierce. "I see that tonight is not an exception."

Pierce's cheeks flushed, and he was thankful for the thick beard covering his face.

"It is said," Douglass began, "what will you do with the slave if emancipated? They can't take care of themselves; they would all come to the North; they would not work; they would become a burden upon the State, a blot upon society; they'd cut their masters' throats; they will cheapen labor, crowding out the poor white laborer from employment; their former masters will not employ them, and they would necessarily become vagrants, paupers and criminals, overrunning our alms houses, jails and prisons. The laboring classes of the whites would come in bitter conflict with them in all avenues of labor; a fierce war of races would be the inevitable consequence, and the black race, of course, being the weaker, would be exterminated."

The audience hissed and booed, willing participants in Douglass's parody.

"In view of this frightful, though happily contradictory picture, the question is posed with a show of sincere solicitude for the welfare of the slave himself: What shall be done with the four million slaves if they are emancipated?

"Our answer is, do nothing with them; mind your own business and let them mind theirs. Your doing with them is their greatest misfortune. They have been undone by your doings, and all they really ask and need at your hands is just to let them alone. The Negro should have been let alone in Africa—let alone when the pirates and robbers offered him for sale in our Christian slave markets—let alone by courts, judges, politicians, legislators and slave drivers—let alone altogether. Be assured that they must now make their own way in the world, just the same as any and every variety of the human family. When you, our white fellow-countrymen, have attempted to do anything for us, it has generally been to deprive us of some right, power, or privilege for which you yourself would die before you would submit to have taken from you."

One person clapped wildly and the audience erupted into spontaneous applause.

"We answer those who are perpetually puzzling their brains with questions as to what shall be done with the Negro—let him alone and mind your own business. If you see him plowing on the open field, leveling the forest, at work with a spade, a rake, a hoe, a pick-ax—let him alone. If you see him on the way to school, with spelling book, geography, or arithmetic in his hand—"

Douglass paused, and the audience completed the sentence: "Let him alone!"

"If he has a ballot in his hand and is on his way to the ballot-box to deposit his vote for the man whom he thinks will most wisely and justly administer the government—"

"Let him alone!"

"If you see him on his way to the church, exercising religious liberty in accordance with this or that religion—"

"Let him alone!"

"We would not for one moment check the outgrowth of any charitable concern for the future of the colored race in America, or anywhere else for that matter; but in the name of reason and religion, we earnestly plea for justice above all else. Benevolence with justice is harmonious and beautiful; but benevolence without justice is a mockery. What shall be done with the Negro if emancipated? Deal justly with him. Give him wages for his work, and let hunger pinch him if he doesn't work. He knows the difference between fullness and famine, plenty and scarcity.

"But will he work, you ask. Why should he not? He is used to it. His hands are already hardened by toil and he has no dreams of ever getting a living by any other means than by hard work.

"But would you turn them loose? Certainly! We are no better than our Creator, and he has turned us all loose.

"But would it be safe? No good reason can be given why it should not be. There is much more apprehension from slavery than from freedom.

"But would you let them all stay here? Why not? What better is *here* than *there?* Will they occupy more room as freemen than as slaves? Is the presence of a black freeman less agreeable than the presence of a black slave?

"The mental objections to emancipation are amazing; there are all sorts of excuses—political, economical, social, theological, and ethnological—designed to barricade the anti-slavery sentiments. But when this accursed slave system shall once be abolished, and the Negro gathered under the divine government of justice, liberty, and humanity, men will be ashamed they were ever fooled by the flimsy nonsense they allowed to hold millions enslaved in our land. That day is not far away."

The audience sprung to its collective feet, but Pierce remained seated, unconvinced. *Admirable words, Mr. Douglass; but blacks will not be ready for freedom until their merit is proven.*

CHAPTER 20
PREPARING TO GO SOUTH

E dward Philbrick and the other Port Royal-bound workforce had spent their first day in New York traipsing through federal offices, wading through red tape. Finally, late afternoon, they were ready for the last step in the drawn-out process—taking the oath of allegiance to the United States of America.

The oath was to be given by Port Collector of Confiscated Goods, Hiram Barney. Night had settled by the time the group arrived at his estate and he personally greeted them at the door. Philbrick, taking in the home's opulence, concluded the Collector's government-appointed position must be very lucrative.

Barney ushered them into the deluxe library, where they joined fifty or so others. Edward Pierce, accompanying the entourage south, rushed to greet them. After brief pleasantries, Philbrick stepped away, fading into a corner. He'd guided the young teachers and superintendents through the governmental bureaucracy most of the day, and now he'd had his fill of them. The group had disclosed a lot about their educational prowess but Philbrick had serious doubts about their ability to grow cotton.

"Tea, sir?"

A young maidservant interrupted his musings, and he was instantly aware of a calming aromatic mixture of exotic tea leaves and peppermint cake. Generous slices of the pink confection lined a porcelain tray.

"Yes, thank you," he replied.

He'd expected the oath-taking to be sterile and brief. *This simple undertaking has become a social affair. It will take all night to be sworn in.*

As the girl poured the tea, Philbrick's gray eyes swept the room. Some of the faces were familiar—fellow Bostonians. But there were several ladies he did not recognize.

"Milk...sugar, sir?" said the server.

"Milk, please—no sugar."

He stirred the mixture, blending the heavy cream. As he sipped the steaming brew, he continued to survey the room, puzzled by the presence of John Murray Forbes, an anti-slavery advocate. Forbes's disdain for Boston's non-violent abolitionist groups was well-documented, referring to them as ignorant zealots. The wealthy railroad industrialist had openly supported the militant John Brown, helping finance his Bloody Kansas insurrections. Philbrick was convinced the affluent entrepreneur was not a part of Pierce's little band. But why, he wondered, was Forbes, a very wealthy man, now associating with mundane abolitionists. He decided to investigate and glanced about for Pierce. Collector Barney, however, chose that moment to command the room's attention.

"Good evening and welcome again. To those of you who've not made the acquaintance of these lovely ladies—" he waved his hand to indicate the unidentified group of women, "they're from Washington City, senators' wives who've volunteered to go to Port Royal. One of their tasks will be to distribute clothing to the contraband." Barney paused for the smattering of applause. "Thank you," he said. "Also among us is Miss Susan Walker, representing The Honorable Secretary of the Treasury, Salmon Chase."

Susan Walker, a large, strong-minded woman, stood and waved briefly.

Philbrick frowned. *Is he going to introduce everyone?*

"Now," said Barney, "to begin the ceremony. Since our number is so large, the oath will be administered in groups of six."

Well, that should speed things along, thought Philbrick.

Barney picked up his Bible. "Any volunteers?"

Philbrick stepped forward and three young men—Edward Hooper, William Channing Gannett and Samuel Phillips—immediately joined him. Austa French—Rev. French's wife—stood beside him. Ellen Winsor took a position beside Mrs. French. Pierce had initially crossed the young woman off the list, but her Commission sponsors had insisted she be hired.

Barney faced the small group, instructing them to place their right hands on the Bible.

They clustered about him, reaching to touch the book.

"As you recite the oath, please insert your name. Repeat after me:

"I, *your name*, do solemnly swear...

"in the presence of Almighty God...

"that I will faithfully support, protect and defend...

"the Constitution of the United States....

"That I will support all acts of Congress...

"passed during the existing rebellion...

"with reference to slaves....

"I will faithfully support all proclamations made by the President...

"during the existing rebellion, so help me God."

After they'd all repeated the oath, they signed the pledge form and Collector Barney, with a degree of solemnity, called them up and singly presented their passports. They were now duly authorized to board the *Steamship Atlantic* and sail behind enemy lines.

The cabriolet driver had barely completed the turn into Canal Street before he reined in his horse, bringing the two-wheeled vehicle to a complete stop. *Now what's happened?* thought Philbrick. He half rose from the seat and craned his neck, peering into the morning's dank dreariness. The silhouettes of dray carts, gurneys, teamster wagons, and other horse-drawn vehicles stretched ahead, stock-still.

"Well, this is a fine fix," he mumbled, turning to the cab driver. "Is the traffic always a logjam here?" he asked.

The man bit off a plug of tobacco before answering. "Yeah, it sure is. And a miserable day like this one always make it worse." He chewed slowly, the wad jutting out from his scraggy jaw. "No need to get in a huff over it, though—a constable'll get it moving in no time." The driver stared into the gloomy distance, grinding the chaw.

"I certainly hope so; the steamer's set to sail at six o'clock."

"Six o'clock, eh? I don't think you'll have *that* to worry about." He gave Philbrick a knowing look and chuckled dryly. The buggy just ahead began to slowly move. The cabriolet driver spat a sepia glob onto the rain-slick cobblestones and flicked his horse's reins.

They arrived at the port and Philbrick readily saw why the driver had said he needn't worry—the *Atlantic* would not be leaving any time soon. A conglomerate of people, cargo, livestock, and merchandise stood shoulder to shoulder, crate to crate, packing the area. Philbrick exited the cab and found himself in the midst of a hundred or more young army recruits. They stood fresh-faced, awkwardly trying to console the clutching, teary-eyed women bidding them good-bye.

A collection of teamsters, dock workers, and stevedores hustled about, struggling to get everything loaded as quickly as possible.

The foul weather made the work difficult, and the clamorous, meandering passengers—wet and impatient—caused the situation to be even more contentious.

He walked toward the wharf and was still some distance away when the stench assailed his nostrils. Reaching the water's edge, the source of the smell was evident as brawny stevedores loaded hundreds of caged animals onto the steamer's lower deck, seemingly oblivious to their raucous squawks, oinks, barks, and fetid odors.

The seedily dressed steerage class came aboard next, scrambling onto the same lower deck as the animals. The passengers moved as quickly as their bundles of foodstuff and beddings allowed, scouting for leeward coverage and the least offensive floor space among the cages.

Philbrick turned his attention to the steamer. The boat's powerful paddles were already engaged and churned mightily—creating froth and spewing icy water. The huge vessel seemed as impatient as Philbrick to get underway. But it wasn't until noon that the tons of freight, trunks, food, clothing, medicines, seeds, farm equipment, and other supplies finally disappeared into the boat's gigantic hold. Philbrick began to relax. *At last, the adventure begins.*

CHAPTER 21

DINNER AT SEA

Rough weather buffeted the steamer, rendering most of the passengers seasick and miserable. The two o'clock dinner was served on schedule, and Philbrick, one of the robust few, entered the nearly empty dining saloon. Pierce and his fellow townsman from Milton, Massachusetts, John Murray Forbes, were already seated. Philbrick approached their table.

"Is this seat taken?" he asked.

Forbes glanced about the nearly deserted room and grimaced at the intrusive stranger. "If it *is* taken, you certainly have your choice of others."

"Oh," said Pierce, quickly rising to his feet. "Philbrick, this is Mr. Forbes, your cabin mate. Mr. Forbes—Edward Philbrick."

Forbes' clean-shaven face reddened slightly as he rose to shake Philbrick's extended hand. "I do apologize. Perhaps we were in the baggage hold when you came aboard." Forbes went on to recount how he'd sent his bags and trunks ahead by wagon, but when he later arrived by carriage, the trunks, bags, *and* the wagoner were nowhere to be found. After the man was finally located, he swore that the baggage had been placed aboard, though buried in the baggage hold's bottomless pit.

"A terrible dilemma!" said Philbrick. "What did you do?"

"What could I do—just got on board without as much as a toothbrush, trusting my friend Captain Smith would provide for me."

As they took their seats, Philbrick gauged Forbes' slender figure. "You're welcome to wear some of my clothes, although they may hang a bit loose."

"That's very kind of you, but we eventually located the trunks." Forbes smiled and his keen face became less agitated. "Now. Let's eat! That whole comedic episode has given me an enormous appetite." He signaled one of several hovering waiters and the man hastened to their table. His white, spotless jacket gleamed against his deep ebony complexion.

"Good evening, gen'lemen." His smile was bright; his tall, lanky frame slightly bowed. In no time he'd placed steaming platters before them—generous entrées of meat and fish, delectable vegetables, a variety of breads, and a wide assortment of desserts. As they dined, the waiter's service proved to be as impeccable as his jacket.

The men ate, chatting amiably and Philbrick and Forbes discovered they had a connection—Philbrick's father-in-law and Forbes had once conducted business. Forbes revealed his trip to Beaufort was two-fold—doctor's orders for a nagging bout with bronchitis and an extended visit with his son, Lieutenant William Forbes. The conversation drifted to slavery and abolitionism.

"I'm as much against slavery as you are," declared Forbes. "It's the pig-headed, do-nothing abolitionists I'll have no dealings with."

Philbrick and Pierce exchanged guarded looks.

"Present company excluded," Forbes amended. "But the thought of simultaneously unleashing four million Negroes upon society....Well, for a time I was totally against it, certain it could only result in slave rebellions—requite with murder, fire, and rape. However, I've come to alter my thinking."

"Oh, why did you change your mind?" asked Philbrick.

Forbes finished his dessert and paused, gazing about the ornate, sparsely occupied room. "What a terrible waste of good food!" He signaled the waiter. "I'll have two more of the same," he said, pointing to his empty dessert plates.

"Yes, suh," said the waiter, "coming right up, suh. Would you gen'lemen care for someth—."

Philbrick shook his head, an emphatic no. Pierce ignored the man and turned to Forbes. "Now, as you were saying—you've altered your view regarding emancipation; why is that?"

"After giving it much thought, I believe emancipation would be economically disastrous for the rebels."

"How's that?" asked Pierce.

"Well, war is expensive and this rebellion has been going on for nearly a year; the Confederacy's tangible wealth—bonds, credit, foreign loans—is nearly drained. Their only remaining assets will be the slaves."

The waiter returned and Forbes alternately sampled the Brown Betty pudding and cherry pie. "Mmm, delicious!" Then he continued. "Economically speaking, slave-based wealth is fictitious wealth; once the slaves are freed, their value as property, as well as their labor, vanishes."

"Yes," replied Pierce. "I see your point."

"I've advised President Lincoln to move quickly toward emancipation; but he continues to waffle, intent on pacifying the Border States." Forbes dipped into the pudding.

"But it will be folly to just send four million blacks on their way; the government must establish a new labor plan for them," said Pierce.

Philbrick leaned forward. "But there's a bigger picture than just the black man's labor," he cautioned. "When slave labor is abolished, the entire Southern labor system will be destroyed. The new free labor plan must also include poor whites and the small farmers."

"You're right," Forbes rejoined. "Slave labor is what's kept poor white trash from having decent work in the first place; this war was started by the planter aristocracy, and as poor whites continue to support the Confederacy, they support a system that will keep them in poverty."

The other two nodded as the ever-hovering waiter refilled their teacups.

"There's also the issue of putting the Negro back to work," said Philbrick.

"True," said Pierce. "If that issue isn't addressed by the end of the war, the government might enter some half-cocked compromise when the rebels reenter the Union—maybe allow the planters to reclaim their slaves or something. And if *that* happens, we'll betray thousands of blacks—loyal men and women who are risking their lives to support our cause."

"I agree," Forbes replied, "but let's not be overly concerned that this bloody battle is to abolish slavery, or even to reunite a Democratic Republic." He began to cough, and pushed the unfinished pudding aside.

"Water, suh?" offered the waiter.

"Yes, please." He took a sip, then went on. "No, our concern must be on the approaching industrialized age—an era destined to remove men from the farms and into the factories; there will be a demand for a new kind of labor." He paused and took another sip. "I see this war bringing a balance between capital and labor, giving all men—including emancipated slaves—the choice of free labor."

"Then," said Philbrick, "the main economic question to come out of this war is, how do we establish a profitable relationship between laboring, capital-less men, and wealthy capitalists who need labor?"

"My sentiments exactly," said Forbes, picking at the cherry pie's golden crust.

"The Port Royal experiment is an excellent beginning," Pierce stated, "and with God's will, it will result in a definitive plan for emancipation *and* free labor." He pushed away from the table. "Now I really must get back to work; this experiment is an on-going, time-consuming project."

They bid each other a pleasant good-day. As Pierce struggled with the slippery, gale-swept exit door, their waiter stepped forward to assist him. Pierce looked directly into the man's face and for a second, the waiter seemed familiar. Pierce almost asked his name, but dismissed the encounter. *They all look the same,* he thought, trudging against the wind.

CHAPTER 22
BEAUFORT BOUND

Stormy weather slowed the *Atlantic* all the way to Cape Hatteras, causing the ship to arrive at Port Royal Sound after high tide. Captain Smith dropped anchor at the Sound's entrance, almost exactly between Fort Walker and Fort Beauregard, set to drift through the night.

As they waited for the tide, Pierce summoned the group—forty-one men and twelve women—to the saloon. His tone was affective. "No others, not even those arriving on the Mayflower, have undertaken a more important mission than you. Yours will be no small task, expunging centuries of ignorance to prepare the Negro for citizenship. But you are endowed with practical capability and talent, more than equipped for success." He talked about the contrabands' deprived, malnourished condition, stating, "They live in wretched disarray but as evangels of civilization, you will bring order, cleanliness, and healthy habits into their lives. I cannot fathom a more noble undertaking."

Then he motioned Rev. French to join him. "Many of you have not officially met this accomplished man of God. In addition to serving as a revivalist, he's also a teacher, writer, and former president of Xenia Female Seminary, one of the many colleges he's helped to establish. I met him during our exploratory visits to Port Royal this past January, where we discovered a mutual friend in Treasury Secretary Chase. We also discovered our goals were similar—to provide for the Negro's physical needs and help his transition into freedom. Based on that, we decided to join forces, with me seeking funds from Congress and the people of Boston, as he appealed to the American Missionary Association in New York." Pierce effusively waved his arms toward the young people. "You, an elite group of evangelists, are the product of our campaigns. As word of our efforts went out, a new cadre was organized in Philadelphia and will soon join us in Port Royal." He paused for the group's jubilant applause, then turned to the portly gentleman standing beside him. "Ladies and gentlemen, the Rev. Mansfield French."

After greeting the group, Rev. French introduced his wife, Austa, then gave remarks. "It is only divine grace that has fitted you for this mission, and you must be ever mindful to show an appreciation for that which you have been entrusted. You will come upon unusual situations, but be mindful to withhold any ill-will or scorn against the Negroes. They have been objects of derision for centuries, and we, no matter how valiant our principles, cannot expect their immediate trust." His oratory was strong as he offered counsel, cautioning the rapt listeners to respect the Negro's right to worship in his own way, regardless of how disconcerting or emotional that worship may appear. He then read passages from the Bible and Mrs. French led the New York assemblage in a spirited hymn. Rev. French ended the meeting with a passionate prayer and the group immediately dispersed. But Pierce, Philbrick, and Gannett, Philbrick's assistant, lingered.

"Well, what do you think of the Rev. French?" asked Pierce.

Philbrick normally withheld his opinions, but this time he was candid. "I praise Mr. French's Christian demeanor, but I don't think much of his leadership ability. He has the spirit, the *theory* of the work, but not the hand that takes hold."

"He lacks depth," said Gannett, himself a Unitarian minister. "And as to his remarks regarding emotional worship—the AMA fellowship can teach the *contrabands* a thing or two about that." He chuckled softly.

"Yes, it seems the Methodists lean more toward religious expression than intellectual fulfillment," Philbrick remarked.

"Frankly, I don't believe Mr. French used good judgment in selecting the New York delegation," said Pierce, revealing his own misgivings. "Still, it's too early to form opinions," he concluded.

"That's true," Gannett said. "And since we are all yoked together, we must earnestly pull together."

"We shall see what—." Philbrick stopped mid-sentence, suddenly aware of someone hovering near. "Who's there?" he demanded. "Come out where we can see you."

The shadowy figure ventured closer, and Philbrick recognized their attentive waiter.

"Uh, excuse me, suh; I don't mean no harm, but can I have a short word with you?" Avoiding eye contact, he nodded toward Pierce.

"Yes, what is it?" said Pierce, still confounded by the man's familiar aura.

"Excuse me, suh," he repeated. "But we gonna disembark tomorrow and I...er, I need to know—what you said, about slaves on Port Royal—being free and all—is that true?"

"Yes, of course it is. Why would I lie?" replied Pierce.

The waiter's eyes stretched wide. "Oh, no suh! I don't mean no offence. It just be that...." He shifted his weight and glanced around furtively.

"What *do* you mean?" Pierce asked.

"Well, uh, you see, suh...." He stared at the floor and his words were barely audible. "A long time ago, twenty-nine years, I run away...to Canada...."

Pierce stepped forward, immediately intrigued. "Oh? From where?"

"Port Royal, suh…."
Aha! Thought Pierce, *maybe that's why he's so familiar!*
"I got kin on St. Helena…if anybody left there." The waiter lifted his head slightly. "But I want to be sure about it—about freedom—before I chance going back."

Pierce hesitated, then placed his hand on the man's shoulder. "You have nothing to fear; your freedom is assured."

"Yes," added Philbrick. "The Sea Islands are now United States territory, under the control and command of the Union forces." Philbrick had no idea just how intense that control really was.

It was noon the next day when the tide came in. A pilot boat escorted the *Atlantic* into the great Hilton Head harbor. Four months had passed since the Confederates surrendered the forts, and Hilton Head was now headquarters for the Union's Department of the South. Recently built huts, barracks, and a hospital fronted the beach; scrappy military men, refugee slaves, prisoners of war, and enterprising civilians had increased the island's population to over 40,000, turning it into a small city. Hilton Head harbor, the deepest and largest on the eastern seaboard, served as the center of operations for the whole Atlantic Army.

Philbrick stood on the deck, looking toward the shore. Comparing the rigid silhouette of pitch pines to New England's gently sloping dunes, he found the trees monotonous. The flat, sandy expanse reminded him of the Egyptian seaside, but without Egypt's enterprising windmills. *This uncivilized state does not even provide water power,* he observed. But he was awed by the magnificent scene of over fifty transports and steamers anchored in the harbor, oblivious that governmental red tape would provide him plenty of time to enjoy the view.

General Sherman had directed the missionaries to disembark in Beaufort, but in order to get there they'd have to transfer to a smaller riverboat, one that could maneuver the shallow shoals.

Government regulations required the civilians to have shore passes before leaving the ship. They waited all day, but it was night before the Provost Marshall arrived with the papers. Philbrick sat on the side of his bunk, writing in his journal. *"March 7, 1862, The Provost Marshall delivered the visas around eight o'clock, much too late to unload or travel. More valuable planting time squandered. However, he did offer advice, saying the negroes were easily governed if we are firm and just with them. He said the officers in charge are more than ready to have us take them off their hands."*

The men spent the next day, Saturday, transferring freight and baggage to a small river steamer—the *Cosmopolitan*. The 15-mile trip up the channel began around three o'clock, but halfway there, the boat ran aground on an oyster bed. There was nothing to do but wait until the tide rolled in. Philbrick, chafing at yet another delay, spent the time reading cotton production manuals.

The steamer freed herself around nine-thirty and as she poked along under the splendid moonlight, sounds of discordant singing enveloped the night. Forbes and Philbrick, inquisitive as to the melodies' source, left their cabin to investigate. They found the missionaries sitting on the deck, conducting a song fest of hymns and abolitionist ditties. The young folks broke into a robust rendition of "John Brown's Body," completely ignoring the other passengers' curious stares.

The *Cosmopolitan* reached Beaufort around midnight and the weather suddenly changed into the coldest night of winter. The deck was covered in hoarfrost the next morning, but the rising sun quickly dissipated the chill, rendering the day bright and beautiful. As the energetic Northerners set to work, idle spectators—both black and white—looked on, watching the men unload the *Cosmopolitan*.

Pierce had obtained rations from a nearby regiment and arranged for breakfast at a Negro's cabin across town. As they trekked along Beaufort's sandy, oak-lined streets, Philbrick observed the charming little town's neglected state. Broken liquor bottles lay strewn in the weed-infested yards, and dilapidated fences fronted the once-grand, but now desolate houses. They reached the elderly woman's cabin and she provided them with soap, bowls, and towels. They washed up at a chain-pump out in the poultry yard, then ate.

Housing was the next order of the day, and Pierce, through military intervention, managed to secure a townhouse for the men. The deserted house belonged to a wealthy planter, and although it had been plundered—either by slaves or soldiers—its marble mantels and gilt cornices remained intact. Rev. French was not quite as resourceful in finding lodging for the women, and at first they shared cramped quarters with a good-natured minister. After scouring the island, Rev. French installed the women in a mansion next door to the men. Everyone made do with scant, damaged furniture—not only because of vandalism—but because the treasury agents, acting under the guise of Colonel Reynolds's confiscation orders, had removed everything of value.

Finally, after settling in, there was nothing more to do except wait until Pierce personally transported each to their designated plantations. Philbrick wrote to his wife Helen that he'd been given three plantations, among them Ivy Oaks, the largest on St. Helena. *My assistant, William Channing Gannett, is agreeable and hardworking. But like several of the others, he's too young to be in control of organizing labor.* He ended the letter by telling her that waiting was the hardest work he'd ever done.

Upon the evangels' arrival, Beaufort was already overrun with Northern cotton brokers, store-keepers, civilians, sutlers, journalists, and Southern loyalists. The soldiers, assigned to dull tasks of distributing supplies, refueling ships, and chasing unarmed blockade runners, saw little action beyond picket duty. The oft-bored men criticized the civilians, saying they made them fight in fetters. The soldiers held special scorn for the abolitionists, saying they'd descended like locusts and mockingly referred to the idealistic reformers as the swarm of Gideon.

But the missionaries, zealous in their battle to conquer evil with good, literally did see themselves armed with torches of enlightenment and took the derisive name-calling to heart. By the time they settled in on their posts, they'd thoroughly embraced the term Gideonites and would be forever known as Gideon's Band.

It had taken Pierce two weeks to place everyone and finally, towards the end of March, the assignments were complete. Gideon's Band was greatly relieved, as their bickering over religious differences—Boston's emphasis on principles and ethics, versus New York's church-centered evangelism—had become a source of public comment, creating more fuel for the soldiers' derisive fires and fodder for Northern newspaper reporters.

CHAPTER 23
CRECIE CARRIES ON

A week after Isham's funeral, the quartermaster met with the people at Brick Church. Stripped of their food and possessions by unruly soldiers, the desperate workers were certain military authorities would share the tons of corn, potatoes, and grain they'd taken from the planters' huge storehouses.

Crecie felt hopeful when the Chief Quartermaster, Captain Rufus Saxton, rose to address the group. He was the only officer that had shown a jot of kindness toward them. But his words were not encouraging, telling them there was little food left, most of it having gone to feed the army and the thousands of refugees that flooded the contraband camps. He promised to do all he could, but the people left the meeting as empty-handed as they'd arrived. Crecie overheard one officer say, "The contrabands are housed in muddy tents, where ever they can; at least the islanders have a roof over their heads."

But that was little consolation as she went home to face her hungry children.

Crecie placed the oddly-shaped patties on the table and Sham immediately began to eat; Leona and Willie however, gaped at the unappealing lumps.

"What this, Ma?" Leona asked.

"Biscuit," said Crecie, reaching for the broom. "Eat it befo' it get cold." She began to sweep the floor, furtively watching the children. *They* got *to eat it,* she thought. *There ain't nothing else left.* Sham quickly devoured his portion and eyed the other two plates.

"It don't *look* like no biscuit," said Leona.

"I want some beans," said Willie.

Leona gingerly touched it. "It don't feel like biscuit neither." She bit into it. "Ugh! This don't taste like no biscuit." She held it in her mouth.

"I don't care what it taste like. Swallow it!" Crecie gripped the broom handle and began to sweep faster. "You, too, Willie."

Willie took a bite, gagged, and promptly shoved the tin plate aside. Sham reached for it.

"Leave it be, Sham!" said Crecie, slamming the plate back in front of Willie. "This be *he* food, and him got to eat it."

"But Ma," complained Willie, "I want some be—."

"I told you, we ain't got no mo' beans; this all we got—cattail flour and groundnuts, and not too much o' that even!" She crisscrossed the cabin floor—sweeping furiously and muttering. "Ungrateful scamps—ain't thankful fo' nothing." But all the while she was sending up prayers. *Please God, put a good taste in they mout' so they'll eat it; if just enough to keep 'em alive, please, please make 'em eat.*

Sham had left the table, but the other two sat quietly, their eyes trained on Crecie. Finally she put the broom aside and stood over them.

"Alright, ya'll can get up now, but when you get hungry enough, that biscuit'll be right here waiting for you."

Days and weeks passed and the lack of nutrients was beginning to take its toll on the already malnourished people. As the situation grew worse, folks' eyes became jaundiced and their hair fell out in clumps. Many people had runny, ulcerated sores, and two of Midway's children succumbed early on. Crecie was overwrought, worried that her children would be next. She thanked God Sham and Leona ate whatever she could forage, fighting to survive.

But Willie could not digest the unpalatable roots. He grew weaker and Crecie sent word to Dr. Traylor in Beaufort, making an appeal for medicine, food, anything that would help him. Both she and Bentoo had worked side-by-side with the physician for many years, caring for the sick, both slave and free. Two days passed before he sent a message, telling her he couldn't help and to let freedom do the healing. Once again Crecie felt alienated in a world she didn't know, trapped in freedom's disorienting snare. She caressed Willie's stick-thin arm. *I got get help soon, or I gwine lose my child.*

The next morning she set out to do something she'd never done before—go on a journey to buy food. She'd secured her paltry sum of hired-out money in a snake-skin pouch and tied it around her waist. In the predawn shadows of murky creeks and brackish backwaters, she navigated the bateau toward Hilton Head. Dodging low-hanging branches, and mindful of the water moccasins that often hung from them, a thousand doubts and fears ramped through her mind; the wickedness soldiers did to women like her was foremost. But the image of her children wasting away conquered the fears and she gripped the oars, pressing on.

It was daylight when she reached the shore, and she was amazed by the changes Hilton Head had undergone. She'd never seen so many people, carts and wagons coming and going. There was a row of stores and businesses near the waterway, but she was too intimidated to enter. Besides, Mose had told her the vendors set up shop near the beach, so she began walking in the direction he'd given. She reached the beach and the outskirts of the camp. Ignoring the stares and jeers of a few soldiers, she chose a sutler whose face seemed welcoming.

"I-I come to buy food," she told the man.

"Well, this is the place. What do you want?"

It was hard to decide. She knew how to barter, how to make a fair exchange; but the use of money was strange and threatening. Finally, after warily choosing a quart of dried lima beans, a five pound sack of corn meal, and a small can of pork, she extended the handful of crumpled bills to the peddler. He glanced at the money and shook his head.

"I can't take that—it's from the Bank of South Carolina; Confederate money's not worth the paper it's printed on."

"'Federate money? Ain't money *money?*"

"Maybe to the rebels, but this is the United States, and that's what we use—United States money."

Despair overwhelmed her and Crecie's eyes welled. She bowed her head as warm drops trickled down her cheeks. *I come so close,* she thought, watching the tears fall to the ground. *But I can't go back with nothing fo' them chillun—I just can't.* She lifted her head and for the first time in her life, purposefully stared into the eyes of a white man. Again, she extended the money.

"S-suh, I done come all this way...and...." Her voice wavered and although she began to weep profusely, her eyes remained riveted to his.

His face flushed beet red, and he turned away, seemingly embarrassed. "Look," he said, "keep your money. Here, you want to make a trade?" He thrust the food toward her. "That's a fine-looking pouch—belt, too. They just might be worth something."

She stared at him, unsure of her good fortune. Then in a flash, she whipped off the belt and handed him the pouch.

That night Sham and Leona feasted on slow-cooked beans, hoe-cake, and bits of stringy pork. Crecie had made a thin gruel of corn meal and bean soup, and as the older children ate, she sat on the floor beside Willie, spoon-feeding the gruel. He squirmed, half-nodding as she cradled his head, forcing the watery mixture through his parched lips. Much of it dribbled out; but her joy knew no bounds when he swallowed a few drops. Finally, after he'd taken in enough to satisfy her, she gently released him and went to clear the table.

The crumpled money was strewn among the tin plates. She picked up one of the bills, studying the image on the dollar as she smoothed it out. She couldn't read, but the picture of slaves picking waist-high cotton gave meaning enough. *First master, now the gov'ment—cotton and money. Can't eat neither one.* She ripped the bill in half. *Isham knowed that; that why he plant he own crop. Food—a body got to have sus'nance.* She continued ripping the bill into uneven pieces. *Cabbage'll be ripe sometime in March, but that still two, maybe three weeks off.* She looked at the slumbering children, their boney knees drawn up to their hollowed chests. *Can they hold on till then?*

She had done all she could, even taken Ossie and Louise back to Bentoo. Since many of the parents worked collecting cotton, Colonel Reynolds provided rations for the nursery. Crecie knew that even the little bit of food Ossie and Louise got at Bentoo's was far more than she could've provided. *Maybe I ought to go back, too, work for Colonel Nobles.* She gathered the worthless scraps of money and stood in front of the fireplace. *But gang labor, working from sun-up to sundown, I won't have time fo' Isham's crop; it'll fall by the wayside.* She threw the money into the fireplace and tempered the blaze. Then she craftily hid the remaining food, hoping that by not eating any of it herself, she could stretch it until the crop ripened.

She eased down beside Willie, listening to his labored breathing, caressing his freckled face. "You look so much like Isham," she said, smoothing the boy's wooly, rust-red hair. Then, cradling his wasted little body next to hers, she gently rocked him, whispering a prayer. "I trusting in you, Lord; ain't got nobody *but* you. You feed Elijah and you save the widow woman and her boy, and you gwine save me and mine. Thank you, Jesus. Amen." She felt a sense of peace and soon fell asleep.

But that very night, as if trying Crecie's faith, the supernatural mist made its first appearance.

CHAPTER 24

SOMETHING GOT A HOLD ON ME

Crecie was usually asleep when the mystic fog came, but this predawn hour found her awake, warily watching the icy vapor swirl above her. An eerie chill filled the room, yet she felt warm, hot even, a sign of what was to come. She clutched the tattered quilt, dreading the specter's strange lure. Then she felt it—felt her essence willingly ebb, rendering her no longer a person, but fractured parts of mind, body, and soul. She tried to move, to cry out, but her physical self was a stiff hollowed shell. Unfettered, her soul floated up, vacillating between the beguiling apparition and her inert body. Then suddenly her psyche glimpsed the awful terror of a nether-life, and she screamed through clenched teeth, pleading for escape.

"Crecie! Crecie!" Bentoo cried, shaking her granddaughter's rigid shoulder. Crecie's soul returned, jolting her lifeless body.

"Y-you alright?" Bentoo asked, holding a candle close.

Crecie nodded once, her unfocused eyes staring into the light. Three weeks had passed since the apparition's first terrifying appearance, leaving her shaken and exhausted.

"You moan and groan all night long," Bentoo whispered, cautious lest whoever, or whatever, still lurked among them. "Do...do you think it be Isham...Polly, maybe?"

"Yes...no....I-I don't know," Crecie replied. "True, I be seeing them spirits, but...but I ain't never *feel* nothing like this befo'."

"Do it be *talking* to you?"

She shook her head from side to side, bewildered. "No, I don't never hear nothing, but I just feel like it *want* something." She buried her face in her work-worn hands. "I just don't know...." She faltered, then started again. "I been hoping if I be here with you, it'll stay away, but...." The move had proved futile and as the manifestations continued, Crecie was as tired and tormented as when she'd first arrived.

Trembling, she sat up on the pallet, head bowed. *Lord, I wish for the day Isham, Polly, and all these haints would just stay away and leave me be.* Bentoo draped the quilt around her thin shoulders but she threw it off.

"I got to get up," she said. "I told Titus and Hamp to come early today; we got to water the cabbage first off, then start on the onions."

"You feeling all right, Crecie? Good enough to work?"

"I got to, Bentoo." Bringing in a crop was a matter of life and death.

The older woman nodded as she folded the quilt. "Crop oughta be ready soon."

"Uh-huh," said Crecie, feeling revived. "Isham plant that winter crop about two months ago, January." She stood, and began to get dressed. "Yes, ma'am, cabbage'll be ready around the end of this mont'."

Bentoo shuffled over to the table, rummaging among her baskets of roots and herbs. "I'm gwine fix you something to eat befo' you go."

"Thank ya," Crecie called over her shoulder. She glanced guardedly around the room before pulling on Isham's beat-up old brogans, then centered her thoughts on the children. The corn meal *had* mysteriously lasted, and although Willie wasn't doing as well as she'd hoped, she took things day-to-day, thanking God for every morning he awoke in the land of the living. It had been her sheer force of will that had kept all of them alive.

Bentoo placed a steaming bowl on the table. "Here, drink this acorn soup. You been working so hard; you need to eat, keep up yo' strength—."

Crecie held up her palm, refusing the food. Acorn soup was edible if all the bitterness was boiled out—which Bentoo usually failed to do. "Er, no, Bentoo, you drink it; I'll look for some groundnuts or something on the way to the field."

"Well, then, I'll give it to Titus or Hamp," she mumbled.

A timid knock sounded at the door.

"That must be them now," said Crecie, flinging the door open. "Ya'll want some ac—." The words stuck in her throat. The man standing before her was not Titus. In fact, he was not anyone she'd ever seen before. "Wha...who you?" she stammered, stunned by the strange way his face mirrored hers—high cheek bones, almond-shaped eyes, ebony skin.

"What the matter, Crecie?" Bentoo asked, looking toward the door. "Oh, my Lord!" she exclaimed and the tin bowl clattered to the stone hearth. "Randy?" The name was a soft whimper and she started toward him. But her knees buckled, and she sank to the earthen floor. "Randy? Is that you?"

The man brushed past Crecie and helped Bentoo to her feet. A nervous laugh escaped his lips and he blinked rapidly as if trying to hold back tears. "Yeah, Bentoo, this is me."

"Crecie!" Bentoo yelled. "Come see—." But before she could finish, the babies, awakened by her excited outburst, began to cry. All of the children—great-grands and charges alike—burst into the room, creating a ruckus as they curiously eyed the tall stranger.

Crecie stood at the open door, away from the commotion. She watched as Bentoo's hands poked and prodded the man's body. The older woman tip-toed to get the feel of his hair, and he bent down to accommodate her. It was as if she needed reassurance, that the vision standing before her was not another deceptive dream.

Finally convinced her son was indeed real, Bentoo collapsed in his arms, sobbing. "I never know if you been dead or alive, but I pray every day—first thing every morning, last thing every night—*every day, every night*—I ax God to show me yo' face again." Her weeping was in earnest and she held him tightly, fearful he might disappear for another twenty-nine years. "It been so long-a-time... so long-a-time...thanks be to God fo' answering my prayers...."

Crecie eased into the yard and waited. Titus and Hamp soon arrived.

"Wuh-what gwining on in there this t-t-time uh, uh morning?" asked Hamp.

"Yeah," said Titus. "The chillun up bawling, Bentoo crying and laughing all at the same time...."

"Ain't nothing fo' you to worry about—or *me*," Crecie retorted. "Come on, us got work to do."

CHAPTER 25

CATCHING UP

B entoo couldn't keep her hands off Randy. Gently, she touched his stubbly chin. "You ain't had this when you run aw—gone away from here. Still got that thick hair like yo' pappy; getting a little gray, now, though."

He laughed. This time it was deep, genuine.

Her hands spread across his broad chest, and she pinched around his ribs. "You got meat on yo' bones, alright. What you been eating all them years?"

Randy held up two large carpetbags filled with food. "Look in here and see for yourself."

The *Atlantic's* cook had plied him with leftovers as a farewell gift, a few slices of this, dabs of that, and containers of whatever. Not much of any one thing, but the people had a saying: "A stomach full is a stomach full."

Bentoo looked around. "Crecie, come see—."

"Ma already gone," said Leona, peeping from behind Bentoo's skirt.

"Who's Crecie?" asked Randy. "And where's Polly?"

"We'll talk later," Bentoo replied.

She hurriedly fixed carpetbag-goodies for the children, and shooed the older ones to eat in the other side of the duplex. Then she pulled the rocking chair up to the fire, keeping an eye on the younger ones as they ate.

"Come sit," she said, directing Randy to the slatted, high-back chair. "A lot done happened since you left."

As Bentoo summarized the twenty-nine lost years, he sat quietly, immersed in her words. She spoke first of the dead—his Papa, Polly, and the young lad who was always tagging after him, Isham. She spoke of all the others who'd gone to the other side, and a sense of gloom seemed to permeate the room.

Then she told him about the Big Gun Shoot, and the coming of the soldiers, and how the army and the government, instead of the master, now controlled everything.

She brought long-forgotten people and events to his remembrance—friends, family, harvest-time, crab boils—and he reveled in the memories, not realizing she hadn't mentioned the woman she'd called Crecie.

Finally, Bentoo took out her corncob pipe; it was now her time to listen.

"First thing I want to know is how you got away. Ol' Massa Boson was fit to be tied when the boat came back and you wasn't piloting it."

"Yeah; running wasn't easy. Seem like the slave hunters were everywhere."

"They was. Massa had 'em looking for you north *and* south. Did everything he could, still couldn't find you. How you do it—get free?"

"Well, you remember how the black boatmen from up North always use to sneak them abolitionist newspapers to me; you know, the tracts I brought you."

Bentoo nodded. "Yeah, I read a lot o' them papers befo' I burned 'em."

"Well, one of the tracts had the name of an abolitionist group that ran a station on the Underground Railroad—a safe place for runaways." Randy recounted how he'd memorized the information and waited for the opportunity to use it.

"So, when massa hired you out on that north-bound steamer...."

"...I jumped ship in Boston and connected with the Underground Railroad. They showed me how to forge my first set of manumission papers and helped me get to Canada. When they found out I could read, the Canada abolitionists hired me to teach the new runaways."

Bentoo gasped. "You was a *teacher?*"

"Yeah, but not for long. Even in Canada I didn't feel safe. I was always moving, always working—shoveling coal on the railroad, houseman in Boston, longshoreman in New York, cook, riverboat pilot—always moving, always working. Except for this last job; been waiting tables on steamboats for...mmm, maybe twelve ye—."

Suddenly a fitful cry interrupted their conversation. Bentoo went to tend the fussy baby as Randy stared into the fire. She returned to the rocker and placed the baby face down over her lap, gently rubbing the little girl's back. Randy watched the scene.

"What's her name?"

"Mary."

Randy looked into the fire. "That's a pretty name. I never had any children; never stayed one place long enough."

Bentoo smiled knowingly and continued rocking until Mary fell asleep. She took the baby into the adjoining room, then joined Randy. She'd saved the best for last. Leaning in close, she looked directly into his eyes, wanting to see his reaction when she told him.

"That girl, the woman who open the door for you—Crecie—she be your daughter."

It took two seconds, then Randy stood suddenly, overturning the chair. "My...my daughter?" He averted his face when he whispered the name Polly. "She was the only one."

"Her name the baby Lucretia, after she own mama," said Bentoo.

"B-but I...I just can't believe—after all these years, me one—no family, no home, nothing...and now I-I got all of this—you, a daughter. And all those children, who they belong to?"

Bentoo chuckled. "Just three be yo' grands—Sham, Leona and Willie."

He shook his head in disbelief then stood in front of the fireplace, his back to Bentoo. She watched his shoulders slope forward as he silently wept, remembering the little boy who never wanted anyone to see him cry.

"I'm sorry, Bentoo," he said, regaining his composure.

"I know, son." She patted his hand. "It been a long row for me to hoe, too; a long row."

Later, Randy filled a tin pail with food and set out for the fields, seeking his daughter. He walked along the deserted road in Slave Row, thinking how everything still looked the same, yet knowing that nothing would ever be the same again. The people, the times, all had changed. But change had been good for him. It was a change of clothes, disguised as an old man, that had aided his escape. He'd frequently changed jobs, houses, countries even, to avoid capture. Change was the only reason he could return to Ivy Oaks as a free man. But the greatest change was discovering, at forty-six, that he was a father.

Polly had been nineteen, almost two years older than he when they initially became lovers. It was his first time being with a girl, and he had been awkward, clumsy. But they'd learned together because he had also been her first. Now, according to Bentoo, he had also been her last. He hadn't known she was two months pregnant when he left; never even knew she had died. *How could she do that, hang herself? She loved life; the baby was just a year-old. Would she have done it if, if....No Randy, that's then and this is now; you can't go back....*

He began to whistle as he drew nearer the cabbage field.

CHAPTER 26
FATHER MEETS DAUGHTER

Randy found Crecie at Muddy Creek. It was the morning break and she sat under a weeping willow tree, crunching ground-nuts. "Morning, Crecie," he said, looking down at her. He tried to sound cheerful, attempting a confidence he didn't feel.

"Morning," she muttered, not looking up.

Crows perched high in the trees cawed back and forth. The rest was all stillness.

Randy's hands felt clammy. He hadn't been this nervous since he'd jumped ship in Boston, searching for the safe house. He knelt in front of her, but she looked down, avoiding his eyes. The birds flew away, and the silence between the strangers lengthened.

Randy spoke first. "Um...you know who I am?"

"No."

It wasn't the answer he'd hoped for. "Bentoo's your gram, so that make me your pa." He half-chuckled. "Why, even a blind man can see that."

She remained aloof, dusting off the little tubers before eating them.

He tried again. "Why did you leave so quick this morning?"

"Why *you* leave?" she said, still averting her eyes.

He was taken aback by her response, but sat down anyway; close, but not exactly beside her. He held up the pail. "To bring you something to eat."

"No; that ain't what I mean. Why you run away from Ivy Oaks?"

Randy surmised he was being judged and made a big to-do of placing the pail between them, stalling. He angled the container toward her, offering the food; she ignored the gesture.

"I wanted to be free," he said.

She glanced sideways at him. "What you know about such a thing; cause you to leave yo' family and all?"

"Polly told me about it—how freedom feel."

Crecie bolted upright. "Polly? How *she* know about such a thing?"

"She was born free. Didn't she tell you?"

"Uh-uh; I been just wean when she...she die."

"Well, Bentoo shoulda told you; she knew."

"Bentoo never tell me nothing about nothing—except herbs and healing." She stared directly at Randy. "*You* here now, though; you tell me."

Randy relaxed; relieved she was showing interest. He took some bread and ham from the pail, made a sandwich, and presented it to her.

She shook her head.

"What you want to know?" he said, forcing a smile.

"Everything," she said, not smiling back.

He bit into the sandwich, chewed, then began to tell Polly's story.

"It was raining the day Old Massa brought her to our cabin and told Bentoo to look after her. She was soaking wet, shivering. Her long hair—straight like yours—was plastered to her body. I never saw anybody with hair that long. At first she wouldn't talk, wouldn't say nothing. We thought she was deaf and dumb."

He took another bite, then went on. "She was so pretty. But she had a crazy look, like a animal caught in a trap. Living free like she did, I guess she did feel trapped."

He finished the sandwich then continued.

"Anyway, after a few days, when she see we didn't mean her no harm, she told us little bits and pieces about herself. Said her mama was a Seminole Indian and her pa was a full-blooded African slave, a runaway from a plantation in Georgia."

"A runaway? How come he massa ain't catch him, take he back to the plantation?"

"A whole lot of runaways lived deep in Florida territory, free, with the Seminoles. The Spanish people owned all that land back then, and they didn't send slaves back."

Crecie listened, completely engrossed.

"But sometimes," Randy continued, "white men raided the territory and captured every black person they could get their hands on—slave or free, it didn't make a difference—then they sold them to slave traders. That's what happened to Polly and her pa. Old Massa bought her at the slave market in Charleston, but far as I know, she never saw her pa again. I remember her talking about him; how he and her ma was married—."

"Married?" said Crecie.

"Yep! They didn't jump the broom like slaves; they married for *real*, in the sight of God."

"By a preacher?"

"Oh, yeah, by a preacher; in a church."

Crecie stared at him, open-mouthed. Then she asked, awed, "They had they own church in them woods? Where they could sit down in?"

"Yeah, but it was more than just woods where they lived. Polly said they lived in little villages, towns; with houses, and trading posts, just like the white folks had."

Crecie shook her head in disbelief.

"And they wore the same kind of clothes the white folks wore—dresses and shirts and such. Polly told me the white folks call the Seminoles a civilize tribe or something like that, because they took up white folks ways. When she talked about those days, about being free, her eyes just glowed. Then, *whoosh!* It would be like wind blowing out a candle and she'd get real quiet."

Crecie shook her head slowly. "I ain't know none o' this befo' now."

"She talked about being free a lot. Maybe she was trying to hold on, not to forget...." His voice trailed off and he was silent, as if reliving his own memories. "But you know what the best thing was, what the Spanish people did—they had schools and everybody could read *and* write."

"Uh-huh, I know," said Crecie matter-of-factly. "Not about Polly, though; about Bentoo."

Now it was Randy's time to be surprised. "Bentoo *tell* you she could read?"

"Ain't I just say Bentoo ain't tell me about *nothing?*"

"Well, how you know that?"

"Once, when I was little, she thought I been sleep, and I see her looking at a paper, talking to it. Then, later, when I see Massa and them do the same thing, I ax Bentoo to show me how to talk to the paper, too. I been too little to know they been reading. Well, Bentoo whip me something terrible that day; said not to never talk about such things no mo'. And I never did, not 'til this very day."

Randy nodded. "You did a wise thing."

"Can you read? Talk to paper, too?"

Randy smiled proudly. "Why, yes; I can. Polly sneaked and showed me, one letter at a time; then I showed Bentoo how."

Randy sensed an immediate change as Crecie's jaw tightened and she leaned back against the tree, distancing herself.

She looked at him accusingly. "But she ain't learnt *me!*"

Randy searched for the right words, and his voice was gentle when he spoke. "Crecie, slaves got whipped, killed even, just for *saying* the word 'read'."

She nodded, having been whipped by Bentoo a time or two; but she knew that didn't compare to the agony cruel overseers gave out.

"Bentoo couldn't take that chance," said Randy. "I was gone; Polly dead. You all she had left …it was too dangerous to show you how to read." He closed his eyes, trying not to imagine Crecie experiencing such peril.

"It ain't hurt *you* none," she said.

It didn't help much, either. North or south, the first thing white folks saw was my black skin; never about what's in my head. He didn't want to think about it anymore—the humiliation, the fear, the loneliness—he just wanted to feel free, safe, and at home with family.

"Bentoo told me you married Isham," he said, changing the subject.

The dodge worked. Crecie's eyes sparkled. "You know Isham?"

"Know him? I nearly raise that boy. He was about six or seven years younger than me; didn't Bentoo tell you?"

Crecie frowned and pursed her lips. "Ain't I tell you—."

"Oh, I forgot—Bentoo ain't tell you nothing about nothing." This time when Randy smiled, Crecie rewarded him with a tight-lipped grin.

"Well, anyway, Isham was my little shadow. That boy followed me 'round foot-to-foot." He reared back against the tree, reminiscing, and their shoulders touched. "Isham must of been around five that time I took him to the crick and a baby gator took his bait. That thing woulda pulled *him* in, if I didn't grab him by the seat of his britches."

Crecie softened at Randy's memory, recalling the day a big catfish took Leona's bait. Still, she was not to be deterred. "You got satisfaction? Glad you leave Bentoo, Polly...." Randy felt she wanted to add, *and me.*

"What did they tell you about me, Crecie, while you were growing up?"

"Bentoo ain't say much; just she be my gram 'cause her son be my pa. I think the load been too heavy for she, not knowing if you alive or not. But you still ain't tell me—you glad you find freedom?"

He tried to answer honestly.

"I didn't know about you before I escaped, but I can't say I woulda stayed even if I did know. Polly and Bentoo, they couldn't leave, but God knows I couldn't stay—not after everything Polly told me about being free." He paused, giving her a chance to speak. She remained quiet, so he continued. "I was gonna either die a slave or die running. I made up my mind to die run—."

"Freedom mean all *that* to you?"

"I had to try." He reached for her hand, but she pulled away. "No," he said, "I can't say I'm satisfied with the way everything turned out—especially not knowing about you. But deep down inside, looking back—yeah, I'm glad I took the chance, broke the yoke."

A horse whinnied in the distance and Crecie saw Hamp and Titus leading Rex toward the field.

She stood up. "I got to go to work."

Randy stood, too, extending the pail. "There's food enough here for the men."

"Well, give it to 'em," she said, walking away.

Randy watched his daughter retreat, wondering if she'd lived with loss so long, she couldn't recognize gain. *Well, I'm back now, and she just gonna have to accept it.*

CHAPTER 27
CHANGES—BIG AND LITTLE

I t was early afternoon when Crecie and the young men left the field. She sat astride Rex; Hamp and Titus trooped alongside.

"You still gwine be at Bentoo cabin in the morning?" Titus asked.

"Yeah, far as I know," she replied.

"Wah-we'll see ya in the muh-morning then," said Hamp.

"Yep, in the morning," she said.

The men took the fork to the right, and Crecie continued on. She was tired and hungry, but her mind was still on work. *I gwine rustle up something to eat while Sham take care Rex; maybe take a little nap befo' checking on the yard garden at Midway. No telling what need doing since I been gone.*

Crecie crossed the meadow, hearing laughter coming from Bentoo's cabin even before she entered Slave Row. She reached the cabin and curtly greeted the people standing around in the yard. Their response was just as terse. *Well, that's one thing ain't change— people acting funny with you 'til somebody get sick and need you to come see about 'em.*

More good-humored chatter came from inside the house, and Crecie suspected folks were there because of Randy. She handed the tether to Sham and entered the cabin. Her suspicion was right. He sat cross-legged on a pallet in the middle of the floor; six or seven people clustered nearby on straw mats. The conversation was lively, and as the group's memories meshed and flowed, each recollection was a lead-in for another. The stories and laughter grew more raucous with each new saga.

"Hey, Crecie," someone called from the group. It was Mose. "Ain't you happy your pa back home?"

"I, um—." Crecie began.

"Sho, she is," Dahlia interjected. "This be a happy day fo' all o' we."

Bentoo stood beside the table. "Crecie, come; I fixed you some food."

She approached the table, hoping it wasn't acorn soup. She was relieved to see green beans, pieces of chicken, and two thin slices of beef. She knew Randy had brought the food but she was so hungry she would have willingly downed the bitter soup.

She ate, listening as Randy talked about his escape and how the Boston abolitionists had aided him. He ended his story and the listeners gradually made their exit.

Mose, however, stayed behind. His work at the army camp on Hilton Head made him privy to the latest news, and he was eager to share.

"Well, General Sherman shipping out," Mose reported. "He say ain't enough action going on 'round here fo' him."

Crecie felt dismay well up. *Oh no. Something else change again.* She'd come to regard General Sherman as fair, hiring Isham and the other drivers after the Big Gun Shoot.

"No telling who gwine take his place," said Bentoo.

"Oh Mr. Lincoln done already pick the best man for the job," said Mose, "General David Hunter. He a abolitionist; he gwine take care the black folk."

"Give us land and we can take care of our self," said Randy.

Crecie glanced up sharply. *Humph! At least I side with him on one thing.*

"For sho, you right," said Mose, plopping a tattered Union cap on his bald head. "Well, I got to be going. G'night, Bentoo, Crecie. I know ya'll glad Randy back home."

"Oh yes," said Bentoo, beaming. Crecie stared down at the empty plate.

"C'mon, Mose, I'll walk you to the wagon," said Randy, heading for the door.

Crecie stood, stretched, and started to make up her pallet. But Bentoo stopped her.

"Oh, wait Crecie. I giving Randy that space. You gwine bed-down with the chillun."

"You giving him *my* spot?" She scooped up the pallet and stormed into the adjacent room. "Damn Randy!"

Bentoo marched lockstep behind her, scowling. "What be the matter with you? You been acting the jackass ever since Randy come home. Why you act like that—you oughta be glad yo' pa back."

"*My* pa? No—him be *yo'* son. I don't know diddly-squat about that man." She threw the bedding to the floor, grumbling. "And fo' true, he don't know nothing about me."

"Yeah, him my son, and at the same time yo' pa, too; ain't nothing gwine ever change that. You ain't got no cause to be acting all jealous and such."

"You the one acting different; you ain't never make all this... this to-do over me! Everything be fine 'til *he* come."

"You ain't been gone twenty-nine years."

"Well, I'll be gone back to Midway t'morrow, then you can make all the fuss you want over him."

"I done already thought ahead o' you, gal," said Bentoo. "And if you know like *I* know, you best try to take yo' pa with you. *Somebody got to look after yo' behind when that hag get to riding you again* and it might as well be him. But you the big woman now, so suit yo'self." She turned and left the room.

Terror gripped Crecie and she sank slowly to the pallet. *Oh, God, no! Them spirits...that...that bad feeling. Lord, no—I can't go through that by myself no mo'.* She was still huddled on the floor when Bentoo returned. Crecie waited until she'd bedded the children, then spoke. "Bentoo?"

"Yeah, what you want?"

"If, er, if Randy want to come stay in Midway, it be alright with me."

Bentoo headed for the door. "I'll ax him," she mumbled over her shoulder.

Crecie plumped up the moss-filled ticking and soon dozed off. For some mysterious reason, it was the first sound sleep she'd had in weeks.

Randy gladly moved in and the two of them formed an uneasy truce. He kept peace based on his need for stability and family; her peace revolved around fear of the supernatural. Although she was barely civil, she found his presence comforting; mainly because the ghostly haze had not reappeared since he'd come into her life.

CHAPTER 28

WORKING A NEW WAY

B lacks and whites sat side-by-side, jammed into every cranny of Brick Baptist Church. The six-year-old edifice at St. Helena, built by slaves for white parishioners, was host to the first meeting between the contrabands and Gideonites. Field hands, artisans, and domestics spilled out into the yard, waiting to hear what the latest newcomers had to say.

Crecie and Bentoo entered the church. Crecie, out of habit, went straight up the stairs leading to the balcony. She'd almost reached the landing when Bentoo called to her.

"Why you head fo' the balcony, gal? You ain't got to stand up there no mo'."

Crecie turned slowly, uncertain.

Bentoo continued into the church. "C'mon," she urged, "we gwine sit in a *pew*, like Massa and the Missus use to do."

"It be too bunch-up down here," Crecie muttered, eying the crowd.

They reached the packed front pew and a young white man rose, offering his seat. The others shifted to make room. Crecie squeezed in beside Bentoo and anxiously looked around. Rev. French and Edward Pierce were the only whites she recognized.

This ain't right, she thought. *White folks standing and blacks sitting; downstairs, too—in the pews.* "Why you come all the way down here?" she whispered. "I could o' gone to the balcony just as good."

"Shhh! They fixing to start," hissed Bentoo.

Mose stood and faced the audience. His squeaky tenor rang out the first line of "There's a Meeting Here Tonight," indicating the start of the meeting.

I take my text in Matthew and by the Revelation, he sang.

The Gideonites watched, tight-lipped and wide-eyed, as the people enthusiastically joined in, rhythmically clapping their hands and tapping the beat.

> *I know you by your garment,*
> *There's a meetin' here to-night.*
> *There's a meetin' here to-night,*
> *Oh! There's a meetin' here to-night;*
> *I hope to meet again, There's a meetin' here to-night.*

They ended the repetitive verses and Reverend French offered a fervent prayer, evoking the presence of the Holy Spirit. The contrabands responded with resounding "Amens."

Pierce, who had been standing beside French on the podium, now took a position behind it. He opened the Bible and read from Luke, 4:1; ending the reading at verse eighteen: "...He hath sent me to heal the brokenhearted, to preach deliverance to the captives, and recovering of sight to the blind, to set at liberty them that are bruised." He looked out over the audience. "Good evening," he began. "It is a pleasure to be back among you, to set at liberty the bruised and brokenhearted, deserted by their masters. But I bring good news. Mr. Lincoln, the Great Man in Washington, has this whole matter in charge and was thinking about what he could do to help you. The trouble with doing for you though, is that your masters have said you are lazy and won't work."

A disgruntled pall crept over the room.

"Where we come from, all are free, both black and white. And they all *work* freely, for wages—just as you will learn to do."

The mood lightened.

"We do not have captives where we come from," Pierce continued. "We do not sell children or separate families. Our intention, in spite of what your master has told you, is not to carry you off to Cuba, but to guide you into freedom. That's why Mr. Lincoln sent us here—to see if you are willing to work on your own. You must show him that you will not go gadding about, but will remain on the plantations and continue to raise cotton as before."

At the mention of cotton, grumbling and dissention reverberated across the room. A young man standing along the wall voiced his thoughts.

"I don't mean no disrespect, suh, but far as I know, I speak for all o' we when I say we looking to grow sustenance crops—corn, potatoes, peas, and the like. Can't eat cotton."

Crecie turned to see who'd been bold enough to speak his mind. Surprisingly, it was Frazier, one of the most reticent men on the plantation. *Talk o' freedom done open many-a mout'*, she thought.

The crowd grew noisy, agreeing with him; Pierce raised his hand to resume order.

"That's all well and good, but you know this is a hard time for all of you. If you choose *not* to work cotton, if you don't do your part to help win this war, Mr. Lincoln will have to give up helping you and you must give up hope for anything better in life. Your children, your grandchildren, even your great-grandchildren a hundred years hence, will be worse off than you. Now, before you come to a bad decision, let me introduce you to Superintendent Philbrick. He will tell you how we're going to help you."

A short, thickset man approached the podium. "Good evening," said Philbrick. "I look forward to working with you, helping you learn to live free productive lives. What I have to say is very important, so you must listen carefully. I know you feel that grow-ing cotton and working in gangs is the same as being a slave. I'm sorry to say that the new superintendents are going to continue the gang labor system started by the cotton collection agents."

Loud protests again filled the room, and Philbrick lifted his arms for silence.

"But here at Ivy Oaks, and at the other two plantations I'm su-pervising, the task system will be used, giving you time, as before, to spend on your own."

He then went on to explain the workings of the new system. The army would provide shelter for the mainland refugees, and if the former island slaves wanted to remain in their cabins rent free, they would *have* to work cotton. If they choose to work elsewhere, they'd be charged a small fee. If they moved from the plantation all together, their homes would be rented to the refugees.

"It is prudent you keep your houses clean, your yards free of useless oddments and rubbish." He nodded toward the senator's wives who'd accompanied them on the *Atlantic*. "These ladies will be distributing clothes and food to you. They are also here to guide you in the art of creating neat, comfortable homes, representative of a free people."

Crecie held on to every word. Isham's status as a slave-driver had afforded them a larger cabin, nicer than the others. The thought of having to leave it terrified her. Her leg nervously shook, and the words, *Change, change, change,* echoed inside her head. She pressed down on her leg, stilling it, then willed her mind to concentrate on the speaker.

"Those who work cotton will be allotted land for their own gardens," Philbrick continued, "and the government will initially provide food and clothing for you. After the cotton is sold, you'll re-ceive wages and be responsible for your own well-being. Everyone, including families, will be assigned as much cotton land as you feel you'll be able to work. The government will pay you twenty-five cents a day for planting and hoeing, and later, two and a half cents per pound for picking." The people listened closely since they'd not yet been paid for the work they were currently doing—collecting last year's cotton.

"Plantation stores will be established. There, you'll use your wages to purchase food, clothing, and other reasonably priced goods befitting a free people. Should the need arise, rest assured you'll be protected in the event your former owners return to lay claim to you," said Philbrick.

The people remained stoically uncommitted.

"If you work cotton, we will provide doctors and teachers for you."

Crecie bolted upright when she heard the words *doctors* and *teachers*.

Philbrick introduced the men standing on either side of him. "This is Dr. John Vickers. And this is Mr. William Gannett; he's a Unitarian minister and my assistant. He will also teach at Ivy Oaks School. I will oversee *all* the schools on the island. In addition, I will personally provide the salaries for some of the teachers."

"School? Ya'll gwine learn our chillun how to read?" said the woman sitting beside Crecie.

"And spell?" called out another.

"Yes; and we'll teach you, too, if you so desire," replied Philbrick. "If you respect our agents, are willing to work, and keep your houses clean, as time goes by you will be allowed to own land and be as well-off as Northern white people."

Pierce stepped forward. "President Lincoln has sent us to do everything we can to guide you into freedom. We've brought with us a shipload of food, clothing, and medicine. More teachers and supplies are on the way. But you must be of good authority for each other, show you are deserving of freedom. If you don't, all of you will suffer ill repute from the bad deeds of a few."

Doctors and medicine was all Crecie heard. *Thank you, God, fo' answering my prayers.* When the meeting ended, she hurried to Pierce, telling him about her sick son, pleading for help.

CHAPTER 29

FAMILIAR FACES

It was common knowledge Crecie made the best chow chow around. Randy had tried to persuade her to sell the peppery relish to the soldiers at Hilton Head, but she'd refused, claiming she had more than enough work to do already. Still, the cabbage yield had been exceptional, and she was determined to preserve all she could for the family, including chow chow.

She was alone in the yard, shredding the cabbage when the army wagon pulled off the road. Two white men alighted from the wagon and began walking toward her. She glanced around anxiously for Randy and Sham; the sound of wood being chopped reassured her they were near. As the men drew closer, she was relieved to recognize Pierce and Philbrick.

"Good afternoon, Crecie," said Pierce. "You remember Superintendent Philbrick, don't you?" Philbrick tipped his hat in much the same manner Pierce had done two months ago.

She responded with a little curtsy. "Yes, suh. I remember him from the meeting."

Pierce unbuttoned his coat; the snakeskin belt she'd given him came into view. Crecie beamed, pleased he was wearing it.

"We went by the field, looking for Isham," said Pierce.

Crecie's hands darted to her lips and she stifled a gasp.

"What's wrong?" Pierce asked, stepping toward her.

"I-Isham...him dead," she said softly.

"Dead?" Pierce drew back, stunned. "When? What happened?"

She regained her composure and took a deep breath. "It be better I tell you inside."

They entered the cabin and Pierce looked around. The once-brimming shelves were now empty; a black kettle simmered in the fireplace, sending out the pungent aroma of cabbage. Two children, a frail boy and a thin girl, sat on a pallet in the corner. The girl, fingering her long, thick braids, stared at the strange men.

"Is that your son, the one Dr. Vickers came to see?" Pierce asked.

"Yes, suh, that be him—Willie," she said proudly. "And this be Leona, my gal chile."

Pierce bent down and spoke to the little girl. "Are you ready to start school?"

Leona nodded shyly.

"And how's *he* doing?" asked Philbrick, looking at Willie.

"Oh, he come a long way since he see the doctor. I so thankful to you and Massa Pierce. If you ain't been here—."

"Yes, yes," said Pierce. "But tell me about Isham."

She sat down at the table and the men joined her. "Oh, Massa Pierce. It been terrible; the soldiers teef we things, and when Isham try and stop 'em, they, they....beat him so bad."

"I see," said Pierce. "You needn't say more. I'm so sorry for all you've been through."

"Yes suh," she said, bowing her head.

"If the government expects these people to work, it must protect them," said Philbrick.

"Well, when General Hunter takes command, I'm sure he'll—."

Suddenly the door swung open and a man carrying an armful of firewood entered. He dumped the load on the hearth, then doffed a weather-beaten hat.

"Afternoon everybody," he said.

Pierce and Philbrick stared for a few seconds, then spoke simultaneously.

"Aha!" said Pierce.

"It's the waiter," said Philbrick.

"From the *Atlantic*," said Pierce, rising slightly. "I didn't get your name on the ship; I'm Edward Pierce, Treasury Agent for the United States Government."

"I'm Randolph, suh; Randolph Panther, but I go by Randy."

"Hmm, Panther; that's a rather unusual name," said Pierce.

"It came from my…my wife, Polly; she was part Seminole and I took her totem."

"Totem?" said Crecie. "Bentoo never mention no totem to me."

"I guess you already know Crecie, my daughter," said Randy.

"Yes," said Philbrick. "And I must say the resemblance between the two of you is striking. I'm Edward Philbrick, the new superintendent here at Ivy Oaks."

"Superintendent? You taking over the cotton collection?" Randy asked.

Philbrick chuckled. "No, their work is nearly complete. They'll be leaving in a month or so."

"And good riddance!" said Pierce. "With all the disruptions from them *and* the army, it's a wonder we've been able to get anything done."

Randy pulled up a rough-hewn bench and sat down. "I ain't been keeping up with everything; just trying to get used to being home again. But I hear about what's going on."

"Yes, what with the army, the navy, the cotton agents, and now *us*—there's a lot going on," said Philbrick. "We're going to need everyone's help to get the work started again."

"Work? That's what I'm looking for. What kind of work you talking about?" asked Randy.

"Growing cotton," said Philbrick.

"Cotton?" said Randy. "Free men don't grow cotton—that's slave work."

"Not necessarily. Even the liberated must work and growing cotton is honest labor," said Philbrick.

"But it ain't about the work, Mr. Philbrick, it's about the *crop*. The way I see it, growing cotton for the government is the same as growing it for the master."

"But the government isn't *forcing* anyone to work," interjected Pierce. "Besides, we must all work in order to survive."

"Yes, but free men work for their *self* to survive, not to make other people rich," Randy rejoined.

"That's right; as a rule, they do," said Philbrick. "But now truthfully, do you think the black man is *ready* to work for himself, independently without the whip?"

Randy scowled and pushed away from the table.

Crecie's hands grew damp. "Leona, you and Willie go outside with Sham."

The room remained quiet as the children exited.

"As I remember, sir," said Randy to Philbrick, "there never was much whipping going on at Ivy Oaks to start with; master was always off the place, just like all the other Sea Island planters. But we still worked; kept the place up, planted crops—all without a overseer beating us half to death."

Crecie sat quietly, her head bowed.

"Now all the masters are gone, for good this time, and crops still flourish." Randy walked to the window. "Come look, see for yourself." He pointed to the yard gardens and beyond. "Black man plant all of that, same as he planted it for the white man." He paused and his broad fingers ticked off the South's money-making crops. "Tobacco, rice, sugar, cotton—even indigo once upon a time—all for the master's gain. But *that* corn field, *that* potato patch—black man plant that to feed his *own* family."

"I'll grant you that," conceded Pierce, standing. "The evidence of hard work, the abundance of crops; that does indicate the Negro's diligence."

"But ain't that why you brought us here in the first place—to work? If our labor was useless you woulda left us in Africa. We been here now some three hundred years, more maybe, working all that time. Clearing land, digging coal, loading boats, hammering iron, laying railroad ties—three hundred years breaking our backs for this country, and don't own so much as a thimbleful of dirt to show for it."

Pierce and Philbrick stared, unmoved.

"But the time's come for our work to show," Randy continued. "All we need is a little land—a toehold." He eyed Pierce and Philbrick beseechingly. "Don't ya'll owe us at least that much?"

The two men exchanged questioning glances, then Philbrick spoke. "In due time, after you've proven yourselves, demonstrated your ability to be responsible citizens. Then I'm sure you'll be granted the right to own land."

"Yes," said Pierce, "and right now it is imperative we get next year's cotton in the ground. The outcome of your freedom depends on it. Now, we must be on our way. Planting is already behind schedule."

Philbrick stood. "I trust *you'll* be reporting for work, Crecie."

"Oh, yes suh, I gwine be there."

She followed the men out into the yard, and even though Randy remained at the window, she felt the weight of his sullen disposition.

The wagon disappeared around the bend and her father joined her outside. She took a deep breath, prepared to meet him head on.

CHAPTER 30

A FALLING OUT

Randy scowled at Crecie. "You gonna work cotton? For *them*?"
"Ain't that what I say? I ain't picky like *some* people." Her tone
was surly.

"No need for that kinda talk; I'll find suitable work soon."

"Work is work."

"Slaving in cotton ain't; not when freedom staring you dead in
the face. But you can't see that."

"Oh, I see it, alright; but 'til I get some land to go with it, freedom ain't nothing I got a taste fo'."

Randy sighed. "Uh-huh. So how you plan on getting land?"

"I ain't thought that far yet; Massa Lincoln gwine see to it. We
just got to be patient, wait and see."

"Patient? Didn't you hear what I told them—three hundred
years is a long time to be waiting and seeing."

"Humph!" she said, turning toward the cabbage-laden workbench. "I got chow-chow to fix."

Randy struggled to remain calm, but weeks of tolerating her
rude behavior had come to a head. He grabbed her arm and swung
her around, facing him. "I got something to say to you, Crecie, and
you better listen good."

She jerked away from his grasp and darted behind the rickety workbench, creating a barrier between them. "Don't be putting yo' hand on me!"

"Just be still and hear me out. The only thing we got in this world is our labor. And that's what the white folks want, what they need. As long as we give 'em what *they* need, they ain't got a reason to give us what *we* need—land."

She ignored him and began arranging the cabbage in a row. After lining them up just so, she looked at him, challenging. "How *you* know what white folks want? Nobody know what they gwine do 'til they do it. But for some reason I just believe, in they own time, they gwine do right by we."

"Is that what you think? *They* gonna do right?" He walked behind the table and stood beside her. "Can't you see, Crecie; if we have our own land, grow our own crops, then we won't need them. We can work for our self just as hard as we work for them—harder even."

He continued to pressure her, and she began whacking the cabbage, trying to drown out his talk about change and independence. Finally, she turned and faced him.

"What you say might be true *after* we get land, but white folks got all of it right now. If us want them to throw we a bone, us best walk around 'em tippy-toe and stay out they business."

"Damn it, Crecie! After everything I said, you still—." Frustrated, he grabbed her by the shoulders and shook hard. "You *got* to stop thinking like that; this is a new day."

"Loose me," she demanded, struggling to escape his grasp.

"No! Not until you understand what I'm saying to you."

"Saying? You ain't got no say! Buckra be in charge o' everything. Yesterday, today, and come t'morrow, he gwine still be boss."

"Listen to me—the times changing and you got to change, too."

She continued to struggle. "Ain't nothing change! Except maybe you—runaway Negro, come back here talking good trying to tell we what to do."

Resigned, he stepped back, releasing her. "Now I see why everybody stay clear of you—you just a damn fool. 'Yessuh, massa; whatever you say, massa'. The more they put on you, the harder you work your ass off!"

"Now hold on, Randy! What right you, *or* them lazy-good-for-nothing Negroes, got to talk about *me?* Ain't none o' them got a crust o' bread fo' to give. Who keep we from starving? Who bring medicine, doctor to keep Willie alive? The white man—that's who! No I ain't shame to work hard fo' the buckra—I *know* what side my bread got honey on." She picked up the knife and began to feverishly cut the cabbage into haphazard strips. "And anyhow, you just like the rest o' them po-ass bastards—ain't got a pot to piss in or a window to throw it out."

Randy stared at her, dismayed and speechless. She continued to mumble as she lacerated the cabbage. Each slash of the knife seemed to pierce him, killing his hope of a loving daughter, a stable family. When he felt calm enough, he spoke. "Well, I'll tell you *one* last thing—you ain't got to worry about me throwing no piss out *your* window; I'm leaving! Bentoo was right, you—."

The slicing came to an abrupt halt. "Bentoo?" Crecie stepped toward him. "Bentoo been talking to *you*...about *me?*"

He hesitated, realizing he'd struck a nerve. "Yeah. Anything wrong with that?"

"What she say? What she tell you about me?"

"Things I missed—how you learn real fast, heal the sick; she told me about the time you killed your first snake. And the spirits—she said you see ghosts and such. She tell the truth about that?"

Crecie picked up the cleaver and banged its sharp edge into the wood, anchoring it. "She ain't got no right to—."

"Oh, for God sake, Crecie; I'm your *pa*." He worked the cleaver out of the wood and slammed it on the table. "Ain't nothing gonna change that—let it be!" He turned and stomped toward the cabin.

Let it be…let it be…that ain't easy fo' everybody to do. She retrieved the knife and, finding her rhythm, rapidly minced the cabbage strips. *I be just like this cabbage—little scraps and pieces just floating everywhere, anywhere, nowhere.* She scooped up the confetti-like bits and dumped them into a huge wooden bowl. *Just to be whole again, like befo' this war come and change everything….* She thought about all she'd lost; heart-sick that the dearest, Isham, could never be replaced. *No, I ain't gwine be whole no more—never.*

Randy emerged from the cabin; from the corner of her eye, she spied his carpetbag. She kept slicing and dicing, ignoring him, but it didn't matter because he didn't venture any good-byes. When he entered the road, she laid the knife aside, watching until he rounded the bend. He was out of sight when she realized he had not looked back, not even one last time. Crecie blinked back tears of angry betrayal. *The hell with him; the hell with all o' them.* She picked up the knife. *I ain't got time fo' this foolishness.*

CHAPTER 31
GETTING STARTED

It was twilight by the time Philbrick and Gannett set out for Ivy Oaks plantation.

"Do you think we'll get there by midnight?" asked Gannett, guiding the oxen along the rutted dirt road.

"We should; but if Ivy Oaks is anything like the Cooke place and Shell Grove plantation, I'm not particular about getting there anytime soon," replied Philbrick.

Inspecting the two smaller plantations had been the superintendents' first-day priority, but the visits hadn't gone well. Their appraisal of the workers, the land, the equipment, had been physically exhausting, alerting them to problems that lay ahead. The contrabands, harassed and victimized by the Treasury's cotton collectors, were sullen, reluctant to cooperate with the latest faces of white authority.

"Why on earth did they smash the cotton gins?" asked Gannett.

"I have no idea," Philbrick replied. "Who knows what goes on in their dark minds; they certainly are a brooding lot."

"Do you believe their story about the missing livestock?"

"That the soldiers slaughtered cattle at will and stole the mules? I think they spoke the truth—as best as I could understand them, that is."

"What *is* that language—their words all run together, and so fast! It sounds like gibberish!" said Gannett.

Philbrick chuckled. "You'll get use to it; the syntax grows on you quickly."

"I hope so. But, yes, I agree with you; they are a guileless bunch, believing every lie the soldiers tell them—even that they're completely free, under no obligation to work. Can you imagine!"

"It's the Confiscation Act; it's made the people more assertive, knowing the army won't return them to their former masters."

"Yes, I noticed as much at the Brick Church meeting," said Gannett.

The wagon creaked into the shadowy night, and the discussion turned to Ivy Oaks.

"That plantation is the largest on St. Helena, yet it hasn't had a real manager in months," said Gannett, "just cotton collection agents provoking the Negroes. And according to Pierce, there's a lunatic in charge of the place."

"Yes, a Colonel Nobles. General Sherman hired him soon after the army landed, a stopgap to getting the Negroes back to work. But then Chase brought Colonel Reynolds aboard, and Nobles was demoted to second in command. Between him and the blacks, my work is cut out for me," said Philbrick.

"Well, in two months or so all the cotton will be picked, baled, and shipped; after that, the agents will be gone for good!"

"And I'm sure the workers' disposition will improve once I reinstate the task system—that's how they're used to working. Nobles has them laboring in gangs."

"Working from sunup to sundown, as I understand it," said Gannett. "That has to be extremely hard."

Philbrick shifted his weight on the wagon's planked bench. "Harder than this seat, you think? Thank God the road to Ivy Oaks is just ahead."

Philbrick and Gannett alighted from the wagon as the outline of two men loomed in the doorway.

"Good Even—," began Philbrick.

"Stop right there," Nobles ordered, walking onto the veranda. The other man, one of the colonel's henchmen, stood close, brandishing a firearm.

"There must be a mistake," said Philbrick. "I'm—."

"I know who you are—a nigger-loving jackass come to coddle these lazy blacks. I've seen you and the rest of them strut around the plantations as if you owned the land *and* the nigs."

Philbrick's face reddened as Nobles lambasted the Port Royal experiment, calling the abolitionists a bunch of dimwit do-gooders; wasting the government's money as they pretended to be gentlemen planters and Southern belles.

"Gideon's Band!" Nobles decried. "You're more like Gideon's Fools. I'm going to put a stop to your posturing; mark my words— the blacks'll not get one free handout when I'm through."

Gannett touched Philbrick's arm, a silent plea for them to leave; but Philbrick shook him off, seething.

Nobles continued his rant. "I know what you're up to—all of you; especially your so-called leader, Pierce. Always poking his nose where he has no business; snooping around *my* jurisdiction and whining to Chase about what he's seen. But I'm going to put an end to his underhanded schemes—the nit-picking little bastard. Now you get off these premises before I have you shot for trespassing."

The henchman raised his gun and Gannett, pale and shaken, turned to leave.

But Philbrick would not be intimidated. "We're not going anywhere. If anyone leaves, it will be you."

Nobles stepped toward Philbrick, his fists tightly balled. "How dare you speak to me that way!"

Philbrick also moved in closer; so close Nobles could see flecks dancing in his cold gray eyes.

"I talk to scoundrels anyway I choose," said Philbrick. "When Secretary Chase hears of your threats, you'll be dismissed on the spot."

"The hell with Chase; I'm in charge here."

"No, General Sherman is in charge; and if you don't step aside, I will have his entire army come to remove your ass." His voice was calm, compelling, but his lower eyelids, transparent blood-lined rims, betrayed the intensity of his anger.

Nobles recognized that the man who stood before him did not suffer fools. Grudgingly he stepped aside. "Tell 'em where to sleep," he ordered and stamped away.

Philbrick and Gannett followed the lackey's directions, parting at the stairs' dusty landing. The manor was large but its austere simplicity left Philbrick unimpressed. He turned the knob to his bedroom door but it was blocked. Forcing it open, he found the room crammed with furniture and bales of cotton. *A-ha! So this is why Nobles doesn't want us here. I wonder what else he's hiding.* He recalled Pierce telling him of the agents' unscrupulous claims to anything of value. In line to receive five percent of the profits from confiscated goods, they steadily shipped expensive merchandise and tons of abandoned cotton north for auction. *I've enough to worry about, I don't need to add Nobles's shaky deals to the list.* Meeting with the workers and inspecting Ivy Oaks was foremost on his mind, adding to his fatigue and mental exhaustion. But as a trained engineer, solving problems was his forte. He shoved an ornate chest aside to reach the bed; then removing the gilded chairs stacked atop it, immediately fell asleep.

Philbrick stood in front of the mule barn, unperturbed as Gannett paced. "Didn't we send word to meet us here this morning?" He glanced at his watch. "It's past six o'clock; these people must be taught proper work ethics—punctuality being number one."

"Yes, time *is* money," Philbrick remarked. "But they'll learn to value their labor when faced with either work or starvation."

The workers arrived at six thirty. Crecie, the only worker to arrive before six, emerged from the wood lot across the road where she'd been waiting. Philbrick repeated the labor terms he'd outlined at Brick Church, mildly rebuking the people's lateness. He paused for questions. The young man who'd spoken up at the church voiced a concern.

"I ain't one to complain, but—."

"What's your name?" asked Philbrick.

"Frazier, suh."

"Yes, Frazier; go on."

"Well, now's the time fo' planting cotton seed, but the fields ain't been muddied yet—."

Gannett looked to Philbrick. "Muddied?"

"Fertilized. Something that should have been done in February," answered Philbrick.

"—and the beds need turning," added Frazier.

Another worker voiced his concern. "Mid-spring drought just a mont' away; us want to be ahead o' that."

"I know, I know. Everything you say is true," said Philbrick. "But we plan to provide you with new equipment, show you better, different ways to grow cotton."

Crecie, standing at edge of the crowd sucked in her breath. *Why they got to come changing things again?*

"We will also work beside you, showing you how things are done," continued Philbrick.

The workers grew quiet and exchanged incredulous glances.

"You gwine do *what*?" a woman asked. "Even poor white trash don't work cotton."

Philbrick smiled. "You're speaking of *Southern* men. We're from sturdy New England stock; we thrive on working hard—every day!"

"That's our way," added Gannett. "A fair day's wages for a fair day's work."

The woman shook her head in disbelief. "Massa ain't never hit a lick at a snake."

"What do you mean, a 'new' way to grow cotton?" Frazier asked. "What wrong with the way us *been* growing it?"

That's what I want to know, thought Crecie.

"Nothing, I suppose, if you don't care to make progress and money," Philbrick answered. "Your tools, your ways of doing things are slow, out of date. You now have smart young men to supervise you and work with you; you'll learn a lot from them."

Frazier looked out over the fields as if searching for a response, but the words eluded him. If they had come to mind, he would have said that you must have knowledge to grow cotton—know everything from picking the right seeds, to ginning the bolls, to packing the bales. You have to know how to keep young sprouts free of weeds and what to do in case of an early drought or a late frost. Most of all, you must know the workers' strengths and weaknesses before giving out tasks. But he couldn't put his thoughts into words. Turning back to Philbrick, all he could say was, "Sense— you need cotton-growing sense to grow cotton."

The people stood quiet, listening as Philbrick bolstered the merits of new tools and machinery. Finally, he completed his talk, and the people, knowing that the roofs over their heads depended on their labor, reluctantly agreed to his terms. But as the crowd dispersed, they made certain their objections were within the superintendents' earshot.

"I work fast enough already; ain't got reason to go no faster...."

"Humph! What decent white man gwine do field work...."

"Can't no machine do what these hands can do...."

Philbrick soon discovered he needed more than just forward-thinking laborers to get the project up and running. Nobles had carried out his threat, withholding farm equipment and draft animals, keeping progress to a minimum. Philbrick appealed to Pierce, who in turn complained to Colonel Reynolds. But Reynolds refused to chastise Nobles, trying to reassure Pierce that all the cotton would soon be collected and the agents gone. It was to no avail as Nobles continued to wield control, making the inept superintendents grapple for the simplest tools and supplies.

CHAPTER 32

WHO'S IN CONTROL?

The work advanced slowly as the baffled hands, accustomed to the master's orderly chain of command, now found themselves trapped between the unpredictable demands of three entities: the military, the cotton collectors, and the Gideonites. Used to an efficient, well-run plantation, the people referred to the chaos as a time of great confusion. Laboring to build seedbeds without hoes and plow furrows without mules, the Negroes walked warily between the white folks' contentious power struggles.

——+—+——

Treasury Secretary Chase's assistant removed two letters from their envelopes. "I think you need to personally speak to these, sir."

Chase looked up from his desk. "Why? Who're they from?"

"Pierce...and Reynolds."

The Secretary's exasperated sigh filled the room. "Had I but known five months ago....What is it *this* time?"

"Reynolds is accusing Pierce of taking a high tone with the cotton agents, bragging about his superior influence with you. He writes 'I, along with the Treasury agents, and most of the army officers, feel that Pierce is overstepping his bounds'."

"Humm," replied Chase. "What else?"

"According to Reynolds, most of the missionaries are totally unfit for their positions, depending on the Negroes to direct *them* in cultivating cotton."

"And Pierce? What does he have to say?"

"Oh, quite a bit. He supplied names to support his allegations this time; here's his letter—it's a bit long."

Chase stood to accept the missive, mumbling as he scanned Pierce's complaints:

"'Colonel Nobles has disclosed that 2,500,000 pounds of cotton will be shipped this year, bragging that after bills are paid he's going to receive $40,000.00'."

The Secretary stopped reading and sat back down. "Why, army officers receive only two, maybe three thousand a year." He continued to read, slower this time. "'…and though I suspect something unscrupulous may be afoot, I take no personal interest in this matter and avoid him and the agents as much as possible. The agents uphold the vendors' exorbitant prices—three dollars for shoes that cost eighty-nine cents at home, a dollar a gallon for watered-down molasses. Muslin that sells for eight cents a yard at home goes for twenty-five cents. I think that if it were not for Nobles's disreputable behavior, the other agents would be more agreeable. But for some reason, Colonel Reynolds is hesitant to make a row with him'."

Chase glanced up at his assistant. "Why do you suppose he's reluctant to deal with him?"

"I have no idea," he replied. "Colonel Reynolds *is* his superior isn't he?"

"Well, yes. Even though Nobles was hired first—posthaste by General Sherman—it was left to Reynolds to keep him on." Chase continued reading, silently perusing Pierce's litany of grievances until he reached the last page. "'The agents have the profoundest contempt for the Negroes'," he read aloud, "'and one of Colonel Nobles's henchmen daily subjects them to a reign of terror. I personally heard him pour a torrent of abuse upon the Ivy Oaks workers. One agent at the Jenkins Plantation distributes whisky to the workers and invites army officers to coerce them to dance, making sport of their drunkenness. I reported this to General Hunter, and though I admire his stance against slavery, he appears a bit eccentric; I cannot rely on his judgments. Ever since his arrival he has acted without forethought—issuing orders and recalling them the next day.

"'The Negroes are demoralized and confused as they try to follow the orders of so many new 'masters.' Also, they have not been paid for work began in November.

"'Colonel Nobles is beside himself in his talk and conduct; using language in the presence of Miss Walker and the other ladies that was so indecorous, Colonel Reynolds was forced to rebuke him. All of this can be verified by Miss Walker herself. There are others who can offer testimony: Mr. Barney's son, Lewis; Superintendent Philbrick and his associate, William Gannett of Boston.

"'I implore you to discontinue Colonel Nobles from the service of your Department, accompanied by an order from the War Department. He should be ordered to leave Port Royal at once; if he should remain, he will strain every nerve to defeat all my efforts…'."

Chase stood up. "Well! It appears my advice to Reynolds has gone unheeded. Maybe my new directives to General Benham will encourage him to act."

"Yes sir," replied the assistant, sitting down at the small writing desk. *To Brigadier General Henry Benham, Post Commander,* he wrote. "I'm ready, sir; you may begin."

The Treasury Secretary's orders, to be executed under General Benham's authority, were brief, demanding that the Negro communities and the entire plantations be off limits to military personnel. He forbade *anyone*—military, cotton collectors or superintendents—to remove livestock or equipment unless authorized by Pierce. Lastly, he ordered Reynolds to meet with Pierce and address the accusations made against his agents.

Reynolds was crestfallen when he related the news to Nobles. "Chase upheld Pierce's charge that the Negroes had been swindled," he said. "I'm ordered to deduct all overpayments from the agents' commissions and give the money to General Benham. He'll divide it among the Negroes." It was a vindication for Pierce, a slap in the face for them.

"What! That's not fair," exclaimed Nobles.

"Fair enough," said Reynolds. "You procured those deceitful vendors, knowing they were the agents' friends. Now somebody's got to pay."

Nobles was livid. "That damn Pierce! Sneaky shyster—he's not seen the last of me."

Reynolds frowned, fiddling with the papers on his desk. "I'd let sleeping dogs lie if I were you."

"But you're not me," fumed Nobles.

"Do what Chase says and don't borrow trouble." He stood, indicating the conversation was over.

Nobles headed for the door. "Pierce will get his comeuppance—I'll see to it!"

The opportunity came sooner than Nobles expected. As he exited Reynolds's quarters, he spied Pierce approaching General Benham's quarters.

"Pierce!" shouted Nobles. "I warned you, you bastard!" Straightway he ran up and boxed the shocked man on the ear.

"Wha—stop! Stop it!" yelled Pierce, trying to ward off his assailant. But Nobles struck another blow and he crashed to the ground.

"You bootlicker!" shrieked Nobles, straddling the defenseless man, punching him in the face. "This'll teach you to keep your mouth shut."

The colonel's rage was unrelenting. Pierce, shouting for help, tried desperately to get to his feet. Soldiers on guard duty heard his cries and rescued him.

General Benham, alerted to the melee, rushed outside. He took one look at Pierce and promptly assessed the situation. "Good Lord, man! You've been knocked into a cocked hat!"

Pierce, dazed and bloody, stared at the general with his one good eye.

Nobles immediately alleged affront, railing against the general. "You're making a terrible mistake Benham. This is a travesty; my appeal to the War Department will prove it so!"

Benham ignored the irate man's rants. "Can you walk?" he asked Pierce.

"Yes." His voice was strong in spite of his swollen lips.

Benham turned to one of the guards. "Go fetch Dr. Vickers before he bleeds to death. And take *this* scoundrel to the stockade!"

As the soldiers escorted the bellicose Nobles away, his threats faded in the distance, "I'll have your stars, Benham, just you wait. I have relatives in Congress…."

Benham leaned against his desk, watching Dr. Vickers bandage Pierce's head.

"You'll have headaches for a few days, but I foresee no permanent injury," said the doctor.

"Do you know why he attacked you?" the general asked.

"No, I've no idea," said Pierce. "Our most recent dispute was over the use of a horse and saddle."

"My word!" said Dr. Vickers. "Such a row over a horse and saddle."

"I agree. But he knows I've asked Secretary Chase to discharge him," said Pierce.

"And there's the overage money to be given to the contrabands," offered Benham.

"I'm sure that had some bearing," said Pierce, "but I didn't *personally* provoke the attack. I deliberately stay away from him and his colleagues."

The doctor gathered up his bag and medical supplies. "Well, let me know if you find out. Right now, I've patients to see. Good day."

The doctor left and the men resumed their talk.

"If Chase had sent him away when I requested," said Pierce, "this would not have happened."

"True," said Benham. "But now that most of the cotton's been shipped, there are fewer agents to contend with."

"But Nobles is still here. That man's impossible to work with, but I've promised to remain until my replacement comes. When will General Saxton arrive?"

"He was scheduled any day now, but then Lincoln ordered him to Virginia to assist McClellan; I imagine he'll be here as soon as that's under control." Benham pulled a chair over and faced Pierce. "You know, it *is* within my jurisdiction to dismiss Nobles, but I'll not risk losing my rank over it. You heard his threats."

"Drivel!" said Pierce. "There's no danger in that. Chase and Stanton know of your unwavering support for this mission. They also know the discord Nobles has brought upon it."

"Very well, then," said Benham. "I'll order an investigation."

Based on the investigation's outcome, Nobles and Reynolds were charged with corruption and mistreatment of the Negroes. In addition, Nobles was found guilty of committing personal assault upon Pierce and shipped out on the next steamer bound for New York.

Reynolds's illegitimate deals and profiteering soon surfaced. His reports to Chase indicated he'd underreported ten percent—nearly $50,000.00—of the cotton revenue. Secretary Chase wasted no time firing him and, because of the sudden dismissal, Reynolds was unable to balance his books. He willingly forfeited his five-percent commission as a Treasury Agent in order to avoid charges of fraud.

With a fortune to be made in the cotton trade, Reynolds and many other Union officers engaged in secret partnerships with Southerners that bordered on treason. The irony of it all was Reynolds's arrest two years later—the result of illegal trading in contraband cotton with Chase's son-in-law, William Sprague.

CHAPTER 33
A MATTER OF TRUST

The freedmen, having been ridiculed and exploited by soldiers and treasury agents prior to the Gideonites arrival, had formed a distrust of all whites. The abolitionists made the situation worse by insisting the Negroes adopt white customs and traditions, proving they were worthy of freedom.

The former slaves, however, felt that freedom was not predicated on lifestyle changes, but on an expansion of privileges they already enjoyed—privileges based on unspoken agreements shaped by centuries of interdependence; privileges that defined an understanding of when, where, and how much work was expected of them. Any demands violating those precious entitlements were met with strong resistance.

The disparities between the two groups became greater as Gideon's Band persistently preached a middleclass concept of cleanliness, piety, and toil, while the contrabands doggedly clung to their own separatist, self-sustaining vision. Their view of freedom meant independence, working their own land. At the very least, they expected fair wages for their labor. Anything less meant a step back, toward re-enslavement. Freedom meant different things to different people. No one had bothered to ask the Negroes what it meant to them.

That feeling of distrust was apparent the day Philbrick went to the field and found no one working. *What now?* he wondered. *They're only here half a day as it is.* He kept going until he saw some women at the far end of the field, planting seeds.

He called out to the nearest worker. "Where is everyone?"

The woman was careful to secure her seed-filled sack before looking up.

"Morning suh," she greeted. "Sup'tenant Solte—the one who ginned the good seed with the cotton—well, he come and take all the men away."

"Take them? Where?"

"Don't know, suh."

"Where are the other women, and the older children? Everyone should be working; we've no time to waste."

"Well, suh, when they see all the men leave, they start grumbling, saying 'Mista Solte let the men go work for they self and leave us to do all this work by we self. We gwine go tend we own field'. So then they all go—foot hasty!"

Philbrick shaded his eyes and peered across the field; row upon row of rebuilt beds remained unseeded. *This experiment is doomed.* Exasperated, he turned to her. "Why are *you* still here? Don't you have crops, too?"

"Yes suh, I do. But I tend to 'em on *my* time and give you what due *you*."

Her answer surprised Philbrick, bringing to light characteristics he'd assigned only to his own kind: diligence, fairness, dependability. For the first time he saw the workers as people, subject to the basic emotions of all human beings. He stared at the woman.

"Y-you all right, suh?" she asked, sneaking a glance at him.

"Yes; yes, I'm fine," he replied. "I met you before, but I don't remember your name."

"Crecie, suh."

"Ah…yes. Your child was sick."

"That's right, suh. Little Willie."

"And your father—the waiter; he was looking for work. Did he find any?"

"Yes suh, up in Beaufort. He keeping care of a gentleman up there. Massa Fobs, I believe."

"Fobs…Fobs…? Do you mean *Forbes?*"

"Yes suh; that who Mose tell me—Massa Fobs."

"I know him. He's a fine gentleman."

"Yes suh."

He nodded in the women's direction "Who are they? Tell me their names."

He jotted the names as she relayed them.

"A shipment of clothing is coming from Philadelphia soon. When Miss Walker sets up the distribution, tell the women to give her their names; you'll be given clothes before the others this time."

Fifty boxes of clothing had arrived with the first group of missionaries, but after doling out garments to the sick and elderly, the field workers had received short shrift.

Crecie's eyes widened and her smile brightened. "Oh, thank you, suh! I tell 'em fo' sho."

Philbrick noticed the women had stopped working and now stood watching. *Any little thing distracts them.* "Well, I'm going to find the others. I want this field seeded today."

He was barely out of sight before the women rushed over to question Crecie.

"What he say about we?"

"He say us gwine get clothes first next time," Crecie reported.

"Oh, thanks be to God!" one of them exclaimed. The jubilant little group encircled Crecie, laughing and light-hearted. For the first time she felt something close to acceptance.

During the coming weeks Philbrick launched his plans to gain the contrabands' confidence. Knowing the value they placed on education, he immediately commandeered the plantations' parlors, the contrabands' praise houses, Brick Church, and any available space, using them as classrooms. Children age ten and under were taught from ten o'clock to twelve. Older students, after working in the fields, arrived at noon. Whenever the opportunity presented itself, the superintendents, though already over-worked, taught reading basics to the weary but eager adults. Even during short breaks throughout the day, workers gathered in haylofts, cotton fields, or under shade trees, fervent for learning.

Philbrick, unlike the other superintendents who continued the gang-labor system, employed the task system, allowing the people time to work their own crops. He further bolstered the workers by intermittently paying them a small, good-faith wage from his own resources and encouraged those who could, to purchase reasonably priced clothing donated by Northerners. Those without money were given clothes, especially for Sunday and school.

The money the people spent on clothes was used to establish the first plantation store. It was a simple step, but Philbrick's actions led the workers to see that their labor was not just a means of producing food, but a way to acquire goods.

The people often commented on their new employer's steadfast nature, leading Crecie to remark, "I don't trust the buckra, but I trust Massa Philbrick." It was the closest she'd yet come to accepting a new way of life.

CHAPTER 34
FORBES AND CAPTAIN SMITH

R andy placed the half-filled brandy snifters on the round tea table and bowed slightly. "Would that be all Mr. Forbes?"

"Why, yes, Randy. You may retire if you wish, just leave the decanter."

"Thank you, suh, good night. Good night to you, too, Captain Smith."

The captain gave a quick nod and Randy left the room.

Forbes reclined on a plush chair and gently swirled the brandy. "Ahh, this is the life," he said, taking a sip.

"You've adjusted to Beaufort quite well," said the captain, reaching for his glass.

"Yes, but I was filled with misgivings initially."

"Why is that?" asked Smith.

"Well, with the military in control of everything, it was impossible to find decent quarters. Happily, my enterprising son used his army connections to rent this house. Now I'm at home, perfectly content." He raised his glass. "I propose a toast to Lt. Forbes for finding this idyllic abode, and to you, my dear friend, for finding the perfect...perfect...what *is* Randy, anyway—houseman? Valet?"

Captain Smith smiled and sniffed his cognac, inhaling its heady, aromatic bouquet. "Whatever his duties, I'm glad you hired him—dinner was delicious! When he came to the *Atlantic* seeking reemployment, I instinctively knew he was the help you needed. I was right, too, judging from your improved color." The captain raised his snifter. "Cheers to your good health!" The glasses chinked in a crystal-pinged salute and the men downed their drinks.

Forbes poured refills. "Yes, I'm definitely feeling better. Randy doesn't let me lift a finger—not even to open the mail. Another month or so of his excellent care, along with this wonderful weather, and I'll be rid of this bronchitis in no time."

"That's great news," said Smith. He sat back, surveying the elegant French Empire décor. "This *is* a grand house. You're lucky General Sherman's replacement hasn't snatched it from under you. "

"Oh, Hunter? You needn't worry about him; he's too busy freeing the slaves."

Smith grinned. "I know. Just imagine—usurping the president and declaring his very *own* emancipation proclamation!"

"He's a mad one alright; no sane person would've arbitrarily freed every slave in South Carolina, Georgia, *and* Florida."

"At least it's more than Lincoln's piecemeal efforts. If he had his way they'd all be colonized, shipped back to Africa," Smith replied.

"Ah, but it will be the military's loss. With the army's labor shortage, the contrabands have taken up the slack, doing much of the menial labor. My son tells me the soldiers are dead set against returning runaways when their masters come looking for them."

"Perhaps. But what Lincoln should *really* do is quit coddling the Border States and emancipate the slaves. That's what Hunter has done, even if it's not official. There's also a rumor that the general plans to arm the blacks, form a Negro unit."

"What?" Smith gasped. "Where'd you hear that?"

Randy, out in the hall listening, pressed his ear against the door.

"Senator Sumner. According to him, fifty thousand extra weapons and fifty thousand red breeches have already been shipped to Hilton Head."

"That bit of news calls for a refill." Smith reached for the decanter and poured them both another round. "Has that information been verified?"

Forbes accepted the drink and took a sip before answering. "Oh, I'm sure it's true. Governor Andrew is trying to get Lincoln to authorize the same thing in Massachusetts, using free blacks."

"Ah—but that's different—*they're* ready and willing to fight. I don't see that happening at Port Royal," said Smith. "These people have a long way to go in their thinking."

"True. But they're improving, enamored as they are with education. According to Pierce, young and old are flocking to the schools—he can't recruit enough staff for his Port Royal experiment."

"I know. New teachers came with me on this trip, most of them from Philadelphia. Do you know a Laura Towne? She's part of that delegation."

"No, I haven't heard of her," said Forbes. "But there are so many dedicated abolitionists in the rank and file these days; it's hard to keep up."

"She's hardly rank and file. I know for a fact that Miss Towne arrived with a ton of donated clothing and $5,000.00."

"Humm, I'm impressed. I'm sure *that* made Pierce happy. Who else came? Anyone from Boston?"

"A few. Philbrick's wife arrived—."

"Yes, Helen—her father's a business acquaintance."

"As she informed me," said the captain. "Her friend Harriett Ware accompanied her."

"Good. But where will they live?" asked Forbes. "Surely not at Ivy Oaks. Philbrick and Gannett are sharing that house with cotton agents."

"No. Miss Ware told me they're going to be at the Cooke plantation now that those agents have gone. Philbrick and Gannett will join them; then when Ivy Oaks is vacated, they'll all move there."

"That sounds like a workable plan. The sooner all those rowdy agents leave, the better life will be for everyone," said Forbes. He lifted the nearly empty decanter. "Another?"

Smith stood, stifling a yawn. "No; I'm embarking early in the morning. I'll need to reach Hilton Head by dawn."

Forbes rose to his feet. "Yes, of course. Randy already knows he's to escort you."

"Good. Are you joining us?"

"We'll see. It depends on how I'm feeling."

"Well, if not, it was a lovely visit, my friend," said Smith. "Thanks for your gracious hospitality."

The men shook hands and walked unsteadily toward the door; neither of them heard Randy creep away.

Randy and Captain Smith arrived at Hilton Head early the next morning, leaving Randy plenty of time to visit Bentoo on St. Helena. The oxen moved slowly toward Slave Row, but he didn't mind; it gave him time to think, sort things out. *My wits getting as dull as these oxen—I shoulda known the general was starting a Negro troop. But how did Forbes get the news? It didn't come by mail—I get that first hand.* He patted the letter hidden deep in his inside pocket. *Well, at least I know what this one says.* It was the last letter he'd collected from the post office; later he would re-glue the flap, making a big show of opening it in front of Forbes. *Got to stay a step ahead; never know what these white folks gonna do next.*

CHAPTER 35

RANDY VISITS BENTOO

Bentoo was angling a pan near the fire when Randy walked in. "Come, sit," she said, "I made yo' favorite." She sat beside him. Mother and son talked easily, exchanging news. She gave her opinion about church services and preaching styles. "Rev. French—now you can *feel* the spirit when he get up to preach; but some o' them other ones, like Massa Gannett, they be so dry, put me to sleep— snoring even," she said, laughing.

He told her what he'd heard about General Hunter forming a black regiment.

"I'll believe that when I see it!" she exclaimed. She went to the fireplace and returned with a pan of hot savory biscuits.

Randy picked up one, juggling it to cool. Then he sopped it in the thick molasses, mumbling between bites. "Mmm-umph! Taste good as I remember, Bentoo." He finished and handed her the letter addressed to Forbes. "This came from Edward Atkinson; he's the boss of some cotton factories up North."

She read the letter, laboring over some of the unfamiliar words, then handed it back. "Look like they want the gov'ment to sell 'em some o' this land massa and them run away from."

"Yeah, and I bet Philbrick know about it, too. He promised to help his workers get their own land. You hear anything about that?"

"Nope, nothing." She put another biscuit on his plate. "Here, this one good and brown."

"Crecie mention anything?"

"Un uh. I doubt she's say if she did."

"How she and the children getting along?"

"Fine, I guess. That gal working them fields like somebody standing over her with *two* whips."

"Who's helping her with Philbrick's cotton?"

"Well, I *know* she got Dahlia, Hamp, Lizbet, and Titus; no telling who else—oh, and Sham, too. She riding herd over all o' them."

"Bet she's working hard right beside them."

"Fo' sho. Then at night she cook, wash, and clean like it ain't no tomorrow— 'specially since Miz Philbrick and them women come around inspecting the cabins. I tell ya, Randy, with Isham gone, everything fall to her one."

"That didn't have to be," said Randy, standing.

"I know; but even teeth and tongue fall out. I just wish ya'll could get along."

He frowned, then his face brightened. "She's still my daughter and I ain't giving up on her. Well, I better head back to Beaufort, see about Mr. Forbes."

"You like yo' job?"

"He's a decent man and it's better than nothing. I rather be working on my own land, though."

"You still my son and I ain't giving up on you." They laughed as she echoed his words. They were still chuckling when Crecie walked in.

Randy tried not to stare. Even though food was more plentiful, she'd lost weight. She turned, as if to leave.

"Crecie, stay," said Randy. "I-I...you the most important thing I got."

She hesitated then entered the room. "Then you ain't got much. Bentoo, I brought you some turnips. Collards gwine be coming in soon."

"My goodness, Crecie; this is fine looking bunch. I gwine wash 'em right now and cook 'em today." She headed out the door.

Randy took Crecie by the hand, "Come sit."

She pulled back slightly.

"You know, you the best daughter I got," he said.

"I be the *only* daughter you got—far as I know." She smiled and Randy felt her hand relax.

Sitting across the table from each other, he continued to hold her hand. "Right! And I mean what I said—you *are* the best daughter, the best granddaughter, the best mama…always working so hard for everybody. When do you sleep? Are you still having those bad dreams?"

She nodded. "They come and go. But I be so tired these days, sometimes I just sleep right through 'em."

"You ought to slow down. Why in the world you keep working so hard?"

He felt her hand tense.

"It ain't no mo' than I been doing all my life."

"Yes, but for Boson, for free—."

She snatched her hand away. "Ain't we done talk about this befo'? Besides, I need land if I gwine work for self."

"We all do. I just heard something, about the government putting the planters' land up for sale. I just wondered if it was true, if Philbrick let ya'll know about it."

"Land? He ain't tell we nothing about that. And if him did, what us gwine use fo' money?"

"I mean, if the government plan to sell, maybe they can set some aside for us."

"I don't know nothing about none o' that, Randy. I just know what Massa Philbrick do fo' me and my chillun—us got bittle to eat, clothes on we back, roof over we head. Got a church even." She pushed back her chair and stood. "I ain't got no truck about what Massa Philbrick know and what the gov'ment gwine do; ain't got money to buy, no how."

"Listen, Crecie. I don't want us to argue and I'm not disputing what you say. If that's how you want to live your life, working for—."

"Yeah; that be how I gwine live it—working fo' Massa Philbrick 'til *he* say I ready fo' land." She turned toward the door. "Tell Bentoo I heading back to Midway."

"Tell her yourself!" he jostled her aside, nearly toppling Bentoo as she walked in.

"You and Randy be like oil and water," she said, shaking her head. "Why, Crecie?"

"'Cause he can't leave me be like I always been. Why he coming from nowhere trying to change *me*?"

"I don't know, Crecie; that be something you got to take up with *him*."

Crecie sat down. "You right, Bentoo. But not now, I got too much on my plate—working fo' Massa Philbrick, tending my own cotton and the field at Possum Point; and them abolition women—never know when they gwine come poking around."

"You know Randy don't mean you no harm, telling you about things."

Crecie opened a biscuit, poured a little honey in between, then gingerly replaced the top. Finally she said, "You right. Maybe later I find time to talk to he."

Bentoo added another biscuit to Crecie's plate. "It be up to you, daughter, but don't wait too long. Never know what gwine happen or who you gwine need."

Crecie pushed the plate aside. "I know, Bentoo. I know so well." Thinking about Isham, her eyes began to water.

CHAPTER 36

IMPRESSMENTS

Wispy smoke curled from beneath the black wash pot and the damp smell of lye-soap permeated the air. Crecie hiked up her dress and knotted the hem, keeping it clear of the smoldering fire. Gripping a long, sturdy stick, she pounded the boiling clothes.

She paused, hearing Leona's voice. "Ma! Ma!" she shouted. Crecie looked up to see Leona running toward her. "Look, Ma! I got a book! I be the only one, too."

Crecie went back to pounding the wash. "Uh-huh. Why you the only one get a book?"

"'Cause I can *read*. Mr. Fill Up say I the smartest one in the school."

Samuel Phillips, having failed miserably at plantation management, had found his niche when Philbrick assigned him to teach at Ivy Oaks. The school was set up in the praise house and, with the best attendance on St. Helena, pupils often spilled out under the trees.

Crecie smiled, knowing Leona's boast to be true. Not long after the Big Gun Shoot, Bentoo had begun teaching her the alphabet. The little girl absorbed it all so quickly Bentoo began teaching her words from old handbills. Leona soon learned those, too, rereading the faded posters so many times she'd committed them to memory.

"Come on, Ma." She tugged at Crecie's apron. "I gwine read for you."

Crecie hesitated, looking down at the soggy laundry. *If I don't do this now, I gwine have that much mo' to do t'morrow.*

"And look Ma, it got pictures."

Crecie focused on the girl's exuberant face. *Well, it just be a little book; can't take* that *long to read.*

Mother and daughter settled side-by-side at the table.

"Sham and Willie gone on to Amos shed?" she asked Leona. Ever since Isham's death, Amos had taken up time with the boys and Crecie was very grateful.

"Yes'um, that where they be." Leona held up the book. "Now see this, Ma. Mr. Fill Up say this be the cover." She pointed to the title—*McGuffey's The Eclectic First Reader.* "I don't know all these words...Mr. Fill Up say it be the name o' the book."

Huh? Book got a name? Look like chicken scratch to me. "Alright, then just read what you know."

Leona opened the cover to reveal a picture of two flaxen-haired children. She cleared her throat, pointed to the first word, and began. "'Lesson 1. The New Book. Here is John'."

Crecie sat quietly, remembering how Bentoo had whipped her for wanting to 'talk to the paper' like Leona was doing.

"'There are Ann and Jane. Ann has a new book'." Leona paused and looked up. "Just like me," she said, grinning.

As Crecie looked upon her child's face, long-forgotten memories tumbled through her mind, and she saw herself standing in the Big House, fanning flies from a dinner table she could barely see the top of...

"'It is the first book,'" Leona intoned.

...and the babies—so many babies to take care of...

"'Ann must keep it nice and clean'."

...rocking them, changing them...babies sucking on pap-soaked rags. She became lost in one work-filled memory after another until she heard Leona speak directly to her.

"Now, Ma, I done read you the whole book."

Crecie felt awed, touched by the wonder she'd just witnessed: *It be a book in this cabin and my chile can read it.* She blinked back tears, aware that Isham and Randy had been right about at least one thing, the times had truly changed. She pulled Leona close and hugged her. "You read that book real good. Mr. Fill Up right—you *do* be the smartest one in the school."

Leona beamed. "Ma, can you cover my book, so it can stay clean?"

The clothes soaking in the wash pot crossed her mind; but then she remembered Randy's reprimand about always working and began rummaging through her scrap basket. "This piece of slave-cloth ought to keep it clean," she said.

She was about to cut it to size when Willie rushed through the door.

"Ma! The soldiers—."

The scissors froze mid-air. "Soldiers? The general tell 'em to stay from Midway."

"But they be at Uncle Amos place and they put all the boys—."

Boys? "Sham!" Crecie dropped the scissors. "Ya'll stay here," she ordered, dashing out the door.

It was a short jog to Amos's shed. A huge army transport wagon stood out in the road, jam-packed with forlorn young boys and men. The soldiers had given them tobacco and silver coins, an attempt to cheer them on; but the would-be inductees remained a stoic, unwilling lot.

Women and girls clamored at the rear of the wagon. Their cries and pathetic wails co-mingled with their angry shouts of "No

Cuba!", "No sugar-cane plantation!" Crecie saw Titus and Hamp squeezed in among the wagon's huddled mass; she also glimpsed Amos and Frazier, but there was no sign of Sham. After a frantic search, she turned toward home. *Maybe he run to the cabin.*

Then she saw him. Half-hidden behind a tree, he was clearly agitated, his eyes wild. She gently took his arm, feeling tremors race through his rigid body. "Come on, Sham, we—."

"Hold it right there," a crusty voice commanded. Crecie was filled with foreboding as the soldier approached.

"Please, suh," she said, "this ain't no man—he just a big chile."

"He look to be eighteen or nineteen to me," the soldier remarked.

"Oh no, suh. He ain't but thirteen—just a big boy."

"I'll be the judge of that." He snatched Sham away from Crecie and the force sent her spilling to the ground.

Sham broke loose and ran to his mother. "Crecie!" he yelled, looking up at the soldier. "You hurt Crecie!" His outburst silenced everyone and Crecie knew from his anguished sobs he was upset, subject to do anything. Scrambling to her feet, she stood in front of him, shielding him from the soldier.

"Get outta the way," the man snarled. "The general sent me to collect negras and that's what I aim to do."

"B-but, suh, he be a little...a little touch in the head."

"The army'll *untouch* him. Now step aside."

Crecie felt Sham cowering behind her and held her ground, remembering all the trials they'd weathered. In her mind he was still a little five-year-old boy, learning how to grip a spoon, dress himself, and what the outhouse was for.

"I'm giving you to three," said the soldier, "that is if you can count that far."

She stood wide-eyed, watching him heft the rifle and angle it across his chest.

"One!"

He positioned the firearm.

Sweat-beads dotted Crecie's already damp forehead. It was the first time she'd ever stared down a gun barrel.

"Two!" He braced the gunstock and slowly took aim.

Oh Lord, this be for real. Her heart went awry, whomping out a strange new rhythm.

"I'm telling you for the last time, darkie, get the hell out the way."

The soldier cocked the hammer and Crecie shut her eyes tight. *Lord, if he want Sham that bad, I gwine die this day.*

The blood pounded in her temples, obscuring sound. As if from afar, she heard someone yell, "Crecie! Muh-m-move!" She opened her eyes to see that Hamp had gotten out of the wagon. The gun was no longer pointed at her, but at him.

"Get back in that wagon, boy."

"N-no! L-l-leave her be," said Hamp, moving toward Crecie. A gang of soldiers quickly wrestled him to the ground. As Crecie watched the scuffle, Isham's savage beating flooded her mind; the women began to wail, joining her hysterical shrieks. The men constrained on the wagon grumbled, threatening to leave. But the bayonet-carrying soldiers thrust their rifles forward, warning them to stay where they were.

Then the sound of gunshot ended the chaos. Crecie looked to see Philbrick straddling a mule and she couldn't decide if she should laugh or cry.

"What's happening here?" He re-holstered his gun and climbed off the mule.

"Who're you?" demanded the soldier.

"I'm Superintendent Edward Philbrick." He gestured toward the wailing women and the men crammed on the wagon. "These people work for me. Why were you aiming at them?"

"Aww, I was just funning, trying to scare them."

"From the looks of things, you succeeded."

Crecie was still shaking. She tried to explain but her words were incoherent. "Oh, Massa Philbrick, Sham just a boy, suh. And then he point the gun—that what the soldier he do—and then they beat Hamp and I get—."

"Be quiet!" said Philbrick, turning to the soldier. "What's going on here?"

"We got orders—men aged eighteen to forty-five—round them up, bring them to Camp Hilton Head."

"I'm well aware of General Hunter's orders," said Philbrick.

"You say you're in charge here, maybe *you* can tell me how old he is," he said, pointing the rifle in Sham's direction.

"Well, no, I can't; not truthfully," said Philbrick.

"Somebody in authority will have to vouch for him or we got to take him too."

Philbrick exhaled slowly. "Step aside, Crecie; let them do what they came to do—for now that is."

"But suh—."

"Look! I don't have time to waste on this. I've got to get these men released and back to work." He climbed back on the mule. "I'm sure General Hunter has no intention of harming any of them. Your boy will be in good hands until we get things straightened out."

Good hands? She glared at the man who'd just held a gun on her, then at Philbrick's departing figure. *Why ain't Massa Philbrick stop 'em? Massa Boson wouldn't o' let 'em take none o' we—not even Sham.* She shook her head, bewildered.

The soldier stepped forward, ordering Sham and Hamp into the wagon. Hamp climbed aboard, but the boy began to scream, clinging to Crecie. Three soldiers took hold, intent on forcing him into the wagon.

But Sadie, a middle-aged woman who was known to speak her piece, stepped to the fore. "Stop," she said. "Can't you just let this one go? Anybody with a grain o' sense can see he ain't right in the head."

"This ain't your business, auntie, so stay outta it," grunted one of the tussling soldiers.

Sadie squinted her popeyes. "I ain't yo' kin," she said, "so don't be calling me auntie." Then she targeted a well-dipped gob of snuff juice in his direction. The runny blob splatted within half an inch of his boot. The man's sudden leap brought laughter and cries of "Bull's-eye!" from his comrades.

"You better watch where you spitting," he threatened, trying to save face. But he didn't call her auntie again and stalked away.

Amos had climbed down from the wagon. "Come on, Sham," he said, extending his hand. "It gwine be alright, son."

"That's right, Sham," Titus called from the wagon. "Take hold Amos hand."

"We gwine keep care of him for you, Crecie," Hamp promised.

Sham, crying still, took Amos' hand and climbed aboard. As Crecie watched the wagon roll down the road, Sadie came and stood beside her.

"I know you and me done had our ups and downs," said Sadie, "but if it anything I can do...."

"I be grateful if you get word to Randy, tell him to come and—."

"He'll get word today, Crecie, sho as my name Sadie."

Crecie wiped the tears with the back of her hand, remembering Bentoo's words: "You never know who you gwine need in this life."

CHAPTER 37

PROTEST AND PRAYERS

Pierce immediately descended upon Camp Hilton Head. Upon questioning the recruits, he discovered that only one man from Port Royal had volunteered for Hunter's proposed regiment; the rest had been coerced.

Brushing pass a startled clerk, an infuriated Pierce barged into Hunter's office. The young man hurried after him but the treasury agent would not be contained. Both men simultaneously burst into the general's office.

"I'm sorry, sir," sputtered the clerk, "he just rushed—."

"I'll take it from here," said Hunter. "Well, Mr. Pierce, I see you've made a miraculous recovery."

"My recovery is not at issue here," stated Pierce, self-consciously touching his bandaged head. "Do you have any idea what you've *done?* You promised to ask for volunteers, which was fine with me—but to force these men into service! It took months to gain their trust; you've destroyed it in a day."

Hunter remained seated. "I've destroyed nothing; if anything, I've—."

"The Negroes think they're being sold, no longer confident we'll protect them."

Hunter sprung to his feet. "Good! As soldiers, they'll gain their own confidence."

"Soldiers? These timorous creatures are not ready for that; they still need our leadership, our guidance."

"Army life will make them ready. If, after two weeks, they still want to leave, they'll be allowed to do so."

Pierce lifted his hands in despair. "Two weeks! The fields will be overrun with weeds by then, destroyed. I demand you release our workers immediately!"

"*Your* workers? No!" said Hunter, banging the desk. "They're not *your* workers—they're men! Men who'll be trained to fight for their freedom."

Pierce took a deep breath before continuing. "General Hunter, I don't think you understand. These people have labored tirelessly, planting over four thousand acres of cotton and sustenance crops in just two months. All of that will be lost if they are not returned to the fields."

Hunter sat down, seemingly reflective. "I'll release the foremen and plowmen."

"Is that *all*?" asked Pierce.

"Until the two weeks are up—yes."

"Then I'll appeal to Washington. There are higher ranks than yours."

"I'm sure there are, but I shall hold fast to my principles. The Negro's place is not in the cotton field, but fighting for his freedom on the battlefield."

"That's *your* opinion. Your oppressive tactics will be accounted for," avowed Pierce, stamping away.

"Do as you please," the general called out after him, "my orders stand."

The A-framed praise house sat at the edge of a woodlot, two miles from Ivy Oaks manor. Fan-shaped palmetto fronds decorated the cedar-grey walls and crude, knotty pine benches lined-up beneath them.

Bentoo stood at the moss-covered altar and in her own confident way, recited Bible verses.

"*James 5:16.* The one who walk straight with God, they prayers got great power and God gwine answer 'em for sho'.

"*Matthew 21:22.* When you pray for something, if you believe God gwine do it, then for true it gwine happen.

"*Acts 12:5.* Peter been in the jailhouse, but the church people been praying hard for 'em."

Cadres of prayer warriors, women who'd ignored Philbrick's back to work orders, had maintained prayer vigils throughout the day. Kneeling at the benches, they petitioned a Higher Power. As fervent pleas resonated throughout the room, the women's words and phrases invoked an aura of divine energy. Some requests were overt, "I come begging, Lord Jesus, please don't send 'em to Cuba." Others beseeched softly, "Please Jesus, bring the men home from the camp; I trusting in You."

Dusk had just settled when Crecie entered the room and her eyes readily adjusted to the candles' subdued glow. She'd not heard from Randy, and her heart was heavy as she knelt, uttering her appeals to God. As she prayed, her mind became less troubled and she welcomed the mystical presence of the Holy Spirit.

Then, by some innate signal, the women ceased praying and rose silently to their feet. Someone in the back of the room began to sing and the others quickly joined in. *I want Je-sus to walk with me...I want Je-sus to walk with me. All a-long this pil-grim journey, I want Je-sus to walk with me.* The song became a corporate prayer as the women clapped softly, tapping their feet to the rhythm. *In my trials, Lord walk with me, In my trials, Lord walk with me, When the shades of life are falling, Lord, I want Jesus to walk with me.* The refrain faded into a somber hum as they continued to clap and pat their feet. Suddenly the door swung open and the humming stopped; the women were amazed to see Frazier and the other foremen enter the praise house. Shouts of "Hallelujah!" filled the room and they rushed to greet the men.

"Praise the Lord!" said Bentoo. "*Acts 12:16*. Everybody praying for Peter to get out o' the jailhouse, and he already been there, knocking on the gate. God done answer we prayer, too."

Crecie searched the men's faces before approaching Frazier. "D-did they let go everybody?"

He shook his head. "No, not everybody—just the foremen and the plowmen."

"Oh," she said, turning away.

Just then, Bentoo called out to her. "Crecie, come look!"

Randy stood in the doorway. He waited a few seconds then stepped aside to reveal Sham standing behind him. The grinning boy ran to Crecie, throwing his arms about her.

"Oh praise God!" she cried, hugging her son. She looked at Randy, knowing he felt her gratitude.

Later that night, after the children were asleep, Randy and Crecie sat at the table, sipping mulberry wine. The fire burned low and shadows danced.

"Crecie, I need to talk with you, but I don't exactly know how to say what I need to say."

"What about?" Her voice took on an edge and a feeling of dread came over her. *Not tonight; I can't fuss and argue tonight.*

"Well, when Mose came and told me what happen to Sham today, that you wanted *me* to come, I didn't know what to do. I never had a call to free anybody before and I...I just felt so helpless, not knowing what to do."

Crecie exhaled, relaxing. "Oh, I be feeling that way all the time."

"I know. That's how they make us feel—helpless. And it was even worse for me—a run-away slave. All that time, helpless. But now...now I'm supposed to be a free man. Yet and still, there was no way I could go down to Hilton Head and tell the army to give me back my grandboy. They probably would've thrown me in there with him."

"I tried to tell 'em, but them soldiers wouldn't listen to *me*. They would o' listen to Massa Philbrick, though."

Randy winced at the word 'massa', but didn't censor her. "Then, Crecie, I remembered something you always say—'Buckra got the power'. That's when it come to me—a powerful white man was sitting right in the next room and I worked for him, Mr. Forbes. I needed his help, but I was scared, not knowing if he would help me or not."

"Praise God, Massa Fobs see fit to."

"Praise God I had sense enough to ask him. I learned a whole lot from this."

Crecie nodded. "Me, too. What come to yo' mind?"

"That you're right—partly. White folks do have the power. Freedom don't mean separate—we all still got to depend on one another. That make any sense to you?"

"It make a lot o' sense 'cause I learn *black* folks got power, too. Course, not as much as white folks—but still....Anyway, *I* ain't had no leeway to go to Massa Fobs, but *you* had his ear; *you* had that power."

"Yeah, I guess so. He went straight to General Hunter and got Sham out."

They sipped the homemade brew, then Crecie picked up the basket of scraps she'd abandoned earlier. "You know, all these little itty-bitty scraps ain't worth nothing by theyself. But when you sew 'em all together, you wind up with something strong, hard-wearing."

"Yeah," he agreed, "a nice, warm quilt."

She ran her hand through the scraps, fluffing them. "And it be a pretty thing, too; all these different colors—just like people."

"It won't be right if everybody be the same, look the same," he said.

"And if you want all the scraps to be the same, you ain't gwine never have enough for a quilt to cover with," said Crecie. "I ain't gwine be left out in the cold."

Randy smiled and enfolded her hands in his. "Me neither, daughter, me neither."

This time she didn't pull away.

CHAPTER 38

NEW DAY, NEW TIME

General Hunter's untimely orders created a labor shortage at the most critical, labor-intensive stage of cotton production—hoeing the young plants. As the shoots peeked through the soil, they had to be weeded constantly or succumb to wild grass and weeds.

Philbrick and the other superintendents were worried. If the Port Royal experiment failed, not only would the theory of free-labor's superior economy remain unproven, the government would lose a much-needed source of revenue. As the Southern states kept their cotton off the market, fierce competition developed among Northern mills for the limited supply. The cost of cotton per pound soared. Philbrick, determined to succeed, assembled everyone, including the sick and elderly, to the mule barn.

The people arrived early, milling around as they waited for Philbrick. Crecie, Lizbet, and Dahlia stood together.

"Ya'll think Mista Philbrick hear something about the men folk?" Lizbet asked.

"Why else he send for all o' we?" offered Crecie.

"That might be," said Dahlia, "but I hope he bringing we wages. Plantation shop got plenty stock now—frying pans, glass buttons, and bonnets—that's what I want—a new bonnet."

Sadie sat within earshot. "They price 'em fair, too. Miz Towne and them ain't try to gouge out we eye like them agents. I glad they gone from here!"

"I too glad!" said Lizbet.

"Miz Walker gwine put a bonnet aside for me when some more come in," said Dahlia. "Everybody buy 'em so fast the first time, I ain't get none. Crecie, what you plan on buying?"

"Huh? Buying?"

"Buying from the plantation store," said Dahlia. "Where yo' mind gone, gal?"

"Probably where it always be," chimed Lizbet. "In the field... somewhere working."

"I *got* to work," replied Crecie. "I done plant a little bit o' cotton on the side, too, just like Massa Philbrick. Besides, I ain't got no money to be buying things."

"You don't need none. Mista Philbrick put it down in the book 'til we get wage," said Lizbet. "And anyway—you just crying poor mout' like you always do. I *know* you got something stash away."

"I ain't saying I do," said Crecie. A sly smile tugged at the corners of her mouth. "But *if I* do, it gwine stay stash away. Remember, them cotton agents take four months before they pay we."

A plowman, squatting on his haunches beside Sadie, spoke up. "But Mista Philbrick ain't treat we the way the cotton agents treat we," he said. "He say us get paid when all the cotton planted, and I believe him."

"I believe him, too," said Crecie, "but that ain't mean I got to spend—."

"Look ya'll," said Dahlia, pointing toward the road. "Here come Mista Philbrick now, him and Mista Gannett."

"Whoa," said Superintendent Gannett, reining in the mule-driven cart. The people were solemn, watching the men walk toward them.

Philbrick stood before the crowd. "You can rest assured the army is not sending your men to Cuba; they'll be free to leave camp within a few weeks—if they so desire."

There was faint applause. "That be good news!" someone in the crowd exclaimed.

"That be sweet to my ears," Dahlia whispered to Crecie. "Amos'll be home."

"And Titus and them'll be back to help *me*," Crecie whispered back.

Philbrick beckoned to Frazier. "Tell us, Frazier...you were with the men last, how did they appear to you?"

The young man stepped forward. "Well, suh, we wasn't in camp for long, but in that short time nobody mistreat we or nothing. Most the hands seem to settle in, make peace with the situation; except the ones who couldn't stomach the army rations. General Hunter come talk to we; say the army was gwine make we into soldiers and—."

"Soldiers!" a woman exclaimed. "Us need help with this cotton; us ain't got time fo' them trying to be soldiers."

"But he make it sound real good," said Frazier. "Tell we the gov'ment gwine pay the men to fight, like they pay the white soldiers. I believe some o' the men might stay on."

"Stay on?" said Sadie. "To fight massa and them? Do that be true, Mista Philbrick?"

"I'm certain the general isn't going *that* far," replied Philbrick. "Maybe he'll use them as pickets, to guard the cotton against marauders."

Cotton, thought Crecie. *That all it ever be about—cotton.*

A woman pushed her way to the front of the crowd. It was Hagar. She had been a plantation laundress when the Big Gun Shoot occurred.

"Mista Philbrick," she said, "you promise to pay we after the cotton get planted. Well, it all be in the ground now, suh. When we get we money...today?"

"You'll be paid," he answered. "But with the men gone, there will be changes."

"What kind o' change?" she asked guardedly.

"First off, *everyone* will have to work; the elderly, the children, even those who can only do a lit—."

"You gwine pay wages?" an old woman asked.

"If you work well, yes. And all of you must now work beyond noon, all day if need be."

How we gwine tend we own crop? thought Crecie.

"The cotton must be kept free of weeds," said Philbrick.

"We know that better'n you, Mista Philbrick," rejoined Sadie. "But if we gwine do more work, ain't we gwine get mo' pay?"

"Yeah!" a woman shouted. "How much you plan on paying?"

"I ain't working in no gang, neither," said Hagar.

Grumbling carried across the yard. Philbrick seemed flustered, baffled by the women's insistent questions and demands. But had he been familiar with plantation hierarchy—white man, white woman, black man, black woman—perhaps he would've found their questions prudent.

No other woman in the United States or the Confederacy had as much cause for vigilance as the female slave. She'd been forced on to the auction block, stripped of clothes and dignity, trembling as her teeth were counted, her belly poked, and her body sold. Denied rights as a mother, she'd been beaten in her children's presence and witnessed them beaten in return. No other woman in America toiled like a man by day and labored in the home throughout the night—cleaning, cooking, washing; ginning, spinning, weaving. Unprotected by law or man, the enslaved black woman was punished without justice, raped without appeal, sexually exploited then labeled a slut. Disparaged and defiled, no one in America had more reason for such vigilance than the black woman.

But the war had left the door ajar, allowing for a flicker of hope. Enslaved women took hold, clutching each beam of independence, safeguarding every glimmer of gain. Unwavering in their quest for a better life, the women challenged the smallest threat to freedom's possibilities, determined the door would never again be slammed shut.

"Well, er, if I *owned* this plantation," said Philbrick, "I could answer those questions; but as it now stands, I'm not at liberty to say whether or not you'll receive more money—that will be up to the government."

"Seem to me the gov'ment ought o' do that—pay more," said Dahlia.

"And pay on time," said Hagar. "More work, more pay—that be the right thing to do."

Others took up the cry, becoming loud and boisterous.

Philbrick held his hand up, silencing them. "You're right, that *would* be the right thing to do. I will continue to press Mr. Pierce, just as I've done in the past. But the government is slow to act and I have no control over when or how much it chooses to pay."

"But if the gov'ment see to it that us get land," said Sadie, "us don't need no wage—us take care we own self. Then you and the gov'ment can go, leave we be."

Their clamorous demands started anew and Philbrick quieted them down again.

"But it was the government that came to your aid when your owners left you starving and naked," he reminded them. "And didn't we, your friends, bring you God's word, set up schools for your children, provide goods for your pleasure? Don't the superintendents deliver your rations each week—your bacon, your herring—bring you real coffee and tobacco? And salt—don't forget your monthly quart of salt."

A few people muttered, "Thank you; I appreciate what you do, suh," but most of them stared back, silent and sullen. Crecie, torn as usual, appeared noncommittal.

Philbrick continued. "And as to land—the government knows of your desire, your need. But it will be many years, maybe after the war even, before this land can legally be sold…"

But Randy say gov'ment looking to sell land soon, Crecie remembered.

"…or until clear titles can be issued. When the time comes, I will do everything I can to help you receive deeds to the land. But until you are able to provide for yourselves, the government will continue to provide for you. These are trying times, but refugees arrive daily from the mainland. Perhaps I can hire some of them to help."

"Who? From the contraband camps?" asked Sadie. "Ain't nobody there but women and chillun; the rest be the same as we—old and sick."

"Fo' sho'," said Dahlia. "All the able-body men leave them crowded shacks soon as they get over here, go live someplace else."

Crecie had seen the young men wandering about the island. Giddy over their newfound freedom, they worked here and there—for the quartermaster, the officers, even for other freedmen—choosing the cotton field as a last resort.

Philbrick was persistent. "If we all pull together, put forth every effort, we *can* save the crop. The government aided you at your lowest; the time has come for you to do the same. I expect everyone who can stand long enough to lift a hoe, to be in the fields at dawn tomorrow." Then he and Gannett climbed on the cart and left.

Crecie dared not look around. She knew what most of the people wanted, and it wasn't to work for the government. They wanted independence, education, and separation from all things white; but they needed land to sustain them. Deep within, she longed for the same things, especially land. But feelings of doubt and dependence still weighed heavy upon her and she remembered how desperate her condition was before Philbrick arrived. Now, even though life was still harsh, her family had food and two sets of clothes. Sham was safe, Leona could read, and Willie, snatched from death's door, was healthy. The crowd's agitated comments grew louder as Crecie quietly left, headed for Isham's field at Possum Point.

CHAPTER 39

THE HOSPITAL

Crecie worked at Possum Point longer than usual that day. Though exhausted, she still tossed and turned most of the night, awaking with remnants of the haunting dream swirling in her head. Her body felt stiff, tense; still she felt grateful—the specter had stayed away for months this time.

She threw open the splintery shutter, letting the dawn filter in. *Dang! I done shut my eye too long.* She grabbed the water dipper and filled the chipped enamel basin. Though the cold water made her grimace, it cleared her head. *Thank God for Bentoo—I ain't got to fool with them chillun this morning.* She snatched a threadbare rag off a nail, dried her face, and dressed quickly. Hurrying out, she dumped the basin of water on the hydrangea.

The road leading out of Midway was deserted. *I must be the only one not in the field yet.* She picked up her pace as she neared the slave hospital. Suddenly its double doors opened, revealing the people inside. Dahlia rushed out to meet her.

"Crecie! I been just coming fo' you."

"Why? What ya'll doing in there?"

"Oh, I forgot—you been gone when us say us gwine meet today. Come on, everybody already here."

Crecie hesitated. Before the war, the hospital had been her domain. Master Boson, recognizing her healing skills, had put her in charge, minimizing his bills to doctors. In addition to Crecie's regular field tasks, she'd run the hospital on a need-to basis—recommending continual care for some, relegating others back to work immediately. Her herbs usually cured the illnesses, but when the doctor or store-bought medicine was needed, it was Crecie who'd informed the master and secured the medicine; at times she'd also administered it. Her authority was absolute, her attitude haughty, and she'd ruled with pride, distancing herself from the people. But they tolerated her because she possessed the power of healing.

No, she had no desire to go in, revisit the past. But Dahlia was already pulling her along, insisting she come inside. She entered the twelve-bed hospital—*her* hospital. They'd commandeered it without so much as by your leave.

Sadie stood at the far end, near the pine-wood medicine cabinet, talking to the crowd: "...and whatever we gwine do, we need to be o' one mind."

Crecie followed Dahlia along the row of beds. The one-story building was jam-packed with elders, women, and children. Many of the older people had been field hands, but some had also worked as blacksmiths, artisans, and other tradesmen. No one spoke and their eyes trailed Crecie's every move. Taking a stand beside Sadie, she felt like an intruder in her own realm.

Suddenly a strong voice called out. "I don't know what ya'll gwine do, but I done already decide." It was Hagar. "You see them great big wash tubs at the Big House, just sitting out in the wash yard, doing nothing? Well, the army be needing clean clothes, and I be needing money. Probably stand a better chance o' getting paid from *them*, than working cotton for Philbrick."

"You right about that," said an elderly man. He'd collected cotton for the Treasury agents. "Massa ain't pay me nothing, then Colonel Nobles come and pay the same."

"And that be what Philbrick doing," said an old shoe cobbler. "I can mend army boots for more'n what he pay."

"Which, right now ain't nothing," the elderly field hand responded.

"He always pushing we to work harder," said one of the women. "Say time be money. Well, *my* time be money, too. If I gwine do mo' work, I want mo' money!"

"Well, we need to be together on whatever we gwine do," said Sadie. "Them who gwine keep working cotton with Philbrick—raise yo' hand."

Crecie raised her hand and glanced around. She was startled, only a few hands went up. If they didn't work the land, there'd be no reason for Philbrick to keep them on. He'd already ousted some native islanders who'd neglected their fields, hiring mainland refugees to work their acres. For Crecie to lose her cabin, aside from losing Isham, would be one of the greatest tragedies she'd yet to face. She couldn't let the others walk away—jeopardize their homes.

"Well, well," said Hagar, strutting over to Crecie. She wagged a wrinkled, potash-tinged finger in Crecie face. "I might o' know *you* gwine stick with the buckra."

"Not now, Hagar," said Dahlia. "This ain't the time for that."

The laundress had resented Crecie and the attention Bentoo gave her ever since they were in the nursery together. The resentment had grown through the years, but when Master Boson had chosen Crecie for Isham, allowing the couple to jump the broom, Hagar's envy had became full-blown.

"Get out my way *Hag*ah," said Crecie, emphasizing 'hag' as when they were children. "I ain't got no time for your mess right now."

"And no sense, neither. You always been crazy as a bedbug—killing snakes and talking to dead folks."

Crecie waited until the snickering subsided, using the time to think. "If you had just a *little* bedbug sense, you'll keep working fo' Mas—Mista Philbrick. It ain't gwine be like working for them cotton collectors. Now move out my way, Hagah. I got to go."

"No, wait, Crecie," said the cobbler. "Tell me, why this time gwine be different."

Crecie turned to the old man. "You know, Uncle Pete, I can't read, and you can't neither. But Leona can, and if Mista Philbrick don't do nothing else, he keeping up all the schools on these islands. Our chillun ain't gwine be ig-nant like we."

"Yes, suh," Pete intoned, slowly nodding his head. "Washing soldiers' dirty drawers ain't gwine get you no schooling."

Crecie waited until the snickering subsided then said, "And another thing, ain't we trying for land? Ain't Mista Philbrick promise to help we? I gwine throw my lot with he, give he time to do what him say." *And I hope to God him do; he mout' sho ain't ring true about the land yesterday.*

The people's whispered agreement encouraged her.

"And suppose the weeds *do* take over the cotton," she said, "Mista Philbrick ain't plant that cotton." She gestured around the room. "Us did! Four thousand acres'll be gone for naught."

"Crecie," said Sadie, "I just thought o' something. What if the gov'ment *really* depending on that cotton? What if the rebels win?"

Crecie looked Hagar straight in the eyes. "Then all o' we gwine keep washing dirty drawers and sweating in the cotton field."

"You know, time getting short," said Sadie. "Now, I ax you again—who gwine work cotton fo' Philbrick?"

This time nearly every hand went up, including Hagar's. Crecie exhaled; relieved that at least for now, nothing had changed. *I gwine worry about the land when the time come.*

The workers headed for the fields and Crecie walked proudly among them, feeling a kinship that had always eluded her. Before today, the people never heeded her advice about anything except death and sickness. The war had brought changes all around.

⚊⧏ ⧐⚊

In spite of the people's reluctance to do so, they'd taken hold of the cotton. The old and the sick—working as free-laborers for the first time—had done remarkably well. In two weeks all the cotton had been weeded at least once, and the corn, except for the recently planted portions, had been hoed.

The crops were thriving and Philbrick had been pleasantly surprised, marveling that the workers had put forth such great effort without payment. Their diligence had saved the cotton, and with the increasing demands of Northern cotton mills, Philbrick was determined to extract even more labor from them.

But they remained averse to the extra work, and as the hands wrangled for more free time, Philbrick had to stay a step ahead. If he didn't, the workers' sustenance crops would continue to flourish while the money crop—cotton—receive less care.

Philbrick noticed that whenever the freedmen received a little money, they acquired the niceties they'd so long been denied. He hoped their liking for the best and as much as they could afford, would wean them from subsistent farming. Preparing to capitalize on the workers' new-found appreciation for manufactured goods, he kept the plantation store well-stocked. By creating a need for money, the people's survival would depend on currency, not crops. Philbrick intended to provide the drive to complete the people's transformation, which in his mind, evolved from ignorant slave to wage-earning freedman.

CHAPTER 40

COTTON! COTTON! COTTON!

The Gideonites continued to foist their middle-class values upon the contrabands—telling the Negroes they must first become father-providers and stay-at-home-mothers to be eligible for freedom. But in their quest to enlighten, none of the whites suggested black men become land owners and black women quit the cotton fields.

The Ivy Oaks workers struggled to save the cotton, but Philbrick's zealous New England work ethic demanded they continue the labor-intensive regimen. He was now convinced that the half-day system, no matter how productive, was a waste of precious daylight hours and launched a coercive campaign, demanding the people work beyond fixed tasks and on Saturdays and Sundays. The more he hounded, the more they resisted.

The hard rain eased to a drizzle, and the motley group of workers slogged through the mud, heading to the tool house. The older children walked ahead, the elders shuffled behind, and the women plodded between the two groups, airing their displeasure.

"Philbrick always snooping around," said Hagar, "preaching cotton and work!"

"He come to my cabin one day," said Rosa Lee, one of the younger women. "Tell me I leave from the field too early, and I must go back. I say, 'Me sick, got female trouble'. Him tell me, 'Go see Crecie'."

"You go?" asked another woman.

"Heck, no; I ain't been *that* sick! I go back to the field, but I been moving re-e-e-al slow."

The women chuckled appreciatively as they entered the tool house.

"Philbrick ain't even pay the twenty-five cents a day he promised we," said Lizbet.

"That little bit o' money ain't gwine do me no good no way," said Dahlia. "I owe the plantation shop double that much."

"What about the pay Amos get from the army?" asked Rosa Lee.

"Pay? Amos and them ain't get no pay; just a uniform and rations—and the rations make him puke."

President Lincoln had chosen to neither acknowledge nor disband General Hunter's regiment. But the General was determined to launch a segregated camp at Hilton Head, placing white officers in charge. He'd scrounged up uniforms, food, and weapons, but the promised salaries, the allocations from Washington, never came. As far as the government was concerned, General Hunter's Negro regiment simply did not exist.

"It ain't right," said Hagar, snatching her hoe from the wall. "All o' we work like jackass to save the cotton, and what Philbrick do? Pile mo' work on we. I should o' follow my mind and quit the first time." She confronted Crecie. "All this be yo' fault—crazy fool."

"*You* the fool, *Hag*ah," said Crecie. "I ain't hold no gun to yo' head."

Dahlia, standing in the center of the group, raised her hands. "No! It ain't nobody fault. Until us get us own land, white man gwine keep we tied to cotton."

"And us got to bind together to get we land," said Lizbet.

Crecie left the discussion; balancing the long-handled hoe on her shoulder, she headed for the field, distancing herself from the others. Her mind was uneasy; Philbrick constantly drove them to work harder and it was taking a toll on everyone. Even with her stellar work habits, she was hard pressed to keep up. With Titus and Hamp gone, the fifteen acres of cotton she'd committed to Philbrick took up most of her day. Sham did his best on the yard garden, but was barely keeping it alive. Then there was the rooster, the chickens, and the horse. The cow had long-since disappeared— no doubt butchered by the soldiers. And the children—she couldn't recall the last time Leona's hair had been combed, and her attendance at school was almost nil. After Mr. Philips had sent her home a few times for wearing dirty clothes, Crecie had kept her out of school, leaving her with Bentoo. What little extra energy the young mother mustered went to her side-plot of cotton and Isham's five acres of vegetables.

Crecie reached the field and began chopping the weeds, careful not to damage the plants' roots. She glanced up to see the elders and their cohorts hobbling toward their chores. The other women had come to the field but stood idle, chatting within Crecie's earshot.

"Ya'll know," said Lizbet, "even though Crecie talk up fo' Philbrick, it ain't her fault him pushing we so. It be the cotton. That all him talk about—growing cotton cheaper than massa did."

"Yeah, but massa *know* what he been doing," said Dahlia. "Even collecting cotton for Nobles wasn't bad as this—us had plenty strong men to help."

"Well, I ain't gwine drop dead in no field," said Rosa Lee. "I be a free woman now; plenty other places I can go work."

With a population of over 40,000, including 20,000 Union troops, the women of Ivy Oaks knew they could find work among the store keepers, army hospital, and military personnel on Hilton Head Island. The camp at Beaufort also offered employment opportunities.

"Fo' true you right," said Lizbet, sitting on the ground. "And you won't have to work from dayclean to dusk dark like with Philbr—." Suddenly she jumped to her feet. "Watch out—here he come nosing."

The women stood their ground, watching insolently as he approached.

He returned their contemptuous stares, muttering under his breath. "…rather work with ten men than a hundred of you wenches…."

Crecie stopped chopping and leaned on her hoe to watch. The elders had shuffled in a bit closer, too.

Philbrick attempted to cajole. "You must get back to work, or I shall tell Massa Lincoln you are too lazy to be free."

The women stared silently. When they looked to Dahlia, she stepped forward.

"Mista Philbrick, suh, I believe I speak fo' all o' we when I say Mista Lincoln ain't care about we. If him did, him would o' let Gen'ral Hunter free we all the way."

The people and the missionaries had rejoiced at General Hunter's proclamation to free all slaves in South Carolina, Georgia, and Florida. But their hopes were dashed when two weeks later the President officially renounced Hunter's decree, declaring '…that neither General Hunter, nor any other commander or person, has been authorized by the Government of the United States to make proclamations declaring the slaves of any State free…'.

"That may be true," said Philbrick, "but you've all agreed to take on the cotton. You must get back to work."

"Us get back soon as us know about we money," said Dahlia.

"I've told you," he bristled, "you'll get paid when the Treasury Department sends it. When that will be, I don't know." *They've weeded the cotton four times already; I doubt these ingrates will do the rest without receiving some remuneration. Damn the government's blundering system!*

"I'm prepared to personally advance a portion of your wages, just as I did in the past." *That should keep them working for a time.*

"You ain't give we nothing since that first itty-bitty money," said Hagar. "You say you gwine pay soon as seed get in the ground."

Crecie ducked her head, recalling that Philbrick had also promised to help them get land; now that he'd lied about its availability, she didn't know what to think. She shrugged off her doubts, trusting that Randy would get to the straight of things.

The women continued to deliberate.

"No, suh, us want we pay," said Hagar. "We know Mista Pierce been stuffing that big iron box; it must be about to bust by now."

Pierce had already explained that the money from last year's crop had to be set aside to safeguard this year's crop.

"Now you listen to me," Philbrick blustered. "I—."

"No, suh, us done listen to you." Sadie had joined the group. "It high time you heed what us have to say."

The women pressed forward. Some expressed grievances, some demands. But all were adamant about getting paid. Having been denied the right to farm for themselves on their own terms, they regarded growing cotton without pay as re-enslavement. It galled the people to continue working cotton. Their feelings of good faith had been tried, especially since they had to work on Sundays.

"Massa Boson ain't never work we on Sunday," said Dahlia, "and just half day on Sat'day. Us want fifty cents a day for working Sat'day and Sunday."

"And us ain't working in the rain and the mud, mending no mo' fences, either," said Rosa Lee.

"I ain't been brought up to work *all* the time," added Lizbet. "I through working extra and ain't getting nothing fo' it. Gwine do my task, then use my time as *I* see fit!"

After the women completed their litany, Sadie said, "We say we piece, Mista Philbrick. *Now* it be yo' time."

"I will advance a part of your wages until the government releases the money. Your work has been assigned, I suggest you get back to it." He walked away, but the women's loud voices followed him.

"Work and cotton! No time fo' nothing except work and cotton...."

It wasn't hard work to which the women objected, they'd done it all their lives. It was Philbrick's unrelenting, all-consuming demands to perform it. They deemed it unjust that the few precious privileges attained as slaves—fishing, crabbing, not working on Sunday—were denied them as freed people.

CHAPTER 41
TIT FO' TAT

The women obeyed Philbrick's orders and returned to work. But as they whacked away the cotton *plants* instead of the weeds, he wished they'd stayed away. They also wreaked havoc on the equipment; the hoes were their main targets. Most of those who chose to show up at all left the fields early. The ones who stayed worked at a snail's pace, rarely completing their tasks. When Crecie and the others continued to work, condemning the slowdown, the slackers resorted to rude taunts and ridicule.

Using disruptive measures, the disgruntled women were determined to be treated fairly, to not work pass quitting time, and to no longer perform extra grueling labor. The plantation routine became mass confusion as Philbrick, Frazier, and Gannett chased animals from the fields, hunted down absentee workers, and condemned dawdlers for their lackluster efforts.

"I ain't never see nothing like this befo', suh," said Frazier. He threw the bar across the barn door, securing the cows that had mysteriously appeared in the fields. Much of the young cotton had been trampled to bits.

"There seems to be many strange things going on lately," said Gannett.

"Yes," said Philbrick. "And I intend to make them even stranger. Listen, Gannett, this is what I want you to do...." He outlined his instructions.

⚊⊹⊱

The people wandered about the plantation's work yard, affably chatting as they waited for Gannett to deliver the weekly rations. Finally, a self-appointed sentry spotted him and alerted the others. The loaded wagon creaked to a stop in front of the detached kitchen. The workers quickly gravitated to it, forming a circle.

Gannett's movements were unusually slow as he arranged and rearranged the huge stacks of cornmeal. Then he straightened bundles of tobacco and coffee tins. Finally, he concentrated on the jars of molasses, scrutinizing them one at a time.

The people paced about, impatient. Except for better wages and working conditions, the one other thing the hands were quick to dispute was the quality and quantity of their food. Any disparities in distribution of their provisions immediately raised their ire. They enjoyed eating the best that was available and as much as they could get, leading to frequent raids on plantation smokehouses.

Finally Gannett completed his bogus inspection and began to mete out the supplies. It wasn't long before angry outbursts echoed across the yard.

As Gannett weighed one woman's meat, she loudly protested. "What I gwine do with that lil' bit o' bacon?"

"I got chillun to feed," cried another, watching him measure a reduced portion of cornmeal. "That ain't enough to feed *me*."

One by one the people approached to receive their rations. Some walked away quietly satisfied. Others complained, ranting loudly.

Crecie stepped up to the wagon, and though she received her usual allotment, she frowned, resentful. *Ain't I done gone ahead o' everybody else—work harder, stay past quitting time? I should get mo'.* She saw Hagar and Rosa Lee eyeing her then walked over to Gannett.

"How come Crecie get her same allotment and you give we less?" she heard Hagar demand.

"I don't know; ask her—or Mr. Philbrick," Gannett said, climbing back on the wagon.

"Oh, I gwine do that, alright," said Hagar.

"Do as you please," he said, flicking the reins. "Giddy-up!" The wagon rolled out, headed for the next plantation.

Hagar looked back to Crecie, but she was gone. "Where you think she be?"

"Wherever she be, I bet she working," replied Rosa Lee.

But Crecie wasn't working. She'd gone looking for Philbrick and finally found him in the tool house.

"Good day, Mista Philbrick, suh."

"Good day, Crecie." He held up broken hoe parts. "You had anything to do with this?"

"Oh, no, suh! I—."

Philbrick laughed. "I know you didn't. You're the best worker I have at Ivy Oaks."

The compliment warmed her. *That what Massa use to say.* Then she remembered: *This be a new day and Massa ain't in it.* She took a deep breath and rushed to the purpose of her visit. "That why I come to see you, suh."

Philbrick was attaching the blade to the hoe's shaft. "Yes?" he said, not looking up.

Crecie's mouth felt dry and she paused to swallow. Then the words flew from her lips—rapid-fire. "I work mo' than the others I oughta get extra ration." *Lord-a-mercy! I been say it!*

That got Philbrick's attention and he looked at her. "Yes, I know you do; but there is a formula for distributing the food."

"A formla, suh?"

"It's a special way the government wants us to distribute the food—a system— based on how many people are in each household. Why do you think you need extra?"

Ain't you hear me? I done work extra fo' it. "Well, you see, suh, my boy Sham—he got a heavy belly, he eat mo' than a hoss—and my other two chillun ain't far behind."

"I've seen them—Willie's a bit small, isn't he? And Le-Le...."

"Leona, suh."

"Yes, Leona," he said, turning back to his repairs.

Crecie was not deterred. "Befo' all the men got took away, I could scrape up a lil' mo' food here and there, go fishing and the like, stretch the provision. But now us been working full days, I ain't got no time fo' that now."

"I understand. But the shortage was brought on by the generals."

Crecie was well-aware of the army's frequent demands—it was high on the women's litany of complaints. "Why should us go lacking," they'd argued, "and the army get the corn us work so hard to grow?" No one had an answer for them.

"Besides," Philbrick continued, "if you're given more than the others, everyone else will want the same; it'll open a floodgate." He rummaged about the tool room, locating supplies, sorting broken parts.

Crecie waited. When he didn't say anything more, she spoke up. "But, suh, you ain't give we no pay neither."

His face turned red and, clearly annoyed, he slammed the broken parts on the workbench. "Haven't I told you people time and again—the money is on the way!"

Crecie stepped back, intimidated. "Uh, well suh, thank—." She abruptly stopped. *Thank he? What fo'?* She'd expected something— hope, empathy, reward for loyal labor—anything. She turned and left. *I come here with nothing and I leaving with the same.*

CHAPTER 42

THE HOMECOMING

Crecie trudged along one of the field's many well-worn paths, trying not to think about the work she'd left unfinished. It was odd, leaving a job half-done, but haggling with Philbrick had tired her out—mentally and physically. *Ain't get nothing fo' working extra no way; might as well do like the rest—work less, get less.*

But she stayed true to her belief. *No! Me, Dahlia, and the rest o' them, done plant fifteen acres o' cotton—won't have nothing to show if I walk away.* She plodded along, feeling the sun siphon even the little energy she usually kept in reserve. *Mista Philbrick got cotton fever fo' true, driving we hard every day o' the week. I believe him drive we all night, too, if us let him.*

She smiled wryly. *But he sho' fix 'em with them rations. I wonder how long it be befo' they get back at him. One thing I know, they ain't gwine listen to nothing I got to say—especially that Hagar.* Feeling terribly used and completely alone, she entered the road leading to Midway. "Why, Isham?" she whispered softly. "Why?"

She approached her cabin and from a distance saw two figures working in the yard garden. One was Sham but who was the other? He seemed familiar. "Sham," she called out. "Come take these rations in the cabin."

The boy rushed to meet her. "Then I go to Amos shed, Crecie?" he asked.

"I reckon; but don't leave that shed."

She reached the man and peered into his face. "Hamp?"

"This me, Crecie. I been in the army so long you done forget about me?"

"Goodness gracious, Hamp! Come here!" She gave the young man a big hug. He patted her on the back, self conscious.

Crecie glanced about. "Where Titus and them?"

"Titus ain't come back. He barbering now...doing real good, too, cutting black and white hair. Say he gwine stay a while, see what army life be like. Amos come back, though. Guess he gone to be with family....I ain't got no—."

"And you come to be with yours," she said. "Come on."

They chatted as they walked toward the cabin. Suddenly Crecie stopped. "Hamp!" she cried. "You ain't stutter no mo'!"

"I wonder how long it was gwine be befo' you say something," he said, grinning.

"When you stop?"

"That day the soldiers come get we; when I climb back in the wagon, I ain't stutter since then." They resumed walking. "Sham say you be gone all the time."

"Fo' sho he ain't lie. Mista Philbrick make all the women do ya'll part; lots o' crop fall by the wayside, though; it been too much fo' we."

"Well, some o' we back; the load be a little lighter now."

Hope so...poor as you looking. "You look, um, a lil' different, Hamp. You still fond 'o stew chicken and gravy?"

"Oh, yeah!"

"C'mon then, let's go catch one o' them fat ol' hens."

His presence had renewed her spirits and they headed toward the chicken coop.

"I much appreciate a good meal, Crecie. Army food ain't agree with me; been hard to keep down."

"I sorry to hear that. Us sent what lil' food us could spare. Ain't that suit you none?" She quietly slipped behind a pecking hen and grabbed its legs.

Hamp stopped, shaking his head. "Food? I ain't get no food from you."

The bird began to squawk. "What?" she said, turning to Hamp. "Mose say he give it to the company sergeant. Ain't you been in Company A?"

"Yeah." He grew quiet then he said, "Crecie, you know them soldiers what…what stole all yo' winter store?"

Crecie's disposition changed and her face became an angry mask. "Yeah."

"You remember the one who smash Isham head with the gun— the red-beard?"

She nodded and carried the flapping chicken to a bloodstained tree stump.

"He be the sergeant over Company A; name Johnstone, but us call him Brimstone 'cause he be the devil seed. He take all the food you send."

Her legs went weak and she pinned the struggling bird to the stump. "He the devil seed alright. I ain't gwine never forget that demon!"

Hamp readied the pail.

She brought the hatchet down with a ferocious swoop. "Never!" The cackling immediately stopped and the animal's life gushed into the pail.

Crecie hung the bird upside down on a low branch. "I know God be the one to fix evil, but I got it in my mind to do some fixing on my own."

"Follow what yo' mind tell you to do, Crecie."

"That be what I gwine do."

The women remained adamant against growing cotton, but they had families to feed and no one to depend on except themselves. Under duress, they decided to trust freedom's promise and returned to the cotton fields.

Hamp had figured correctly; things were a bit better when the small male cadre returned to work. Philbrick lessened the women's workload, affording them more time to work their own crops, and scheduled a workable day that didn't include extra labor. It was enough for the women—for now.

CHAPTER 43

A DARING DEED

Frazier and Philbrick looked out over the picturesque scene of diligent workers bending over endless rows of cotton, wielding long-handle hoes. But pictures can be deceptive and neither man mentioned the men and women's ominous ongoing demeanor.

Philbrick removed a crumpled handkerchief from his pocket and wiped sweat from his broad forehead.

"Hot enough fo' you, suh?" asked Frazier, dipping a tin cup in the oaken bucket.

"I'd say. It's only the first of June; I hate to think of what summer's going to be like."

"It'll be too hot fo' white folk, suh, that's fo' sho." He gave the cup to Philbrick. "'Specially them living near the swamps."

"What's that talk—about the air being sick?" He accepted the water. Glancing into the cup he gingerly removed a flailing ladybug.

"Oh, that be mo' than just talk, Mista Philbrick; the malaise be a dangerous thing. But ya'll be fine at the manor house, all that ocean breeze coming through." Frazier dipped another cup for himself. "Fo' truth, though, it be time for white folks to leave."

I can't leave now, thought Philbrick. *If these lazy ingrates stop, they'll never get started again.*

"I'll speak with the other superintendents, see what their plans are for summer." He gulped the tepid water and gave the cup to Frazier. "Have the workers meet me here this evening, at the loading platform. I've decided to advance a part of their wages since the government is so late paying them."

"Yes suh!" said Frazier, grinning broadly. "Maybe that'll cheer the women up—money to buy all them new doodads in the shop."

"I'm counting on it," he said. The plantation stores were stocked with cologne, tableware, dried peaches, pipes, and other enticing wares, in hopes the freedmen's fondness for factory-made goods would create a cash-dependent economy; transferring their dependence from farm-grown subsistence to wage labor. Philbrick knew all too well that no other group possessed the freedmen's cotton-growing expertise. He was determined to keep them working it.

Three rows of steps ran the length of the cotton house platform. Many of the women had plopped down on them, grateful for the chance to rest their aching backs. Some workers leaned against trees, while the older ones perched atop stumps or slumped wearily on the deck itself. Several of the men half knelt, crouching on their haunches.

Philbrick and Gannett soon arrived. Those lolling on the steps rose to allow them leeway to the platform. "Well, Frazier, I see you have everything in place," said Philbrick, sitting down at the table.

"Yes suh; thank you, suh," said the foreman.

Philbrick opened the table's drawer and stuffed the greenbacks inside. He'd wanted to pay the workers in specie, since they were more familiar with that monetary exchange. But the scarcity of coins had increased the use of paper money. He picked up the pay roster. Crecie's name was the first one he called.

"Yes suh," she said, rising from her spot on the far end of the deck.

Philbrick counted aloud as he laid the U.S. Government greenbacks in front of her. "Five...six...seven. Is that your due?"

Not if everybody else gwine get the same. "If you say so, suh." She picked up the legal tender, ignorant of its value and the stern face that stared back—Treasury Secretary Salmon P. Chase. She'd just returned to her place beside Lizbet when a horse-drawn army wagon veered onto the edge of the clearing. The driver hopped down and started toward the group.

"Oh, my goodness; is that...." whispered Lizbet, peering at the approaching figure. "It *do* be him!" She leaped from the platform and ran to the man.

Crecie also recognized him. He was one of the men Boson had let go to work for the Confederate Navy. The last Crecie had heard, they were working on a big rebel ship in the Charleston harbor.

As everyone looked on, Lizbet walked up to the man and shyly greeted him. "How...why you back home?"

"I come to fetch you and the chillun." His voice was loud, decisive, not at all like the timid person Crecie remembered.

Philbrick, already short of workers, immediately addressed the couple. "What's going on here; who are you?"

The man doffed his hat. "Oh, excuse me, suh. Most folks around here know me. My name David Jones."

"H-he be my husband," Lizbet offered.

"Does that give you the right to come fetch her?" Philbrick asked David.

David carefully removed a folded piece of paper from inside his coat pocket and handed it to Philbrick. It was a pass from army general Isaac Stevens, Subordinate Commander at Beaufort, requesting that David Jones be permitted to relocate his wife and children to Beaufort.

"He sent a boat and a crew to carry we back to Beaufort," said David.

"What's the purpose of this? Why is he making this request?"

"Because of the *Planter*, I guess; that ship be carrying a load of weapons—a 32-pounder cannon and a 24-pounder howitzer aft." He didn't mention the two eight-inch Columbiads captured from Ft. Sumter a year ago. The Confederate steamer was also armed with a rifled forty-two pounder, one thirty-two pounder, and a large supply of ammunition.

"What does a rebel ship have to do with *you?*" asked Philbrick.

"A whole lot, suh. But I tell you like this—it be a long story."

"I have time and I'm certain everyone else wants to know, too," said Philbrick. The people moved in closer.

"Well, it all start with Robert Smalls. Him born in Beaufort, but he master hired him out in the Charleston shipyard when he been twelve. He mama's people from Ladies Island."

"Yeah!" said Sadie. "I know he ma, Lydia. Mista McKee been her massa and he take her to live in Beaufort when she been just a little girl."

"Yes'um, Aunty," said David. "You 'zackly right. And when Massa Boson send we to work with the rebel Navy in Charleston, Robert already been the wheelman on the *Planter*. They put me on as a fireman. Alfred and John was the engineers. The rest of them— William, Gabriel, Samuel, and them two Abrahams—Abraham Jackson and Abraham Allston—they been the crew."

Philbrick exhaled impatiently. "Yes, go on," he prompted.

"Well, I was teasing Robert one day, telling him how good he mocked the captain—had his walk, his talk, and all, down pat. And Robert, being smart, come up with this plan...."

He sho ain't mealy-mout' like he use to be, thought Crecie, *but he ain't tell we nothing about the big boat.*

"The plan was to capture the *Planter* and take we to freedom."

A shocked hum rippled through the crowd.

"And not just us men, neither," continued David. "Robert's wife and baby, too; and four other women even and they two chillun."

The people gasped in disbelief.

"What!" said Lizbet. "Ya'll gwine do what?"

"Let me tell the whole story," he replied. "Alright, now this be what happen."

David began, relating how he, Robert Smalls, and the others had plotted their escape then waited for the *Planter's* three white crewmembers to spend a night on shore. Finally, the opportunity came, and the slaves put the plan in action, hiding the women and children on a boat moored nearby. Then, in the wee hours, Robert, and all except one black crewmember who refused to go, fired up the *Planter* and picked up the women and children who were hiding on the other boat.

Freedom was within the Union blockade, just seven miles away, but the *Planter* had to clear five Confederate forts before reaching open waters. As they passed the first three garrisons, Robert, an expert seaman, gave the correct whistle signals. But a low tide slowed the ship and by the time they reached Ft. Sumter, dawn was breaking. The *Planter* had to pass right under the fort's high walls, close enough for the guards to see Robert's dark face. His crew urged him to speed through; but he knew that would arouse suspicion, so he quickly put on the captain's wide straw hat to conceal his face. The ship maintained a slow, steady pace while Robert stood on deck, arms crossed, mimicking the captain's stance. The ruse worked. Ft. Monroe, the last one before open waters, was the easiest. After clearing it, the *Planter* picked up speed.

But the real danger lay ahead. The *CSS Planter*, flying the Confederate flag and the South Carolina Crescent, now moved full speed toward the Union blockade. The captain of the *USS Onward*, thinking he was about to be attacked, swung his ship around, aiming its broadside guns at the rebel ship. It was a tense situation as the *Planter's* frenzied crew removed the Confederate flags and frantically hoisted their sign of surrender—a white sheet. The slaves could only hope the blockaders spotted it in time.

Then just before the command to fire, a sailor spotted the sheet billowing in the wind. He sounded an alarm, halting the order to shoot. Tensions eased and Robert guided the *Planter* to the blockader's stern.

"Well," said David, ending his account, "Robert drew the vessel up beside the *USS Onward*, and leaning on the rail, shouted to the captain: 'Morning, suh! I got some of the good old United States guns fo' you!'"

CHAPTER 44

I KNOW I BEEN CHANGED

Lizbet stared at him. "B-but David, what would o' happen if...if they had o' catch ya'll?"

"We had another plan," he muttered, avoiding her eyes. "We was gwine fight to the end—if that what it come to..."

Crecie strained to hear. *Did him say fight?*

"...then blow up the ship."

Oh, Lord! Fo' true him say that!

"No!" Lizbet exclaimed, gripping his arm.

The people sucked in a collective breath. The magnitude of David's words stretched beyond anything they could imagine, and they struggled, not sure whether to brand him a liar or pay tribute.

Suddenly old Pete leaped from the stump he'd been sitting on. "Praise be!" he exclaimed, breaking the communal spell. The people exhaled with shouts of admiration.

"Glooo-*ry!* Hallelujah!" a woman shrieked.

A male voice rang out. "Thank God—Him spare their life!"

They gathered around David, astounded he had lived to tell his story. Superintendent Gannett grabbed David's hand, vigorously shaking it. "I am in *awe!*" he said. "Commandeering that ship was—why, it was *beyond* courageous!"

"Yes suh! Thank you, suh," David replied, grinning.

Philbrick remained aloof, his face void of expression. When the cheering subsided he turned to David, who stood basking in the attention. "As I understand it, you were forcefully taken from this island and all that you knew." Philbrick's tone was patronizing. "Indeed, you must have been desperate to return home, taking on such peril."

David's smile vanished and he seemed puzzled.

"It's obvious that if *Charleston* had been your home," Philbrick continued, "you would have been content, unwilling to take on such risk."

Now David understood. He shook his head. "No suh. That that ain't the way it been."

"Oh, that *must* have been the reason. We all know you islanders are unwilling to fight. Finding a brave Negro in this district is a rare find indeed."

David frowned. "I don't know what kind o' Negro you trying to find, suh, but I ain't chance my life just to get back to St. Helena—I been determine for freedom or die trying."

Crecie was shocked by David's bold words. Never had she heard a black man contradict a white person, daring to speak his *own* thoughts. She glanced sharply at Philbrick, expecting a reprimand, but the superintendent appeared unperturbed.

"Well, as *you* say," Philbrick replied, smirking.

David turned away, steering Lizbet toward the wagon as Philbrick addressed the workers, reminding them of their obligation to the cotton crop.

"Work and cotton!" exclaimed Dahlia. "That's all he talk about." She rushed to join the others as they crowded around David and Lizbet, bidding them good-by.

But Crecie, too stunned by all she'd seen and heard, was desperate for solitude. David had entered a place she didn't know existed, broken rules she thought were forever. *Freedom got the power to do that? Make a slave act like a real man…a real woman?* It was quiet behind the cotton house and she leaned against its huge double doors, struggling to calm emotions she hadn't felt since she was a little girl. Trailing Bentoo in the woods, it had been a time she'd felt most free. The birds fascinated her—flashing red cardinals and jewel-toned hummers were her favorites. Even though she was just a toddler, she sensed their freedom. But as she grew, so did slavery's confining barriers. She was barely four when she questioned Bentoo about reading. Her grandmother had whipped her, throttling the child's inquisitive nature in the process. After that, Crecie resolved to substitute work for wonder, replacing her love of learning with labor. If she hadn't found a way, her life would have ended like Polly's—swinging from a rope tied by her own hands.

Crecie paced behind the cotton house, struggling to corral her racing thoughts. She'd felt superior, knowing she was not a lazy, ne'er-do-well, doing just enough to avoid the whip. "I been one o' Massa *good* niggers!" she uttered. But the admission brought no sense of pride. The words hung in the stillness then ignited her consciousness. As the pain of truth emerged, she struggled to stay focused, to seek a self so deeply buried she wasn't even sure it existed. *What good all that work do? Every day, every night, nothing but work, work, work! Fo' what? To make mo' money fo' Massa to buy mo' land, to grow mo' cotton, to buy mo' slaves?*

She stared at her calloused hands, at the cuts that had healed on top of scars. *It ain't help me none, all that work.* She bowed her head, ashamed. *That evil taint ain't never gwine leave. Massa own me same as he own the cows, the horses, my body, my mi—.* Suddenly she stopped. "No—I *give* him my mind!" She had found her truth, and the certainty of freedom's compelling force, its life-changing power, exploded within her. *Freedom ain't something outside o' me; it be in me, natural, like air holding up them birds.* "My air just been suck out fo' a time that's all, but the time done come to suck it back in."

The revelation moved her to tears, and although she tried to blink them back, the free-spirited girl-child within would not be denied. She wept until her eyes hurt. Gasping for breath, she welcomed her inner self.

CHAPTER 45

PIERCE'S FAREWELL

It was an early June morning, but the air was already muggy, another torrid day in the making. Crecie stood beside Randy and Hamp, waiting as the steady stream of people approached them. Willie and Leona ran to join the children darting in and out of the group.

Pierce, having fulfilled his obligation to Treasury Secretary Chase, was returning to Boston and the people were intent on saying good-by.

"This be one hot day already," said Crecie, falling in step beside Dahlia.

"You right about that," she replied, batting sand flies away.

"I hope Bentoo and Sham start out early," said Crecie. "Brick Church ain't gwine hold but so many."

Dahlia chuckled. "If I know my aunty, they been there before the rooster crowed."

Crecie laughed. Randy glanced at her, taking in her calm eyes and springy step. *She's more at peace these days,* he thought. *Don't even look the same.*

"Look yonder—Rosa and Hagar. Let's go catch up with 'em," said Crecie, hurrying away.

"Hagar? That *really* is new," Randy muttered.

"What you say?" asked Hamp.

"Is Crecie acting different to you?"

"If you mean 'cause she ain't working as much, yeah, she different, alright."

"Uh huh, that's what I say, too," said Randy.

Crecie and the others settled in among the Gideonites as Rev. French approached the podium. "There is still much work to be done," he said, "but because of Special Agent Pierce's untiring efforts, the worst conditions of poverty and neglect are no longer with us. Because of him, churches that were once closed are now welcoming retreats, places where the people can freely worship."

A few amens could be heard.

"Because of his appeals, there is money for teachers' salaries. Thousands of you and your children are learning to read, taking away the pall of ignorance."

Hearty amen's rang out this time.

"Your diligence can be seen on every island. Fields are lush with corn, potatoes, peanuts, and of course, cotton. You have proven to the world that you *will* work without the whip. The ideals of citizenship have been firmly planted. The outcome is up to you. And now, I present Mr. Pierce."

The Gideonites and the freed people gave Pierce a standing ovation, applauding wildly.

Although Pierce and other abolitionists privately criticized Lincoln's reluctance to free the slaves, he began by praising the President.

"As I depart from you," he said, "you must remember that President Lincoln is your friend and has your best interest at heart. He has sent a man more powerful than I, a big general, to continue my work and look after you. Many of you already know of General Rufus Saxton. You must respect and obey him just as you've done me."

The people began to whisper their approval. Saxton had served as Chief Quartermaster right after the Big Gun Shoot. Many in the audience remembered the slightly built captain as one of the few officers to show any interest in their well-being. They'd lost a friend when he was transferred.

"To you, Mr. French," Pierce continued, "who, in addition to preaching the Words of our Savior and taking on so many special duties…I offer my eternal gratitude." He went on to extend appreciation to many others, thanking the superintendents, the benevolent associations, the military generals, the female teachers and volunteers—whom he'd fondly dubbed the Port Royal Ladies—letting everyone know how much their support meant to him. "And also to New York Port Inspector Hiram Barney. Without his expertise, the business part of the experiment could not have gone forward.

"But more than anyone else, I am under special obligation to you, the people who have been under my charge. I am grateful for the confidence you entrusted in me and for your uniform kindness. You have served me more than any white man ever could."

He paused, seemingly overwhelmed before continuing. "You have come, time and again, even after receiving words of criticism or authority, to express self-reliance and demonstrate your tenacity.

"I believe that God, in His infinite wisdom, has predestined that no race be doomed to eternal bondage, not even the Africans. You have given me your prayers and benedictions and I should be ungrateful indeed, to ever deny them or forget any of you."

He took his seat and the people began to bless him, praying out loud. Crecie was among those who pressed forward to shake his hand. She was pleased to see he was wearing the snakeskin belt she'd given him. "I gwine miss you, suh," she said. He nodded, too emotional to trust his voice.

Pierce was leaving at a time the experiment, although still in its infancy, was generating national pros and cons. The editor of the newly organized Beaufort *Free South* praised Gideon's Band for calling attention to the real issue of the war: the slaves' inevitable emancipation. But a *New York Times* reporter challenged the Gideonites' authority since they knew so little about slavery and cotton. Some correspondents charged the missionaries with catering to the contrabands' every whim; others accused them of personally profiting from the Negroes by establishing plantation stores.

The opposing views of various abolitionists also added to the debate. Wendell Phillips, in spite of his nephew Sam Phillips' work as a Gideonite, had little respect for the group's efforts. The elder Phillips publicly condemned the Port Royal experiment at an Anti-Slavery Society meeting, saying, "The blacks of the South do not need those benevolent people. The freedmen only ask this nation to take the yoke off their necks and they will accomplish the rest. I ask nothing more for the Negro than I ask for the Irishman or German who comes to our shores—an opportunity to thrive."

Pierce felt it was easy for the distant critics of the Port Royal Experiment to declare the Negroes didn't need help, but he and the abolitionists in the field knew that the people's extensive emotional, physical, and educational needs were far from being met.

CHAPTER 46

WAR GAMES

General Hunter, engrossed in the reconnaissance map spread across the table, didn't hear General Saxton enter the office. "A-hem," said Saxton, making his presence known.

Hunter looked up. "Ah, Saxton, welcome back; the Port Royal Negroes have been awaiting your arrival."

"I know; but other duty called first, sir."

"Yes, I'm aware." Hunter pulled a chair from the huge conference table and the men sat opposite each other. "It was a duty you handled brilliantly, diverting Stonewall Jackson at Harper's Ferry. He was marching directly toward Washington."

"But he made a hasty retreat when he realized our troops *and* artillery outnumbered his."

Hunter looked down at the reconnaissance map and traced a route with his finger. "The news is still good—McClellan's Army of the Potomac is within five miles of the Confederate capital."

Saxton leaned in. His side-whiskers completely contrasted with Hunter's clean-shaven face. The men's leadership traits also differed, but their strong anti-slavery belief provided enough common ground.

"The artillery's in place and the works are completed," said Hunter. "McClellan should be closing in on Richmond now."

"Why, that means if he captures Richmond—."

"*If!* What do you mean, *if?*" exclaimed Hunter. "He's in command of the most powerful army in the country; over 100,000 men with the best armaments, the best training; God knows he took long enough to prepare them—three months, if a day."

"Of course," amended Saxton, "*when* he takes Richmond, slavery and this rebellious farce will end. Lincoln had better act quickly though—unless he plans to follow through on colonization."

"Colonize four million Negroes? I doubt that."

"I think your solution for emancipation would have worked. Why did he revoke it?"

"I supposedly breached protocol because he found out about it in the newspapers," Hunter replied. "But I know the *real* reason—he's trying to appease the Border States and McClellan." He began to pace in front of the table. "Why he keeps that jackass of a general in command is beyond me; he lacks boldness and his tactics are flawed. Maneuvering to capture territory, pandering to traitors—it's absurd!"

"What can you expect from a pro-slavery Democrat?" said Saxton. "Someone who declares blacks aren't fit to fight in a white man's war."

Hunter stopped pacing and banged the desk. "Damn it to hell with his so-called *civilized* tactics—our armies need to demolish their houses, burn their fields, free their slaves!" Trembling with rage, he sat down. "We need all the help we can get—Robert Smalls proved as heroic as any white soldier." Fixing a somber gaze on Saxton, he stonily intoned: "The South is fighting unto death, and unless we acknowledge what's at stake, the war is lost and so is the Union. If the Peninsular Campaign fails, we are in for a long bloody war."

Lost for words, Saxton shifted uncomfortably in his chair. Finally he said, "I understand, sir, but with McClellan so close, closing in on Richmond…well, what can go wrong?"

By July 2, just two days later, everything had gone wrong; and it was all because that past June, the wily General Robert E. Lee had succeeded the wounded General Joseph Johnson. Lee, defending Richmond as the new commander of the Army of Northern Virginia, out-maneuvered the overly cautious General McClellan, leading him to believe he was vastly outnumbered. McClellan ordered his great army to retreat again and again, beseeching Lincoln to send even more troops. With Lee in dogged pursuit, McClellan finally secured his army on the James River. On the fourth of July, at the end of the engagements known as the Seven Days' Battle, the Army of the Potomac morosely camped on the banks of the river, their cries of "On to Richmond" silenced. McClellan's much-touted Peninsular Campaign had failed to end the war. Secretary of War Stanton, fearing a Confederate attack on panic-stricken Washington, ordered his field commanders to immediately send reinforcements to protect the city.

Many Union newspapers had prematurely predicted the war's end and now heaped blame upon Lincoln, Stanton, and McClellan. Northerners, coming to the realization that the South really *could* win, demanded a hard fight to a real war. President Lincoln agreed. Closing out the Peninsular Campaign, he brought General John Pope, an anti-slavery Republican, to command the Army of the Potomac. War on the Eastern front became punitive as Pope confiscated private property, demanded loyalty from Southern Unionists, and allowed the execution of captured guerillas. Southerners protested the war's forceful turn, but Lincoln supported Pope's aggressive tactics, stating, "The war could not be fought with elder-stalk squirts charged with rose water."

⟰⟱

"Hal-looo," called Mose. "Anybody in there?"

Crecie rushed to the cabin door. Opening it wide, she stepped outside and closed it firmly behind her.

"You give Titus the basket o' food I send?" she whispered.

"Yeah, and he send this fo' you," Mose whispered back, handing her a small snakeskin pouch.

She pulled the drawstring and peeped inside.

"That what you want, ain't it?" he asked.

"Yeah, this it alright." She tightened the drawstring and secured the bag in her apron pocket. "How Titus doing? He like being a barber?"

"Must like it fine...all the men go to him fo' hair cut; white ones, too."

"I know," said Crecie, giving the bag a little pat. "C'mon, let's go inside."

Randy sat at the table, eating. He looked up and the men's grunts served as greetings.

"I'm through cooking," said Crecie. "Want me to fix you something?"

"What you cook?" asked Mose.

"Never mind what I cook—you gwine eat or no?"

Mose pulled out a chair and Crecie bustled about fixing his food.

"What going on with Hunter's regiment?" asked Randy. "They still camped at Smith Plantation?"

"Yeah, they still there, but they ain't doing much o' nothing except drilling. They ain't get no pay neither."

Crecie placed a steaming bowl of boiled fish and hominy in front of the elderly gentleman.

"This sho look good; smell good, too." He picked up a spoon. "You got any red pepper sauce, Crecie?"

"Right there in front o' you," she said, sitting beside him at the table.

Mose doused the sauce on his food.

"Whoaaa!" Randy warned. "Better go easy on that; you got to either be a *real* man—or Crecie—to eat that stuff. I can't make it hot enough for her."

"You can't make it hot enough fo' me neither," said Mose. He put the spoon to his lips and his eyes immediately watered; tears streamed down his stubby cheeks and a rust-red hue crept over his tan face. He fanned frantically, stirring the air with his tattered Union cap. "Hot damn," he whispered when he could breathe again. "This what them boys in Hunter regiment need; it'll keep they blood flowing alright!"

"Then they better get it soon," said Crecie "because Gen'ral Saxton say Richmond fixing to fall; won't be no need fo' soldiers."

"No, Crecie, the shoe's on the other foot now," said Randy. "McClellan didn't capture Richmond like they thought he would."

"How come you know so much?" Mose challenged. "I ain't hear no talk like that."

"You don't have to be first to know everything," said Randy. "Why you think I keep that telegraph office so clean every day?"

"Because they pay you?" said Mose.

"Yeah, that too. War Secretary Stanton told Hunter to send five thousand infantry men to Washington, help protect the city."

Crecie looked up sharply. "But Gen'ral Hunter done already send a bunch o' army mens up North to help." She placed a pitcher of water on the table, her hand shaking. "Who gwine watch over we if they take all the soldiers? Ya'll know what happen on Hutchinson Island."

Neither man answered, but remembering the carnage, knew Crecie's fears were legitimate. The attack had occurred in June,

236

when three hundred or so rebels sneaked onto the island before dawn, surprising the Negroes. They'd butchered those who couldn't escape and shot others. Wreaking havoc, they set fire to the church, Mrs. March's abandoned house, and the food supply. The secessionists escaped before the Union sentries arrived, taking some of the Negroes captive. Talk of the raid had remained foremost on everyone's lips for months.

"Hunter's taking care of that," said Randy. "He's bringing the soldiers from Edisto to take over for the ones he's sending to Washington. We'll have less protection, but it's better than nothing."

Crecie poured a jarful of water and sat it in front of Mose. "But that gwine leave the folks on Edisto open to the sesesch rebels," she said.

"No it won't. Hunter's shutting Edisto down, everybody got to come to St. Helena—if they want to be safe," Randy replied.

"But what about they cotton crop and the food they plant fo' winter?" asked Crecie. "The best cotton come from Edisto!"

"Well, they gwine have to choose between the land or they life," Mose remarked. He turned to Randy. "The wire bring any mo' news?"

"Oh, plenty."

"What!" said Crecie in a huff. "And you ain't tell me? You just like Bentoo."

"Man got to work in the silence. Don't want the dispatchers pointing at me if the news get out too soon."

"Well," said Mose, prodding. "What else you got?"

Randy leaned back in his chair, folding his hands atop his full stomach.

"Oh, I got more, but you got to keep quiet until it comes back around to you."

The two nodded and leaned in.

"Well, first off, Yankees ain't won a real battle since April."

Mose leaned back. "Shucks! Everybody already know that! Some say the North about to lose even."

"But something come on the wire today, put *all* the operators in a tizzy!" He paused. "Any coffee left, Crecie?"

"Coff—no! What the telegram say?"

"It said the white folks up North mad as hell because they're losing—especially at McClellan for not capturing Richmond. They told the government to *do* something and be damn quick about it. So the government did what it always do—hurried up and put some new laws together."

Mose leaned forward, interested again. "What kind o' law?"

"You know about the Confiscation Law, right?" said Randy. "Government claims to own everything, any contraband that can help the rebels."

"Yeah, I hear that," said Mose.

"Well, the government added something to *that* law, calling it the Second Confiscation law. Now the law say if a slave can get to Union territory his master can't claim him—he's free. And something else—you know that land the planters left behind? The government gonna sell that land to pay the back taxes."

"Sell to who?" asked Mose.

"Anybody with money, I guess. I ain't for sure."

Crecie's face flushed, remembering their terrible argument when Randy last mentioned land sales to her.

"And that's not all. They pass something called the Militia Act. Negroes can be soldiers in the army now, work at the camps for pay. They gonna be free if they join, and their wives and children and mamas, gonna be free too."

"Like all o' we on St. Helena?" asked Crecie.

"Yeah, if they can prove their master is a rebel, helping the Confederates."

Mose sat still, seemingly deep in thought.

Finally he spoke. "Randy, tell me this: Mista John, on Opella Plantation ain't run away like the other white folks—he a loyal Union man—so what be the outcome for *his* slaves; they free, too?"

Randy cocked his head quizzically. "You know, Mose, I didn't think about that; I bet the government didn't either."

Mose stood. "Well, buckra gwine do what he want anyway, nothing us can do about it." He plopped his cap on and started toward the door. "I best be leaving befo' it get dark."

"Wait," said Crecie, "take some hot sauce—."

"Oh no, I don't—."

"No! Not for you; for Titus and the men. I got chow-chow fo' *you*."

Mose grinned sheepishly. "How *you* know? *I* might want some o' that hot sauce, too."

"I don't believe you do," said Crecie, grinning.

CHAPTER 47

JULY FOURTH

"Hurry up, Crecie," Hamp called from the yard. "We gwine be the last one to get there."

"Oh, we got plenty o' time; sun just rising," she yelled back. "You just get Rex hitched up; Leona, stay still while I tie yo' bow!"

Randy entered from the adjoining room. Sham and Willie, dressed in their best, strutted proudly behind him. "The boys look right smart, Crecie. You did a good job."

Remaking the Northern donations into clothes for the children had been a joy. She'd snipped and sewed through many a night, whispering to the dancing shadows. "You been right, Isham, black folks can do fo' we self. I believe that fo' true now."

"Crecie, ya'll not ready to go *yet*?" Randy's loud voice interrupted her thoughts. "Why the woman always take longer than the man to do everything? Hamp been ready to go."

"That's because the woman got to *do* everything," Crecie replied. She stepped away from Leona, eyeing her handiwork. "Now that be a good bow!"

Leona spun around, showing off her 'new' baby-blue dress and matching hair ribbon. Ivy Oaks school was one of three that would sing at the program.

"My, my," said Randy, smiling at Leona. "Don't my grandboy look pretty!"

Leona stopped twirling. She placed her hands on her boney hips and glared at Randy. "I ain't no grandboy—I be a girl!"

"Don't pay PawPaw no mind," said Crecie. "He just joking you." She looked at Randy and frowned. "You still got on yo' old clothes. Ain't you coming to the cela'brashin?"

"No, I—." Randy began.

"Cel, cel-a? What that be?" asked Willie.

Not knowing herself, Crecie remained quiet.

"Mr. Fill Up say it be a special day fo' we," Leona prattled, "and there gwine be fire lighting up the sky."

The Fourth of July was indeed a special American holiday; but only whites celebrated, having picnics, parades, fireworks, to honor the tradition of freedom. But the day of festivities held dread for many slaveholders. Fearing rebellion and unrest, some planters made the slaves work longer hours and the very mention of Independence Day was cause for the whip. Masters and overseers celebrated, but remained on high alert. It was not by accident more plantation fires occurred on July fourth than any other day of the year.

"Well, Willie," said Crecie, attempting to answer his question, "this cela'brashin thing—it be a day fo', fo'...." She faltered, having no concept of the day's significance. Her eyes sought Randy's help.

He chose to ignore her silent plea. "You gonna be the prettiest girl at the Fourth of July picnic," he told Leona, giving her a quick hug.

Leona grinned shyly. "Mr. Fill Up say we gwine sing fo' the new gen'ral, Gen'ral Saxby. That be why I look so good."

Randy smiled. "His name is Saxton, Leona."

"That what I say," she replied, skipping out the door.

Randy turned to Crecie. "What you waiting on? They're waiting for you in the wagon."

"You sho you ain't coming, too?" she asked.

"Sure as I can be." Taking her arm, he guided her out to the wagon. "This is your first Fourth of July, go and have a good time!"

Randy watched them pull away then went back inside. He filled a tin cup with steaming coffee and began to rummage through his travel satchel. After finding the well-worn pamphlet, he settled at the table and read its title aloud: "*What To The American Slave Is Your 4th of July?*" Frederick Douglass had posed that question to the Rochester Ladies Anti-Slavery Sewing Society in 1852. Randy had read the speech so many times, he'd almost memorized it.

"'Fellow-citizens,'" he recited softly, "allow me to ask, why am I called upon to speak here today? What have I, or those I represent, to do with your national independence...it is shared by you, not by me'."

Randy read silently, alternating between cooling the hot drink and sipping it, savoring both the words and coffee. Then, reaching his favorite part, he laid the paper aside, recalling his fugitive days. He had soon learned that running from slavery didn't necessarily mean escaping to freedom. Even free Negroes were considered unfit for citizenship and in many places, forbidden to attend the patriotic events.

Randy stood and walked over to the open shutter. Looking toward a field void of workers, he knew that this one work-free day in July didn't add up to a liberated life. But it was a start.

He recalled another passage of the speech, mulling it in his mind: *This Fourth of July is yours, not mine. You may rejoice, I must mourn. To drag a man in fetters into the grand illuminated temple of liberty, and call upon him to join you in joyous anthems, were inhuman mockery and sacrilegious irony.*

He walked back to the table and picked up the pamphlet. "'What, to the American slave is your 4th of July'?" he read. "'I answer: a day that reveals to him, more than all other days in the year, the gross injustice and cruelty to which he is the constant victim'."

Randy scanned the lengthy speech, seeking familiar words and phrases. "'Your celebration is a sham; your boasted liberty an unholy license....I do not hesitate to declare with all my soul, that the character and conduct of this nation never looked blacker to me than on this 4th of July'!"

Despondency loomed and he read no further. After gulping the last of the now-cold coffee, he put the pamphlet back. *Maybe next year, Leona*, he thought, fastening the satchel's worn straps. *Maybe then I'll go to see fire lighting up the sky.*

━◆ ◆━

Rex's slow gait rocked the tired children to sleep almost immediately. Crecie angled the pine-wood torch toward Hamp, peering into the young man's face.

"You ain't sleep, too, is you, boy?"

"Naw, Crecie. After all what gone on today, I be too worked up to sleep."

"Yeah, it been a fine time, ain't it?"

Satisfied that Hamp was indeed awake, she relaxed, thinking about the Fourth of July events.

The celebration had begun with two columns of marchers singing and waving greenery, making their way to the old Episcopal Church. Superintendent Gannett led one group and Edward Hooper, Pierce's former assistant, led the other. A huge American flag, a gift from General Saxton, hung between two towering pines, marking an entrance to the church grounds. Superintendents, teachers, and military personnel, sat on a bunting-draped platform, facing the flag. Crecie recognized most of them: Philbrick and his wife Helen; Laura Towne, the healer; Superintendent Gannett and a few of the other superintendents. Hooper, outfitted in a captain's army uniform, sat beside General Saxton, his new supervisor. Many of the young teachers, lonely and homesick, had returned to the North. But Sam Phillips, Leona's Mista Fill Up, sat in the midst of several newcomers.

The procession halted beneath Old Glory, and the people performed stirring Negro Spirituals. The platform guests, sitting beneath the ancient oaks, applauded enthusiastically throughout, but especially for the closing favorite, "Roll, Jordan, Roll."

"Yeah, it been a good day," said Hamp, interrupting Crecie's thoughts. "What be that song—the one the chillun sing?"

"You mean *"America"*?"

"No, the one what say *Glory, Glory*."

"Oh, you talking about the "John Brown Song.""

"Yeah, that one."

Crecie sang softly and Hamp joined in:

John Brown body be a-moulderin' in the grave,
John Brown body be a-moulderin' in the grave,
John Brown body be a-moulderin' in the grave,
He soul be marchin' on!
Glory, glory, hallelujah!
Glory, glory, hallelujah! He soul be marching on!

"I like that song," said Hamp. "You remember the rest o' the words?"

"Sho do." Crecie knew the words to all the songs, Leona sang them so much.

She started up again and they went through the rounds, their voices louder on each verse. By the time they got to *They will hang Jeff Davis to a sour apple tree*, they were belting it out. But when they reached the last stanza—*Now, three rousing cheers fo' the Union*—their voices echoed throughout the dark, dense woods, and they ended the disjointed duet in a fit of laughter.

One of the children stirred, but quickly drifted back to sleep.

"It been a good day, alright," Hamp said, catching his breath.

"Yeah it was. What you like most about it?"

"Well, if I got to pick one something, it gwine be the smoke herring and the hard tack, and the molasses water, and then—."

"Hold on—that be mo' than one!" she said.

"I know...and then I eat and drink all I want. What you like best?"

"The speech making—just to hear talk about Washington City where President Lincoln live; and about how John Brown die trying to free we. That place name Harper Ferry—Gen'ral Saxton fight there, too."

Frowning into the darkness she thought about the things she'd enjoyed but hadn't shared with Hamp; the shivers she'd felt, listening to Miss Nelly Winsor play "*America*" on the organ; and her heart almost popped out as Leona sang "My country, 'tis of thee, sweet land of liberty, of thee I sing...." Those feelings had been her best things. She sat quiet the rest of the way home, wondering where she fit in the sweet land of liberty, land of the noble free.

CHAPTER 48

THE BEGINNING OF AN END

Crecie looked about furtively before unlatching the storehouse door. The room reeked of onions, radishes, and other hardy staples. Reaching behind a sack of rice, she retrieved a ragged bundle and untied the knot. Two items lay on the checkered cloth—the snakeskin bag Mose had brought and a moss-stuffed effigy. She examined the bleached-burlap doll, noting its twisted lop-sided mouth; the result, no doubt, of her secret, often hasty, handiwork. "Well, this just gwine have to do," she muttered, shrugging off her failing. But the figure's neatly stitched blue uniform, coupled with perfect circles of iridescent oyster-shell eyes, gave her a sense of accomplishment.

Removing the bag's contents, she carefully arranged the tufts of red hair and fingernail clippings in a precise, mystical fashion. Then, as the crisp aroma of sticky pine-resin permeated the room, she glued strands of red hair onto the doll's smooth head. She was almost done gluing the beard when Hamp's loud call interrupted her.

"Crecie!" he shouted. "Where you?"

"In here, getting some taters," she yelled back. "What you want?" She threw a few sweet potatoes onto the cloth and quickly retied it.

"Come see," he said.

She gathered her cache and exited the shed.

"Look who done come back," said Hamp, grinning.

Crecie peered into the gathering dusk. "Titus!" she exclaimed, rushing to greet him. "I *too* glad you back. You done left the camp?"

"Well, yes and no," he said. "Ain't no mo' camp, but I still gwine be in the regiment."

"Huh? What kind o' fool answer is that?" she asked.

Titus laughed. "This what happen. General Hunter never get we no pay from the gov'ment, so he close the camp, sent the men back to the fields; all except the first hundred that join on they own."

"But you ain't join on *yo'* own," said Hamp. "Soldiers make you go, same as everybody else."

"I *know* all that, Hamp; but you see, I be the one who cut General Hunter and them hair, shave they whiskers and such; that why he ain't send *me* back to the plantation."

"Uh-huh," said Hamp. "So cutting yo' massa hair been good fo' *something*, eh?"

"Fo' sho you right. You be surprise, how getting a haircut can set a man to talking, loosen he mouth. Let me tell you—."

"Tell we inside," said Crecie, swatting a mosquito. "These skee-tuhs about to eat me to death."

Randy sat in front of the fireplace, nodding as he half-listened to Leona read. He perked up when he saw Titus.

"I'm glad to see you, boy," said Randy. "I hear you all working for no pay—same as slavery times."

Titus laughed. "Oh, I gets *paid*, ol' man."

"Who're you calling old?" said Randy, rising from the rocking chair. "That army made you mannish, but I can still ride your frame."

Titus backed away, grinning as he feigned fright. "OK! OK! I believe you!"

Crecie shooed the children into the other room and turned to Titus. "Tell me, how you still be in camp if Hunter done shut it down?"

"Yeah," said Hamp. "You *in* or *out*?"

"I be *in*, fo' sho'," said Titus, taking over the rocking chair. The others gathered close, eager to discover the latest news in their ever-changing lives. "I already tell you Gen'ral Hunter done shut down the camp, right?"

They nodded.

"Well, Gen'ral Saxton was waiting for me to trim he beard after I finish cutting Black Dave hair so—."

"Black Dave?" said Hamp.

"General David Hunter," Randy offered.

"So Black Dave tell Saxby—."

"I know who that be," said Hamp. "Saxton."

Crecie pushed back her chair and stood up. "Now you just tie yo' mout', Hamp; you too, Randy, and let Titus give account." The men exchanged droll glances as she sat back down. "Go on, Titus."

"Yes ma' am, Miz Crecie!" said Titus. "Well, Secretary Stanton— oh, ya'll know who that be?"

"I ain't ignorant," said Crecie. "He the one over the whole war; don't have to answer to nobody—except Mista Lincoln, maybe."

"Right. He ordered Black Dave to send five thousand o' his men to help clean up the mess Gen'ral McClellan made. I thought Saxby was gwine have a fit, he been so mad when he hear that. He say 'Ain't gwine be enough soldiers left to protect the people'."

"Fo' true," said Crecie. "That's what happen on Hutchinson Island when the rebels sneak over there and the black folks ain't had no soldiers to save them and—." She stopped, noting the men's annoyed stares. "Uh, go on with yo' story, Titus."

"Thank ya. Well, Saxby say he gwine write Mista Stanton a letter, tell him that if these islands can't get mo' white soldiers, they gwine have to get black ones—else the gov'ment ain't gwine have no cotton."

"That's how it should to be," said Randy. "We're already doing everything else in the army, from cooking to building bridges; might as well get a gun and do some soldiering, too."

"Black Dave went along with that," said Titus. "Tell Saxby to go ahead, write the letter. But guess who gwine *take* the letter to Washington City—Mr. French!"

"That ain't nothing special," Crecie sniffed.

"Yeah. But who he taking with him is. I hear they might even get to see the president." The group waited as Titus maintained an affected pause.

Finally, Randy sighed. "Who are you talking about, Titus??"

"Robert Smalls. He gwine tell his story about the *Planter* in Washington, then he gwine tell it in New York."

"Fo' true?" Crecie whispered.

"If it be a lie, Black Dave and Saxby tell it," said Titus. "I hear it with my own ears from they own mout'."

"Well, if anybody can make Stanton see the light, it gwine be Robert," said Hamp. "He got a story to tell."

"Yes suh, I believe things about to turn around for us black army men," said Titus. "Now's the time to come back, Hamp."

Hamp stood and poked the embers, reviving the dying fire. "Uh-uh, Titus. You know me and Brimstone don't set horses."

The checkered bundle had not left Crecie's hand. She gripped it tighter.

"Sergeant Johnstone? Ain't Mose tell ya'll about him?" said Titus. "He had a stroke o' the brain, face all one-sided, can't talk even."

The mout', she thought, *the crooked mout'!*

"No, I ain't hear that," said Hamp. "Where him be now?"

"Where him be now is helpless; army sent him back to Ohio, to he family."

Hamp shook his head. "What go 'round, come 'round."

"Fo' true," said Mose.

"Oh, Crecie, I almost forgot," said Titus. "The men want to know if you got any mo' chow-chow and hot pepper sauce. They gwine pay you fo' it."

"Yeah, got plenty in the storehouse. Hamp can get it fo' you."

Titus stood. "Thank yo' kindly. Well, I best be getting back to camp befo' they think I run away."

The men followed him to the door. "You coming, Crecie?" asked Randy.

"Huh? Oh—no, I got to do something. I glad to see you, Titus. Come back, now."

"I will," he called over his shoulder.

Crecie removed the sweet potatoes before tossing the bundle into the fire. *No need fo' this now.* The resin flared, consuming the bundle. The smell of pine, snakeskin, and burning hair assailed her nostrils. *Vengence be left up to the Lord, I guess.*

CHAPTER 49

WORKING OUT THEIR FREEDOM

It was late August when Rev. French and Robert Smalls returned from Washington City, authorized to organize 5,000 persons of African descent as volunteer employees for the United States Army. War Secretary Stanton's official edict arrived a few weeks later, giving General Saxton legal permission to uniform, equip, arm, and receive Negroes to guard Union-occupied plantations. The letter stated that the new soldiers would have license to raid southern plantations and salt works; they'd escort willing slaves to Union-held territory, lessening the Confederates' access to labor. Stanton's order ended with the affirmation that, "By recent act of Congress, all men and boys received into the service of the United States who may have been slaves of rebel masters, are, with their wives, mothers and children, declared to be forever free."

The one hundred men held over from Hunter's Regiment became Company A and were sent to guard St. Simons Island in Georgia. The company, consisting entirely of former slaves, was the first government-recognized regiment, a segment of the

First South Carolina Volunteer Infantry, U.S.C.T.—United States Colored Troops.

⟻⟼

Edward Pierce once remarked that the slaves possessed a mysterious spiritual telegraph: if a single slave on the Potomac learned of an emancipation edict, his brethren on the Gulf would soon know it too. Such was the reaction to the passage of the Second Confiscation Act and the Militia Act. Immediately after the word went out, a stream of enslaved people left the plantations and stealthy made their way through the war, risking their lives to make a difference in the fight for freedom.

As hundreds of runaways reached Union camps, they were immediately put to work— repairing and building wharfs, tending military gardens, digging graves, cooking, and chopping wood. The Negroes also served as boatmen, engineers, laundresses, carpenters, teamsters, dockhands, stable hands, and hospital attendants, giving support to the white volunteer army.

Throughout the war, President Lincoln's field generals reported on the contrabands' contributions. It soon became evident to him that emancipation of the slaves related directly to winning the war.

In July 1862, Lincoln assembled his cabinet, telling them that "The slaves are undeniably an element of strength to those who have their service; and we must decide whether they shall be for us or against us. Emancipation is a military necessity, absolutely essential to the preservation of the Union." He then presented his handwritten Preliminary Emancipation Proclamation. It was evident he had taken great care with his four-page wording, scratching out sentences and attaching newspaper clippings to booster his position. The Proclamation warned the Confederate states to return to the Union by January 1, 1863, or their slaves shall be thenceforward and forever free. The United States military was authorized to enforce the congressional acts, prohibiting the return of fugitive slaves.

Most cabinet members supported the President, but because the war had been going badly all summer, Secretary of State William Seward advised Lincoln to delay announcing the Preliminary Emancipation Proclamation to the public.

"This is a time of discouragement," said Seward. "Wait until you can give it to the country supported by a military success. Otherwise, the proclamation may be seen a cry for help...our last shriek on our way to retreat."

Lincoln followed Seward's advice. Then, on September 22, he summoned his cabinet to a special meeting. It was five days after the Battle at Antietam, the bloodiest day in American history, the source of more than twenty thousand Union and Confederate casualties.

"I think the time has come," Lincoln told his cabinet. "I wish it was a better time....The army's action against the rebels has not been quite what I'd expected. But they have been driven out of Maryland."

Having feebly chased the rebels out of Maryland, it was a dubious win. But with northern newspapers amplifying the battle as a victory, building morale, Lincoln announced the Preliminary Emancipation Proclamation to the country. The war to save the Union was now also a fight to free the slaves.

CHAPTER 50
THE MOTHERS

The cabin door flew open just as Bentoo placed a huge bowl of mush in the center of the floor. She looked up, surprised to see Philbrick standing there; but she was even more astounded by those who stood with him. Nine months had passed since the Big Gun Shoot and Alina Boson's retreat to upland Spartanburg, taking several workers with her. Now five of them had returned.

"Good morning, Bentoo," said Philbrick. "Do you know these women?"

"Oh, yes suh—that be Yoruba, Margaret, Charlotte, Fatima, and Medina. I too glad to see ya'll," she said, giving each a hug. "I know these chillun glad, too." She nudged the little ones forward.

But the children clung to Bentoo, peeking at the strangers from behind her long skirt. Disappointment clouded the mothers' gaunt faces and they stared longingly, anxious to hold their children.

"Don't worry," consoled Bentoo, handing each woman a small wooden spoon. "Just feed 'em—they'll come around." The women positioned themselves around the mush-filled bowl and the children hurried over. Bentoo softly chuckled and winked.

Philbrick stood at the door. "Bentoo, come outside; I need to speak with you."

"Yes suh," she said, baffled by the request.

They walked toward an autumn-decked sycamore tree, the leaves crunching under their feet. The morning was cool, but Bentoo's hands felt clammy. She wiped them on her apron, waiting for Philbrick to speak. He didn't hesitate.

"I've hired these women to work for me, but they'll have look after their own children. I'm closing the nursery."

"Suh?" Bentoo wasn't sure she'd heard correctly. "What you say, suh?"

"The island is overflowing; Edisto refugees have taken over St. Helena Village and mainland runaways are spilling out of the contraband camps, living anywhere there's a bit of shelter—sheds, barns—even the jail."

"B-but suh, this be my home, and…." *My home ain't yours to give,* she thought.

"I understand that, Bentoo; but this is the only available place."

"But where I gwine go? This where I live all my life, just like my pappy and mammy."

"With Crecie, perhaps?"

She turned away, too proud to reveal the welling tears. *Crecie! Sham, Leona, Willie, Randy, Hamp—and God know who else she got piled up in there; where they gwine put me?*

"When I got to go, suh?"

"This afterno…by tomorrow. The cotton has to be cleaned, baled, shipped—I need these women to get started immediately."

"Crecie know?"

"Not yet. I'll tell her today." He climbed up on the wagon. "The women will help you gather your things."

Her shoulders slumped and she returned to the cabin.

Margaret, Ossie's mother, rushed up. "I tell him us can go to the contraband camp, but him say no, too much sickness there."

"That be true enough," said Bentoo. She and Crecie often visited the cramped unsanitary camp, administering to the ragged hordes that arrived daily. Racked with consumption and covered with open sores, the runaways continually infected and re-infected each other.

"I too sorry you gwine have to leave yo' cabin," said Margaret.

"Ain't yo' fault," said Bentoo, settling in the huge rocker. The women stood around, cuddling their offspring. Margaret sat on the floor, cradling her son Ossie *and* her niece, Louise.

"Where Hester?" asked Bentoo.

The women sat down on the floor, encircling Margaret.

"She, she…oh, my po' sister…." Margaret began to weep, holding fast to Ossie and Louise.

Bentoo caressed the woman's scrawny shoulder, speaking in a soothing tone. "Let it go, daughter. Let that yoke fall."

It was as if a dark cloud had been lifted and all the women began to sob, unleashing their pent-up anguish.

"Let it all out," urged Bentoo.

Their laments grew louder and the wide-eyed children fled to Bentoo.

The women expressed torrents of grief before the wails gradually became whimpers.

"Ya'll gwine feel better now," said Bento.

"Yes'um, Aunt Bennie, I do," said Margaret. She blew her nose and dried her eyes. "This be the first time us grieve proper fo' Hester."

"Us been too dry inside to make tears," said Charlotte.

"It been a trying time, Aunt Bennie; us getting back," said Fatima.

Bentoo prodded the children toward their mothers and leaned forward. "Tell me, what happen?"

"One day us been chopping weeds in the cotton field and hear guns shoot; us been *too* scared," said Medina.

"Well, the rebs and then the yanks come marching through," said Fatima. "They take all the food; even strip the corn what ain't ripe yet. What lil' bit o' food us grow keep we from starving."

Yoruba took up the story. "Then all them runaways start coming, slipping through the night. I ax 'em where they heading. All o' they say to the low country; tell me they gwine be free in the islands."

"So that's when us make we mind up, to get back to Ivy Oaks," said Fatima. "But it be much danger between there and here, so us press through the woods, off the road where nobody can see we."

Bentoo nodded; she'd noticed the gashes and raw cuts covering the women's faces and arms.

"None o' we been too strong to start with," said Margaret, "but Hester been the weakest on account she can't catch wind."

"I know," said Bentoo. "She had breathing fits ever since she been lil'."

Margaret's eyes began to water.

"Take yo' time, daughter," urged Bentoo.

She blinked back the tears and took a deep breath. "Us forage along the way—roots and nuts—that be the only thing us eat. No water, neither; just dew befo' the sun dry the leaf." She paused, looking down at her hands. "Then come the rain—Lord, how it beat 'pon we—all night, all day, sopping wet, no roof fo' we head." She wrapped her arms tightly around her thin waist, reliving the bone-chilling cold. "Then it stop. But Hester wheezing real bad now and moving slow. I ax her, you alright, Sis? And she say fine and us must keep going. I know she ain't fine, but ain't a thing I could do about it; not one thing I could do...."

Charlotte took up the story. "Hester been hot with fever, burning up."

"Ya'll search for some *life everlasting*—herb and such?" asked Bentoo.

"Yes'mam; us give her every plant us find, but ain't had no fire, no water to boil tea, so us just put the leaves all over her. She be so hot, soon as we lay 'em on, they burn crusty! Us do that all through the night—putting leaf on, taking leaf off. Hester lay quiet, just watching we. Her trying hard now, to catch wind." Charlotte buried her face in her hands, shaking her head from side to side.

"But the fever ain't break," said Medina. "Then befo' dayclean, she...she stop trying."

The women grew silent in their remembrances.

Then Yuroba said, "Us find sticks to dig a shallow grave with."

"Then us pray fo' Hester, that she spirit cross over to the other side," Medina said. "But us ain't cry...can't make tears, us so dry inside."

"Then us cover she best us could," said Yuroba. "Then do like she tell we—us keep going."

"The next day us come 'pon Yankee camp," said Fatima. "Some runaways been camp close by and help we. That be how us get back."

Bentoo pulled Hester's little daughter close. *Motherless little one, homeless old one; all in need of care.* This time she wasn't too proud to let the tears flow.

By the time Randy and Crecie arrived, the mothers had packed Bentoo's belongings. They helped load the wagon and the little family set out for Midway. The cabin had sheltered four generations—five, counting Crecie's children—but Bentoo, Randy, and Crecie never looked back. No one wanted to be first to break down.

The mood was suppressed as the trio returned to Midway, their usual banter buried beneath anxious thoughts. It wasn't until Randy steered Rex into Crecie's yard that the tacit silence was broken.

"Bentoo! Bentoo!" yelled Sham, running to the wagon; Leona and Willie followed closely. Sham reached out for his great-granny's hand. "I help you," he offered.

Bentoo grasped the boy's hands and maneuvered down. "These ol' bones thank you, son." The children began fussing over her, ending her doubts about moving in.

But Crecie wasn't sure. Bentoo coming to live with her wasn't a problem—they would make room for one more—it was how it came about that caused her concern.

Hamp joined the welcoming committee. "Evening Aunt Bennie, good to see ya."

"Good to be here, Hamp…good to be anywhere—alive!"

Hamp laughed. "Oh, you got a long time left to be alive!"

"Make yo'self useful, Hamp," Crecie snapped. "Help Bentoo get settle in; I got to work in the shed." Randy and Bentoo exchanged befuddled glances as she stalked away.

CHAPTER 51

DECISION TIME

The shed now held more food than the amount the soldiers stole, but Crecie was not at peace. Upset over Philbrick's action, she compared the differences between him and Malcolm Boson. Her mind whirled from one thing to the next as she rearranged the already neat shelves. It dawned on her the two men had at least one thing in common—power. The slave owners controlled everything before the war but now the new white folks had taken over. *They done change things to they way o' thinking,* she surmised. *Black chile toting book and black man toting gun. Yeah, that be power alright.*

She reached for a sack of rutabagas. *But that what Philbrick done... Bentoo born in that cabin, live there all she life—how he just put she out like that? 'Cause he can, that's why.* Trying to sort her thoughts, she lined the bag up beside the others. *Ain't that what you want, Crecie— white man be in charge?*

She reached for another sack, but stopped mid-air. "No!" she exclaimed, vigorously shaking her head. "Not if he gwine sweep an old woman out like...like...dirt out the door." She lifted the sack and lined it up. *But then come January, Mista Lincoln gwine free we. But fo' what us be free?* She sat down on a sack of onions, thinking hard.

"I still knee-deep in cotton," she muttered, "new massa just don't carry no whip."

She remained stock-still, struggling for a peek into a strange new future. Suddenly, a field mouse darted across her foot, startling her. "I bet it be mo' where he come from." Searching for the animal's nest, she stumbled upon Isham's tattered straw hat. She dusted it off, savoring its sweat-stained essence—Isham's essence. The unraveled fringes curled around her fingers and she recalled Isham's back-breaking labor, how he'd turned bramble-filled acres into fields of corn, potatoes, and onions. She looked about, surrounded by sacks and jars of life-giving sustenance. Her heart nearly burst with the wonder of what Isham had begun and she'd finished.

"This be *us* power," she whispered. "The land and what it give back to you. That where true power be." She plopped the hat on her head. "Isham, I too glad you ain't listen to my foolish talk. You been right all along—freedom ain't worth nothing if you can't *live* like it worth something." She cocked the old hat to the side, angled the brim and headed for the door. "White man say we free? I gwine find out fo' sho'!"

⎯⎯✦⎯✦⎯⎯

Philbrick always arrived at the tool shed before the workers, but this morning a worker was there waiting for him. "Morning Crecie," he said. "You're here bright and early—that's good."

She didn't return the greeting. "I come to pay you the two dollars, suh."

"Pay *me*! What on earth for?" He forced back an amused grin.

"The rent, suh." She extended the crumpled bills. "You say us who don't work fo' you must pay rent."

Philbrick scowled, ignoring the money. He needed all the hands working, especially skilled ones like Crecie. "Are you quitting?" he asked.

She nodded.

"Why? Because of Bentoo?"

"Naw suh." She lowered the money. "I ready to do something fo' self."

"And what might that something be?"

"I gwine take up vending, suh." She held out the money again.

"Vending! That's not steady work! Oh, none of you are dependable!" His face became a stone mask and he stood silent. Finally he said, "I see. Then your two dollars is not enough."

Her arm went limp at her side and she stared at the ground.

"Those acres you're farming at Possum Point—that's permissible only for those who work on a government plantation. You're no longer entitled to farm those acres."

Crecie suppressed a sly grin and looked up. Many of the islanders hired each other to work their crops, just as Isham had done when he took on Hamp and Titus. Knowing the government took months to pay, and the destitution Margaret and the others faced, she'd offered them a plan. "Oh, I know that suh. Them women you put in Bentoo's house—they yo' workers and they done took over them acres."

Philbrick immediately knew that Crecie, by turning her fields over to the women, had basically hired them. He snatched the money and stalked away, livid.

Crecie's plan was successful. While their mothers worked for Philbrick, Bentoo returned to the cabin each day to watch the children. After the women completed their tasks, one mother remained with the children, while the others tended Crecie's fields. She made sure no one went hungry and they all shared the harvest. It was in everyone's interest to combine forces.

It was a demanding pace, especially for Crecie, cooking late into the night and rising at dawn to get her goods to market. After vending, she canned fruits and vegetables and fashioned snakeskin products in the evening. In between, she helped care for the sick. Even with Bentoo and the children's help, the work was grueling.

━━━

It didn't take long for Crecie to develop a clientele at Hilton Head. The soldiers bought chow-chow, sweet potato pone, vegetables, and Randy's hot sauce daily, but still she worried. Her independence, the family's survival, depended on land that could be snatched at any moment. But the pride of knowing she owned her own labor, that whatever she earned was hers, brought renewed strength each day.

CHAPTER 52

MIDWAY MAKES ROOM

It was late afternoon and Crecie bustled about, packing goods for vending. "Randy, you got any mo' hot sauce fo' market tomorrow? Ain't but a few bottles left on the shelf."

Randy put the newspaper aside, Beaufort's *New South,* and glanced up. "You already sold what I made last week?"

"Just about." She eyed the rest of the goods. "We be a little low on chow-chow, too…and the snake-bone earrings. I can't make them things fast enough."

Randy chuckled. "You just can't account for what folks spend money on. I can see hot sauce and chow-chow—but earrings made out of snake bones?"

Crecie laughed. "Yeah; soldiers send 'em back home to they lady friends. They done take a liking to the belts and wallets, too."

"They make good souvenirs up north, I guess. Yeah, I got some hot sauce out in the shed." He paused and held up the paper. "But first, let me tell you what I re—."

"Halloo!" a voice shouted from the road.

Randy went to the door. "Crecie, that look like Frazier."

"What he want this time of day?" she said. "I got work to do."

Frazier, Philbrick's foreman, steered the wagon into the clearing. "Whoa!" he said, reining in the oxen.

They joined Frazier outside, surprised to see Margaret, Charlotte, Fatima, Medina, Yoruba, and the children huddled in the wagon. The women clutched their meager possessions and stoically stared out.

"What's this all about?" asked Randy.

"I know," said Crecie, looking up at Frazier. "Philbrick turn 'em out on account o' me, ain't it?"

"He ain't zactly say why," Frazier replied. "He just tell me to hire Edisto refugees because these women ain't strong enough to—."

"He lie on we!" said Margaret. "Us work fo' him *and* Crecie every day."

"Fo' true us work hard," said Charlotte. "And 'cept fo' Sunday, us ain't miss a day."

"I know that be the truth," said Frazier, "but him the boss and him tell me to take 'em to the contraband camp. But that place ain't fit fo' hogs, let alone people. That's why I bring 'em home to you."

Home? thought Crecie. *None of we got a toehold nowhere these days.*

She was right in her thinking. Now that Philbrick had replaced the mothers with other workers, Crecie lost access to Possum Point. The land that had provided sustenance and independence was no longer available for her use.

The Midway residents congregated around the wagon and the toddlers began to fidget, squirming to get out. The women looked to Crecie, uncertain of their next move.

"Don't worry," she reassured them. "Ya'll gwine be alright." *God see they get back home alive, He ain't gwine let 'em die in that camp.* Crecie faced her neighbors and addressed the women's homeless situation. She was careful not to accuse Philbrick, as the majority of the workers held him in high esteem. His stature had grown steadily as he maintained the schools and advanced his own money to cover the government's late payments. Pandering to the freedmen's want of manufactured goods, he kept the plantation stores well- stocked. As the end of the cotton harvest drew near, Philbrick had presented some of the workers with at least a yard or more of milled cloth. All except the malingering slackers were pleased with the windfall.

Crecie ended her appeal for the women with carefully chosen words. "Ya'll know these women born and raise right here on Ivy Oaks. They don't belong in no contraband camp with them outsiders. Us got to take care we own. Plenty folks living in my cabin, but we gwine make room fo' one, two, mo'. I know ya'll can find room in yo' heart to do the same."

Amos was first to step up. "You right, Crecie. They part o' we, close kin to some. Me, Dahlia, and us chillun gwine be packed tight, too, but Medina, you and yours welcome to live with we."

Medina, too relieved to speak, nodded. After handing her two children over to Dahlia, she climbed off the wagon and stood beside her benefactors.

Rosa Lee reached out to Charlotte. "Charlotte, you and yo' chillun can stay with me."

Charlotte grasped Rosa Lee's extended hand. "I too glad you take we in, cousin."

Within five minutes the other women and children had been given shelter and gone home with their sponsors.

Later that evening Bentoo led the family in prayer before they discussed solutions to their desperate situation.

"I hear it be a black woman name Harriet Tubman at the army hospital, could use some help," said Crecie. "I can work there fo' sho'."

"She the one they call Black Moses," said Margaret. "She done start a laundry at the contraband camp, washing fo' the soldiers. I gwine see if they need some mo' help."

"How the snake things selling, Crecie?" asked Bentoo. "I can help you make 'em."

"And I can work fulltime at the army camp," said Hamp. "Lots o' them officers be wanting they own manservant."

Randy had quietly listened, then he spoke. "I won't be so quick to count out us having a winter crop." He held up the newspaper. "It say here the tax commissions are in Beaufort, figuring out which plantations going to be put up for sale. If we pull together, maybe we can come up with enough to buy a few acres." He paused and addressed Crecie directly. "I mean, if that's alright with you, Crecie."

The blood rushed to Crecie's face and she felt ashamed, remembering her fierce objections when Randy had previously mentioned land ownership. She looked directly at her father, but her words were for everyone. "I want ya'll to know I be a change woman now. I ain't gwine argue against standing on my own no mo'. Tell us what you read about, Randy, so we know which way to turn. Us ain't gwine be free 'til us get we own land."

CHAPTER 53

THE TAX COMMISSIONERS

I t had been eight months since the initial group of abolitionists landed at Port Royal and many of the young people, homesick and isolated on outlying plantations, soon returned north. Several new faces had come and gone, but a core group remained. Buoyed by their weekly visits to Brick Church, they usually arrived early to collect their mail, socialize, and comment on the Negro worshipers' choice of Sunday attire.

Small clusters of Gideonites stood on the church grounds, enjoying the camaraderie and the late November morning. One trio's conversation centered on the Federal tax commissioners and the upcoming land auction.

"It was quite a task for just three commissioners," said Charles Ware, a Bostonian and Philbrick protégé. "But they researched those deeds in record time; the sale's already scheduled for February eleventh."

"They were locked away in the courthouse for a month," said Captain Hooper. "It's too bad they've divide the land in large lots, without set asides for the freedmen."

"No, that's good; very good!" Gannett exclaimed. "How damaging that would be, giving them land they haven't worked to acquire—they'll fail to appreciate it."

"I agree," remarked Ware. "I'd rather see them work for speculators before being handed anything."

"But speculators aren't concerned about the Negro's welfare,"
said Hooper.

"Oh, they couldn't treat the blacks any worse than the government has," said Ware. "Congress's bungling is the reason our cotton crop fell way short of last year's."

"Didn't we plant over 3,000 acres?" asked Hooper.

"Yes, but our yield was twenty-five percent less lint cotton per
acre; ninety thousand pounds less than last year's harvest," said
Gannett.

"The caterpillars got in the cotton, but apparently the Negroes
didn't," remarked Ware.

"No, let's be fair," said Hooper. "They wanted out of the cotton,
remember? And the way the treasury agents ridiculed them—and
us—well, that was hardly an incentive to good husbandry."

"I knew you'd make excuses for their indolence," Ware testily
replied.

"And don't forget the government's involvement," countered
Hooper, "or lack of it—low pay, late pay, and loads of red tape.
How could that encourage diligent free labor?"

"Ah, yes," said Ware, "but now that General *Saxton's* in charge
of Negro Affairs, and with *your* able assistance, I'm absolutely confident the free labor experiment will show a greater profit next
year."

Hooper flushed. "Say what you will—the low yield wasn't
the freedmen's fault. But your boss Philbrick's the new Cotton
Collection Agent; that makes *me* absolutely confident next year's
harvest will be a bountiful one. No matter what the figures in
Washington show, the first free labor crop was a dismal failure!"
He turned on his heels, heading for the church.

Hooper was right. The Port Royal experiment's first year *had* re-
sulted in a $75,000.00 government deficit. But Treasury Secretary
Chase buried the loss by combining the slave owners' 1861bumper

crop with the Gideonites' lesser harvest of 1862. He justified the mergers, stating that the hiring of Negroes as free laborers saved the 1861 crop. The subterfuge worked and Chase's *Congressional Farm Report* showed a $501,278.76 profit. His figures became the official reference for the Gideonites' first crop, motivating congressional approved for another year.

The men stared at Hooper's retreating figure. "Mmm," said Gannett, "I wonder what his old employer would say to that!"

"Pierce would be having a conniption over it...." Ware became silent as a wan young man walked up.

"Greetings, gentlemen," said Samuel Phillips.

"Sam!" Gannet exclaimed. "When did you return?"

"Two days ago. Of course Mother thought it was too soon, but I won out. I missed the islands; especially the children."

"And they missed you, too," came a voice from behind him. Laura Towne and another woman had quietly joined them.

"Oh, Miss Towne," said Ware. "Good morning."

"Good morning, gentlemen," she replied, and turned to the young Negro standing beside her. "This is Charlotte Forten, one of the new teachers; the Philadelphia AMA is sponsoring her."

"Forten?" said Gannett. "Any relation to Robert Forten?"

"Why, yes, he's my father," she replied. "Do you know him?"

"Only through his abolitionist work; William Lloyd Garrison and John Greenleaf Whittier often spoke highly of him—*and* your grandfather—James Forten."

Miss Forten smiled. "My father is zealous in the fight to end slavery—as was my grandfather; it's my family's legacy." Her speech indicated culture and refinement.

Phillips bowed slightly. "Welcome to St. Helena, Miss Forten. You'll be challenged but it will be worth it."

"Speaking of challenges," said Miss Towne, "how is your health?"

"Much improved," he said, taking her hand. "I never thanked you for nursing me through that horrid bout with malaria."

"Your recovery is all the thanks I need," she said. "You were so sick when you sailed for Boston. I...I only wish Mr. Barnard and the others could've pulled through; I did everything I could...."

"You did your best, Miss Towne," said Gannett. "Perhaps in this instance we all should've listened to the Negroes; heeded their warnings and gone away for the summer."

"Yes, perhaps," said Phillips.

The group stood quietly for a moment, then Miss Towne remarked, "Well, on to the latest news—the land auction. It's a pity the lots are so large. Without set asides the freed people are definitely excluded."

"That's the way it should be," said Ware.

"But why should—," Miss Towne began, but a gang of children interrupted her.

Leona led the way. "There him be!" she shouted. "I *told* ya'll Mr. Fill Up was gwine come back." The youngsters clamored around the young teacher and nearly cried for joy. Any further attempt at conversation was curtailed.

"Well, it seems I must now take my leave," said Phillips, allowing his frail body to be tugged toward the church where another group of enthusiastic students waited.

"I've never seen a teacher so beloved," remarked Miss Forten. "Hopefully, I will be so as well."

"I'm certain you will, dear," said Miss Towne. "But back to you, Mr. Ware; do you object to the freedmen owning land?"

"I'm certain they will eventually arrive at a point where they'll earn that right," he replied, "but for now, they need white men to carry them through. I've seen *some* improvement, but they still have a long way to go."

"I concur," said Gannett. "Without Yankee guidance it's questionable they'd ever become free laborers; certainly not under their old masters."

"Their emphasis is on sustenance farming, not cotton production," said Miss Towne. "And they need land for that."

"I beg to differ, Miss Towne," said Ware. "The more I work with these people, the more I'm convinced they should receive payment only for services actually performed. Under no circumstances should they be given anything. They're not yet responsible."

"Fortunately, General Saxton doesn't see it that way," she replied. "He feels the land should be preempted to the people, or else divided so that they can buy it. Hopefully he and Rev. French will succeed in their appeals to Congress."

"If they are appealing for Negro asides, that will be most *unfortunate*," said Gannett. "It's not—."

"Excuse me, Mr. Gannett," said Miss Forten. "May I speak? My people have suffered a ruthless system of injustice for hundreds of years. If any group is entitled to receive land, it is those who have toiled upon it with no reward."

"Miss Forten, perhaps you are unaware that Congress has appointed a Commission to address your concerns," said Gannett. "General Saxton has been instructed to investigate the character, ability, and prospects of the freed people. When more is known about their capacities, I'm sure the Negroes' needs will be addressed—which may or may not involve land."

"That proves my point: It is you, in part, who are responsible for the degradation of which they've been exposed, yet *their* character is to be investigated. Some members of your race continue to stand in the way of the Negro's progress—progress that necessitates land acquisition."

Miss Towne smiled broadly. "Well said, Miss Forten, well said. Now, gentlemen, off to church, shall we?"

CHAPTER 54
A WAY OUT OF NO WAY

It was early morning when Randy and Crecie arrived at the beach on Hilton Head. After he helped her set up, Randy left to do odd jobs at the telegraph office. She was soon busy, haggling with the soldiers as they put their best bartering skills to use. But the Northerners were no match for Crecie and the other astute island-ers, paying dearly for the small luxuries the Negroes provided.

Business was brisk. By noon, Crecie had sold everything. After furtively securing her earnings and packing up the utensils, she headed for the telegraph office to wait for Randy. She'd been too busy to notice the moon-faced white man across the way, his eyes frequently trained on her makeshift market.

The specially-built cart slid easily across the sand and Crecie was grateful Amos had fashioned it with runners. Deep in thought she was unaware of the man trailing her. *Soldiers want chow chow, okra soup, sweet potato pie—I can't make enough fo' 'em!* She sidestepped the incoming tide, and the man did the same, following her. *They buy earrings then no mo' that...they want things to eat. How I gwine make biddle with no land to grow crop?*

The stalker quickened his pace. When he'd narrowed the dis-tance, he shouted "Hey, you!" Crecie glanced back. Seeing a rotund man swiftly approach, she started to run. But the wet sand slowed her down. The man's shouts grew louder—he was gaining on her. She made a frantic effort to outrun him, but tripped in the sand. The cart overturned and he was instantly upon her. Terrified, she peered up at his flushed, puffy face.

"Please, suh…," she begged.

"Don't be scared." He smiled, revealing a wide gap. "I've been trying to find you for almost a year now." He extended his hand. "Here, let me help you up."

She shook her head, refusing his offer. "Find *me*?" she asked.

"You make items out of snake leather, don't you?" He kept his hand out.

She ignored it, struggling up on her own. "Yes suh, I make 'em." She brushed the sand from her face and, sneaking a closer, suddenly recognized him. "It be *you*—you give me the food." It was the vendor who'd made the trade with her nearly a year ago. "That been such a blessing Mista….."

"Smiley. Arthur Smiley."

"Thank you, Mista Smiley. You snatch my lil' boy from death door."

Smiley nodded. "You're welcome, er—what's *your* name?"

"Crecie, suh." She began gathering her utensils.

"Glad I could help you, Crecie." He picked up a pot and handed it to her. "You know, that pouch and belt we traded…soldiers in all the camps want to know where they can buy trinkets like that."

"I know, suh. I do sell a lot o' them. Soldiers send 'em back home, up North."

"And I want to make sure they *keep* sending them. Do you have enough snake leather on hand, can you make a few dozen wallets and things for me?"

"Yes suh; I do."

"Good! I'll buy all you can make; pay you three cents for each item. How many can you bring me?"

"Many as you want, suh. Only thing, it gwine cost you same as what soldiers pay—five cents and up. I ain't working fo' free no more."

The vendor smiled. "Fair enough. Bring some samples tomorrow and we'll work out the particulars."

"Yes suh. I be right here on this beach tomorrow."

⚔

As Randy rowed back to St. Helena, he listened to Crecie prattle about Smiley, glad that at least *she* had some good news.

"He gwine sell all my...my—what he call 'em—trinkets?"

Randy nodded.

"Anyway, with him buying so many, that'll help we scrape up more money to buy a few acres. How much us done aside?"

He'd been dreading that question. "Twenty-one dollars and some change, but that ain't the worse of it. The Tax Commissioners won't be selling the land in small parcels—they're selling in big lots, starting at 320 acres."

"Three hundred and twenty acres! Where we gwine get *that* kind o' money?"

"No place I know of," he said.

"Maybe the gov'ment can...," she began, but stopped, remembering Isham's murder and the soldiers' free reign. "No...gov'ment ain't gwine help we. Besides, here it is December and they still owe *me* fo' working July and August."

"You and everybody else."

"But they ought to be paying soon; that'll put a little clink in everybody pocket." She looked out over the grassy waters, thinking. "Maybe that's what us at Midway can do—put we little money together and try to buy one o' them big lots. It'll be a start. Ax 'em about it, Randy."

"*Me?* You thought of it—you ask them."

"They ain't gwine listen to me."

"They took in Medina and the others when you asked them. Put it before them, they might do it."

"Gov'ment ought o' just let we work the land and pay for it lil' by lil'…like Philbrick do at the plantation store."

"That'd be too much like *right!*" said Randy.

"You know, all these white folks say they come to help we, but seem mo' like us helping *them*, working cotton same as ever. Now us get chance fo' own land, but they muddy the water.…" She watched a seagull swoop down, then take to the sky, clutching a fish in its beak. "Seem like *somebody* ought o' help we."

They were entering the shallows when the idea came to her: "Mr. Fobs! What about axing him? I bet he got mo' money than the gov'ment."

"Yeah, you might be right about that. I'll ask Laura Townes to write him."

"They still don't know you can read and write?" she asked.

"That ain't their business," Randy replied, approaching the St. Helena shoreline.

"Well, *somebody* ought o' write him. He get Sham free, it be worth a try to see if—." She stopped short, recognizing a little figure on the landing. Leona stood between Miss Towne and Charlotte Forten. "Hurry up, Randy," said Crecie. "Something done happen—I feel it."

She jumped from the boat before he had a chance to tie it up. "What be wrong?" she asked Miss Towne. Crecie reached for Leona, all the while inspecting for blood.

"I have some sad news," said Miss Towne. "Very sad. Mr. Phillips died this morning."

"Oh, no," cried Crecie. She pulled her daughter close, peering into her eyes. "How you doing, Leona?"

The teary-eyed child looked up, but said nothing.

"I ax you, Leona. How you feel?"

The child opened her mouth, but it seemed as if she was gasping for breath, no words came out.

Crecie looked to Miss Towne. "Wh—what wrong? Why she ain't saying nothing?"

"I...we don't know," Miss Forten answered. "When we told the children of Mr. Phillip's passing, Leona fainted. When she came to, well...she's not said a word since."

Crecie had never encountered a freeborn black, and had not known what to make of the new teacher—a Negro who acted and talked like white folks. She directed her question to Miss Towne. "How long it been since she talk?"

"Hours ago," Miss Forten answered.

"Hours! Oh no, that ain't like her." Crecie grabbed the girl by the shoulders, shaking her. "Say something! Why you not talk?"

"What's going on?" asked Randy, joining the group.

No one answered. He looked questioningly to Miss Towne and she explained the recent events. "She's just in shock, Crecie," he said. Draping his arm around Leona's shoulder, he led her toward the wagon. "She'll be fine after we get her home."

But Leona was not fine. She remained mute, resorting to pointing and gestures.

CHAPTER 55

AT YEAR'S END

The children had strewn greenery and late-blooming wildflowers about the casket, paying tribute to Samuel Phillips. Now they solemnly sat, listening as Rev. French delivered the eulogy.

"Samuel Phillips was a religious young man," he said, "a devout Episcopalian who never boasted about his beliefs…he lived them. This past autumn he went home for a vacation; though still ailing, he rushed back to see about you, those he called his people."

He paused, looking over the mourners packed in Brick Church. "His students never tired of praising his good deeds, telling of all he did for them; providing precious books and slates, patiently bequeathing knowledge. All of the superintendents generously made time for teaching, but none were as generous as he."

Crecie glanced at Leona. Tears streamed down the child's face, but no sound escaped her lips.

"Recently," continued Rev. French, "I inquired of the more advanced students who was it that taught them their letters. Most responded, 'Mista Fill Up'."

Leona pressed her mother's hand and Crecie quickly pressed back, hoping to hear a word—a grunt even. But there was nothing.

"Sam Phillips was a considerate, well-mannered humanitarian," said Rev. French. "A young man who possessed a kind heart, who loved his work and loved you. He never returned to perfect health, but you diligently nursed him during his sickness, tending to his every need. Your love for him was complete, as was his love for you.

"Though his remains will be returned to his bereaved family in Boston, his gentle, compassionate spirit will forever be here, on St. Helena."

The mourners filed past the coffin, grief-stricken; but Crecie saw hope in this final act. She and the family had done everything they could to help Leona—cajoled, threatened, pleaded—but could not break her silence. She grasped the girl's hand and led her to the casket. "Say 'bye to Mista Fill Up," she gently urged. The child opened her mouth, her lips quivered, but she could not utter a sound.

An unbearable helplessness came upon Crecie and she began to wail in angry frustration. Leona snatched her hand away and ran to Bentoo. Hagar, standing near, whispered loud enough for those around to hear. "See! Ain't I tell ya'll—Crecie be crazy—and her girl, too. Hoodoo! Somebody done rooted she fo' sho!"

Crecie fell to her knees, grieving not so much for the dead as for her mute child. The people continued to pay final respects to the dearly departed Mr. Phillips, stepping around Crecie as she knelt before the casket.

Crecie, like Hagar, had not dismissed the possibility of hoodoo, and put forth a counter attack, forcing Leona to drink bitter teas, pray before a makeshift altar, and wear a seashell amulet around her neck. Fearing some new calamity might befall her daughter, she rarely allowed Leona out of her sight, insisting the girl sit near as she fashioned the snakeskin trinkets. Crecie knew she should go to Hilton Head and meet with Smiley, but she couldn't bear to leave Leona—not even for a day.

But Leona had lost her voice, not her mettle, and after two weeks of her mother's constant scrutiny, she became irascible. Crecie finally decided to heed Bentoo's advice and let Leona attend school, now housed at Brick Church, but she went with her.

When they got there, Crecie sat on a nearby stump, watching Leona run into the building. Miss Forten, Mr. Phillips' replacement, had not yet arrived. Jerome, Hagar's ten-year-old son, stood in front of the class, pretending to be the teacher.

"Alright students," he said, pointing to a map of the United States, "what be the name o' this island?"

The children giggled and responded in unison. "St. Helena," they yelled.

"And what be the name o' this state?"

"South Carolina!"

"What be the name o' this country?"

"The United States of…."

Leona burst in and a hush fell over the room. The children stared then began to mock the fish-like puckering of her silent lips. Jerome snickered and pointed the yardstick at her. "What be she name?"

A boy yelled, "She name Fish Mout'!" Leona jumped on him like white on rice. They were tussling in earnest when Miss Forten, followed by Crecie, rushed into the room. The teacher rapped on the desk for order and Crecie grabbed her daughter's arm. "Come on, we gwine go home!"

"Please wait," said Miss Forten. "I—."

Crecie brushed pass her, headed for the door. But two men, lugging an upright piano into the church, blocked her way.

"Where you want we to put it, Miz Charlut?" one of the men asked.

"There, at the front of the church."

The entry cleared and Crecie started out. But Leona held back. She, along with the others, was fascinated by the piano.

Miss Forten sat on the piano bench and the children gathered around, singing as she played. Leona stood beside Crecie, looking on. Her eyes filled with longing, but the words remained locked in her mind's memory.

Miss Forten noticed the forlorn little face and called to her. "Come, Leona. Sit with me on the bench." She didn't have to ask twice; Leona quickly wiggled in beside her.

"Would you like to play a song?" the teacher asked.

The child bobbed her head. Miss Forten pressed a key, directing Leona to do the same. In no time at all, they were playing a two-finger duet. The others looked on, amazed. They applauded when Miss Forten led Leona in a bow, content to be her friend again because *she* knew how to play the piano.

"It's time for school," said Miss Forten. The students hurried to their seats, but Leona remained on the bench. She looked as if she wanted to stay there forever. Crecie went outside and sat on the stump to wait.

"I have another surprise," the teacher announced. "My friend, John Greenleaf Whittier, is a poet who once lived in Philadelphia—."

"That be in Pennsylvania," a student proudly volunteered. "Mr. Fill Up teach us that."

"Yes, very good....Well now, I asked Mr. Whittier to write something special for our Christmas program, and he did! The title is "His People Are Free." Listen as I read it to you."

"Oh, none in all the world before
Were ever glad as we.
We're free on Carolina's shore;
We're all at home and free!
Thou friend and helper of the poor,
Who suffered for our sake,
To open every prison door
And every yoke to break,
Look down, O Savior, sweet and mild,
To help us sing and pray;
The hands that blessed the little child

Upon our foreheads lay.
Today in all our fields of corn,
No driver's whip we hear,
The holy day that saw Thee born
Was never half so dear.
The very oaks are greener clad,
The waters brighter smile,
Oh, never shone a day so glad
In sweet St. Helen's Isle.
For none in all the world before
Were ever glad as we.
We're free on Carolina's shore;
We're all at home and free!"

"Wasn't that lovely?" she asked.

"Yes ma'am," they chimed.

"The program will be held Christmas Day. If you'd like to take part, raise your hand."

All hands went up immediately. "Me! Me! I do!" the students exclaimed.

"Good. The poem will be sung to the tune of "I Will Believe", which you know already. And we've been practicing the Christmas carols…all you need to do is memorize the poem. Oh, I'll be playing the piano."

"Yea-a-a!" shouted the children.

Leona slid from the bench and walked slowly outside to Crecie. She threw her arms around her mother's neck. "I gwine be in the Christmas program," she said softly.

The words rolled like thunder, yet Crecie doubted her ears. Holding Leona at arm's length, she stared at the girl's pouty little mouth. "S-say again," she uttered.

"I gwine sing in the—."

"Oh, praise God!" Crecie exclaimed, pulling her daughter close. "Thank you, Jesus, thank you!"

Leona wholeheartedly set out to memorize the poem, and Crecie, assured that her child was herself again, returned to vending. Two weeks had gone by since the aborted meeting with Smiley. Reluctant to ask his whereabouts, she kept a watchful eye, but there was no sign of the vendor.

≌ ≍

The church had been beautifully decorated for the program. A wreath of red holly and broad leaves adorned the pulpit. Little American flags, encircled in greenery, were attached to the walls and the words to John Greenleaf Whittier's poem hung opposite the pulpit. The teachers wore black skirts and blue garibaldi blouses; the gilded shoulder buttons sparkled as they bustled about with last minute arrangements.

Dressed in their best, and eager to entertain the audience, the students tried not to fidget. Lieutenant Colonel Liberty Billings, a Unitarian minister in the First Regiment South Carolina Volunteers, spoke of the coming Emancipation Proclamation Day, January 1, but the children were too excited to pay much attention. Miss Forten spoke of her friendship with Whittier and the poem he'd written especially for the school. The poem, "His People Are Free", was the finale and the young voices harmonized the words and music to perfection. The students bowed to a standing ovation. But the best was yet to come when the teachers surprised them with gifts of clothing.

Hearing Leona sing, Crecie's joy was boundless. *I get the best gift of all,* she thought.

≌ ≍

It was the last week of 1862 and as Crecie vended on Hilton Head, she kept looking for Smiley. One day as she was packing up to go home, a young soldier from Vermont, a regular customer walked up. She dared to ask him about Smiley.

"It's been a few weeks since I last saw him," he answered. "Probably moved on to another camp."

"When he be back?" she asked.

The man held up a jar of pickled okra, a taste he'd acquired upon coming south. "Is this all you have left?"

"Yes suh, but I got fine wallets and belts right here."

"Nope; okra's all I want." He handed her the money. "He most likely won't be back until next year—the end of February, first of March."

"B-but that be two mont's from now."

"He covers a lot of territory, even Florida. What do you need? Maybe another sulter has it."

"No, nothing, suh," she muttered, turning away. "I thank ya, though."

CHAPTER 56

WATCH NIGHT

It was early afternoon when Crecie returned from vending. Bentoo and Margaret, doing laundry, looked up and waved. But Crecie ignored them and hurried inside. Bentoo thrust a basket of wet clothes toward Margaret. "Here, hang this up; I be back d'rectly."

"Yes'um, Aunt Benny," she said, taking the basket.

Crecie was standing at the medicine table when Bentoo walked in.

"How everything be today?" asked Bentoo. "You sell a lot o' them snake things?"

Crecie nodded.

"Then what be wrong?" asked Bentoo.

The young woman pressed her hands against her temples. "Everything. Smiley gone; ain't coming back 'til the end o' Feb'rary—*after* the sale."

Bentoo pulled a chair out from the table. "Here, sit."

But Crecie didn't move. Bentoo put some white, grainy powder in a jar, added water, and stirred. "Here, drink this," she said.

Crecie sloshed the contents then swallowed. "Phew!" she said.

Bentoo sat down in the rocker. "Your head gwine feel better now. It get to hurting every time you get to worrying."

"Can't do nothing but worry, the way things be; ain't hardly room to breathe in this cabin, let alone sleep—and there be ten mout's to feed."

"Worry ain't gwine put one crumb in nobody mout'," said Bentoo.

"There be another worry, too—only God know who gwine buy this plantation in Feb'rary."

Bentoo looked up sharply. "Thank God ain't none o' *we* gwine be on the auction block."

Crecie rushed to her grandmother's side. "Oh, Bentoo, I too sorry." She knelt beside the chair. "I...I ain't mean to open up that wound."

Bentoo looked away. "But you did."

January 1, a day the slaves referred to as Heartbreak Day, was the source of that wound. Centering on the planters' custom of adjusting their accounts at the end of the year, the beginning of the new year could be devastating for the enslaved. If the year had been profitable, the plantation's structure and operation remained unchanged. But if the planter had suffered a loss, then farm equipment, along with slaves and livestock, were sold to satisfy debts. On the night of December 31, the enslaved secretly huddled in cabins, praise houses, bush hollows, warily watching the old year go out, praying the master's house would be in order when the new year came in.

Bentoo stared at her clasped hands. "Heartbreak Day gwine stay with me 'til the day I die."

Crecie, familiar with the story, waited quietly.

"Old man Boson been a hard gambling man," said Bentoo, "and we know things ain't been right when he sell off some plows and such. Then at the end o' the week, him and the slave trader come out to the quarters. They come to my cabin. Randy been a lil' thing, crawling on the floor. I scoop he up, hold 'em tight in my arms. I ain't know who massa come fo'—me, Tom, or the baby—but I start screaming and begging, 'Please, suh! No, no!' But he sell Tom anyway."

A lone tear slid down her grandmother's cheek and Crecie wiped it away. "I know, Bentoo, I know," she consoled.

"Tom go, humble-like. But he eye tell me everything him feel inside. I never see he no mo'—him just gone, gone…."

"But change done come," said Crecie. "Ain't that what you tell me?" She patted her grandmother's hand and stood up.

"Yeah, you right," said Bentoo, managing a little smile.

"And I gwine say a different prayer at Watch Night tonight; one I never had cause to say befo'."

Neither woman noticed Randy had walked up to open shutter. "BOO!" he yelled.

"Oh Randy!" exclaimed Crecie.

"Why you sneak up on we?" said Bentoo, clutching her chest.

He grinned and came inside. "You shoulda been watching." He glanced at the hearth. "Any food ready?"

Bentoo stood, her mood brightened. "I gwine chunk-up the fire, make some bittle fo' you."

"That's good by me." He sat down at the table. "So…Crecie, what kind of different prayer you're saying tonight?"

"Fo' Rev. French and General Saxton to help we get land."

"Yeah, that's different, alright."

"You hear from Mr. Fobs yet?"

"Not a word—unless he wrote Miss Laura and she didn't tell me."

"No, she would o' say if she did. Lots o' them abolition folks helping, but us got to do fo' self, too,"

"Well, if you make one step, God'll make two…so they tell me," said Randy.

"Only step I can think of is axing them Midway folks to put we money together."

"Tonight will be a good time, at the Watch Night meeting."

"Sho you right, Randy. Ax 'em!"

"Oh no, I already told you I'm not gonna do that. Besides, I'm helping Titus and his regiment; they roasting ten oxen for General Saxton's Emancipation Day to-do."

"You helping with *that*? You ain't do nothing fo' the Fourth o' July—ain't even go to the celebration."

"Oh, this is different—that was for the white folks; this one belong to us."

"What us celebrating fo'; us already free. 'Mancipation ain't gwine bring land with it. I ain't even gwine go."

Bentoo placed a steaming bowl of stewed mullet and a tin pan of hoecake on the table.

"Hot food fo' a hungry man," she announced.

"It smell good," he said, diving in. "Taste good, too." He turned to Crecie. "That's left up to you if you don't go. Emancipation's not about the government giving us land—it's about the freedom to get it on our own."

Bentoo stood at the table. "You know, Crecie, Titus gwine be drilling with the South Carolina Vols."

"Uh-huh," she replied. "Maybe I go just to see Titus. Right now I got to think on what I gwine say tonight."

Crecie walked into the praise house and, upon seeing all the people, felt a glimmer of hope. She felt even better, noting Hagar was not among them.

Mose began the meeting, leading the people in song. Many of them gave testimony, looking on the past year with thanksgiving. A soldier from Saxton's new regiment preached, reminding everyone that this night marked a declaration of freedom, the first

Freedom's Eve. At eleven-thirty they all went to their knees, preparing to usher in the new year.

As over four million enslaved people across the South bowed their heads, Watch Night prayers took on new meaning. Some prayed softly, others whispered, and many prayed out loud—a cacophony of fervent voices thanking God for His faithfulness, that freedom was on the horizon, and families would no longer be torn apart.

CHAPTER 57
CRECIE MAKES AN APPEAL

The people were still on their knees when the plantation yard bell heralded in 1863. Crecie, intent on seeking support to buy land, arose and stood at the moss-covered altar. She was surprised to see Hagar had slipped in, sitting right up front. Ignoring the woman's intense stare, she began to appeal to the people, hoping they would favor what she had to say.

"If Rev. French and them can't get the gov'ment to set land aside fo' we, us need be ready to get us own." She searched their bland faces for a reaction; seeing none, she pressed on.

"Ya'll know lots o' them missionaries fighting hard for we to be freeholders, but us got to jine in the fight. If us put we lil' money together, when the time come fo' bid, us can have we say, too. What ya'll say to that?"

When no one responded, Margaret spoke up. "I say we go along with Crecie; won't hurt to try."

Frazier, Philbrick's foreman, stood in the rear. "Buying land— that may be the thing fo' you, Crecie—but I don't want no part o' it. I satisfied making a wage…and from the looks o' the rest o' you, ya'll satisfied, too."

The people nodded, proud of their new possessions. The Gideonites had established five plantation stores across the islands, offering credit at each. The freed people sported new bonnets, store-bought shirts, and factory-made shoes. The hated slave cloth was replaced with milled fabric; goods made in the industrialized north—clocks, dishes, forks, and candles—were treasures in their lowly homes. The teachers, doubling as shopkeepers, were hard-pressed to keep up with the demand for goods. Within the year, the workers at Ivy Oaks had purchased more than $800 in products and $300 in clothing.

Crecie smoothed the front of her homespun dress, scrunching her toes in Isham's old brogans. "All o' we don't want wage-labor or new-fangle things, Frazier." Then she addressed the crowd. "Well, what ya'll want to do—work fo' wage or work yo' own land?"

A nervous cough was the only response.

Then Amos walked up to the front. "I got to have my say. I know why they ain't talking, Crecie, and it ain't 'cause they don't *want* land—it be 'cause they ain't got no chink to put in the pile."

"No, Amos," said Crecie, "the gov'ment come up with the money; Philbrick just pay all o' we back wage—I get eight dollars myself."

"Yeah, but you ain't turn right around and pay the store."

Crecie addressed the people. "That be true?"

Most turned away, not answering.

"They ain't gwine say, so I gwine say for 'em," Amos proclaimed. "They ain't got two cents to rub together."

"That ain't yo' worry about what folks got," Frazier shouted. "People work hard, worthy o' whatever they want."

"Yeah," a man rejoined. "It left up to *we* how to spend we money."

"And I gwine spend it the way *I* see fit," a woman said.

"*All* o' ya'll ain't nothing but fools!" Amos retorted. "You spending the way Philbrick see fit."

"Hold on," said Frazier. "Ain't no call talking about Mr. Philbrick like that, after all he done fo' we. Besides, *you* work at the army camp—not Ivy Oaks. Mr. Philbrick be a good man to work fo'."

"You right, Frazier," said Crecie. "He be a good man to work *fo'*...but I want to work fo' *me*—Crecie!"

Amos stood beside Crecie. "And I aim to work fo' *Amos*. Me and Dahlia adding what lil' us got to the land pot."

"I ain't got much, either," said Rosa Lee, "but I putting in, too."

"Ya'll can follow Crecie if you want to," said Frazier, "but now ain't time to buy land—you need to wait, learn how to work fo' a living!"

All eyes transfixed on Frazier, and the word *work* hung in the air. Then the room erupted in laughter. When the guffaws subsided, Bentoo caught her breath, saying, "Learn how to *work?* Thank ya, son—you make a good joke!"

"But what I *mean* to say was, free labor be the—." Frazier looked into the bemused faces. "Aw, to hell with all o' ya'll," he growled, stamping out.

Margaret, still grinning, asked, "How much money we gwine need, Crecie?"

"I ain't fo' sho, but according to Randy, us need three hundred fifty or mo'."

"Dollars?" Margaret quickly sobered. "That be a lot o' money to come up with...."

"In a lil' bit o' time," Yoruba added.

Crecie moved to the center of the group. "Now ya'll just hold on—remember how hard us work fo' massa and fo' Philbrick—ain't none o' that kill we; working fo' self ain't gwine kill we neither."

"That ain't no lie," said Mose. "You know, maybe them at Slave Row will put in with we. They doing that at the Taylor plantation—putting they money together."

"And us gwine do it at Ivy Oaks," said Crecie. "Give all us can, make a sac-a-fice. Amos can hold the money and Bentoo can keep account, write yo'—."

Everyone in the room gasped. Charlotte jumped to her feet. "Write!" she exclaimed. "Bentoo can write?"

"And read, too," Bentoo said, chuckling.

"That be what I trying to say," said Crecie, "times done change— us ain't got to hide no mo'. Now *all* o' we can get educate, get we own land. Bentoo gwine keep up with what you put in, and Amos gwine keep watch over it."

"Who gwine watch over Amos?" Hagar demanded.

"You putting in?" snapped Crecie.

"Well…yeah; much as I hate to say, yo' plan got some strength behind it."

Crecie stared at her, flabbergasted. "Wonders never cease," she mumbled.

⊷⊶

For the contraband of Port Royal, Lincoln's proposed signing of the Emancipation Proclamation signaled the legal end of en-slavement; but other than that, nothing else would change much. They'd lived as a freed people for over a year, ever since the Big Gun Shoot in November, 1861. Their hopes had been sustained by General Hunter's failed attempt at emancipation. Thousands of adults were learning to read and the children were in school, ensuring literacy for coming generations. The people freely chose their own labor, earned money, and to some extent, charted their own course.

Hunter's aborted regiment became part of the First South Carolina Volunteers, a legitimate unit of the newly formed United States Colored Troops. The men flourished under the leadership of Colonel Thomas Wentworth Higginson, a Boston abolitionist, hand-picked for the post. Volunteers from Georgia, Florida, and South Carolina descended on Port Royal by the thousands, and another Negro regiment—the Second South Carolina Volunteers—was created.

As the once enslaved Sea Islanders greeted January 1, 1863, they already felt free, ready to move forward.

CHAPTER 58
JANUARY 1, 1863

President Lincoln had announced the Preliminary Emancipation Proclamation in September, offering the Confederate States a chance to reenter the Union by January 1, 1863, or else the final Emancipation Proclamation to free slaves in many of the states would go into effect. The Confederacy refused, and on January 1, 1863, abolitionists in major Northern cities filled huge assembly halls, awaiting news the president had signed the proclamation.

Boston

Messengers lined the street leading from the telegraph office to Tremont Temple Baptist Church, ready to relay news that a copy of the Emancipation Proclamation had been sent. Many in the integrated audience had waited all day, but when light faded into dusk, and dusk into darkness with still no word, their hopes began to wane.

Frederick Douglass arrived at Tremont in the early evening, joining another former fugitive, William Wells Brown, on the stage. During the first hour, they and other platform guests delivered speeches to the enthusiastic, yet restless audience. Nine o'clock came and no news arrived. The crowd's ardor began to fade. Douglass, along with Brown, a prolific novelist, orator, and playwright, continued with speeches and songs, hoping to bolster the throng. At 10 o'clock, and still no word, an elderly lady loudly proclaimed, "He's not going to sign it." Douglass refuted her words, saying, "Abraham Lincoln may be slow; Abraham Lincoln may desire peace, even at the price of leaving our terrible national sore untouched, to fester for generations, but Abraham Lincoln is not the man to reconsider, retract and contradict words and purposes solemnly proclaimed over his own signature."

But when another hour elapsed, Douglass also began to doubt, remembering the threat of Union soldiers to throw down their weapons before they'd fight to set Negroes free. Democrats had won seven November state elections, including Illinois. Kentucky's legislators vowed the Border States would leave the Union if the President signed the decree.

Douglass worried that conservative Republicans had pressured Lincoln to abort the Proclamation. He leaned in and whispered to Brown, "I wish Lincoln had made the Preliminary Proclamation effective in September instead of this long, conditional wait."

"So do I," said Brown. "But Lincoln's party, as far as emancipation goes, is like Jacob serving Laben for Rachel. Hopefully we don't wake up one morning to find we have Leah."

"The suspense is painful," he muttered, slumping back in his chair.

The abolitionists may have doubted Lincoln's intentions, but the rebels were convinced the Proclamation was a done deal that would create disturbances among the blacks. Confederate soldiers wrote to their superiors, begging leave to go home and protect their families. "The Negroes are making their brags," they'd written, "saying that by January 1 they'll be as free as we are." Indeed, the grapevine *had* alerted slaves all across the South that the Proclamation existed and they were confident it would be issued as promised.

Washington City

On January 1, President Lincoln awoke to a dry, sunlit morning; but his arduous agenda held no cheer. His day had begun early, with a contentious meeting between General Burnside, General Halleck, and War Secretary Stanton. Lincoln's previous attempt to resolve differences between the men had required his utmost diplomacy, and he'd manage to keep the war on track. But not today. After hours of discussion, nothing had been resolved. The meeting ended at nine a.m., as argumentative as it had begun. The parties left in a huff, agreeing only to meet again later that day.

The president turned to the next thing on his agenda—the Emancipation Proclamation. He reviewed its wordings, meticulously including his Cabinet's suggestions. After fine-tuning the document, he sent it to the State Department for the official calligraphy.

At ten forty-five, as Lincoln dressed for the Executive Mansion's traditional New Year's Day Reception, Secretary of State William Seward delivered the Proclamation. After he'd hastily signed it, the superscription caught the president's eye: *In testimony whereof I have hereunto set my name and caused the seal of the United States to be affixed.*

"Seward," he said, "I don't like the word *name* here; that's more fitting for a treaty than a presidential proclamation."

"I agree," Seward replied. "It's a pity we didn't notice it before."

"Substitute *hand* for *name*; I think that will be more appropriate."

Just then a presidential aide entered the room. "It's eleven o'clock, sir. The guests are arriving."

"I'll have the Proclamation redone," said Seward. "It'll be ready when you return."

"Thank you," said Lincoln, hurrying downstairs to his next executive duty. He wouldn't be able to sign the document until after the reception.

Lincoln greeted his cabinet, the generals, and foreign diplomats in the Blue Room. They left at noon, when it was time for the public hordes to arrive. As the Marine band played, the dictates of protocol kept him shaking hands for three hours.

It was past two o'clock when he returned to the Cabinet Room. The Proclamation was spread out on the desk and Seward stood nearby, waiting. Lincoln sat down, his hand so tired he could barely hold the pen.

"I've been greeting callers and shaking hands since seven o'clock this morning," he said, "my arm is stiff. But this signature will be looked at very closely; if they decide my hand trembled, they will say 'he had some *compunction*'. But anyway, it is going to be done." Then he slowly and carefully wrote his name at the bottom of the Proclamation. "I never was so certain in my life that I was doing right by signing this paper." The signature turned out to be uncharacteristically firm and bold. He looked up, smiling. "That will do," he said.

Lincoln had made no effort to be ceremonial that day. He didn't convene his Cabinet and no delegations of abolitionists or Negroes were present; he'd visited no slave family, nor did he make a speech. A few staff members wandered into the room—curious witnesses to history.

After Seward signed his name, the document was taken to the State Department where the great seal was affixed and duplicates made. The Emancipation Proclamation was then deposited in the Government Archives and copies given to the press. But Lincoln's day was far from over.

The act to admit West Virginia into the Union was waiting for his signature, as well as an agreement to provide a freedmen's colony on an island near Haiti. Then there was the meeting with the delegation of anti-slavery leaders, demanding that the Proclamation be issued as an act of justice rather than a military measure. Another meeting with Burnside, Halleck, and Stanton was of utmost importance. His *day* extended far into the night.

It was late when Lincoln made his regular visit to the War Department's telegraph room. A young telegraph operator, Edward Rosewood, greeted him then hurried back to his work. Curious, the President went over to see what he was sending out. It was the Emancipation Proclamation. He watched for a few minutes then calmly strolled over to his favorite chair, the place he'd written most of the Preliminary Proclamation, and propped his feet on the desk. It was, for him, the end of a long, satisfying day.

Boston

It was almost midnight when a messenger ran into Tremont Temple shouting, "It's on the wires! It's coming!" The audience went wild as the cheers of three thousand shook the hall. All kinds of emotions immediately went into play—tears, praises, hysterical sobs and joyful shouts.

The printed document arrived and the pandemonium quieted down. Douglass addressed the crowd after the Proclamation was read. "I am glad the people of the country are finding out that the color of a man's skin does not disqualify him from being a citizen of the United States. The Emancipation Proclamation has changed the war from mere strife for territory and dominion, into a contest of civilization against barbarism. I rejoice in the deliverance of our race from bondage."

Caught up in the euphoria, Douglass initially only saw the Proclamation's antislavery side. Later, upon closer examination, he realized the document's authority was limited to geographical and military boundaries and the abolition of slavery was presented as a military necessity to save the Union. But Douglass was not dismayed, saying, "I approve the spur-wisdom of Paddy, who thought if he could get one side of his horse to go, he could trust the speed of the other side to follow."

Although the Emancipation Proclamation did not actually free slaves in the Confederate-held states and did not address slavery in the loyal Border States, it did have three positive effects: First, Union-held lands were free-soil country and the army was legally bound to maintain freedom within them. Next, the edict demonstrated to the world that the United States was committed to the rights of labor and to ending slavery. Finally, nearly all blacks regarded the document as an official declaration of liberation, inspiring thousands to flee the plantations, putting their much-needed labor at the Union's disposal. The foundation of slavery's peculiar institution rapidly began to crumble.

CHAPTER 59

EMANCIPATION
PROCLAMATION DAY

Millions of people enslaved throughout the Confederacy secretly welcomed in the New Year by declaring their freedom. But secrecy was not the order for the contrabands on the Sea Islands, especially not at Port Royal.

General Saxton had planned a grand Emancipation Day celebration for thousands of people, providing roasted oxen, hard bread, and barrels of molasses. There was even tobacco, fermented vinegar, and pounds of ginger for the adults. Two steamboats and the general's personal craft, *The Flora*, ferried hundreds of sojourners to Beaufort, then scores of rowboats took them over to Camp Saxton. A beautiful grove of live oaks adjacent to the camp served as the celebration site.

Crecie and her family arrived early, choosing a spot under an expansive moss-draped oak. Stout branches formed the tree's canopy—spiraling into a twisted, helter-skelter maze. Its limbs, gnarled by the weight of centuries, ran parallel to the ground. The children were immediately drawn to it, clambering over the low-hanging boughs.

Hamp helped Crecie spread the quilt. "Me and Sham gwine go find Titus and Randy," he said. "They at one o' the roasting pits—I just got to find which one."

"Come let we know when you do," said Crecie.

"Yeah, and keep a good watch on Sham," said Bentoo. "Everybody gwine be jam-up under these trees."

The women and children settled in. Willie straddled a tree limb, fascinated by the cavalry as it circled the grove's wide perimeter. Ossie and Louise darted around the oak's massive trunk, and Leona sat on the quilt, trying to decipher a printed program someone had given her.

The army band played lively tunes as the ragged runaways and better-clad islanders filled the spaces under the trees. A number of white people sat in the shade or remained perched in their carriages.

Crecie watched the crowd then turned to Bentoo. "Anybody put money in the pot yet?" she asked.

"A few, but us ain't gwine worry about that today. Look," she said, pointing to the women's brightly colored head wraps. "I ain't never seen nothing pretty as that."

Leona had figured out the program's purpose. "Ma, this paper tell what we gwine see. The first thing be—."

"Hush!" Crecie admonished. "Let it come just so."

"I just gwine read you *one* lil' bitty thing," Leona insisted.

"You ain't got to," said Bentoo, eyeing the dignitaries seated on the platform. "Somebody already standing up to do something."

But Leona would not be silenced and hurriedly scanned the program. "That be Rev. Fowler," she whispered. "He gwine say the prayer."

Crecie sighed as she and Bentoo exchanged knowing glances. Sure enough, Leona continued to announce each item on the program: the reading of a poem, General Saxton's speech, Colonel Higginson's introduction of Tax Commissioner Brisbane, who read from the Preliminary Emancipation Proclamation, issued September 22, 1862. The audience listened attentively until he read the words, *"...that all persons held as slaves within said designated States, and parts of States, are, and henceforward forever shall be free...."* Deafening cheers resounded over the wide expanse. When the joyful expressions died down, Dr. Brisbane completed the reading.

"Chaplain French gwine be next," said Leona to no one in particular.

Rev. French, now serving as chaplain for the Negro regiment, stood at the podium. "We have Rev. Cheever's church in New York and a benevolent lady in Connecticut to thank for these regimental flags." He held up the two folded banners. "It is with great honor I present them to Colonel Thomas Wentworth Higginson, Commander of the First South Carolina Volunteers."

Just as Higginson accepted the items, a feminine Negro voice, elderly yet strong, arose from somewhere near the platform. *"My country 'tis of thee..."* she sang. Two other female voices immediately joined in.

Leona frantically scanned the program. "That ain't on this paper," she protested.

Then other freed people began to sing. The white platform guests, unsure of protocol, looked at each other and began to sing, too; but Higginson shushed them. Perhaps he felt that this musical declaration belonged to the people alone.

"Sweet land of liberty...." The words resounded through the mossy grove as thousands of former slaves, strong in the hope of a new dawn, resolutely sang verse after verse, declaring freedom for the very first time.

"Long may our land be bright,
With freedom's holy light,
Protect us by Thy might,
Great God our King."

They finished singing and Leona turned to Bentoo. "How you know that song?" she asked.

Bentoo didn't answer right away, simply stared into Leona's bright eyes. Finally, she said, "I been listening to buckra sing that song all my life, chile, and I *know*—I just *know*—one day I was gwine sing it fo' myself." She looked out over the grove, packed with over three thousand newly-freed people. "This be the day."

Up on the stage, Colonel Higginson cleared his throat, visibly moved. "That tribute was far more effective than any speech I can make." He then talked for several minutes before presenting a silk American flag to Sergeant Prince Rivers, and a regimental banner to Corporal Robert Sutton, asking them to say a few words.

Rivers spoke first. "I was getting better wages in Beaufort than from the army, but I'd rather take less and fight for the United States, because I believe the United States is fighting for me and for my people." He ended his remarks saying, "I will die before I surrender this flag!" Then he added, "I sure wish I could show it to the old masters." The people wildly shouted their approval.

Corporal Sutton encouraged the men in the regiment and those in the audience, telling them, "I will not rest satisfied while so many of my brethren are left in chains. We *will* fight because we must show this flag to Jefferson Davis in Richmond!"

Then an old man, a gaunt-faced contraband from the mainland, was asked to speak of his slave experiences. A soldier helped him hobble up on the stage. "Once, the time was," he began, "I cried all night. 'What's the matter? What's the matter?' the missus ax me. Matter enough. The next morning my child was to be sold; and she *was* sold, and I never spec to see her no more 'til the day of judgment. *Now no more that!*

"With my hands agin my breast I was gwining to my work when the overseer used to whip me along. *Now no more that!*

"When I think what the Lord done for us, and brought us through the troubles, I feel that I ought to go into his service. We's

304

free now, bless the Lord! They can't sell my wife and child no more, bless the Lord! *No more that! No more that!* President Lincoln have shut the gate! That's what the matter!"

The crowd applauded, saying, "Glory! Glory!"

Bentoo reached over and tapped Leona's program. "That been on this paper?" she asked. "'Cause if it ain't, it sho ought o' be."

Leona tossed the program aside. "I just gwine see what unfold."

Crecie hid her smile and said, "Oh look, here come Hamp."

"Ya'll having a good time?" he asked.

"Gwine have a better time when we get some o' that barbeque Randy been bragging on," replied Bentoo.

"I got the food right here," he said, handing the pan to Crecie. "Randy send a little vinegar fo' you, too, Aunt Bennie," he said, giving her a wink.

"Go on with yo' fool talk, boy!" said Bentoo. "You know I don't drink that stuff."

"OK, then," said Hamp. "I gwine take it ba—."

"Well, maybe just a lil' sip or two," she said slyly.

"Now don't say I force it on you, Aunty." Laughing, he placed the jar beside her and looked around. "Where the chillun? I gwine take 'em to see the men turn them big oxes on the spit."

"They around here some place," said Crecie, calling to them. Ossie and Louise emerged from behind the tree. "Where Willie?" she asked.

"Horsey," said Louise, pointing toward the prancing cavalry.

"Oh no!" Crecie jumped to her feet and charged into the milling mass. "Willie! Willie!" she shouted, weaving through the crowd. People stopped eating and gave the screaming, wild-eyed woman leeway. She reached the perimeter, but there was no sign of him. Oblivious to the cavalrymen's warnings, she sidestepped between the horses, yelling, "Will-eee! Will-eee!"

Suddenly she heard someone call *her* name; spinning around, she came face-to-face with Smiley. "Mista Smiley! You here!"

"Yes, I came back to sell—." Then staring at her stricken face, he asked, "What's wrong, why are you—?"

"My *chile* gone; I can't find my boy!"

"Crecie! Crecie!" Hamp ran up to her, panting hard. "I look for you all over this place. Willie back now—with Bentoo. I had to stop her from beating the hell out o' him for rambling off like that!"

Crecie took a deep breath, exhaled, then asked, "Where he been to?"

"He go closer, trying to see the horses do tricks; but then him get all jumble up in the crowd. A woman see him-one standing, crying hard. When he tell her about the big ol' tree, she help he find it."

Crecie clasped her hands over her heart. "Oh, thank God somebody find Willie; and thank the Lord Mista Smiley find *me*!"

"Right!" said Smiley. "Well, now; I believe you have some novelties to sell me."

Crecie frowned. "Some what?"

He smiled. "Snake trinkets," he said, "exotic snake trinkets."

"Oh, yes, Mista Smiley. I got a-plenty o' them fo' you."

CHAPTER 60

THE IMPENDING AUCTION

It was the end of January, two weeks before the land sale and Crecie grew more worried with each passing day. She looked on as Amos emptied the sack on his work table and meticulously counted the money.

"Well?" she said when he'd finished.

"A hundred fifty dollars or so," he reported.

"That be all? Count it again," she demanded.

"That ain't gwine make it be mo'."

"You count up everything…the money I get from Smiley, too?"

"Every nickel. Even if the lots sell cheap, this ain't gwine be enough."

"I thought—well, after he bought all the trinkets—I thought fo' sho we be close enough to bid."

"We could o' had mo', but everybody ain't putting in like they should," said Amos.

She helped him put the funds back in the sack. "This ain't gwine turn into dollars no time soon."

"What about Smiley?" asked Amos. "Make some mo' things to sell him."

"Ain't enough time fo' that. Besides, he gone again, vending. Only reason he come back last time was to sell at the celebration."

Amos hid the sack behind a box of wood scraps. "When he coming back again?"

"*After* the sale, as far as I know."

"I don't know, Crecie...things don't look good fo' we."

She knotted her brows. "Us got to keep trying, Amos; get everybody to put mo' in the pot."

—◦+ +◦—

Crecie was not the only one worried about the impending sale. Rev. French lay quietly awake, trying not to disturb his wife. But his breathing lacked sleep's rhythmic flow, and after thirty-one years of marriage, Austa knew he was not asleep. She stirred, turning to him in the moonlit room.

"It isn't going well is it, dear?" she asked.

"Oh, I'm sorry I awakened you."

"It's no matter; I can't sleep either."

He shifted position, facing her. "No, it's not going well at all. The sale's been advertised in all the newspapers and stock syndicates are already preparing to offer shares to the public."

"Why can't General Saxton use the cotton fund? There's at least a half million in it. He can buy the land and sell it to freedmen—or give it to them."

"Yes, that's a good enough plan, but even if Chase liked the idea, he can't authorize using the fund; only Congress can do that, and we've heard nothing from them *or* Chase." He sat up on the side of the bed, his head hung low.

Quickly, she draped a quilt around his shoulders. "It's drafty, dear. You might catch cold."

"No one deserves land more than the freedmen," he said. "The country owes them at least that much."

"Then perhaps General Saxton should go to Washington and persuade them, like he did for the Negro regiment."

"I don't know what he's going to do, but something will have to be done soon. Sharp-eyed speculators are circling like buzzards."

Austa sighed. "It's sad. Even in freedom the Negroes face such a perilous future; but you've done all you can humanly do."

Dawn filtered into the room and he pulled the quilt tighter. "Humanly, yes; but God has the final word. He is still in control."

※ ※

General Saxton summoned his assistant from the adjoining office and Captain Hooper promptly appeared. "Yes sir," he said, standing before the general's desk.

"Have a seat, Edward. I'd like your opinion about something."

Hooper was used to his superior's familiarity. He was the only officer on staff to share Saxton's abolitionist views and the two had developed a sense of solidarity. The others, a band of bigoted army officers, had only disdain for the Port Royal experiment, showing little respect for the teachers and superintendents. Saxton's orders, especially those dealing with the First South Carolina Volunteers, were frequently ignored or sabotaged.

"Here, read this," he said, handing Hooper an envelope. "It concerns the impending land auction."

Hooper read the return address—John Murray Forbes, Boston. A cursory reading outlined the wealthy industrialist's vision for the experiment. "He wants Port Royal to serve as a model for land usage," said Hooper, "carving the South into some kind of feudal territory when the war is over." He returned the letter. "If his plan is adopted, the Negro's lot will be little changed."

"Yes, that's what I thought. Forbes is a staunch Lincoln supporter and I fear his views are influential."

"Have you heard from Congressman Sumner?" asked Hooper.

"No; not even about purchasing land with the cotton fund. I fear Congress is not going to act in time."

"And time is our most valuable commodity. We can't begin planting, not knowing which plantations will remain under our control," said Hooper.

"True. We'll just have to wait and see what the auction brings. We mustn't give up hope."

"No sir, we mustn't," Hooper replied, dejected.

CHAPTER 61

THE DELAY

Randy carefully placed the huge platter on the table and lifted the cheesecloth.

"Oh my!" said Laura Townes. "This little piggie's roasted to perfection."

"Thank you, Miss Laura. All you need to do is pop a apple in its mouth and serve."

"My guests are in for a treat. You know, Mr. Forbes always bragged about your excellent cooking."

At the mention of Forbes' name, he looked at her questioningly, then replaced the cloth.

"Yes," she said, "I *did* receive a letter from him. He suggests Port Royal become a model for Southern land reform, with blacks and whites living on their own land, working side by side."

Randy exhaled, relieved. "That mean he's gonna help us?"

"Well...no." She paused. "At least not right now; he wants the free labor project to continue, get the workers used to being wage earners."

Randy shook his head. "I don't understand. He say everybody gonna be living and working side by side; why would we be working for wages?"

Miss Townes carefully chose her words. "Mr. Forbes sees the Negroes organizing their own communities, building churches, schools; tending to their small farms."

"How small...the farms?"

Sensing his apprehension, she avoided his eyes. "Five to twenty acres, depending on family size."

Randy shook his head. "Depending on size, that's barely enough land to *feed* a family, let alone raise extra for market. How we gonna buy clothes, shoes, coffee—things we can't grow?"

"He says the small farms will be situated between large farms. They're going to need lots of workers."

"*They*? Who's *they*?"

"He expects white men to buy the estates and hire Negroes to continue cotton production."

Randy stood stock-still, his face frozen in disbelief. "He wants *us* to keep working cotton—not farm for our own well-being?"

"He believes that arrangement will provide a better livelihood." She removed the letter from her apron pocket. "Listen—this is his reply to the letter I wrote to him. 'We can avoid the danger of speculation by selling the large plantations to liberal men from the North. The Negroes should be given assistance to purchase small homesteads and the land surrounding their property should be owned by people who can pay them wages and furnish supplies. We must appeal to the Negroes' economic needs, encourage them to *want* to be free laborers'."

She folded the letter and put it in her pocket. "He seems mainly concerned about the Port Royal project, giving it a chance to succeed without government interference."

"You know, Miss Laura, government been meddling ever since it made slavery legal; nobody claimed interference then."

"I know; but things are different today—freedom is coming soon."

"That may be, but if things go like Mr. Forbes want, we still gonna be under the white man's heel."

"General Saxton and many others feel the Negro's future is to be independent of whites; they know you need land to do that. It's all going to work out. I *know* it will!" She hoped her words belied her faltering confidence.

Randy's stoic face showed neither hope nor despair. "Yes ma'am," he said, heading for the door.

━━◦÷ ÷◦━━

Most of the guests left soon after dinner, and Miss Townes, after seeing Charlotte Forten to the door, joined General Saxton and Captain Hooper in the parlor.

"Charlotte should reach home before dark," she said, sitting down on the settee. "Everyone left so early."

Saxton sat beside her. "I apologize for causing that bit of stiffness at the table."

"Oh, on the contrary," she consoled. "General Seymour needed to be reprimanded—General McClellan does *not* walk on water."

"You can't convince Seymour of that," said Captain Hooper. "But you know, his asinine pro-slavery views irritate me more than his worship of McClellan."

"Perhaps after residing in Charleston so many years, he's now filled with Southern *chivalry*," Miss Townes remarked.

Saxton looked troubled. "I was most disturbed by Seymour's argument that we should hold the islands. Why can't he see that the land must be preempted to the people—or bought and sold to them—not greedy speculators?"

"Yes," said Hooper, "it's dreadful the way Seymour and the other officers treat the Negroes. A pity they don't have General Hunter's passion—and *com*passion."

Miss Townes grew quiet. Hooper's words, *General Hunter's passion*, resonated in her head. "General Saxton," she said softly, "have you spoken to General Hunter about the land sale situation?"

"Why, no, I hadn't thought to approach him with it."

"He commands the Department of the South, doesn't he? Maybe he can stop the sale."

"Perhaps. I'm never certain of *what* Hunter is capable of, but your suggestion is worth a try. I'll pay him a visit tomorrow."

⚊⟨⊹ ⊹⟩⚊

Hunter readily agreed to Saxton's suggestion. Citing military necessity, he issued a General Order, stopping the sale on the eve of the auction. He asserted Congress needed to address his department's concerns before selling the land; to wit: Where should he put the refugees that arrive daily? Where would the government get timber? How would crops be grown for his troops? He maintained that the army and the colored population needed land within Union lines.

A directive soon arrived from President Lincoln, adding General Hunter and General Saxton to the Tax Commission and ordering the commission to set aside a sizable amount of land for the government. Congress voted to postpone the sale, giving the five-member commission time to decide which parcels would be set aside, how much of it, and to what purpose the land would be reserved.

⚊⟨⊹ ⊹⟩⚊

The commissioners surveyed 76,775 acres, and struck off 60,296 acres for the government's military, educational, and "charitable" use. The remaining portion, 16,479 acres, would be auctioned March 9, 1863.

Since no land had been specifically earmarked for the freed-men, the President decided to set aside eight 20-acre allotments from the land earmarked for "charitable" purposes, and sold to blacks at a reduced rate in 1864.

CHAPTER 62

THE PLAN

Many Gideonites were overjoyed at the auction's delay, but Edward Philbrick was livid. Sternly denouncing the sale's setback, he arranged an emergency meeting with the superintendents.

Most of the men were late, using travel from distant plantations to justify their tardiness. Superintendents Gannet and Ware had arrived with Philbrick, watching the others file in, filling the Old Episcopal Church.

Philbrick allowed little time for pleasantries and immediately began the meeting. "The quartermaster has refused to issue supplies until the outcome of the land sale is determined," he said. "The hands are struggling to begin, having neither tools nor animals at their disposal. It's all very discouraging. Saxton's campaign to secure set-asides for Negroes was disheartening enough..." He paused, alert to any dissension. Hearing none, he continued. "... but now General Hunter's order to delay the sale has endangered the entire war effort. If planting doesn't immediately get underway, the Port Royal experiment *and* your employ are in jeopardy."

"Why is he so upset?" Gannett whispered to Ware. "We began late last year and still made a crop."

"I really don't know," replied Ware, "but his farms did better than mine, so listen."

"Time is of the essence," said Philbrick. "The outcome of this war depends on cotton and the revenue it brings." He held up a printed sheet of paper. "I've drafted this petition, urging Congress to reinstate the original sale date. You *must* sign it or our purpose here will be of no consequence."

Superintendent Bryant, a member of the Philadelphia delegation raised his hand. "But why the rush to restore the date? Surely a few weeks will not make that much difference."

"I'm positive it will," said Philbrick. "Our crop yielded less than last year's because of governmental bungling and a late start. Relying on my expertise as Cotton Collector, General Saxton has given me *carte blanche* over this year's crop. But if the government's inept interference continues and we start late once again, I have no choice but to return to Boston. " He waited until the men's surprised murmurings abated, then continued. "My decision rests with the outcome of the land sale. General Saxton thinks it won't affect our relationship with the workers, but if the land falls to speculators, I know it will. In order to keep Ivy Oaks out of speculators' hands, I was thinking to buy it—for the good of the experiment, of course—not for profit."

"But there's the likelihood you *will* profit," said Superintendent Bryant. "That's not our purpose here."

"Oh, the free-labor experiment will continue," Philbrick responded, "but under more favorable conditions. I don't see progress any other way."

"But what about the freedmen's need for land?" asked a young superintendent from New York. "Many of us are advocating on their behalf, even appealing to the President."

"Well, if you're successful," Ware drily remarked, "we're all out of work."

"Perhaps the free-holding Negroes will hire us," added Gannett.

The superintendents chuckled, easing the tension.

"Rest assured *that* won't happen," said Philbrick. "This generation of freedmen are too immature to be land owners."

The young super persisted. "But how would that appear to others, one of *us* buying a plantation? I don't believe a man should establish conflict between his humanity and his self-interest."

"The freedmen are not ready to compete with white men in the workplace," replied Philbrick. "By delaying the Negroes' independence, the white man's humanity will surely be vindicated. It would be inhumane to leave him to his own fate, ill-prepared."

Mr. Bryant stood. "I beg to differ—the South Carolina freedmen are not paupers. With little or no help from the government they've raised sufficient food to supply themselves, with even enough to sell to the troops. They perform just about all the work in the quartermaster's department and even furnished a full regiment of soldiers. Besides all this, they have raised, gathered, ginned, and packed seventy-five thousand pounds of Sea Island cotton. With cotton selling for more than seventy-two cents a pound, their labor has greatly benefited our National Treasury."

"I agree," rejoined the young New Yorker. "By owning land the Negro can continue to benefit the country *and* himself. They have the expertise. How many of us can truthfully claim cotton-growing proficiency?"

Philbrick dabbed at his flushed face, saying, "Yes, the blacks have proven themselves to be a hard-working, productive people." Then he quickly redirected the discussion. "One way or another, the sale will be over in a few weeks. Once we know where we stand, we'll get started. The petition is here, please sign before you leave."

Most of the men ignored the paper and left.

"Well, I guess this cancels that suggestion," said Ware, scanning the petition.

"On the contrary," said Philbrick, "I have a plan underway; one that involves you and a few specially chosen others."

Gannett and Ware exchanged curious glances.

"The longer the sale's put off, the more disadvantageous my plan becomes. Are you interested?"

"I am," said Ware, "anything that will get the job done more efficiently."

"And help me deal with these willful Negroes," remarked Gannett. "Sometimes they'll work and sometimes they won't—sometimes stopping before they even begin."

"Well then, here's my plan. I'm going to produce cotton via private enterprise and avoid government interference."

"But that requires capital—and lots of it," said Ware.

"Money's the least of my worries," said Philbrick. "John Murray Forbes is backing—."

"Forbes?" Gannett exclaimed. "That must have been quite a coup."

"Not really. He's an astute businessman who feels that the private sector will establish free labor faster than the government's bureaucracy. I presented my plan and he readily endorsed it, organizing a Boston syndicate to support it. They've invested $12,000 and authorized me to purchase plantations in my name."

"How ironic," said Gannett. "My father proposed something similar, offering to sponsor me. But I've been hesitant, anticipating adverse criticism."

"Especially from French and his New York missionaries," remarked Ware.

"Who cares?" said Philbrick "As long as our motives are for the good of the experiment and not personal gain, I see nothing wrong in privately running the plantations."

"That sounds feasible. How does it involve us?" asked Ware.

"Our mission will remain the same—encourage free labor by making wages more attractive to the Negro than sustenance farming. In the end, we'll prove that more cotton can be grown cheaper with free labor than slave labor."

"How about us," asked Gannett, "will we be salaried?"

"Until your crop comes in, you'll be housed, fed, et cetera. Then you'll receive one-half of your crop's net proceeds…after operating expenses, of course."

Both men readily agreed to the plan.

"Good!" said Philbrick. "Hopefully the auction will get back on schedule and our plan can get underway."

CHAPTER 63

ALONG LIFE'S WEARY WAY

Randy tossed an inch-sized potato cube into the sturdy sweet-grass basket. "I'm through cutting," he announced. "It's getting too dark to be out here using knives."

"Sho you right," said Hamp.

"Yeah, I guess this be plenty to start with," said Crecie. The three of them had spent the afternoon cubing white potatoes, preparing them for spring planting. Crecie was grateful the men had helped, but she still ran her fingers through the basket, inspecting the dimpled squares.

"Mmm, the pieces ya'll cut ain't got but one good eye. Them pieces *I* cut got two or three; they gwine bear more taters than what you and Hamp done."

Hamp grinned. "How you know? Your seed gwine bust through the ground saying look at me—Crecie cut *my* eye!"

She laughed. "Who know...they might; stranger things than that been happening—General Hunter stopping that land sale fo' one."

"Now *that* was something—the way he made everything stand still—just like that!" said Randy, snapping his fingers.

"Well, at least that crazy ol' man finally got one thing right," said Hamp. He hadn't forgiven General Hunter for forcing him and the other young men into the army last year.

"You don't have to worry about conscription no more," said Randy. "Saxton's in charge now; gave his word *that* won't happen again. But if a man got a mind to volunteer...."

"All I can say is, them that got a mind to sign up—fine! That's why they call 'em the First South Carolina *Volunteers*."

"Lots of runaways from Georgia and Florida have joined," said Randy. "Sgt. Rivers' recruiting is bringing them in, too."

Crecie was quiet, listening to the soldier-talk. Suddenly she picked up the basket and balanced it on her head. "I gwine put these in the shed, they be ready to plant in three or four days."

Hamp shook his head as she walked away. "That been a bad time for she. First Isham, then Sham."

"Yeah." Randy replied "That soldier could've killed her, too."

"That impressment was a bad time all around; if they want *me* to sign on, they gwine have to *catch* me first!"

"But you only stayed in the army a week or so."

"*Two* weeks! Two weeks I ain't gwine *never* fo'get."

"That must've been a terri—hush! Here she come," said Randy.

Crecie's mood had lightened. "Well, now; since Hunter put off the sale, I got time to make mo' trinkets, have 'em ready for when Smiley come back."

"When is that?" asked Hamp.

"Last o' Feb'rary, maybe the first o' March. When I get through, he gwine need *two* wagons to carry it in."

"That's less than a month away," said Randy. "You better get to stepping!"

"Oh, no," she replied, "we *all* got to get to stepping."

———※——※———

Crecie began an around-the-clock regimen, working far into the night. Succumbing only when her body refused to go on, she often fell asleep among scraps of tanned snake leather. Bentoo did the best she could—taking on household chores, the yard garden, and the chickens. The elderly lady also looked after the children, even keeping an eye on Sham when he wasn't hanging around Amos's work shed. Work consumed the entire family, rendering them little more than passing phantoms.

"I gwine work in the yard garden now, Crecie," said Bentoo. "Leona and Willie can watch Ossie and Louise 'til I get back. You keep working on them trinket things."

"Yeah, OK," said Crecie, glancing at the boxes piled in every nook and cranny, many of them still empty. Filled with anxiety, she picked up an unfinished wallet. *I got a long way to go,* she thought.

No sooner had Bentoo left, Ossie held up his bowl. "Wanna eat," he cried.

"I hungry," Louise whimpered.

"Dog-gone-it!" said Crecie. "This ain't no time to be stopping. Leona! Come make them some gruel."

Leona stopped sweeping and went to the bucket. "I can't, Ma; ain't no water in the peggie."

Crecie checked for herself, then shoved the wooden container into Leona's hands. "Here; you and Willie go to the well—and hurry back!"

The children struggled with the water-filled bucket and had gotten half-way home when the container began to list.

"Keep yo' side up, Willie!" Leona ordered. "All the water slopping out the peggie."

"I can't," he whined, "it too heavy fo' me."

"Just hold tight the handle, us just got a lil' ways to go."

"My hand ain't gwine hold on."

His side of the bucket tilted, spilling more water over the rim.

"Well, okay," said Leona, "just put it down fo' a—."

Willie's hand slipped and the bucket fell. Water splashed all over their dusty feet, splattering mud on their clothes.

"Dang! Look what you done," said Leona, staring at the empty container. "Now we got to go all the way back to the well. A flea be stronger than you!"

A tear slid down Willie's caramel-colored face. He'd inherited Isham's high cheekbones, but he favored Bentoo—even her diminutive stature. He was five years old, but Ossie and Louise, two years younger, were almost as tall as he.

Leona immediately regretted her words and brushed his tears away. "Don't cry, Willie. You be a big boy."

"No, I ain't! You say I lil' like a flea."

She picked up the overturned bucket. "Yeah, but a flea got a big bite, that what make 'em strong. Remember what Ma say: 'You a lil' piece o' leather, well-put-together'."

Willie brightened. "Yeah; and she say, think big and you be big."

"That's right."

They trudged quietly along until Willie broke the silence. "Why Ma don't be with we no mo', Leona?"

His sister sighed. "I done say to you too many times already—she got to make them snake things so she can get money."

"Why?"

"I don't know. To buy some land or something, I guess."

They reached the well and Leona lowered the bucket. "I ain't gwine fill it all the way this time."

"I too glad fo' that!"

She tugged the rope and he helped her retrieve the bucket.

"But why *us* got to be working all the time," said Willie. "Don't even go to school no mo'."

I know, she thought, misty-eyed. "Ma say working make we strong."

He held the peggie steady as she poured the water into it.

"Mo' strong than a flea?"

She blinked away the tears and smiled. "Oh, yeah; mo' strong than a bull, even—like you!"

Beaming, he grabbed one side of the handle, and they started for home.

Ossie and Louise sat on the floor, wailing and banging their wooden bowls.

"Quiet! Leona be back soon," said Crecie, attaching a belt buckle. "Can't make no gruel without water."

The youngsters hollered all the more.

"Hush that fuss befo' I give you something to cry fo'," warned Crecie, pushing away from the table. She stood and, not seeing Ossie under foot, stumbled over him.

"Damn it!" she yelled, knocking over a chair as she crashed to the floor. The frightened children's piercing screams filled the cabin. "Hush that damn noise!" Crecie shouted.

Just then Leona and Willie walked in, covered with mud. Crecie scrambled to her feet and snatched the bucket. It was less than half full. "What! All that time and this all the water you bring back!"

"But Ma," Leona began, "Willie drop the—."

"Uh-uh," said Willie, "you cuss at me, and then I—."

"And just look at you; like pigs in a mud sty," said Crecie. "I oughta take a switch and tan both ya'll lil'—."

"Ahem. Crecie?" A shadow fell across the threshold and she looked into the eyes of Charlotte Forten, Leona's teacher.

Many of the former slaves, grateful for the abolitionists' support, had developed a rapport with the Northern women. But

Crecie, though cordial, had remained aloof. Tolerating the missionaries' impromptu inspections masked as social calls, she'd kept her cabin clean and in order. But that was then.

"May I come in?" asked Miss Forten.

Seem to me you already did. Crecie nodded slightly. The mingled smell of cooking grease and dirty laundry assailed her nostrils and she saw the cabin's muddled mess through the young teacher's eyes.

"I was concerned about the children," said Miss Forten. "We miss them."

Crecie's face burned with shame. Weeks had passed since they'd last attended school. *Po' lil' Leona…she been working like a woman around here—even helping me make trinkets.* "I gwine send 'em tomorrow," she mumbled.

As Miss Forten chatted with the children, Crecie, from some place far away, fought desperately to hold in her emotions.

"I brought these books for you, Leona," said the teacher. "I know you will share them with Willie."

"Yes ma'am," she said. Her eyes sparkled as she grasped the books. "Ma, can I go outside and read?"

"Yeah," she murmured, looking down at her rough hands.

"I'm leaving now, too," said Miss Forten. "And Crecie, try to get some rest."

The second she was alone, Crecie covered her face and wept uncontrollably.

CHAPTER 64

A BREACH OF FAITH

Bentoo looked up from the row of beans she was hoeing. "You hear from Smiley?" she asked. "The sale start t'morrow."

"No, not a thing," Crecie replied. "Move aside, Leona, I'm coming down that row now."

There was nothing more to say and they worked in resolute silence—Bentoo briskly chopping, Crecie moving at a measured pace. Leona tugged at weeds as Willie stood near, keeping an eye on the rambunctious cousins, Ossie and Louise.

Suddenly Hamp's voice broke the stillness. "Crecie! Bentoo! Smiley done come!"

Crecie dropped the hoe and lifted her hands skyward. "Oh thank you, Jesus!"

"Ain't no surprise," said Bentoo, leaning on the hoe. "God always right on time."

"And not a minute too soon," said Crecie.

"I gwine start loading up his wagon," said Hamp, hurrying away.

"I right behind you," said Crecie, now energized. "Leona, keep pulling them weeds, and Willie…you keep them lil' ones out o' trouble."

Hamp was already moving boxes when Crecie reached the cabin. A group of curious children had gathered, taking in the painted wagon and sneaking shy glances at the red-faced man.

Smiley was shocked by Crecie's haggard appearance, but maintained a cheery façade. "That's quite a haul you put together, Crecie." The containers were crammed with hundreds of belts, wallets and, of course, snake-bone jewelry.

She beamed at the compliment. "Thank you, suh. I done my best."

Smiley examined a well-crafted belt. "Yes, so I see." Watching Hamp load box after box, he turned to the young man. "You're a fine packer; I could use someone like you working for me."

"Oh, no, Mista Smiley," said Hamp. "I ain't gwine ramble too far from Ivy Oaks."

"Yes, you people do cling to the old home place, don't you?"

"Hamp ain't from here; he from the Main," said Crecie, "but he one o' we now; gwine own land, too, thanks to you."

"Hope so," said Smiley, paying her for the trinkets.

She quickly counted the money, then disbelieving, counted it again. "This all? Thirty-five dollars? You pay more fo' the first batch and that been less."

"That's the most I can offer," he said, climbing aboard the wagon.

Crecie was devastated. "B-but you gwine make two, maybe three hundred; just give me seventy fo' the lot, then," she pleaded.

He stared straight ahead. "Sorry, my sales are down."

The children's eyes grew large, listening to the exchange.

Smiley looked down at her. "Well?" he prodded.

Crecie stared at the money then looked up. "Get we things, Hamp; you chillun go help him."

"Don't you pickaninnies touch a thing in my wagon," warned Smiley, climbing down. "Look, Crecie, I'll make a sacrifice, give you fifty for the whole lot."

"Sac-a-fice!" All her trials came to bear. "What the hell *you* know about sac-a-fice!

"Look, take the fifty; I don't have all day to squabble with you."

"Damn you!" She flung the money in his face.

"Why—you, you ungrateful wench!" He struck her with the horsewhip.

Pain, coupled with fatigue, overcame caution. Enraged, Crecie grabbed the vendor, pounding his head against the wagon. By the time Hamp pulled her away, Smiley was bruised and bloodied. The children, having never seen a white man being beaten, especially not by a black woman, ran away screaming.

Crecie continued to lunge at the cowering Smiley, but Hamp, with a mighty effort, held her at bay.

"*I* work, the *chillun* work, ol' *granny* work!" she shouted. "None o' we hardly stop fo' eat, fo' sleep, and *you*—*you* talk about sac-a-fice?" She continued to rant; unmindful of the blood streaming from Smiley's head. Then Smiley, using a white handkerchief, dabbed at his bloodied face. Suddenly the crimson-stained cloth came into focus, jolting Crecie's awareness.

"Oh, Lordly!" Falling back against Hamp, she became rigid, panting in disbelief at what she'd done. "I...I...loose me, Hamp." She extended her hand toward Smiley. "Here, let me help—."

"No! Keep away from me," he shouted, darting around the wagon.

She retreated. "I too sorry, suh. I ain't mean to...." Her voice faltered.

"You've not heard the last of this; I promise you that!"

She began to back away, frightened. "Get we stuff, Hamp," she whispered, "get all we stuff." Then she turned and ran.

"...and then I see the blood running down he face," said Crecie softly. "I don't know why I done such a thing, Bentoo."

Her grandmother sighed. "It been too heavy a load on you, chile. A body, a mind—they be like a jar, or a river even—can't hold but so much."

"What Smiley gwine do? S'pose he go tell Philbrick...he gwine put me off this place fo' sho now."

"He gwine most likely tell the army man," said Bentoo.

"Jail! The army said it gwine put vendors in jail fo' fighting! Lord, if only Randy be here; he tell we what to do."

"No telling when that reg'ment gwine get back; they ain't been gone but two days."

Randy, working as a pilot, had accompanied the *First South Carolina Volunteers* to Jacksonville on an assault mission.

"Things ain't like befo' the war," said Bentoo, "when us know what massa gwine do. New buckra handle things different now."

"I know, I know," said Crecie, pacing back and forth.

"Maybe you oughta hide 'til us see which way the wind gwine blow," said Bentoo.

"Yeah...yeah, that be the best thing." Quickly, she threw a few provisions and matches in a sack and grabbed a pine torch.

Bentoo followed her outside, anxiously watching as she harnessed Rex. "W-where you gwine be, Crecie? You know I worry so."

"No, don't fret; I gwine be fine. Isham say the cemetery be the best hiding place."

Word of Crecie's assault on Smiley spread quickly. The Midway hands knew about it even before they left the field. That evening they descended on her cabin. Bentoo saw Amos leading the way and went outside to meet them.

"Evening, Bentoo," said Amos. "I sorry about all this. I axed 'em to let it keep 'til in the morning, but Hagar here say no, do it now."

Hagar spoke up. "That's right; ain't no sense waiting. Crecie couldn't sell them wicked-looking snake things she been making, so us might as well get we money back."

"I got the list right here," said Bentoo.

"And I got the money," said Amos. "When Bentoo call yo' name, come get what you put in."

Margaret stepped forward. "You ain't got to call my name, Aunt Bennie. Keep it fo' the next land sale."

"Yeah," said Mose, "keep mine, too."

"And I gwine keep adding to the pot," said Yoruba.

"Well, I ain't adding nothing," said Hagar. "I through fooling with Crecie—crazy woman, jumping on white folk like that. I want my money now!"

"Yeah, me, too," someone else demanded. "Messing with Crecie gwine get all us put off Ivy Oaks."

"Where she be, anyway?" asked Rosa Lee.

"Crecie ain't holding yo' money, and she ain't got no list," said Amos, "so where she be ain't yo' business."

"Just give me what I put in, and I be gone," one woman said.

"Me, too," said another.

The crowd pressed in.

"Hold yo' horses," said Bentoo. "No need to be shoving."

The grumbling continued as Bentoo read the names and Amos issued amounts. Some people demanded refunds in the exact denomination they'd given it; others claimed more than they'd contributed.

Bentoo and Amos finally got it all settled and went inside the cabin. She flopped into the rocker and shook her head. "I been knowing that gang all they life, been midwife to some; why in the world they figure I gwine steal from 'em?"

"Or me," said Amos. "I guess the smell o' a lil' money can change some folks. Could be they scared, too, about being put off the place."

"Only thirteen names left on the list," said Bentoo, reaching for her pipe. "The faithful few...."

Amos handed her a light from the fireplace. "Where is Crecie, anyway?"

"Cemetery."

"Uh-huh, I should o' know that. She ain't never been scared o' them haints."

Bentoo got the pipe going then spoke. "Tell, me Amos; is them white folks gwine chastise Crecie over this?"

"Nah, nothing much. Mose say the army gwine stop her from vending—*if* Smiley tell 'em. I doubt he will; no man want folks to know a woman got the best o' him."

Bentoo rocked gently and puffed. "Lord, that be a load off my mind—she ain't going to jail. It'll be a load off her mind, too, if you go tell her."

Amos' eyes stretched wide. "Tonight? In the graveyard?" He moved toward the door. "Nooo, Bentoo; that news can sit 'til in the morning."

"Why? You scared?"

"Well, I gwine put it this way...Crecie get along fine with them haints, but as long as they ain't come looking fo' me, I ain't gwine go looking fo' them."

CHAPTER 65

THE CEMETERY

Crecie dismounted and asked ancestral permission to enter the cemetery. Using the torch to light the way, she located Isham's grave. Peering at the cedar tree that had been planted at its head, her eyes traveled over the rounded mound. She stopped short, shocked by what she didn't see. Except for a few scattered seashells, no personal marker adorned the grave; there was nothing to guide Isham's spirit to the other side, safeguarding it there.

"But I *know* I mark he grave...I break the lil' bowl and then—no, wait. I pick up the pestle, but then...Sham!"

Her brows knotted as she wrestled with the memories of Isham's burial night. The excitement of hundreds of people arriving at the cabin had agitated Sham. He'd burst into the house shouting; then he ran back outside, Crecie and Bentoo in pursuit. Several minutes later Amos caught him and they'd forced Sham to drink the potion. The drugged boy had slept in the wagon, beside the coffin, as the long processional wound its way to the cemetery.

"Oh, no...." Crecie whispered. "I never break the bowl." She'd come to the cemetery for refuge but had uncovered something more urgent. "Lord, have mercy! Isham spirit been roaming free all this time!" She clutched the torch. *That bowl been in my hand when we get here.* She glanced around, frantic. *I got to find it fo' sho!*

The torch cast an eerie glow among the oaks, doing little to dispel the murky gloom. Shadows danced and dodged as she plodded from grave to grave, hovering over the dead.

But the search was futile and she ended up near a briar patch. Looking around, the area seemed familiar, and she struggled to recall the events of that night. *They been fixing to put Isham in the ground and...and...I ain't want to see that. So I been looking—standing right here—looking down at the bowl when Leona...she scream! I run and hold her—but ain't nothing been in my hand then.*

"The bowl! I must o' chunk it down right here!" She secured the light and began tugging at the tangled vines, snatching at the prickly underbrush. She combed the small patch, but finding nothing, slumped to the ground, drained. That's when she saw a glint— something half buried beneath a large stone. She dug the object out and brushed off the dirt. It was a wooden box. Four brass-plated corners anchored the foot-wide sides, forming a square. *This box—I done see it befo'...but where?* The letters AMB were embossed on the front and, thanks to Leona, Crecie could name the letters even though she had no idea what they meant. She grabbed a rock and broke the fragile lock, releasing a fragrant aroma of cedar. Her hands shook as she raised the lid, astounded by the glittering jewels. Earrings, bracelets, broaches, diamond rings, twinkled in the flickering light. She delved into the cache, overwhelmed by the sight of species and banknotes. "Glory be! I gwine take this to Bentoo!" She reached for a sack to put it in but when she turned back around, her heart nearly stopped. A fluted, milk-white bowl, broken into two jagged pieces, sat gleaming beside the box. "Oh, sweet Jesus," she muttered, scrambling to her feet.

Bentoo, too worried to really asleep, was dozing in front of the fire when Crecie slipped into the cabin. So as to not awake the others, she motioned for Bentoo to join her. The two silently walked to the shed.

Crecie looked on as Bentoo examined the jewelry.

"These earrings, this pin—these Miz Alina own," said Bentoo. She pointed to the letters on the box. "A, M, B—that stand fo' Alina McIntosh Boson."

"It been Isham spirit, lead me to this," said Crecie.

"That might o' been why you had them dreams."

"I *know* it been! That be why I make *sho* I pray over that broke-up bowl and mark Isham grave befo' I leave the cemetery tonight."

"He spirit be at peace now. But this box…how in the world *that* get in the cemetery?"

"I don't know." Crecie sighed. "Lots o' things just…well, there just ain't no accounting fo' *everything*."

"Maybe you right," said Bentoo, gazing at Crecie's weary face. "You been through a lot, daughter. Thank God you ain't gwine have to add jail to it." She reached out and touched the young woman's hair, removing bits of debris.

"Wait!" cried Crecie, grabbing her grandmother's hand. "What you take out my hair?"

"Nothing; just this." She opened her hand, revealing leaves and sand spurs.

"That…that be the same thing I take from Isham hair when—." She pounded a fist in her palm. "I know! I know how that box get in the cemetery!" Her words flew in a torrent. "That day—the day o' the Big Gun Shoot—Isham had this box. I remember he move it to make room for me to get on Rex. But I ain't go with he. Later, him tell me he been in the cemetery when the big guns shoot."

"Miz Alina must o' give him this box to hide from the Yankees," said Bentoo. "That make sense to me, the way that box come to be in the graveyard."

"Yeah, make sense to me, too."

335

"What you gwine do with these things?"

"Maybe save the jewelry for when Miz Alina come back—*if* she come back. What you think?"

"Well, if anybody see we with these ring and thing….No, it best us put 'em back in the ground, where you find 'em." She peered into the box. "Anything else be in there?"

"Uh huh." Crecie set a wad of South Carolina bank notes to the side. "I know *this* ain't good for nothing—start a fire with maybe. Plenty species in here, though." She scooped up the coins; they made a metallic jingle as they slipped through her fingers.

"How much you figure in there…enough to buy land with?" Bentoo asked.

"Oh, fo' sho. Even mo' than that."

"Good God from Zion! Let me sit, catch my wind." She eased down on a sack of rice. "If only Randy been here," she lamented, "he could to go to the auction."

Crecie fixed her eyes on Bentoo. "Well, he ain't; so that just leave you and me."

Bentoo met her gaze. "No, that just leave *you*. I too old and tired to go traipsing to Beaufort."

"Oh no, Bentoo—not me one!" She looked away. "Somebody who can talk better than me—read and such—got to go along, too."

Bentoo reached over and picked up two coins—one gold, the other silver. "You see this? This gwine talk fo' you—read too, if need be."

"But I don't know nothing about no auction, not even a *slave* auct—."

"Ain't nobody else to go. Who you willing to trust where this money come from?"

Crecie watched the dawn filter into the shed. Finally she turned to Bentoo, "If I make one step, God gwine make two. He gwine have a ram in the bush somewhere."

CHAPTER 66

THE AUCTION

Crecie watched the early afternoon scene from across the street, in an abandoned doorway. A wooden platform had been erected in front of the Beaufort County courthouse and sutlers' wagons lined the street. Much to Crecie's relief, Smiley's wagon wasn't among them. Clusters of auction-goers, whites up front, a few blacks off to the side, waited for the auction to start. Soldiers lounged under a row of budding crepe myrtles until a colonel approached the platform; then they snapped to attention. Just as the courthouse clock bonged one, the Tax Commissioners exited the building onto the stand. The milling crowd stood still. The auction was about to begin.

Crecie took a deep breath, willed her body to move, then ambled across the street. The colonel was speaking to the buyers, but Crecie, at the rear of the crowd, couldn't hear a word he was saying. *I ain't got no business here, no how,* she rationalized, wanting to leave. But her previous self-chiding to start with one step, kept her from turning back. So she took a step, then another, inching forward until she stood midway the group's outer arc. Secure in her new vantage point, she recognized some of the teachers and superintendents. Rev. French stood to the left, up front. Philbrick and Gannett were in deep conversation, on the right. Guessing the others were speculators, she felt doubly inferior, standing so close to the well-dressed assemblage.

The colonel introduced General Hunter, General Saxton, and the other tax commissioners—Brisbane, Wording, and Smith. "I'm the auctioneer and you may refer to me as Colonel. This public auction is being held for the collection of direct taxes in the insurrectionary...." The word made Crecie's mind spin. *In— insuh...? What in the world he talking about?* She fastened her eyes on the auctioneer and concentrated, shutting out the affluence surrounding her.

"The Commissioners are prepared to accept opening bids of ninety-three cents per acre," the Colonel announced.

Good! I know what that mean.

"If no counter offers are received..."

Counter offer?

"...the lots will go to the opening bidder."

Lots?

"A description of each lot, naming the owner and its exact location, will be read before opening bids are received."

Oh—lots must mean land.

"Lot number seven, Cherry Hill, is first up for bid. It contains one thousand acres and is owned by William Elliot."

Crecie shuffled in a little closer, forcing her mind to follow her ears.

"Bounded north and northeast by Broad River," read the Colonel, "south, southeast by Fish Creek, the property includes Bob Island and Turtle Hammock."

Yeah, I know right where that be. Just that little bit of knowledge encouraged her.

"Do I hear a bid?" called the Colonel. "Do I hear a bid?" His well-modulated voice was now louder.

A man shouted "Ninety-three cents!"

The auctioneered repeated the bid. "Ninety-three cents; do I hear ninety-four? Calling for counter offers."

No one responded. "Going once," he said, banging the gavel. Crecie jumped at the sound.

He hit the gavel again, "Going twice." Then he banged it for the last time and shouted, "Sold! Sold to the gentleman in the brown coat. Please report to the treasurer." He pointed to a bespectacled man seated at a small table nearby.

Crecie saw the treasurer gave the winning bidder a piece of paper. Her confidence waned, watching him read it. But when he wrote on it, what little bravado she'd garnered vanished completely. "Ain't got sense enough fo' this," she muttered, making a sharp turn to leave. The man standing behind her ducked out of her way.

She'd gotten to the rear of the crowd when the auctioneer announced the next lot.

"Possum Point now up for bid...."

At the words Possum Point, Crecie's feet refused to move. The auctioneer's voice seemed far away and a vision of Isham cutting down trees on the Point flashed in her mind. Seeing cornfields where brambles once stood, she hurried back to her spot.

"Lot seven consists of two thousand acres..." continued the auctioneer.

Two thousand acres! Crecie was dumbfounded. *I ain't know it stretch that far!*

"...and is bounded by Ivy Oaks Plantation on the north...."

Gannett turned to Philbrick. "I thought the Point was *within* Ivy Oaks."

"So did I," said Philbrick.

The Colonel finished reading the property description, frowned, and said, "Just a minute, please." He turned to Tax Commissioner Brisbane for a quick conference, then back to the crowd. "Commissioner Brisbane has verified that the owner of Lot seven is unknown. The bidding will now commence. What do I hear?"

"Ninety-three," a man called out.

Crecie immediately recognized Philbrick's voice.

"Ninety-three from the gentleman in the gray coat. Do I hear ninety-four?"

That be what I oughta say...?

"Ninety-four...ninety-four..." said the Colonel.

I gwine say it. She raised her hand and mumbled, "Ninety-four."

"What's that? Did I hear ninety-four?"

"Y-yes suh," she replied.

Philbrick, as did everyone else, turned to see who'd made the counter bid.

"They must have raised enough," whispered Gannett.

The gavel pounded. "Going once..."

"But not enough to buy Possum Point," said Philbrick. "One dollar!" he shouted.

The crowd was certain the bidding would end on that note.

"Do I hear a counter offer?" the Colonel asked. "One dollar five cents?"

Crecie was uncertain until the auctioneer banged the gavel, saying, "Going once, going twice..." She raised her hand, "A dollar five cent."

A hum of surprise raced among the spectators.

"One dollar and ten cents," Philbrick rejoined.

The auctioneer, alert to a bidding war, increased the tempo. "Dollar ten, dollar ten, what do I hear? Do I hear fifteen? Say now, say now!" The words spilled out rapid fire, his voice insistent.

Crecie's heartbeat measured his staccato spiel and she fought the rising panic. She felt all eyes on her, especially Philbrick's piercing glare, and her mind became muddled.

"Do I hear a counter? What's the counter? Dollar fifteen, dollar fifteen?"

What to say? Oh Lord, what I gwine say?

The auctioneer banged the gavel.

She opened her mouth, "D-d-d...." But the words stuck in her throat. *I, I done lose the land.*

Just then, someone whispered in her ear, "Bid!"

She turned to see the man who'd earlier ducked from behind her—it was Frazier.

"Going twice...."

"Frazier, what you—."

"Hurry! Bid the most you can!"

The coins lay heavy in her pouch. Remembering Bentoo's advice to let the money talk for her, she said, "Two dollar, suh!"

The crowd, looking to Philbrick, erupted into noisy chatter. The auctioneer banged for order as a stern-faced General Saxton rose to his feet, glaring at Philbrick.

But Philbrick was already pushing his way through the crowd, leaving.

The auctioneer banged the gavel. "Sold to the Negro woman!"

Crecie nearly fainted and her knees buckled as Frazier lead her to the treasurer's table. Still, she had the presence of mind to ask, "Can you read?"

He smiled. "Enough to take care o' this."

Later that night the group of thirteen, those who'd left their money in the pot, came to Crecie's cabin. Someone had made a smoldering rag fire, and they sat outside on benches and stumps, fanning the smoke and the gnats. The new land owners were excited, eager to hear every detail of the auction. As Crecie talked, Frazier stood near, filling in the gaps. She ended the account saying, "God put Frazier there to be my ram in the bush."

"No, Crecie," said Frazier. "You been *my* help—New Year's Eve night."

"Huh? What I do so?" she asked.

"Yeah, Frazier," said Dahlia, "I remember you running out, saying us ain't know how to work."

The others tittered as Frazier looked on, seemingly ill-at-ease.

"Ya'll hush," Bentoo admonished, "let the man talk. Go on, Frazier; what Crecie done so?"

"It ain't what she done—it be what she say—strong talk about owning land, working fo' self. The mo' I think on it, the mo' it make sense; so I start saving my little money, looking for something to buy. I find out Honey Hill was coming up for auction; it ain't but three hundred acres, but enough to start."

"Man got to start somewhere," said Amos.

"Not to Philbrick way o' thinking, though. When I couldn't scrape up enough money, I ax he to lend me the rest."

"Uh huh," said Crecie. "Did him?"

"He say it be too big a risk and I stand to lose my money. Then him offer to buy it *fo'* me, in he name, and sell it to me after the crop come in."

"He buy seven or eight places today," said Amos. "One o' them gwine be yo' own?"

"Oh no, them be him own. I go tell Miz Laura what him say, that if he buy it fo' me, he gwine keep profit from the crop and give me wage."

"What she say?" asked Mose.

"She say if I want to make money, I must buy the land myself; tell me to go see what Captain Hooper think. Well, I ain't *never* see a man so mad; he say the real risk be Philbrick not selling the land back to me. Then you know what the captain done? Him lend me the rest o' the money to bid with—plus enough to buy tools and such."

"Yeah, Captain Hooper be a good one, alright," said Bentoo. "Right along with Rev. French and General Saxton."

"I won't take nothing for Miz Laura, neither," said Margaret.

"Or Mr. Fill Up," piped Leona.

Bentoo gave her a look and she scampered back to the other children catching fireflies.

Crecie turned to Frazier. "All I can say is thank you; if it ain't been fo' you...."

"No need fo' that, Crecie. I do what I can fo' anybody, I ain't begrudging like Hagar and that bunch. They so jealous because ya'll freeholders now smoke pouring out they ears!"

"The way ain't been easy fo' none o' we," said Crecie. "But God help them who help they self."

"Ain't that the truth," he declared. "Well, I best be going; Honey Hill coming up fo' bid t'morrow and I need to start fo' Beaufort early. You coming, Mose?"

"Yep, might as well," he replied.

Crecie walked with them to the wagon. "Good night, and good luck t'morrow."

"God willing," said Frazier, pulling away.

The others soon drifted to their cabins, leaving Bentoo and Crecie in the yard. "It been a long day, Crecie. I gwine go inside. You coming?"

"Yeah, after I smother this fire." It was the first chance she'd had to be alone, and the solitude, accompanied by the frogs' guttural croaks, was soothing. She eased down on the bench, staring across the road into the pitch-black forest. *Possum Point right over there, on the other side o' them trees...and it be mine.* "Nobody but You, God," she whispered slowly shaking her head. "Nobody *but* You!" Then looking to the star-studded heavens, she smiled. "And you, Isham."

THE END

ACKNOWLEDGEMENTS

The original setting for this novel was Sapelo Island, Georgia, but when the research led to Willie Lee Rose's fascinating book, *Rehearsal for Reconstruction: The Port Royal Experiment*, I knew this was the story I wanted to tell.

I had a wealth of support while writing *Free to Be*, starting years ago with my long-time sister-friends Audrey Gilchrist Roach and Mercita Dahlia Wimberly; and my inspiring daughter, Genay James Jackson. You've been my cheerleaders, reading my short stories and the novels that always ended at their beginnings. But you kept encouraging me, praising my single first-chapter efforts. Thank you for believing in me all those years.

My appreciation for my good friend and 'running buddy' Brenda T. Miller has no bounds. In spite of your busy schedule and numerous projects, you were never too busy to help me. Thank you for your unselfish nature and for adding me to your list of things to do.

I'm extremely grateful to Elvin Proctor for teaching me how to manage massive research files and to Oscar German of *G2 Computers Sales and Service* for keeping my equipment current, operational, and bug-free. Thank you both for guiding me along the dark path of techno-ignorance.

Volumes of appreciation go to my Englewood Writers Workshop cohorts and our eagle-eyed facilitator, John Boles. Thank you for your time, comments, and suggestions. A special thanks to Gae Weber—I looked forward to your in-depth critiques!

For those times when nothing in my creative process worked, I had only to call on my writer-friends—Mary S. Erickson, Sharon Hatton, Kellye Heise, and June W. Overgaard. As we lamented our pathetic word counts and read each other's hard-won efforts, we became better writers. Your excellent critiques, your tireless editing, your encouraging words were invaluable, but it was your insistence that *Free to Be* was a story worth telling that kept me going. Thank you for your enthusiasm, commitment, and laughter. I couldn't have done it without you.

Hugs and kisses to THE man in my life, Tommy James Chandler. You sustained me and never complained about *anything.* Thank you for providing a peaceful and loving place to write.

I am deeply indebted to artist James Denmark for granting the use of *The Goddess of Hope and Mercy* for the cover. Your *striking* work, (pun intended, fellow Rattler), personifies our customs and culture as well as the novel's main character, Crecie. Tommy and I thank you for your generous spirit, not only at this juncture, but throughout the years.

To everyone who offered encouragment, I thank God for you. It is through His Glory we are able to strengthen one another.

PRIMARY SOURCES

Books

Berlin, Ira, Barbara J. Fields, Stephen F. Miller, Joseph P. Reidy, Leslie S. Rowland, eds. *Free at Last: A Documentary History of Slavery, Freedom, and the Civil War,* (1992).

Berlin, Ira, Thavolia Glymph, Stephen F. Miller, Joseph P. Reidy, Leslie S.
Rowland, Julie Saville eds. *The Wartime Genesis of Free Labor: The Lower South,* (1990).

Billington, Ray Allen, ed. *The Journal of Charlotte Forten: A Free Negro in the Slave Era,* (1953).

Camp, Stephanie M. H. *Closer to Freedom: Enslaved Women and the Everyday Resistance in the Plantation South,* (2004).

Cornish, Dudley Taylor. *The Sable Arm: Negro Troops in the Union Army, 1861 – 1865,* (1956).

Franklin, John Hope. *The Emancipation Proclamation,* (1963).

Geraty, Virginia Mixon. *Gullah Fuh Oonuh (Gullah For You): A Guide to the Gullah Language,* (1997).

Gooding, James Henry. *On the Altar of Freedom: A Black Soldier's Civil War Letters from the Front,* Virginia Matzke Adams, ed. (1991).

Higginson, Thomas Wentworth. *Army Life in a Black Regiment,* (1870, reprint 1984).

Holland, Rupert Sargent, ed. *Letters and Diary of Laura M. Towne, Written from the Sea Islands of South Carolina 1862-1864,* (1912).

The I.P. Stanback Museum and Planetarium, South Carolina State University, *Moments from the Past: An Exhibition in Celebration of the Penn Center of the Sea Islands,* (1993).

Levine, Lawrence W. *Black Culture and Consciousness: African American Folk Thought from Slavery to Freedom,* (1977).

Litwack, Leon F. *Been in the Storm So Long: The Aftermath of Slavery,* (1984).

McCutcheon, Marc. *Everyday Life in the 1800's: A Guide for Writers, Students, and Historians,* (2001).

McFeely, William S. *Sapelo's People: A Long Walk into Freedom,* (1994).

Pearson, Elizabeth Ware, ed. *Letters from Port Royal, Written at the Time of the Civil War,* (1906).

Powell, Lawrence N. *New Masters: Northern Planters During the Civil War and Reconstruction,* (1980).

Rose, Willie Lee. *Rehearsal for Reconstruction: The Port Royal Experiment,* (1964).

Schwalm, Leslie A. *A Hard Fight for We: Women's Transition from Slavery to Freedom in South Carolina,* (1997).

Taylor, Susan King. *Reminiscences of My Life in Camp with the 33rd United States Colored Troops, Late 1st S.C. Volunteers,* (1902).

Vlach, John Michael. *Back of the Big House: The Architecture of Plantation Slavery, (Fred W. Morrison Series in Southern Studies),* (1993).

White, Deborah Gray. *Ar'n't I A Woman? Female Slaves in the Plantation South,* (1999, 1985).

The Internet

Beaufort County Library, Beaufort, SC
Cornell University Library, *Making of America*
Digital History, *The Meaning of the Emancipation Proclamation*
The Gilder Lehrman Institute of American History
Harvard University Library OASIS: Online Archival Search Information System
The Jacksonville Public Library, Jacksonville, FL
The Library of Congress, *American Memory*
The Literature Network, *Frederick Douglass-Biography and Works*
The National Archives
Project Gutenberg
Questia, The Online Library of Books and Journals
South Carolina's Information Highway-SCIWAY
The University of North Carolina at Chapel Hill, The Louis Round Wilson Special

Collections Library
The University of South Florida, *Africana Heritage Project*
University Libraries, South Carolina Library Digital Collection
U.S. National Park Service, *Gullah Geechee Cultural Heritage Corridor*

Poem

"His People Are Free"
By John Greenleaf Whittier